Follow The Tracks

First Edition

ISBN: 978-1-7323820-0-8

Jacket design by Michael Hughes and D.W. Wolf
Jacket photo by Michael Hughes

Signature House Publishing provides a wide range of authors for speaking events. To find out more, go to www.SignatureHousePublishing.com

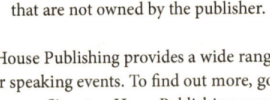

PRINTED IN THE UNITED STATES OF AMERICA

This novel is dedicated to

"You"

Prologue

CONSTANCE HAD JUST PUT IN A LONG TWELVE-HOUR shift at the hospital when the odor of burnt cloth drifted through the cold night air. She paused a moment to smell it. Thinking it was the musty scent of oak smoke out of a nearby chimney, she continued along the sidewalk, passing the low-lying manicured boxwood hedge at the corner of the emergency drop-off. It was there that she heard a faint moaning coming from the hedge.

She followed the noise into the bush. In the dark, the stench of burnt flesh invaded her nose, and her eyes had no choice but to follow. Lying in the bush, in a fetal position, was a severely burned body, obviously in tremendous pain. Quickly, Constance dropped her bag and bent down toward the head of the body. As she moved a hand from the person's face, burnt flesh came with it. The nurse jumped back in alarm, then ran back into the emergency room entrance where she immediately yelled for the trauma team.

"We have a Critical III," Constance yelled, then she looked at the registration nurse. "Page Dr. Stewart immediately!"

Quickly, she directed the emergency crew to the body and instructed them on what to do. As they wheeled the person through the automatic

sliding doors, a few resident doctors and nurses rushed over to the stretcher.

"Nurse Constance, what do we have?" asked Dr. Cox, a middle-aged emergency room physician.

Constance began calling out the distinguishing characteristics of the unknown person. "It's a female; I didn't find any identification."

"So, a Jane Doe?" he emphasized.

"Yes, and she looks to be severely burned."

"Has she lost consciousness?"

While looking at the woman's severely burned face, Constance offered an honest answer. "I'm not sure, doctor."

"We're following trauma center procedures, people. Stick with the ABCs," Dr. Cox yelled, and then added, "airway, breathing, and circulation for you interns."

Two more nurses rushed over to assist the doctors. They wheeled the stretcher into a prep room of the ER and carefully shifted the body to a bed car.

Dr. Cox noticed the blistering and redness of second-degree burns covering various areas of the woman's face. He feared the patient might go into shock.

"Get an IV line and a catheter on her so that we can monitor intake and outtake of fluids. Where did she come from?" Dr. Cox's eyes beamed back at Constance.

"Sir, I have no idea. I found her in the bushes as I left the hospital."

Constance could see the woman's eyes were barely open before one of the residents flashed a light in her face. When Dr. Cox momentarily moved away from the bed, Constance spotted the woman's lips slightly moving.

"What are you trying to tell me?" Constance murmured as she moved in closer to the woman's face.

Everyone began to move around the injured woman and Constance.

"You're going to have to move," said a raspy-voiced, third-year resident doctor.

Constance ignored the command and tried hard to block out the chaos going on around her. Barely audible, the woman tried to speak.

Constance repeated what she assumed the woman said. She broke the word into its syllables.

"Bobby," she repeated aloud before asking, "Who is Bobby? Is Bobby hurt, too? Where can we find Bobby?"

Quickly, Dr. Cox moved back to the bed to inspect the woman's face. Along the jawline, the skin appeared charred brown with white patches underneath the chin.

"She has partial thickness to full thickness third degree burns covering the neck," said Dr. Cox, speaking to the resident doctors. Suddenly, Dr. Cox heard a raspy noise when the woman breathed. "Check the airway to make sure the air passage isn't being obstructed."

Gradually, Dr. Cox's eyes moved from the victim's face to the wet, burnt clothing that partially covered her torso. When he observed her hands, both were dry and white in appearance.

"Critical burns on forearms and on both hands," he informed. He peered over at Constance. "Has she been able to speak?"

"Just faint sounds, doctor."

"So pretty much non-responsive?"

"Dr. Cox," blurted a third-year resident doctor, "I see no direct injuries to her throat, sir, but she still has a disturbance in her breathing."

"Smoke inhalation may accompany the burns. Check for singed nasal hair."

"I did, sir, and nothing."

As Dr. Cox leaned forward with his stethoscope to listen to the woman's lungs, he smelled accelerant on her clothing.

"Put her on an assist ventilator and continue to monitor her breathing. Start evaluating her circulation. I don't need a circulatory collapse on my hands."

Another physician sounded off, "Do we need a culture to confirm infection?"

"Nurse, start an IV drip of antibiotics and continue to monitor her vital signs for symptoms of shock," Dr. Cox commanded.

Before Dr. Cox had an opportunity to continue, the nurse shouted, "Her blood pressure is dropping, doctor."

Dr. Cox wondered if the victim was suffering from some external

bleeding. He didn't have a chance to give it much thought when a resident doctor bellowed, "She has blood coming from her head."

"Determine the severity of the injury," Dr. Cox responded.

"There's too much blood in her hair for me to even see the injury."

"Start cutting her hair."

Abruptly, there was a shout from a second-year resident doctor. "There's blood coming from her side. I'm assuming she suffered a puncture wound."

"Don't assume," Dr. Cox replied. "Find out." He then spoke to Constance. "Nurse, we can handle it from here. You're going to have to step aside so we can help her." His tone dipped. "You've done all you can do, Constance. We'll take good care of her."

Amid the disorder, Constance couldn't help but think there was something important the woman was trying to say. With another look from Dr. Cox, Constance knew that he was becoming annoyed with her insubordination.

The woman's eyes closed, then reopened. Immediately Constance called to the woman, "Stay with me."

"Dr. Cox, there is a puncture wound on her side," confirmed the second-year resident doctor.

Without taking his eyes off the woman, Dr. Cox asked, "What is her BP?"

"Blood pressure is 95 over 60," a nurse replied.

"Okay. For now, gauze the puncture with saline and squeeze out the excess fluid."

"Keep me updated on her BP," ordered the doctor before his attention was drawn again to Constance, who stood close by the bed. "Nurse, you're going to have to leave."

"But she's trying to tell me something, doctor, something about a Bobby. Maybe there are others injured that need our help. I don't want to leave her until...."

"Nurse, please!" Dr. Cox loudly interrupted. "It is hospital policy that once your shift is over, you are not to be here. Now leave! That's a direct order. We have enough nurses and doctors to handle this. You're only in our way. If there are others injured, I'm sure the local emergencies and

authorities are handling that situation. At this point, my main concern is this patient."

When the resident doctors and nurses turned toward him, he realized the elevation in his tone. He lowered his voice.

"Nurse, all you're doing is impeding us from treating this patient; if you want to help her, then leave so we can do our jobs."

Constance felt that sudden request for her departure had less to do with helping this patient and more to do with Dr. Cox and their frequent confrontations.

Reluctantly, she moved from the woman's side but continued to watch her lips, hoping to decipher some important information concerning the woman's family or possibly others in a serious accident.

As Constance was pushed further from the bed, she could still see the woman's mouth mimicking the same two syllables. When the breathing apparatus was placed over the patient's mouth and nose, Constance began to say the word softly.

She allowed the syllables of the word to slowly roll off her tongue, "Bob-by."

With all the doctors and nurses surrounding the bed, Constance could no longer see the face of the patient. She could hear and see only rushed voices and quick movements.

"The bleeding has stopped, doctor," said the second-year resident doctor standing behind the injured woman's head.

Dr. Cox darted back to the patient's head to inspect her scalp. There was a large bump and a few abrasions to the scalp. "She's going to need a head CT to make sure she isn't experiencing any internal swelling or bleeding." He paused to address his team, "Okay, everything seems to be under control for now, so let's determine a disability and perform an exposure."

Dr. Cox paused to study the woman's clothing. "When attempting to remove the clothing, be mindful not to remove any clothing that is sticking to the skin. The burns should not be disturbed. After the clothing has been removed, I need a complete secondary survey from head to toe. Keep the clothing. It might

help to identify the patient."

Meticulously, two doctors began to cut through the patient's burned clothes, while another doctor looked over her vitals and checked for other injuries. Dr. Cox continued with his examination of the burns on the woman's hands, arms, and legs, while a resident doctor commenced examining the pupils for size, symmetry, and reactiveness to light.

Soon the chaos in the room calmed. Dr. Cox announced his intentions of treating the patient as a burn victim and performing a full neurological examination. Suddenly, the disorder returned.

"Doctor, her heart rate is rising."

"What's the BP?" Dr. Cox asked.

"It's 85 over 40, doctor."

"But she's in no distress," replied the raspy voice, third-year resident doctor.

Dr. Cox looked at the monitor, then at the woman on the bed. "Commence shock prevention. I want her legs elevated twelve inches and her arms also above her heart." Dr. Cox took a moment to look at the woman and said in a whisper that only he could hear, "What is going on with you?" Then he looked about the room. "Okay, let's get ready to move her to the burn unit."

Constance stood afar and watched the disarray in the ER. As if she were making one last effort, the woman slowly lifted her index finger and dropped it on her abdomen. This subtle gesture was enough to grab Constance's attention.

It was how the woman's hand landed that alerted Constance. What would appear to be a drop of the finger to many was indeed a last plea to an experienced nurse. All the fingers were curled except the index finger. Mentally, Constance recalled the woman's repeated word in slow motion.

"Bob . . . by." She's not saying Bobby, thought Constance. She looked over at Dr. Cox. "STOP!" she screamed.

Irately, Dr. Cox's head suddenly turned in Constance's direction.

"A baby; I think she's pregnant, doctor."

The room came to an immediate standstill while the doctor glanced

from Constance to the patient. Everyone waited for his command. He scrutinized the abdominal area of the woman. Slowly, Dr. Cox began cutting through the wet blouse. When the woman's abdomen was fully exposed, he noticed more extreme burns. Carefully, he placed his stethoscope over the abdomen to listen for a fetal heartbeat. When he heard a heartbeat, his concerned eyes darted toward a first-year resident doctor, "I need a blood sample immediately. And have an ultrasound machine standing by."

Constance found it to be a perfect opportunity to ask one of the nurses if the attending physician had been contacted.

Dr. Cox's eyebrows rose in disagreement when he heard Constance's inquiry. Then Dr. Cox fired off, "I thought I was clear when I gave you a direct order to leave. We have everything under control."

"Dr. Stewart is the attending physician and head of this trauma team, so it's procedure to give him a call, doctor."

"I thought you did that, so where is he?" Dr. Cox asked aggressively before looking up to the clock on the wall. "This woman's life depends on our response time. Even though you are the head nurse, I'm still a doctor. So, when are you planning to follow my orders?" He looked away from the nurse. "Where is the ultrasound machine?" he snapped.

"We can't seem to locate one, doctor."

"What?" he questioned in disbelief. "Get me a measuring tape and fast."

An intern handed him a tape measure.

Constance looked alarmed, "Dr. Cox, taking a fundal height doesn't necessarily offer an accurate reading of gestation."

Still, the doctor stretched the tape from the woman's pubic bone to the top of her fundus.

"Twenty-four weeks of gestation," he remarked after reading the distance of the patient's abdomen.

"Doctor, the positioning of the fetus could make the patient further along than it appears," Constance exclaimed.

"That's true, but sometimes you work with what you have, and if twenty-four weeks is the best scenario, then I really don't think this baby is going to make it, given the burns and the other serious injuries to

this patient. However, the fetus doesn't appear to be in any distress." Dr. Cox then noticed the team standing around. "Okay, people, let's get busy with placing cool wraps on her legs and arms. After we take care of the puncture wound, we will be moving her." He looked at another doctor. "Call the Department of Neurology and tell them we have a critical burn victim with a head injury in our care."

So as not to challenge the doctor openly in front of the others, Constance came to the side of the bed.

"Dr. Cox, what about the baby?" she whispered boldly. She had a feeling that Dr. Cox had already decided not to focus on the baby, regardless of what the ultrasound machine may later tell him.

"It is my medical opinion that the best course of action is to save this patient," Dr. Cox barked. "She is our primary concern."

"But, doctor, you're weighing your decision on a tape measurement. As I mentioned, she could be further along," Constance continued until Dr. Cox interrupted.

"Nurse, as I said before, the fetus doesn't show any signs of distress." He paused, "Are you challenging my medical opinion and authority to treat this woman the best way I see fit?"

"No, doctor, but shouldn't we wait for Dr. Stewart? He might see the situation differently."

"See the situation differently," he repeated with contempt. "This patient has second-degree burns covering more than 15 percent of her body, and 30 percent of her body suffers from third-degree burns. The systemic effects these burns can cause are life threatening. Therefore, the severity of the burns has determined not only the type of treatment, but also who takes priority."

"But shouldn't the new insight of her being pregnant have some influence on how you treat this patient?"

"I already said how I plan to treat this patient—as a burn victim with a serious puncture wound and a head injury."

"I still feel you should update Dr. Stewart since all emergencies are supposed to be reported."

Defiantly, he charged back at her with scathing words. "So now you're suggesting I shouldn't give this woman any medical care, jeopardizing

her life, until Dr. Stewart shows up?"

"No, that's not what I'm suggesting. Just that you inform him on the nature of the situation."

"Nurse, who are you to tell me who to inform?" His voice was elevated, and he elected not to lower it.

"As you said earlier, doctor, we must adhere to hospital procedures."

"You aren't," he blurted before thinking. He took a second to glance into the eyes of Constance before continuing. "Nurse, when it comes to an emergency of this magnitude, there is no time to inform, just react. And since Dr. Stewart isn't here, I'm the next in command. Now, you are more than welcome to go and find the benevolent doctor. But, until he shows up, I am head of this team, and it goes my way, so move away from this bed!" When she didn't budge, he looked quickly to a nurse, "Call security and have this nurse removed."

To their surprise, an older, white-haired, distinguished doctor, with a semblance of youth, rushed into the room. His mere presence commanded attention from everyone, including Dr. Cox.

The younger resident doctors and Dr. Cox watched as the older doctor slipped on a mask and gloves. Dr. Stewart greeted Dr. Cox with his eyes and a head nod.

"So, what's the situation?"

Quickly, Constance took the opportunity to update Dr. Stewart on the patient's injuries and that her identity was unknown.

Dr. Stewart returned his eyes to Dr. Cox. "Anything to add, doctor?"

Still agitated with Constance, Dr. Cox tried to gain control over his temper. Quickly, Dr. Stewart moved toward the bed, while Constance moved back so that the doctor could take his place opposite Dr. Cox.

He spoke quickly, "Doctor, the patient has suffered critical burns over 45 percent of the body surface area. She has sustained an injury to the head and a puncture to her left side. Because of the degree of the burns, and the high percentage of BSA covered, it is my suggestion we address the burns immediately to prevent shock."

Suddenly, two nurses rushed in with a mobile ultrasound machine. Dr. Stewart gave it a quick glance.

"What's with the ultrasound machine?" asked Dr. Stewart. He peered

down toward the woman on the bed as he moved in closer. Then he looked over toward the nurses standing by the machine. "Is this patient expecting?"

Constance blurted, "Yes, she is, Dr. Stewart."

"How many weeks of gestation is she?"

Dr. Cox interjected, "I didn't have an ultrasound machine to determine an accurate reading, so I measured her abdomen to be twenty-four centimeters."

"That would make the fetus twenty-four weeks of gestation. Without knowing the accurate position of the fetus, I'll give her plus or minus two or three weeks," Dr. Stewart said.

Constance glanced at Dr. Cox. She noticed his angry eyes. She figured he was upset that Dr. Stewart had taken over the trauma team. Dr. Stewart peered over the rim of his glasses to look at the burns on the woman's abdomen.

"I need a more accurate reading," Dr. Stewart said, as he glared at the painful-looking second-degree burns. "But I'm afraid I can't use the ultrasound machine."

"Her blood pressure went up from 90 over 50; it is starting to drop again, doctor," a nurse advised.

With a sudden sense of urgency, the two doctors began to move to diagnose the cause for the low blood volume.

"Could be an excessive loss of body fluids due to the major burns," Dr. Cox said. "It's possible an infection is causing an inadequate intake and outtake of fluids. This could send our patient into shock."

After checking her vitals, Dr. Stewart leaned in closer to the patient's face to check for general symptoms of shock. He looked for cold to sweaty and bluish to pale skin. A diagnosis of shock proved difficult since the patient's skin was already dry and red in appearance as a result of the burns.

"Is her blood pressure holding?" Dr. Stewart called.

"Still dropping, doctor," a responded.

"I'm not sure if the loss of body fluid is causing the drop in blood pressure," replied Dr. Stewart.

Dr. Cox blurted, "She is suffering from a head injury, so she could

very well be experiencing early stages of shock due to excessive dilation of blood vessels. All the more reason why we should be treating her burns and conducting a CT scan rather than standing idle. The more her blood pressure drops before we treat puts this patient in greater danger. Time is of the essence, doctor."

"So is the correct diagnosis for treatment," countered Dr. Stewart as he pressed on an area of the woman's skin to see if the color returned much slower than normal. Her skin was somewhat warm to the touch. His facial expression didn't change as he requested a fetal Doppler device. Immediately, Dr. Cox's face screamed with alarm.

Dr. Stewart looked up at Dr. Cox. "You agree, Dr. Cox, that pressure from the fetus after twenty weeks can also cause a drop in the mother's blood pressure? Not to mention that she is lying on her back."

"Dr. Stewart, maybe you didn't hear me, we don't know why the patient's blood pressure is steadily dropping. This patient could be suffering from an allergic reaction to something or she may be a victim of a number of different types of shock."

Dr. Stewart listened to Dr. Cox while he applied a little pressure to the woman's abdomen area of her uterus. When the woman moved with slight discomfort, Dr. Stewart moved quickly to the end of the bed to inspect her vaginal area.

"There is bleeding," Dr. Stewart announced.

A few of the resident doctors sighed because they knew internal or external bleeding could cause a drop in blood pressure.

"Was there a substantial amount of blood loss as a result of the puncture wound?"

"We managed to stop the bleeding of the puncture wound, and her blood pressure was holding, doctor," said the third-year resident doctor.

"Where is the Doppler?" he asked with a hurried inflection in his voice.

"Right here, doctor."

Dr. Stewart glanced over to the nurse who was covering the transducer of the Doppler with a protected glove, a means to reduce any chance of infection. Gently, Dr. Stewart placed the transducer over non-burned areas of the woman's abdomen in hopes of finding a heart

rate for the fetus.

Dr. Cox peered at the monitor to steal a glance at the blood pressure reading. Suddenly, the number on the Doppler flashed.

"Fetal Heart Rate, 140 BPM."

Even though the fetus's heart rate was strong, Dr. Stewart feared there was a chance the mother may be experiencing internal bleeding as a result of the trauma that befell her, which could eventually put the fetus in distress. He commenced with a vaginal inspection to determine if a major rupture was about to occur.

"Her blood pressure is still dropping, doctor," exclaimed a nurse.

"She's hemorrhaging, but I can't determine if the placenta is starting to detach from the uterus," Dr. Stewart replied, once he finished his inspection.

Dr. Cox took Dr. Stewart's diagnosis as a justification for saving the baby, so quickly he spoke. "Bleeding in this stage of pregnancy can be caused by placenta previa, and shock is a complication of placenta previa. She's likely to go into shock first."

"Bleeding also occurs as the lower part of the uterus thins during the third trimester of pregnancy in preparation for labor. Given the situation, there is a chance the uterus can detach from the placenta before the baby is born. If that were to happen, there would be greater complications than shock that could affect the mother and baby," Dr. Stewart said, then added, "and could be the major reason for the drop in blood pressure."

Dr. Cox retorted, "At this time there isn't an abruption, and we can't be certain if the fetus is in some sort of distress. Frankly, without the ultrasound, we cannot determine what is causing the bleeding. How do you justify what we don't know taking precedence over what we do know? And what we do know is that this patient's blood pressure is continuing to drop. She requires immediate treatment, that's if the mother's life is our primary objective."

"Then, what do you suggest, Dr. Cox?" Dr. Stewart asked.

While the chaos in the ER continued, Constance listened as the two physicians volleyed back and forth regarding the safest method of treatment.

"This is a fragile situation, Dr. Stewart, but treatment depends on severity of the patient's injuries. Clearly, she has sustained a head injury and thermal burns. The longer the body's cells do not receive enough blood and oxygen, irreversible damage will be done to her organs, not to mention the dangers associated with the head injury, such as blood clots or swelling of the brain. Both the burns and the head injuries further increase this patient's likelihood of death as well as that of her fetus. The other crises this patient might be experiencing are secondary. Therefore, it is my recommendation that we stick to medical trauma protocol, control her blood pressure by controlling the bleeding, then treat her critical burns and head injury."

"Doctor, you don't agree saving this baby takes precedence over the mother's burns and head injury?"

"If this were a term pregnancy, then yes, but again, this premature fetus is in no form of distress. Therefore, the option should be to save the patient's life. I don't have to remind you of the risk in delivering a fetus less than twenty-four weeks. The fact that the fetus will be premature, maybe gives it a 50 percent chance of survival. Giving this patient a chance to survive helps the baby survive to a longer gestational age. That is the best care we can give to this patient, doctor," said Dr. Cox, then he continued. "Frankly, the patient may not survive any of her injuries, but it's our job to give her a chance."

"It's our job to give them both a chance, doctor."

"Why are we wasting so much time prolonging treatment to this patient and making her endure more pain?" gritted Dr. Cox.

"I think the mother would want us to in order to save her baby," Dr. Stewart replied.

"Remember your medical oath, doctor, 'to do no harm.' "

"The mere thought of not saving the child is harm enough."

"There is a chance that if the patient dies, the fetus dies, doctor."

"Advice well taken, Dr. Cox," Dr. Stewart replied as he directed the resident doctors to proceed in moving the patient. "Prepare for vaginal delivery."

Dr. Cox grabbed Dr. Stewart's attention immediately. "A vaginal delivery at twenty-four weeks, doctor?" he questioned. "This patient

isn't ready to have a vaginal delivery. If there is a chance of the placenta abruption, the dangers associated with a vaginal delivery are even greater. And given the bleeding, cesarean delivery is the only option," whispered Dr. Cox, who considered it extremely unprofessional to continue going back and forth with Dr. Stewart in front of other doctors and nurses.

Dr. Stewart responded, "There is also a greater danger performing a cesarean section with the mother having such critical burns. The mother could die during delivery while trying to save her baby. The baby has a strong heartbeat, and the separation of the placenta is moderate. We have a small window to induce labor and perform a vaginal delivery, just another means to an end to saving them both."

Dr. Cox's voice raced in frustration. He stepped closer to Dr. Stewart and whispered harshly near his ear, "That's a very small window to risk both of their lives. Even if you are successful in delivering the fetus, it will probably have immature lungs or other complications. Dr. Stewart, what you're doing is medically wrong, and I cannot be a part of that. I've worked too hard to get where I am just to lose it over your medical incompetence. If this woman could speak, I'm sure she would choose saving her life as the first option. And every minute wasted is jeopardizing her life."

Dr. Stewart dismissively stepped away from Dr. Cox. There was silence in the room. The other doctors and nurses stood waiting for instructions.

"Look!" pointed a nurse at fluid running from the patient's inner thighs.

"What is that fluid? Did you cath her?"

"Yes, Dr. Stewart, I did," a nurse said.

Dr. Cox moved to where he could see the liquid. "Since you cathed her, it can't be urine."

"It's her amniotic fluid; she's going into spontaneous labor," Dr. Stewart replied, then looked at Dr. Cox. "I guess she was able to speak after all, doctor. And it appears she chose the life of her child as the first option. Okay, everyone, listen to how this is going to play out. Prepare OR for an emergency delivery. Once we have the baby, we will go back

to treating the burns, head injury, and any other injuries this patient has sustained." He glanced over toward a nurse, "Get a perinatologist, a neonatal nurse practitioner, a neonatologist, a respiratory therapist, a burn specialist, as well as a neurosurgeon here immediately.

"Excuse us, doctor," Dr. Stewart said hastily as the resident doctors and nurses began wheeling the bed car past Dr. Cox.

Dr. Cox watched as the team of doctors and nurses rushed down the hall and into the operating room.

As they prepped the woman for delivery, Constance immediately referred to the woman as Jane Doe. She felt that would at least help during the delivery.

"Jane, listen to me, you're going to have to push with quick breaths when the doctor tells you to push."

Jane's eyes moved from one side to the other, barely giving notice to Constance's instructions.

Once the patient was positioned for delivery, Dr. Stewart ordered everyone to get ready. He gave a head nod toward Constance to begin coaching.

"Okay, Jane, here we go. It's time to push," she said softly, then adding, "Jane, you have to push harder. Come on, you can do it."

Jane's face grimaced as blood seeped from underneath the saturated gauze bandages attached to her side. Her mouth opened to scream, but only faint sounds could be heard.

"Now breathe," Constance ordered as she looked into Jane's fatigued eyes, which filled with tears.

Seconds later, Dr. Stewart instructed her to push again. Constance was on time with her support. She felt the skin of Jane's hand slide around in her palm. Constance couldn't imagine the amount of pain this woman was having in trying to deliver her baby.

After another bout of pushing, Jane's face relaxed. Her grip loosened around Constance's fingers, her shoulders relaxed, her body was exhausted, and she wanted so much to drift away with the contractions.

"You're doing great," encouraged Constance.

"Blood pressure still dropping, Dr. Stewart," a nurse advised.

Dr. Stewart acknowledged the nurse with a head nod; then there was

another head nod to Constance, and the veins in Jane's neck inflated as she silently screamed in agony and pushed with all her might.

"That's it, Jane," Constance screamed, hoping to transfer some of her energy to Jane.

"I see the head," the doctor spoke softly. He looked up and noticed that Jane was barely conscious. "Keep her conscious!"

Constance yelled in her face, "Jane, no, stay with us! Wake up! Come on, Jane."

As the baby's head moved further through the birth canal, Dr. Stewart began having difficulty getting the baby's head completely out of the canal. The umbilical cord had gotten wrapped around the baby's neck and was causing the baby severe distress.

"I have a tight cord times one," the doctor said. "I need two hemostats."

He began pushing the head back into the mother's womb to readjust the baby. The slumping of Jane's shoulders was a sign of defeat. She was worn out. Constance could see there was nothing else Jane could give.

"Listen to me, Jane, I know you're in pain, I know you're tired, but please hang in there. The life of your baby depends on it."

There was no response from Jane.

"Come on, Jane," Constance called, as she bent forward to speak in Jane's ear. "Don't give up now."

Dr. Stewart placed two hemostats along the umbilical cord and then he cut between them to avoid bleeding out.

The baby slid right out of the birth canal into the doctor's hands. "We got it," the doctor yelled.

Constance felt a grip around her fingers. With her last ounce of strength, Jane's shoulders lifted off the pillow so she could see the baby.

Jane fell back onto the pillow, eyes closing as the doctor handed the baby to the neonatal nurse.

"It's not breathing," a voice cried. Jane's vision blurred as she glared toward the team of doctors that surrounded her baby.

"Loss of pulse," Constance looked at the continuous line on the monitor then at Jane. "Flat line, she's going into cardiac arrest. I'm starting compression!" Constance shouted, "We're losing her."

Gradually, the sounds in the operating room started to fade and all

the figures started to narrow from the woman's vision—into blackness.

"I need a defibrillator," Constance demanded, as she frantically pumped on the woman's sternum. Constance began screaming the name she had given the woman, "Jane, JANE!" Her screaming began to fade from Jane's hearing. "Jane! Jane!"

—

Constance stood at the foot of the hospital bed looking at the bandages that covered Jane from head to toe. She wondered how Jane even survived the critical burns that covered so much of her body and portions of her face. There were a few times she thought Jane wasn't going to make it. Hopefully, the worst was over; that's if she comes out of the coma, Constance thought. The more Constance stared at the mummy-like figure lying lifeless in the bed, the more compassion she felt for Jane.

Constance stopped gazing and pulled a chair to the side of the bed to talk to Jane, which had become her normal routine.

"Remember that guy I was telling you about? The one I met online. Well, I went on that date last night. And let me tell you, it was a disaster. Could you believe the nerve of that jerk? He asked me to pick up the tab. He claimed he left his wallet at home. Yeah, right. Let me stop you before you say it. I know, I need a man in my life, but I'm not paying for one. So, you know what I did? I told him no problem. I would pay the bill after I visited the little girl's room. You know, I had to powder my nose."

Constance laughed loudly, then continued, "I headed straight for the door. He's probably still sitting there waiting for me to return, a damn idiot. Or am I the idiot for trying to find love on some online dating site? That's it, no more social networking for me. Well, enough about me; how are you doing today?"

She answered for Jane.

"Can't seem to wake up?" another hard laugh. "I know that was in poor taste, but honestly I can't seem to wake up either from all these bad dates. Well, it must be nice to lie in bed all day and do nothing. Why don't you wake up out of that coma, so we can trade places? It's been five

months now, and you've had your fair share of sleep."

Constance began changing the bandages covering Jane's body.

"The doctor says you are healing very well. Hopefully, it won't be long before the bandages come off permanently. Then, we can see your face, and maybe someone will show up and tell us who you really are."

Before checking Jane's blood pressure, Constance went on to conduct some passive exercises with Jane's arms and legs. Afterwards, she began administering several functional tests. She took a small needle and dragged it along the bottom of the bandages on Jane's feet to evoke a response. She watched silently to see if Jane would respond. When there was no reaction, Constance jotted something down in Jane's medical chart. She then picked up the conversation about her date.

"Well, I figure my prince charming will come by and sweep me off my feet. I hope he has some money; otherwise, I don't want him to show up."

When Jane squeezed Constance's index finger, it prompted a normal reaction between two people that were enjoying each other's company.

"You feel the same way, hon. You can squeeze my finger again on that one."

When Constance realized what she had said, her speech slowed. She took Jane by the palm. "Please God, I don't need to be delusional on top of crazy. I know I felt her squeeze my hand. Jane," she called, "Jane, I need you to open your eyes. Come on, Jane, you can do it. Come to my voice, Jane, and wake up."

Jane's eyes blinked several times before Constance's face came into focus. Tears welled in the corner of Constance's eyes. She brushed the tears away and regained her composure.

Constance reached for the call light and pressed the red button. When she heard the nurse respond through the intercom, Constance yelled, "Page Dr. Stewart immediately."

Over the next few days as Jane recovered from the coma, Dr. Stewart had a team of specialists monitor her closely, making sure she didn't slip into another coma.

Dr. Stewart waited several more weeks until Jane clearly gained a

level of comprehension before attempting to address her true identity and to explain her overall state of health, as well as what the specialists had done to save her life.

Dr. Stewart pulled a chair close to the head of the hospital bed to speak to Jane. "Do you know your name?"

She went to speak, then immediately touched her throat.

"Incidentally, you were severely burned around the throat area, which destroyed your voice box. So, for now, move your head up and down for 'yes' and side to side for 'no.' Do you understand?"

Jane slightly moved her head up, then down.

"Yes," he verbally gave an answer for her head movement. "Okay, good." Dr. Stewart revisited his first question. "Do you know your name?"

Jane moved her head from side to side.

"No. Do you know how old you are?" Again, he waited for her movement before responding. "No. Do you know where you are?"

Her eyes looked around the room. And she shook her head, 'no.'

"You are in a hospital. Do you know what may have happened to put you here?"

Once again her head movement gestured 'no.'

"Do you remember anything prior to today?" He watched her movement and said 'no.' "Nurse Constance has been referring to you as 'Jane.' Of course, when you remember your biological name, you can let us know. Until then, you will be known as 'Jane Doe.' "

Dr. Stewart took a moment to jot down some notes concerning Jane. What alarmed him most was Jane's inability to recall any personal information about herself, as well as her inability to recall events that occurred prior to her arriving at the hospital, including such a serious accident. The fact that she had an injury to her head caused Dr. Stewart to wonder whether she suffered from a head trauma. He wrote an additional note for Jane to have a neurological and diagnostic test performed in order to find the cause of her inability to retrieve such information.

Dr. Stewart peered back at Jane. "Jane, you were found in bad shape on the grounds of the hospital. We have no idea how you got there or

how you came to succumb to so many injuries. Given the trauma to your head, coupled with the other injuries, you slipped into a coma. And you were in the coma until a month ago."

Gradually, Jane began to look at the bandages that covered her from head to toe. Again, she attempted to speak but found it very painful.

"You won't be speaking anytime soon, Jane. Frankly, all of your injuries were very serious, especially the burns that caused infection and inflammation in your body. You had several body organs fail at once, and you experienced respiratory distress, meaning your lungs failed, as well. Both conditions were a result of your immune system attacking your organs, and all of this took place while you were in the coma. It is a miracle that you even survived.

"Because you were in a coma, the healing process of the burns slowed, but the coma did have its benefits. It kept you from experiencing pain as you went through the tub baths, surgery to remove dead tissue caused by the burns, and surgical skin grafts. Unfortunately, a few of the skin grafts didn't take, so we had to redo them. That, too, prolonged your recovery and confirmed my decision to keep you bandaged at all times, except during sponge baths, wound dressing, and bandage changing. Actually, this has helped to reduce bacterial infection.

"The coma, coupled with the damaged tissue, severely limited your mobility and normal functioning of your joints. So, along with the occupational therapy you've been receiving, you will undergo a rigorous, four-month rehabilitation process with the guidance of physical therapists. These standard therapies are meant to increase joint movement and function. If limited function persists, additional surgery may be necessary to remove more scar tissue.

"I won't lie to you, Jane, this is going to be a long recovery, but we're doing everything to get you healthy and out of here."

Jane shook her head, but it was the glare in her eyes that the doctor understood.

"Jane, I know all of this is overwhelming and very upsetting; however, there is some good news. The worst is behind you."

She lifted her hand to touch the bandages on her face.

Dr. Stewart smiled, "Don't worry, I brought in a leading plastic

surgeon who performed all your skin grafts, and I am sure he did a great job on your face as well. Unfortunately, you're going to have to wait until the new skin heals on and around the face. As the skin begins to heal, I will determine if the bandages should be left off. As for your hands, they received the worst burns, so they will probably stay bandaged the longest. Again, there's always a positive in a negative, such as you will never have fingerprints again." His attempt at levity fell on deaf ears. "Anyway, because of the danger of infection, I have confined you to this room, except when attending therapy."

Jane looked as if she wanted to speak; instead, she touched her throat.

"I have a throat and voice specialist scheduled to see you, as well, so don't panic. For the time being, don't even try to speak. Do your best to communicate with this pencil and pad." He placed the pencil and pad on the table while he continued his comments. "Again, Jane, this entire team we've assembled is doing everything to make sure you get out of here in the next four to five months. That depends on how you heal, as well as a few other things." Dr. Stewart decided not to discuss her memory loss as one of those factors that could further prolong her stay.

"Jane," Constance called her name as she began to change the dressing on her hands and arms.

Dr. Stewart moved toward the door. "I will leave you two alone." Then he paused briefly by the door. "Nurse Constance, I am heading to Mr. Ghent's room."

Constance looked away long enough to offer the doctor a head nod.

"So how are you doing today, Jane?" It was evident in Constance's tone of voice that she was happy to hear or see any response from Jane.

Jane's eyes smiled.

"That's good, Jane. My name is Nurse Constance, but you can call me Connie."

Jane nodded, then glanced at the corner of the ceiling where the television had been hanging.

"Oh, Dr. Stewart had the television removed from your room. He felt the speed of the television would be too much for your eyes and mind. Trust me; you are not missing a thing on television except Jeopardy!" She paused to display her affection for the game show. "If the doctor

knew I was allowing you to watch it, I might be out of a job."

Jane squinted her eyes.

"Don't give me those puppy dog eyes. I like my job more than I like your pretty eyes." She let out another laugh. "And, you don't have a radio because the doctor felt the noise would also be a distraction. But those are the doctor's orders."

Jane lowered her eyes before noticing the top half of a book slightly extended from Constance's medical jacket. Jane grabbed at the pencil and pad that was left by Dr. Stewart. Constance assisted her by placing the pencil between the bandages of her index finger and thumb. Still, there was an inability to grasp the pencil tightly as she moved it over the pad. Constance tried making out the scribbled words but could not decipher them. She noticed Jane's stare on the book in her jacket pocket, so she pulled the book out and placed it on the table near the bed. Slowly, Jane moved the book closer to where she could read the cover.

"It's supposed to be a bestseller. Of course, with all the hours I am working, I haven't had a chance to even crack the spine," Constance admitted.

Jane's soft eyes looked up from the book. She then pushed it back to Constance.

"We have a system here that after someone on the floor reads a new book, the book is forwarded to someone else. This eliminates the necessity of everyone having to purchase the same book," she paused to look over the book. "Funny thing, it doesn't look as if it has been read." She began to whisper, "I believe I have a secret admirer because this was put on my desk back in February, February fourteenth to be exact." Constance waited for Jane to respond with her eyes. When she only received a blank stare, Constance blurted, "Valentine's Day. The book was left for me on Valentine's Day." When Jane's expression didn't change, Constance went on with the conversation. "I likely won't get to read it until I go on vacation, or even then because I still have so many medical books to read. So, go on and crack the spine, but promise me you won't tell me the story." Slowly, Jane made a cross over her chest.

"Reading should be okay for the eyes, but take your time. Don't try to read the entire book in one day. Nurse's orders."

Jane looked baffled.

"The doctor said not to talk, not to listen to the radio and not to watch television, but he didn't say anything about reading. It will at least break the boredom."

Constance leaned forward to give Jane a light hug.

"Jane, I have to check on some other patients." She watched as Jane's attention stayed on the title of the book. "I will admit the title doesn't sound interesting, but you can't judge a book by its cover, so I heard," smirked Constance, as she tossed the old bandages in the trash receptacle on her way out of the room.

Jane smiled and watched as the door closed before her eyes fell back on the title of the book, A *Path to the Past,* by Sipul Sinac. She turned to the first page in the book and read, "This book is based on a true and tragic story." She turned to the next page and began to read.

1

IN THE SKY, IMMENSE RAIN CLOUDS STRETCHED AS FAR AS the eye could see but offered no relief to the stifling and suffocating heat that filled the summer night air.

Bland Benthall stood motionlessly under an antique light post. A murky ray of light shone over his body and highlighted his thick, dark hair. He was tightly proportioned and good-looking with chiseled facial bones that extended like the tips of mountains, and valley-like dimples that smiled without him ever parting his lips. His feet hurt from hours of standing on the antebellum cobblestone street, which stretched the full length of the old train station.

Bland placed himself in perfect view of the entire station, especially the silver train tracks. The palms of his hands were clammy from anticipation of the train's arrival. He checked his watch in the light's rays. At any minute, he assumed a loud horn would crack open the peaceful night air. Suddenly, his prediction was brought to pass by a deafening trumpet sound. His eyes frowned before tunneling down at the two steel rails that disappeared into the distant darkness. Another blast preceded the bright light illuminating everything in its path. Bland hurried to the station's balcony.

Moments later, the Crescent 19 thundered its way toward the station's lights. Bland felt the vibration given off by the train as its heavy iron wheels locked hard against the steel rail, forcing the locomotive to come to a screeching halt. He watched from the balcony as porters unloaded the train in regiment form. Far down in the link of cars, Bland could see a sprinkle of passengers disembarking and heading his way. The conductor wasted no time in calling for boarding passengers.

"All aboard! All aboard the Crescent 19 south bound!"

The ticket agent rattled his keys as he prepared to lock the upper portion of the station. He turned hastily while wrestling to put on his jacket and captain-like hat. He then shuffled his way in Bland's direction. He slowed his pace just enough to ask Bland if he had purchased a ticket.

"You're going to Atlanta?" he screamed over the loud engine.

Bland didn't attempt to talk over the din of noise, so he nodded his head.

"Well, come on because after she's loaded, off she goes!" the ticket agent yelled; and then set off in a quick trot. Bland took a long glance at everything before heading down to the tracks.

It was his first adventure on a train, so he wanted to remember everything about the station and his first trip. He readjusted his backpack and, with a brisk walk, gave chase. Bland and the ticket agent scampered down a long flight of stairs before reaching the tracks. They dodged dollies, boxes, and porters as they rushed toward the conductor who saw them coming.

"Only one tonight?" asked the conductor with his hand extended for Bland's ticket. Bland reached into his front left pocket to pull a yellow ticket that the conductor was quick to punch and hand back in one motion.

"Yep! Only one tonight," the ticket agent answered.

The conductor looked down toward the engine of the train as he pointed for Bland to climb the few steps to the hallway of two adjoining cars. The porters had disappeared, and only light patches of steam drifted back in their direction.

"Well, she's loaded," the conductor acknowledged, then tapped the front of his cap at the ticket agent.

While Bland waited for the conductor, he occupied his time studying the narrow aisles that led from the door to the coach cars. He heard the conductor slam the hatch to the lower steps, then come down hard with the top hatch and secure the two with a tight clamp. Bland glanced at the name tag on the old man's shirt. Harry, Bland murmured to himself before stepping out of his path. Suddenly, the train's engine jerked hard to pull the long link of cars, and Bland fell into the wall. Harry whipped his head back at Bland and laughed.

"You gotta hold on, sonny. It can be tricky walking these aisles." Bland smiled at Harry who appeared to have spent much of his life on trains.

"This way," Harry directed, as he headed toward the direction of the train's engine. He maneuvered his way along the narrow aisle with ease while Bland fought to keep his balance. The old man slammed his fist against an iron door with its penitentiary-esque viewing glass. The door automatically slid open to allow entrance to the next seating car. Bland followed Harry into a dark car filled with rows of seats but occupied by very few passengers. Flashes of light from passing streetlights beamed through the windows with open curtains, allowing Bland to scan the tops of seats while moving toward the back of the seating car.

Harry stopped near the rear of the car and pointed for Bland to take his seat. Then he pointed to the luggage rack above the seat and said, "You can put your bag up there, sonny."

Bland followed his orders before taking his seat to wait for any additional instructions. He watched the conductor pull a tag from his shirt pocket and a pencil from the side of his cap. The conductor printed the letters ATL on the front of the paper and dropped it into a gutter, similar to that found on a house, which extended from one end of the luggage rack to the opposite end. Then the conductor shoved the pencil back underneath his cap.

"The dining car is closed, but if you're hungry, the lounge is six cars in that direction." He pointed toward the opposite direction of the train's engine, the direction from which they had previously come.

Bland noticed that the constant flashes of light had long disappeared when the train moved out from the inner-city tracks to the rural tracks.

"They serve all kinds of snacks, cigarettes, beer, liquor, and microwave

foods." Harry paused. "Well, that's it. You have a nice trip, sonny."

Harry started down the dark aisle of the passenger car when he stopped abruptly to turn in Bland's direction. "In case I didn't mention it, we arrive in Atlanta around 7:00 a.m. Don't worry. If you're sleeping, another conductor will come by and wake you." He then continued to make his way down the aisle toward another iron door.

Bland leaned back in the deep cushion of the seat and welcomed the cool air that brushed his face. As he relaxed, his eyes and ears focused on the environment of the car: the slight rustling of a paper bag, the shifting of a few passengers seeking additional comfort, and the continuous clacking of each boxcar rolling over the rails. He realized that he was as restless as the environment around him, so he sought the lounge car.

With the train at full speed, it was difficult for Bland to maintain his balance, but quickly he caught the tops of seats and staggered up the aisle as if in a drunken stupor. He passed through several cars before he came upon a line of passengers who waited to place their orders with a bartender. Once they received their drinks, Bland watched them push a swinging door to an adjoining lounge car. Each time the door opened, out poured merriment of laughter and smoke. Unlike the noise in the passenger car, he found this extremely inviting. When a few more passengers entered the crowded room, Bland took the opportunity to steal a glimpse at the cheerful faces of people sitting around drinking and smoking. A few more bursts of laughter and Bland's curiosity increased. He tried to see over the heads in front of him. Once he reached the bar, he had no need for sustenance. Instead, his appetite for the excitement behind that swinging door surged. His interest was still on the laughter coming from the lounge car when the scratchy baritone-voice of the bartender interrupted his thoughts.

"What will it be this evening, sir?"

Bland surveyed the man who bore a striking resemblance to an early twentieth-century bartender portrayed in the old movies.

"I'll have a cola," Bland replied, while peering into the opening in the doorway. The laughter sounded louder and even more distracting now that he was at the front of the line. The bartender was quick to scoop

some ice into a plastic cocktail cup, grab a soda from underneath the bar and pour it over the ice.

"A dollar fifty," he said before taking the next person's order.

Bland pulled two dollars from his wallet and slid it across the top of the bar.

"Keep the change," he smiled, then sipped the cola from the rim of the cup.

The bartender made light of the tip. "Thank you, big spender."

Bland walked toward the swinging door and delicately pushed against it until the inside of the lounge car was completely exposed. It was a small lounge, having the same décor on both sides. At both ends were two small tables, which accommodated up to two passengers on either side of the table. Positioned between the tables was a small sofa. Intrigued, Bland scanned the area in hopes of finding an empty seat. His attention was drawn to a conversation from his immediate left.

"Okay, the next person who enters the room will decide," said a raspy voice.

"No," sighed the most gorgeous woman Bland had ever seen in his life.

"Why?" asked a thin man, who wore a tank top that revealed the outline of his fragile ribcage. Bland studied the man's hairline, which resembled a predeveloped cul-de-sac.

Bland's eyes darted across the table when another voice chimed in to get his attention. "Please try to pay attention to them because your answer will end a three-hour drawn-out debate." The stranger paused temporarily. "I'm sorry. How rude of me. My name is Elizabeth, but my friends call me Liz." Elizabeth then pointed across the table. "Now, that beautiful woman is," Elizabeth paused long enough to ask sarcastically, "what name do you want to be introduced as?" The beautiful woman looked up at Bland but did not answer. Elizabeth tossed her hands up and without missing a beat, answered for her, "You can call her Grey. And that southern speaking gent beside her is Steven."

Grey sat back in her seat. "Steven, being in love is like being bare in a garden of beauty, and you're not afraid. The key is not to mistake

love for some mere attraction, for then you're susceptible to being taken advantage of."

Steven had a point that couldn't wait to roll off his tongue. "Frankly, anyone is capable of being used." He paused to take a long drag from his cigarette, "So what you are really implying is that love is conscious?"

"No, love shouldn't be conscious to where you are keeping records on what someone does for you."

"According to your theory it is," remarked Bruce, a retired Marine but still dressed in fatigues and waiting for an opportunity to refute any woman who challenged a man.

Bland noticed how it surprised Grey when Bruce's baritone voice spoke up. Grey turned and looked directly in Bruce's eyes and said, "Caution isn't recordkeeping, nor is it a signal for falling in love. It's an advocate for falling in love. You just know it. It sneaks up on you like the idea of falling in love at first sight."

Steven gawked as Grey laughed aloud.

"Steven, you have to learn how to read the signs."

"What signs? You need to stop pacifying yourself with this illusion of love at first sight," mumbled Steven.

"I guess my definition of love is very different from yours," she admitted.

"It very well could be," Steven smiled.

"And that's what this is all about," Elizabeth said to Bland, as she inhaled the tobacco of the cigarette.

Waving her hands as if having a moment of clarity, Grey blurted, "That's the beauty of love. It can be defined and redefined according to the person."

Steven held up one of the miniature bottles to make a toast, "Well, I am here to redefine love as a passionate affection based on sexual attraction."

He nodded in Grey's direction. Grey pressed her lips upward toward her nose. "That's so sad."

"Why? You just said love is defined as I see it."

"Yes, I did, Steven, but honestly, shouldn't love be more than just a sexual attraction?"

"Not my love." He turned his body in the tight space to face her squarely. "Okay, listen, sex is a part of love. You agree?"

"No. It doesn't have to be."

"But it can be?"

"I guess it can be depending on the person who is defining love."

"Then one can go so far as to say sex is the motivator of love; therefore—" Grey tried to interrupt, but Steven put up his index finger, "Wait, wait, wait; therefore, love is sex."

"How sad you should think such a thing and use it as an analogy. That type of love only leads to pain."

"Grey, you can't have love without pain. Try telling me a love you once had that didn't accompany some level of pain." There was a brief silence. "You see," he flipped out an open hand, "love is a process built over time, not at first sight. You're looking to get yourself hurt."

Bland caught himself entertaining the thought of love at first sight. Since the moment he set eyes on Grey, he couldn't take them off of her. Is that love at first sight? He considered it being more than a mere physical attraction. But who truly knows, he thought, since his only experience with love and sex came with an over-zealous crush and a series of wet dreams about his twelfth-grade science teacher. Otherwise, Bland's young and handsome face was the semblance of virginity.

Finally Steven took notice of Bland. "We did say the next person that entered the room would settle our dispute. And here he is—a young and handsome man."

"No, I did not agree to that because the next person that came from behind that door could be a man." She pointed with her hands toward Bland to prove her point. "And his answer will already be biased," Grey exclaimed.

"Calm down, it could have very well been a woman. That's why it's called random selection because we didn't know which sex would enter the room. Now do we both agree that the person's answer will settle the debate?"

"Agreed, but I will ask the question." She looked directly into Bland's eyes and asked, "Is there such a thing as love at first sight or just fragments of lust?"

Bland offered a blank expression. There was only a partial seat in the overcrowded room, which happened to be beside Grey. He peered down at the small space and wondered if his answer would jeopardize him getting the seat. One thing for certain, his feet hurt from standing for hours waiting for the train.

Steven's voice boomed, "Well, come out with it."

"Don't rush him," sparked Grey, while moving tightly against Steven's body, eager to make additional room if his answer pleased her.

Bland stalled on his thoughts before answering.

"I believe in soul mates where love can be built over time or found in a single glance."

After giving his answer, he noticed all their blank faces, so he continued with a more detailed explanation.

"To me, love is an intangible, something that you can't touch, but you feel it in your heart. You feel it all over your body, and that is what touches you. It touches you to numbness and fills you to completion. Honestly, it doesn't have to be sexual."

He heard Grey take a sudden breath and hold it while waiting for him to continue.

Bland continued. "Love invites the opportunity for others to love, the opportunity to please someone, and the opportunity to bond at any given moment, and even the opportunity for lust to exist, as well as pain. With every available minute, your mind and thoughts are conscious of him or her. Just the thought of that person can break you out in a cold sweat."

"Or a hot flash," Elizabeth laughed, while fanning herself with her hands. "This is kind of erotic. Keep going; you're turning me on."

"A modern-day Shakespeare," frowned Bruce, who had his own attraction for Elizabeth.

"I beg to differ," Steven opined.

Bland smiled. "After listening to both of your opinions concerning love and lust, it is my opinion that a man can respect a woman and not love her, but a woman cannot love a man she doesn't respect. And if either desecrates their body for one night, whether it's love at first sight, or lust, then neither will respect the other or themselves. And if it's an

object you're falling in love with, then I guess you don't have to worry about any of that."

"Umhmm," Bruce muttered before taking another puff from the cigarette. "What do you know—a virtuous man!"

Bland grinned. He reflected on his childhood, back to the day his adoptive parents told him they were not his biological parents. Even when they knew the truth might scar him, they believed the truth was important for the growth of his character. They raised him to do the right thing, even in the face of difficulty. His answer reflected what they instilled in him. However, his answer was also motivated by the only seat available in the lounge car, which happened to be beside the most beautiful woman he had ever seen.

Bland asked, "May I sit?"

Steven looked baffled. "I'm not sure if he ever answered the question."

"You earned a seat next to me," smiled Grey.

Bland delivered his answer with such sincerity that it struck her inner core to the point that she turned and stared at him.

"Very well said, young man," said an onlooker, Albert. His soft, British-trembling voice caught Bland's attention immediately.

"Thank you," replied Bland, still studying Albert's voice relative to his size. He couldn't help but wonder how Albert, Elizabeth and Bruce managed to squeeze their bodies in such a tight space without complaining.

Once Albert had successfully opened a pack of cigarettes, he offered the pack for anyone to take a smoke.

Bruce pulled a lighter from his shirt pocket. Steven leaned forward to light the tip of his cigarette, then said, "Please entertain us, sir, with a more formal introduction."

"My name is Bland Benthall."

"Where are you headed, Bland?" Elizabeth asked.

"To Atlanta."

"For business?"

"Pleasure," Bland replied.

"You will find Atlanta to be quite charming. Steven is a native so maybe he will be willing to show you around," Albert suggested.

As the group began to chatter amongst themselves, Bland was fixated on the pale green inscription underneath Bruce's rolled up sleeve. He tried deciphering the tattoo's faded green words when Bruce caught his eye.

"Semper Fi," Bruce said. "It's Latin for Semper Fidelis," his deep voice injected with a sinister expression on his face.

"I beg your pardon."

"It means Always Faithful. It's the motto of the Marines. We leave no one behind. When you go into battle and the shit gets thick when you're in the trenches, we refuse to leave anyone behind, dead or alive."

Steven interrupted, "Don't get him started with those war stories."

The conductor's announcement interrupted their conversations.

"Excuse me passengers, we are running thirty minutes behind schedule. Our next four stops are in this order: Danville, VA; Greensboro, NC; High Point, NC; and Salisbury, NC."

A voice called out from the rear of the car. "When will the train arrive in Charlotte?"

"That's my stop," Elizabeth declared. She was already nudging Bruce out of the seat.

"In about four hours; that's if we don't lose any more time," replied the conductor.

"Why are you in such a hurry? The man said you have four hours," stated Bruce.

"Well, that gives me four hours to sleep."

Bruce saw an opportunity to leave with Elizabeth, so he took it. The train could be felt slowing down, and the conductor motioned with his hand for departing passengers to follow him.

Albert followed Bruce and Elizabeth into the aisle. They all said their goodbyes before exiting the lounge car.

Within a few hours, a domino effect occurred in the lounge car as more and more passengers moved to their seats. Eventually, only Bland, Grey, and Steven were left among empty seats, scattered liquor bottles, overfilled ashtrays, and crushed cigarette packs.

The three stayed wedged shoulder to shoulder. Hours of being

squashed together somehow created a level of comfort none of them wanted to give up right away.

As they sat in rare silence, Grey felt lethargic and dropped her shoulders; she was certain that she would be the next to depart.

"You know I hate goodbyes," Grey said, then pulled a cigarette from a crumpled pack on the table. "Got a light?"

Steven flicked the lighter, and the flame soaked up the tobacco. Grey inhaled and immediately exhaled, blowing circles of smoke into the air. Bland surmised that the cigarette offered her a feeling that he only wished he could have.

Steven shook his head from side to side. "Not me, there are times when I begged for people to leave. Since you two are not going to leave before I do, I'm saying goodnight. So, slide, so I can get out of this cramped space."

When Steven reached the aisle, he took one last pull on his cigarette. He coughed smoke as he spoke to Bland. "What a shame, it could have been lust at first sight. Oh well, don't you kids do anything I wouldn't do."

"What would that be?" Grey asked warily.

"Short of everything," he laughed as he walked down the aisle.

The two of them sat in silence for a long time before Bland broke the tranquility.

"So, is Grey your real name?"

"Why would you ask that?"

"Because earlier Liz asked what name you wanted to be introduced as."

She laughed. "I meet a lot of people, and I've learned through bad experiences to never give my real name to folks. So as not to be rude to people, I abbreviate my last name, which is Brindle, to Brind."

"So, you tell people your name is Brind, but it's really Grey?"

"Well, it's really Greysen."

"Greysen," he repeated. "So, Grey is just another abbreviation?"

She smiled.

"You're confusing," he laughed. "But now I'm curious. How did you get such an unconventional name? Did your mother name you?"

"No, my father named me Greysen after his mother. What can I say? Grey is what stuck."

"It sounds as if you don't like your name."

"Oh no, nothing like that. I plan on handing it down to my daughter. That way, the name will stay in the family."

"And if it's a boy?" he said, before sliding his elbows across the table.

"I'll name him Grayden."

"That's a beautiful name. It sounds like you have it all planned. How does your father feel about it?"

Suddenly her eyes shifted to the table. Immediately, Bland noticed how uncomfortable she became.

"I'm sorry, did I say something wrong?" he asked.

"No."

He waited for her to gain composure before resuming the conversation.

"My parents recently died in a car accident. They died on my eighteenth birthday."

Bland's eyes grew extremely large. His head began to move from left to right, not knowing how else to respond.

"I'm so sorry."

"Thank you. That's the purpose for my trip. I just needed to get away," she said, without making eye contact with Bland.

"Where are you escaping to?"

"As far as this train takes me."

"And once you are there?"

"I don't know."

"What about your relatives?"

"It's just me. I have no one else. Everything I loved I lost in that car accident."

Again, Bland apologized because he didn't know what else to say. Cautiously, he put his arm around Grey's shoulders to console her.

"I hope you don't mind," he said.

She smiled, then wiped the corners of her eyes, "You're a really sweet guy. There's something very special about you. It's like I've known you all my life."

"Maybe it's because we both lost our parents."

She turned toward him, "You too?"

"Well, the only parents I've ever known. I was put up for adoption. My adoptive father died seven years ago, and my adoptive mother died at the beginning of the year."

"Were you angry?"

"Yes, because she was all I had left."

"Do you know who your biological parents are?"

"No, I don't know who they are, or if they are still living. At first I was angry that someone could just give up their child. Fortunately for me, a loving couple was willing to take me. My parents," he paused to correct any confusion, "my adoptive parents were hardworking people who were very loving. At that point in my life that's what I needed. After my mother's death, I needed to get away. I felt I had no direction, no sense of purpose." There was a brief silence. "I'm hoping this trip can help me put things into perspective."

"I'm just hoping time will help me heal," Grey said.

"If you allow it to."

She curled her lips, "Sounds as if we have some things in common, Bland, tragic things, but things nonetheless."

"Well, I was always told that out of tragedy can come something beautiful."

She paused to embrace his words. From a half-smile, suddenly, Grey began to laugh.

"What's so funny?"

"Doesn't Bland mean plain, tasteless and unimaginative?"

If my name meant anything, it definitely was not unimaginative, thought Bland.

"Look who's talking. A name like Grey is pretty dull, wouldn't you say?" he asked with a flirtatious grin.

"Very funny," Grey smiled. "Plain and dull, I guess we are made for each other." The two of them sat in a blanket of silence, shoulder to shoulder, watching the silhouettes of structures outside the lounge windows. Bland quietly watched Grey fondle a locket on her necklace. When he attempted to ask her about it, the lounge door suddenly swung

open, and in entered the conductor with pad and pen in hand. At his surprising entrance, they jerked their bodies upright.

"You two are still here," he smiled. Then he pulled another slip from his back pocket. "Anyone heading to Atlanta?"

"That's him," Grey stated, as she pointed at Bland.

"We're still running behind schedule, sir, so your expected arrival time in Atlanta has been moved from seven to eight in the morning."

"An hour?" Bland questioned.

The conductor tipped his cap and continued through the car. Bland wasn't sure of the amount of time that had passed, but he knew it was getting late. Frankly, he was tired of the lounge car. He wished his back lay against something soft.

Grey offered a solution with a whimsical smirk. "I've been in this lounge car since I left New York. I am sharing my seat with an old woman who constantly thinks my shoulder is her pillow and my shirt is her handkerchief." The thought of the old woman slobbering on her shoulder made her gag. "I was wondering if we could head back to your car."

There was a sudden surprised look on Bland's face. He didn't know how to respond.

"My car?" he paused.

"Are you sharing your seat with anyone?"

"Umm, no."

Again, she asked, "So, can we go to your car?"

"Umm, sure."

He slid out from the table, then immediately pulled her by the hand. As they traveled from one car to the next, Bland noticed how each passenger car was the same in appearance and smell. When they arrived at his designated car, it, too, hadn't changed. It was more than half empty—mainly quiet except for those few passengers who snored. Occasionally, a passing light would skim over the passengers' heads and various empty seats.

Bland offered her the seat closest to the window. She had forgotten how good a cushioned seat felt.

"I must admit," Grey exhaled. "This feels so good. Do you mind if I

slip off my sandals?"

"Not at all, please get as comfortable as you like. I know that hard lounge seat had to have taken its toll on your body."

"That's the truth," she confessed, as she turned her body to place her back against the large window. A penetrating coolness came through her thin blouse to her soft skin. "If you only knew how good this feels." She closed her eyes, as she slipped off her sandals. Bland couldn't help but notice that even her feet were pretty.

"I can imagine."

"May I?" she asked, before lifting her legs to rest them on Bland's thighs.

Bland tensed up. "Whatever makes you comfortable."

Bland couldn't help but notice how her thin skirt rolled up along her thighs. He was hesitant to rest his hands on her toned thighs.

"It's so good to stretch out." She let out more than a few sighs of relief.

"So, Bland, are you going to Atlanta to meet someone, like a girlfriend?" Her eyebrows rose.

"No," he smiled. "I just wanted to take a trip before starting at the University of Virginia this fall."

"That's wonderful, Bland. What does a guy like you study?"

"I want to study English literature."

"So, you want to be a teacher?"

Grey listened while watching the way Bland's mouth moved. He is so wise and articulate, she thought. His eyes expressed deep emotions for writing. He was confident. Listening to him as he revealed his innermost desires opened her eyes to his perfections and somewhat imperfections.

Bland was also seeing Grey in a different light. As he watched her, he considered the question concerning love at first sight, and the possibility of such a thing occurring between them. Silently, he found himself deliberating if this was his soul mate or just a crush.

After fully extending her legs, she shifted from one position to another to find a level of comfort. After several more tries, she sat up. She unhooked her necklace and held the heart-shaped locket in her hand. Breathing a sigh of relief, she slid back into the large seat cushion. Again, she squirmed until she found that relaxing spot.

"What's that in your hand?" he asked.

"It's a necklace with a locket. It's the last thing my mother gave me before she died."

"Is there a picture inside the locket?"

"A picture of my parents," she said, before reaching up to flick on the overhead light. A dim light was cast over the necklace. She opened the locket, then handed it to Bland. "This is all I have of them, so I keep it where they are the closest to me, my heart."

Bland noticed the other picture slot of the locket was empty. "Why is the other side empty?"

She instructed him to turn the locket over. Bland read aloud the inscription on the back of the locket, "My soul mate."

"The person who is my soul mate will occupy the other slot of this locket and my heart." Grey placed her hand over her chest.

Bland smiled, "I like that."

He handed the locket back to her. She clutched it in her hand. There came another moment of silence between the two of them. Knowingly, Bland placed his hand on her thigh, which was smoother to the touch than it could have ever been to his eyes. From the consuming comfort, her eyelids were feeling heavy. He watched as her shoulders slid down the window, triggering her hips to press into the side of his leg. He reached up and turned off the light. Another streaking light from outside the window passed over parts of her face, exposing her moist, silky lips, instigating a moment of passion between the two.

Captured in silence, they stared at each other. Their heads tilted as their lips gravitated closer and closer.

She could feel his warm breath on her face. And their lips joined as two ripples in a pond and vibrated rhythmically throughout their bodies. Sensuously pleasing, their tongues slowly coiled while his hand floated over her satin skin. She slid her fingers through his curly hair as he kissed down around her neck. He detoured with soft kisses to her chest. His hand momentarily settled on her waistline.

The annoyances from earlier in the seat car—paper bags rustling, passengers snoring, and the train rolling over the tracks disappeared. Even the passing light that at various intervals exposed the darkness

that concealed their fervent touches seemed not to disturb them.

Bland found himself in a compromising position. He wanted Grey sexually and selfishly he wanted to disregard his sense of morality. However, his earlier comment about love and respect stopped him from attempting to seduce her in an open seat car.

"Are you okay?" she whispered when she noticed his hesitation.

"I want you, and if we were to do this, you wouldn't think I have any respect for you. Honestly, I'd rather you respect me today, tomorrow, and forever."

Wordless, she sat in the dark, absorbing what he had said. She leaned forward to give him a soft peck on his cheek. "Thank you, Bland," she snickered, "but I never said you were getting some." Her laughter settled before becoming more serious, "I keep thinking about what you said earlier about soul mates finding each other. I know we've only known each other briefly, but I feel this connection with you. But could my soul mate have a name as plain as Bland?" she joked. Once again, she lay back in the seat.

Bland caught her eyelids drooping. "By the way, my name also means pleasantly gentle. Now that's pretty imaginative for a possible soul mate." He smirked and lay his head against her shoulder.

2

BLAND AWOKE TO THE SUN'S RAYS SPREADING ACROSS his face and Grey's head on his chest. Subtle highlights in her hair glistened in the sun. She looks just as beautiful in the early morning hours, he thought. He looked at his wristwatch to check the time—fifteen minutes before seven. A wide smile stretched across his face. He closed his eyes to feel the sun's warmth on his skin. Briefly, his mind drifted before panic sat in. Quickly, he jumped, pushing Grey's head from his shoulder.

Stunned, she asked, "What's wrong, Bland?"

"It's almost seven. We're probably outside of Atlanta as we speak. Can you feel the train slowing down?"

"Bland, calm down," she said, shielding her eyes from the morning sun. She reached up and pulled the curtain across the window to block the light. Then turning back to him, she said, "You forgot. The conductor said we were an hour behind schedule. More than likely, we are an hour from Atlanta, and what you're probably feeling is the train pulling into a smaller station."

There was an expression of relief. "You're right. I had forgotten all about the conductor telling us that last night. Sometimes I get this

nervous energy."

She raised up from the seat and began climbing over his legs.

"Is everything okay? Where are you going?" he asked, once she was in the aisle.

"I'm going to my seat to get my luggage and then I am heading to the shower car."

"There's a shower car on this train?" He looked surprised.

"Yes, I desperately need a hot one," she smirked.

"Are you planning on coming back before the train arrives in Atlanta?"

She offered a perplexed look in his direction. "Bland, I will see you in twenty minutes. If fate will have it, you will still be here when I return."

She turned to walk the aisle when he gently grabbed her arm.

"Grey, if it makes any difference, I'm glad nothing happened last night."

She contemplated his remark and smiled. His awkward facial expression showed his sincerity.

"Well, thank you, Bland, but it doesn't lessen the fact that I feel bad about what did happen. We'll talk later, okay?"

She tapped him on the shoulder and then started up the aisle. He watched her disappear behind the door. Before getting totally comfortable, he noticed the necklace in her seat. It must have fallen out of her hand while she slept, he thought. He held the locket in the palm of his hand and thought about his emotional connection to this stranger. He wasn't quite sure what he was feeling, and an uneasiness came over him. Quickly, he turned to look behind him. She was halfway to the shower cars, he figured. He shook the thought and began to drift back to sleep when a heavy voice pulled him back to awareness.

"Sonny, aren't you heading to Atlanta?"

Bland recognized the voice. It was Harry, the conductor.

"Why, yes," said Bland, surprised to see the old man.

"Well, you have approximately five minutes before the train pulls into the station. You might want to gather your things, sonny."

"What do you mean, five minutes? I thought the train was an hour behind schedule. At least that's what the conductor said last night."

"We were, but a few stops didn't require freight transfer, so we were fortunate to make up a majority of the time."

Bland looked upset, "I thought someone would notify me of any changes."

"Sonny, you were dead asleep. Now, would you have wanted me to wake you up with such a pretty girl beside you?" Harry laughed.

Bland shook his head, "How much time did you say I have?"

"At least five minutes," Harry repeated.

Realizing how much time he had to find Grey, Bland jumped from his seat, turned to grab his backpack and raced off in the direction of the shower cars.

"Sonny, you're going the wrong way!" Harry yelled.

Bland wasted no time maneuvering his body against the train's gravity. He moved quickly from one car to the next in search of Grey. Occasionally, he came upon a car with crowded passengers preparing to get off. Rudely, he pushed his way through. His anxiety increased with every forward step. The doors to the cars could be heard jolting open and porters helping various passengers off. His time was running out, and it wouldn't be long before he too had to exit the train.

By the time Bland reached the bed cars, he had no idea how far back the shower cars were in the link of connected cars. He had an idea to call out Grey's name in hopes she would hear him and come out from behind one of the doors. He became angry that he didn't get her information before she took off and angry that she didn't get his. He called her name with urgency and desperation. A soothing but indifferent relief came over him when the engineer announced over the intercom that the train had arrived in Atlanta. He realized the announcement meant he had to exit the train, but he hoped the announcement would also make her aware of the situation and that it would spark her to search for him.

By allowing the cool water to penetrate her neck and back, Grey hoped to escape the thoughts of what happened early that morning. Bland somehow occupied a space in her mind, which she couldn't remove; better yet, she refused to remove him. Deep inside her, she

knew Bland wasn't to blame for what had happened. He could only do so much of what she allowed him to do. But that posed a problem. After touching him, she knew she wanted more of him. Suddenly, a relieving smile spread across her face. For a virgin, he is extremely knowledgeable of the anatomy, she thought. She massaged some shampoo in her hair and smiled. What am I thinking?

She turned her back to rinse the shampoo from her hair. As the water ran over her ears, she faintly heard a muffled voice coming from the intercom located in the ceiling of the shower car. Her eyes flinched with an attempt to make out what was being said. By the time she cut off the water, the engineer's voice had stopped. Quickly, she turned the shower back on to rinse the remaining shampoo. She couldn't wait to get back to Bland.

Sitting and guarding the entrance of the next several boxcars was a conductor and a porter. Hesitantly, they stood when Bland smashed his fist against the door of the car and waited impatiently for it to slide back. When the door slid open, the broad-shouldered conductor and the short statured porter greeted him with straight arms.

"Sir, do you have a pass to be in this area?" the conductor asked.

Bland didn't answer; instead he tried to proceed past the two men. The conductor attempted to impede his forward motion by pressing his hands firmly against Bland's shoulders.

"Sir, if you do not have the proper pass, you are not allowed to be in this area." The conductor asked again, "Do you have a pass?"

"No, I do not have a pass, but—"

"Unfortunately, I am going to have to ask you to leave this restricted area."

"How is it restricted when the person I'm looking for is back there?"

"You have to pay an extra fee to use these cars."

"Listen, I need to reach a friend that just so happens to be taking a shower."

"Well, sir, unless you have that pass, we can't allow you to enter," the conductor replied.

The porter tried to help, "What is this friend's name? We might be

able to locate him or her for you."

Another conductor's voice could be heard calling, "All aboard!" Bland was growing extremely impatient.

"Her name is—"

Abruptly, another porter came running down the aisle.

"Sir," he called to the conductor, "is your area clear? The train is starting to pull out."

"Yes, it's clear," he said, then turning to Bland. "Sir, I need to see your ticket, please."

"My ticket?" He looked from the conductor to the porters.

Bland reached over his shoulder and took hold of the straps of the backpack. He unzipped the front pocket and pulled out the ticket. The conductor quickly grabbed it from his hand.

"Sir, this is your stop," the conductor's eyes looked up from the ticket. "Atlanta."

"Yes, I know but, as I said, I am looking for a friend who happens to be showering in one of these cars. I need to give her my—"

Bland was interrupted. "Unfortunately, we have five shower cars and there is not enough time to search them all. I am afraid you have to depart the train at this time."

"No! I am not going anywhere until I find her." Bland was defiant.

"Sir, please do not make this difficult."

"You're making it difficult." Bland refused to comply with the conductor's orders.

The conductor pulled his radio from his hip pocket and whispered something into the receiver. Within minutes, two other porters came running through the door.

"What is this?" Bland asked as all the porters surrounded him.

"Sir, I have asked you nicely to leave this train, and I will only ask once more. Will you please exit the train?"

There was a hard jerk through the train and a few of the men and Bland grabbed the wall to prevent falling. The conductor didn't waste any more time.

"Grab him," the conductor ordered the porters.

Bland wrestled with the men and was getting the best of them when

he felt a heavy blow to his head. The conductor had come down hard on his head with the radio. As the train started moving, the porters opened the hatch of the car and tossed Bland and his backpack onto the platform.

When Bland gained consciousness, Steven was standing directly over him.

"What in the hell happened to you?" Steven asked. He set his luggage down to help Bland sit up.

Bland grabbed the back of his head. "I was hit with something."

"Why?" Steven asked, as he looked at Bland's head. "He hit you pretty good, but it doesn't look like stitches will be needed."

He stared at Steven with a look of delusion before jubilation crept upon his face and voice.

"What?" Steven asked.

"You were with Grey for much of the trip?"

"Is that what this is all about?"

"Did you happen to get her number or where she was heading?"

"All I know is she boarded in Buffalo." Steven grabbed the handles to his luggage.

Bland interrupted, then climbed to his feet. "I thought she boarded in New York."

Steven shook his head, "You failed geography? Buffalo is in New York. But I recall her saying she was heading overseas. Somewhere in South America, I think. She said she needed to get away, do something different."

"Did she say where in South America?"

Steven paused for a moment, then replied, "Honduras. Yeah, I think that's it, Honduras."

"Are you sure?"

"That's what she said."

"Then it's official, you failed geography." Steven noticed Bland's confused expression. "Bland, Honduras is in Central America."

The pain from the blow continued. Bland frowned and applied more pressure to the bump. "Yeah, I think she might have said Central America."

"You think?" Steven replied sarcastically. "I think you were hit harder

on your head than you think." Steven shouted, "Hey, I have an idea. I'm sure the transit line has information in the computers about their passengers. Let's go inside because this heat is unbearable."

"Good idea."

The two men made their way up the long incline that led to the station's entrance. Inside the station was a line of passengers that extended from the ticket window to the entrance.

"Hey, I will hold your place in line. Why don't you go and put some cold water on that," Steven said, as his eyes zoomed in on Bland's head.

"Yeah."

Once in the bathroom, Bland examined his scalp in the dirty mirror. He parted the curls back to find his head slightly open and bleeding. His hair had absorbed much of the blood.

"Son of a...," he uttered.

He turned on the faucet. The pipes let out a long squeal well before any water appeared. Slowly, murky water drizzled from the faucet. Bland waited for the color of the dirty water to change before slipping his head under the faucet. He closed his eyes and allowed the water to run over his head and down his face. The water felt so refreshing that he refused to move his head.

Meanwhile, Steven had made his way to the front of the line. From other experiences, he knew it wasn't customary for the company to give out information on passengers; however, he had devised a plan to get some information on Grey.

"Good morning," he smiled and continued, "I happen to have left some luggage on the train."

"What kind of luggage?" the window agent asked.

"Expensive," he smiled. "The luggage was left beside a person that traveled down with me from New York."

"That passenger is still on the train?"

"Yes."

"What is the passenger's name?"

"Her name is Grey Brindle."

The agent made a few keystrokes on the keyboard.

"Sir, that name is not coming up in my system. How do you spell it?"

"The way it sounds."

"Well, it's not coming up. Do you know where she was traveling?"

"Honduras, I think."

"Sir, the train doesn't go to Honduras."

With a sarcastic smile, Steven was quick to rebut. "What, trains can't fly or float?"

"Do you know her boarding point?"

"Buffalo," Steven dipped his mouth closer to the opening in the window. "You do know that's in New York?"

"Yes, I am quite aware where Buffalo is located," sneered the agent. Her fingers pecked on the keys quickly. "I am sorry, but no passenger by that name boarded in Buffalo, New York. Are you sure you have the right name?"

Steven dropped back down to the small window opening, "Where is the train's next stop?"

"It stops in a few smaller stations."

"Is there any way I can give you a description of the person?"

"I thought you were trying to retrieve some luggage."

Steven's voice rose again, "She is the luggage."

"Okay!" acquiesced the agent, "we won't be able to look for her until the train reaches Savannah."

Meanwhile, Bland continued to submerge his head under the faucet. Minutes later he grabbed a few paper towels to wipe around his face and dab up any remaining blood from his scalp. When Bland returned to the main lobby of the station, he was surprised to hear Steven's high-pitched voice coming from the front of the line.

Bland made his way to the window in time to hear the ticket agent say, "Because the smaller stations are short staffed and looking for this passenger would get the train off its schedule."

"How long does it take for the train to reach Savannah?" asked Steven. He looked over his shoulder, and there was Bland. "I'm trying to get a message to her at the next stop."

"What's the next stop?" Bland asked.

"Savannah, Georgia, is the next major stop." The voice of the ticket

agent rose over their voices. "It will take the train approximately forty-five minutes to an hour, and that's not including if the train is delayed at one of the smaller stops. What is the passenger's description and attire?"

Steven blurted, "She is five feet, six inches tall, give or take an inch or two. She has brown hair that comes to her shoulder. She has amber colored eyes. I am not sure what she is wearing." Steven peeped around to Bland, "Did I leave out anything like a mole or a scar?" He turned his attention back to the ticket agent.

"In case we locate this person, is there a number someone can contact you?"

"Yes," Bland said quickly.

"He will be staying with me," Steven blurted. "Let me give you my number."

Bland reached in his front pants pocket and pulled out a small paper, which he slid through the opening of the window.

"I will be staying here. Leave a message for Bland Benthall."

"Bland, you don't have to waste your money on a hotel. I have plenty of space."

"It's okay, Steven; I budgeted for it."

Bland and Steven listened as the ticket agent phoned to the Savannah station. After the agent provided the information that was given to her, the two men left the window, disappointed. They walked to the front of the station where Steven gave off a loud whistle, and a taxi rushed in.

"You want to share a taxi?" asked Steven before getting in.

"No, I'm okay. I want to wait here for the train to reach Savannah."

"Bland, you gave them your hotel information. You don't need to wait."

"Yeah, but I'll feel comfortable waiting here."

"Okay, do what you have to do. Here is my business card. Give me a call if you need anything."

"Thanks, Steven, you've already done enough." Bland watched Steven slip his small physique into the taxi. Immediately, the taxi window rolled down and Steven bellowed out, "I guess there *is* such a thing as love at first sight."

—

Jane's eyes slowed over the words as the tension from a sudden migraine overcame her. She put the book down on the nightstand and closed her eyes in hopes that resting them would cause the headache to pass quickly. Abruptly, the door to the room opened and Constance entered with a chipper face. Quickly, she noticed Jane sitting up in the bed with her eyes closed and hands pressing on her temples.

"What's wrong?" she asked, as she rushed over to the bed.

Jane tapped the right side of her temple. Constance's eyes cut toward the book, "It probably came from reading. Sometimes the mind can't keep up with the eyes or vice versa, so don't attempt to read the entire story in one day. Maybe you should put the book down for a few days; the headache should subside."

Jane shook her head in agreement. Constance pulled two pills out of her pocket and walked over to the sink to fill a cup with water. She put the pills in Jane's mouth and offered the cup of water, "These should offer you some relief." Jane grabbed the cup and sipped the water through the extended straw. In excitement, Constance threw her hands up in the open air.

"I came to tell you something. You won't see me for a week. I'll be in a training class. Finally, I can turn this phone off. I will see you when I return, okay? Please don't come up missing like you did a few months ago when they found you in the prosthetic lab. They were ready to move you to another hospital but, thankfully, Dr. Stewart told the administration he would foot the bill until you were healthy enough to leave on your own."

In the early morning hours, Jane woke in a cold sweat. She tossed the covers off. As she sat in the dark, she wondered what happened in her life that put her in such a place. Suddenly, she realized her headache had disappeared. No longer able to sleep, she reached over to tap the button for her night light. Against Constance's orders, Jane clumsily flipped through the pages of the novel to the place where she had stopped reading.

3

Twenty Years Later

BLAND SAT BEHIND HIS MAHOGANY DESK MAKING THE final edits to a manuscript by a new author when his intercom buzzed.

"Mr. Benthall."

"Yes, Paige."

"Messrs. Stump are requesting your presence in their penthouse."

His eyes lifted from the manuscript. "The penthouse," he repeated with concern. His mind began to search for reasons why. "Now?"

"Yes, sir. Should I tell them you're tied up?"

"No," he replied, grudgingly pulling back from the desk and the manuscript. "Tell them I'm on my way."

S&W Publishing acquired its name from Smith Wilkins Stump, a name handed down through three generations. It was Smith Wilkins Stump III who had a love for books. That love grew from a one-room storefront into a dilapidated two-story building on the southwest side of Washington, D.C., where low-cost paperback editions were printed and sold. The firm grew slowly but steadily.

Smith Wilkins Stump III ended the long tradition of passing the family name to the next generation when he had twin boys. He gave each son one of the traditional last names as a first name.

After the elder Stump's untimely death, his two sons continued the business under the name S&W. Smith assumed principal responsibilities for publishing activities, and Wilkins was concerned chiefly with book production. Smith and Wilkins wanted to have complete control over all business activities, imprints and editors. Thus, they adopted a micromanagement style which allowed the twins to cover all duties from president to publisher and editorial director to editor-in-chief of all its imprints. This approach allowed the firm to keep pace with the larger publishing houses.

Smith and Wilkins had taken the company from a miscellaneous bookstore selling old collections and printing low-cost novels into a renowned publishing house. The company published hundreds of titles a year under a number of imprints, in mass market paperback, trade paperback and hardcover formats. In the process, they had generated a distinguished list of novelists and bestselling authors.

Thirty years ago, Smith and Wilkins purchased land adjacent to their start-up publishing company in downtown D.C. They hired an architect to expand the building to cover an entire city block and demanded it be built as deep and as high as the legal limits the District of Columbia allowed. Below the street level was a private fitness club, and below it, a basement for filing storage with a subbasement under it. On the street level there was a galleria of exclusive shops and restaurants that attracted shoppers, tourists and locals. Various consultant businesses, law offices, and CPAs occupied the second through fourth floors. The publishing house occupied the fifth, sixth and seventh floors. Bland shared a floor with five other editors; they all shared the same administrative assistant, Paige, who also served as liaison to the twins.

The eighth floor was the penthouse, which the brothers shared as their residence. It was their way to continue micromanaging the publishing house. Over the years, the two men had become more than fraternally different. Smith was thin and completely bald, while Wilkins lugged around three hundred plus pounds and had a full head of hair.

Neither of the two men had children, nor did they desire them. The twins were approaching their sixty-sixth birthday and were concerned about the direction of the publishing house.

While Bland rode the elevator to the penthouse floor, he couldn't help but wonder why the twins wanted to see him. In the sixteen years he worked for the publishing house, he could count on one hand the number of times he was summoned to the penthouse. He also remembered nothing was ever in his favor when Smith and Wilkins ordered him to their quarters.

As always, they greeted Bland at the elevator and led him through the foyer to the main study.

The tall and extremely wide windows to the study were on the east side of the building and had a perfect view of the South Capitol lawn. It was breathtaking. Bland often found himself envying the twins' penthouse.

Bland glanced around the plush study with its hardwood floor and high wraparound bookshelves of rich mahogany. Smith and Wilkins kept everything in the room in complete order, much like they did the publishing house. Bland knew that to be in the penthouse meant a change was about to take place. Somehow, he knew he was part of whatever Smith and Wilkins had planned; otherwise, he would not be standing in their study.

"Bland, go ahead and take a seat," Wilkins ordered before flipping open the box of cigars on the large office desk. Bland took his usual seat, the seat nearest the view. For a moment, he watched as Wilkins clipped the end of the cigar, lit it, and inhaled the tobacco smoke. Smith opened the conversation just as Wilkins puffed the smoke from his mouth.

"We called you up here, Bland, because we have been thinking."

Immediately, Bland thought the worst. Even after twelve bestsellers, they looked for better books that produced more revenue.

"We have a proposition," Smith said.

"Better yet, call it an opportunity," Wilkins blurted as he gently rolled the cigar between his puckered lips.

The garden view had preoccupied Bland until he heard the words proposition and opportunity. He turned back toward the two men with

curious eyes and whispered, "Proposition?"

Bland assumed it was another attempt at getting him to write again. They had tried so many times. Still, Bland went along with their conversation.

Smith stepped away from the entrance of the study to stop directly in front of Bland's view of the Capitol Building.

"Yes, a proposition. We're old men without any kids. No family to leave the publishing house to, and we never want it to go public. This publishing house has been in the family for decades; frankly, you've become part of the family."

Bland's eyes shifted slowly from one man to the other. Wilkins made his way around the desk. Bland sat up on the deep cushioned seat. Sometimes Bland addressed the men by their first names; it helped to keep confusion down between the two of them.

"I don't understand, Mr. Smith and Mr. Wilkins."

Smith shook his head and continued, "Just say we'd like you to have a different type of interest in our publishing house."

"Hell, let's stop beating around the bush and speak straightforward," grunted Wilkins.

Smith spoke, "What we are trying to say, Bland, is that we want to extend to you a junior partnership in the publishing house."

"A partnership?" Bland muttered.

"Junior partnership," Wilkins clarified.

"Wow, but, if I am not mistaken, there are no junior partners or partners, except for the two of you."

"You're right," Wilkins pointed out with some sarcasm, then continued, "and we want to keep this house privately owned."

Bland watched as Wilkins frowned before biting down on the soggy tip of the cigar.

Carefully, Bland asked, "What did I do to deserve this?"

"You're loyal," Smith said.

"And conservative," Wilkins added.

"Do you want a drink, Bland?" Smith asked, as he made his way to the bar.

"No, thank you."

Smith continued with his reasons for the offer. "Not to mention, Bland, you're a great storyteller and your books have done well for the publishing house, and in return, the publishing house has made you rich."

Bland didn't respond to something he normally would have debated with himself. He considered his current financial standing, and he was far from being rich.

"From the moment you were hired in this house, we had our eyes on you. As your fame grew, Literature House Publishing Company, and that deceptive recruiter, Brandi, poked her head from her hole and offered you a big contract to jump ship and sign with them, but you stayed committed to this house. That means more than you can imagine."

It was a surprise to Bland that the men knew about the offer from Literature House Publishing. Equally surprising was that his loyalty would play such a huge role in setting up this opportunity. He took a second to think back as one of the men grabbed a few ice cubes and dropped them into two clear glasses, then handed one of the glasses to his brother.

Bland had volunteered as a student writer for the University of Virginia's newspaper. That's where he met Alvin Snead, an assistant junior editor whose stock was rising quickly amongst the other university editors. Impressed with Bland's creative style of writing, Alvin suggested that many of his stories be printed. Based on Alvin's recommendation, it wasn't long before Bland began to edit other journalists' articles.

After writing a few years for the university, writing hundreds of articles, editing thousands of articles and doing hundreds of interviews, Bland wanted nothing more to do with journalism. Instead, he sought something more creative. Alvin told Bland about an interview for an editorial position he had in Washington, D.C., but then Alvin received an opportunity of a lifetime—a position as the producer for the local news station. Alvin went on to persuade Bland to take the interview in his place since that was Bland's passion.

The following week Bland was in the lobby of S&W Publishing, waiting to be interviewed for the editorial position. There was only one

problem—he had to assume Alvin's identity in order to get the interview.

Bland sat there until he heard Alvin's name being called by a middle-aged man. He took his sample work and went to the interview room. During the entire interview, he did nothing to correct the twins' assumption that he was Alvin, afraid he would get thrown out and miss his opportunity to edit for a small but rising publishing house. The twins prided themselves on books that were written with strong storytelling. They believed in growth, but not too quickly. They believed in quality versus quantity. Moreover, the two men upheld a traditional sense of business and their way of doing it. They liked for all their editors to put in a nine to five workday. And, every aspect of business was done in one building.

In the week following the interview, Bland received a call offering him the position. He was surprised to learn the hiring department knew his real name. The twins saw Bland's style of editing working well with the publishing house style and its authors. During the hiring process he was informed of his working hours, rate of pay, vacation days earned and other information he needed to know, including the nine-to-five workday.

Bland didn't mind because the extra time in the office would allow him to dabble with a story he had wanted to write. Eventually, he developed a true passion for telling his own stories. At first, he wasn't sure how the twins would react, so he wrote under a pen name and assigned himself to edit this new author's manuscript. The more Canis Lupis's suspense novels grew in popularity and sales, the more Smith and Wilkins wanted to meet the author. It was impossible for Bland to keep the secret from them.

After learning Canis Lupis was Bland's penname, the twins loved it. Over the course of sixteen years, Canis Lupis wrote twelve bestsellers. Bland's novels were the kind that book clubs adopted and followed for life. His books added to the growing reputation of the publishing house. When Bland abruptly stopped writing, the partners became concerned.

The nagging worry that the partners' offer was too good to be true didn't come right away. However, Bland had a feeling it would sneak up on him, much like the offer to become a junior partner caught him

unaware. Staring at the twins, he knew the two old men were keeping something from him, and he was not the type to hold a question under his breath.

As Wilkins took a drink, very politely Bland asked, "What's today's date?"

"It's the first of the month," Smith answered.

"I wouldn't think you two were into pranks, but is this an April fool's joke?"

"Bland, it's the first day of March," Smith corrected.

"I know, maybe you mixed up the months. Nonetheless, it still sounds like a joke to me."

"Have you known us to participate in such things?" Wilkins replied with a stern face.

"That's what bothers me, that it isn't a joke."

Wilkins's only reply was his normal stern glare toward Bland, a glare with disgust toward him that started when Bland quit writing. Bland believed Wilkins detested him because his books no longer made a profit for the publishing house.

"Is the publishing house in some sort of financial trouble?" questioned Bland.

Smith smiled, "Why would you think that?"

"The fact that you're offering me a partnership."

Smith paused to entertain Bland's remarks. "So, you posit that our offering you a partnership has to do with the house's financial stability?"

Quickly, Wilkins interjected, "Now, that's interesting. If that were the case, wouldn't we be firing you instead?" Wilkins didn't wait for Bland to answer before continuing, "Bland, let us assure you of one thing, we could have easily offered the position to any of our other editors. You know, you're not the only editor in this house and definitely not the publishing house's best literary writer."

Audaciously, Bland countered, "I am the only editor who has written twelve bestsellers for the house. You never made this type of offer before, so why now?"

"You used to be a bestselling author," Wilkins blurted. He continued before Bland had a chance to rebut, "Let us remind you that you haven't

produced a quality book in some time."

"You're two clever foxes," Bland nodded as Smith smiled. "More of a reason to wonder about the offer. What's the catch?"

Briefly, the two men looked at each other.

"Well, there is a contingency to getting the partnership," Smith admitted.

"A contingency?" Bland repeated.

"You have to write another book," Wilkins revealed.

"So that's the catch. My partnership is based on me writing a book? I have heard of many things before, but this beats them all."

"A bestseller," Wilkins corrected. "Would you rather for us not to have offered you the chance of securing a junior partnership?"

"I would rather the partnership be based on my contribution to the publishing house."

Wilkins's neck snapped as he turned to stare at Bland. Wilkins did not have to bring it to his attention; Bland knew his contributions as a published author over the last three years were subpar.

"As you boldly stated, you do have twelve bestsellers, so is that what you consider a contribution to the publishing house?" Smith asked.

"Not to some," replied Bland while looking in Wilkins's direction. Wilkins frowned, then tapped the cigar on the edge of his steel ashtray. Bland focused again on Smith, and then he continued, "Definitely not, if the partnership is based on me writing another novel."

"Bland, don't be confused. A partner must carry his own weight and bring in good writers as investments. Admittedly, your personal writing has been less than stellar for the last three years; however, you have developed several talented writers for the house. You have been a great asset to the house, so we're trying to reward you for your hard work. Hopefully, that will renew that fire from within you to write again. But know this, as a partner, you are seen just like our authors, an investment. Like all investments, we expect to make a return on our dollar. Now, since you are unable to see this opportunity from a business perspective, maybe you can see it from your fans' perspective. They enjoy your books, and I am sure they would love to read one more. I know I would. Plus, it was awful how you treated your fans, just dropping them abruptly.

That is the worst thing you can do to a true fan." Smith completed his comment and took another sip of cognac.

"Far greater men have done more to secure a partnership," growled Wilkins, who was more than tired of trying to convince Bland to take the opportunity of a lifetime.

Smith replied, as he walked across the study, "I concur with Wilkins on that. As we mentioned, we're old men with not much time left in this business; we want to make sure the house stays private. Your becoming a stakeholder will put our minds at ease. That's where loyalty plays a crucial part in our decision to make you a junior partner. Of course, if you accept our offer, there will be a clause in the contract stipulating that long after our deaths, the publishing house remains privately owned."

Bland smirked, "Loyalty with no trust."

Before Smith could respond, Wilkins became even more agitated with Bland's lack of gratitude.

"You are so ungrateful and arrogant," Wilkins scoffed, then turned to look at his brother, "I told you who would be the better candidate."

"Excuse me," Bland snarled. Bland knew exactly who Wilkins preferred—Larry Peterson, his arch nemesis, who had been with the publishing house two years ago.

"Calm down gentlemen, no need to get unraveled," commented Smith.

Bland grunted and looked up to steal a scene from the window, but instead found Wilkins's eyes, double-barreled down and looking straight into his eyes. Wilkins pressed him for an answer.

The few seconds Bland was given to reply to the proposition was just more time added to what he had already come to grips with three years ago: that he had lost his passion for writing. For more than a decade he was critically acclaimed as one of the best suspense writers of his time. Now he had worked down to editing other writers' work. Until their latest offer, Smith and Wilkins had stopped asking Bland to write. They would settle for skills, hoping he could turn some mediocre writer into an acclaimed bestselling author like himself.

Frankly, it was more than Bland's loyalty that kept him with S&W. Bland would have abandoned writing, but much of his earnings had

been squandered in poor financial investments, million-dollar homes, and a lavish lifestyle. All too soon his passion for writing turned from a deep-seeded desire to a hollow necessity for getting out from under a mountain of debt. After other failed attempts to write a successful novel, Bland had resigned himself to the fact that his ability to write a winning novel no longer existed. Yet, he knew, as he drifted away from writing novels, S&W would stop producing those large advances that helped fund his extravagant lifestyle.

One last book, he thought, while sitting there appearing to be uninterested, when he knew this was a great opportunity to never have to write again and to never worry about financial security.

"Well," Smith shifted as he waited for Bland's answer. "Surely, you think you deserve this opportunity. Now, we don't want to pressure you. We are perfectly fine with your editing ability, but frankly, your gift is telling your stories."

"How long before you need the book?" Bland asked.

Wilkins puffed, "How long does it take to write a masterpiece?"

A lifetime, Bland thought. Smith heading toward the door of the study was a blatant announcement to Bland that his time had expired.

Smith stopped in the doorway to add, "Oh, and if you decide to take our offer, we want to have everything finalized by Christmas."

By Christmas! Bland's face screamed.

"Actually, we need at least three to four weeks to print and ship the book so it can be on store shelves by Christmas. Thus, we need the manuscript by the first Monday of December. To be exact, before midnight," Smith said.

Bland put his hand over his forehead to think. "The first Monday of December," Bland repeated. "That's not enough time to make Christmas sales," he added.

"Let us worry about that," Wilkins replied. "Your job, if you decide to take the offer, is to write the book and have it in our hands by midnight."

"Midnight? What's the significance of having the book at midnight?"

"You can get us the book before then, but that's the deadline, Bland. You can take it or leave it," sneered Wilkins.

Bland shook his head at the thought of having a book finished so

soon. He barely had enough energy for his last bestseller, which took him over two years to complete.

His thoughts were interrupted when Wilkins blurted, "We prefer that you write this book like you always have written."

"And how is that?"

"Here, at the house," Smith said.

Bland rose from his seat and made his way to the door of the study while listening to Wilkins, who walked behind him.

"That shouldn't be a problem since you have written all your previous novels here. We believe that's your formula for success, and when you deviate from what brought you success, you're not successful."

Without saying it, Bland knew exactly to what the twins were referring.

"We just want you to stay focused," Wilkins interjected, as smoke rings floated to the ceiling.

Bland stopped once he reached the doors of the study before wryly stating, "As you said, I've always written them here, but this time I just have to stay more focused." The men knew Bland was being sarcastic. "Before I can give you a definite answer, I have to consult with my wife."

"That's why I never bothered to get married," snapped Wilkins, "a man having to ask for permission just to make a decision. What happened to men when they used to be men?"

"True, a man needs to be a man," Smith agreed, then looked over toward Wilkins. "But modern men listen to their wives. So, what will it be, Bland?"

Bland, refusing to look weak, answered confidently, "Okay, I'll do it. What about my editorial duties?"

"Larry will take over those duties."

"Larry?" Bland muttered.

According to Larry, the current assistant executive editor of all imprints, Bland was nothing more than a washed-up writer and mediocre editor.

To Bland, Larry was a scoundrel seeking any advantage that would give him power. Kissing the partners' butts just wasn't enough at times, Bland thought.

Smith cleared his throat, and Bland cleared his thoughts. "Bland, you will continue to receive your senior executive's salary, but the junior partnership salary won't take effect until the manuscript is on our desk."

"So, what is a junior partner worth these days?"

Smith smirked, "Seven figures with a great number of financial bonuses. In addition, you will receive royalties from your book sales. That should be an incentive to get the book done sooner."

As Bland walked to the elevator, he couldn't believe what had just taken place. He contemplated why they would offer a partnership and jeopardize a family tradition. Was there more to the story than they were telling? He scolded himself to stop making more of it than it was. When he thought about the burden of what he had placed upon himself, he could not help but make it more than what it really was. Antipathy increased along with his thoughts. He rested his forehead against the iron elevator door. Yet, there was a hidden smile behind those bewildered eyes, and he reflected on his opportunity to become a junior partner. Could he turn down such an offer? He hoped his wife would understand. The question that lingered on his mind the longest was whether he had it in him to write one more bestseller.

The excitement of the partnership provoked Bland to work half a day. He returned to his office to grab his work. He stuffed the loose papers into his satchel, then headed for the elevator. Larry happened to be in the reception area of the suite and stopped him.

"Smith and Wilkins asked me to relieve you of your poor senior executive duties. Plus, I need the manuscripts you are currently editing."

After trying to get Bland's job since he started at the publishing house, Larry proclaimed his victory with a devious smile.

Bland smirked before chuckling. He dug into his satchel to hand Larry the loose papers. "This is one of the manuscripts I have been working on." He turned to Paige, "Will you please get Mr. Peterson all the manuscripts I was editing?"

As Paige went to retrieve the manuscripts, Bland contemplated telling Larry the news. Then again, why tell him something the twins didn't want him to know. If they did, he wouldn't be standing there with

that silly grin on his face, Bland thought.

"That's all the manuscripts," Paige said, while handing Larry a stack of paper.

"Bland we are not living in the twentieth century. I know you have a flash drive for all these manuscripts."

"You never asked if they were on a flash drive," Bland said, sarcastically. "Can you please get Mr. Peterson the flash drive that has all the manuscripts?"

"Yes sir," responded Paige.

"Thank you." Turning to walk away, Larry announced, "Paige, all calls for the former senior executive editor should be directed to the new senior executive editor, and that would be me."

Paige appeared baffled as she looked at Bland. Bland smiled and stepped into the elevator.

Bland lived in Shelby Grove, a small but affluent community in Montgomery County, Maryland. He pulled his SUV into the driveway and turned off the engine. He sat for a few moments before getting out of the vehicle. Again, he mulled over the meeting with the twins. Why accept the offer? For the power? He shook his head because power never seemed to be an issue with him. So why make his life complicated? Why did he want to be a partner? He answered the question immediately—the security to get rid of his debt would be nice. That security would offer a more solid foundation for his wife and child.

He smiled, thinking of the peace he would gain from being freed from the pressures of money issues. He pledged to himself that he would make wiser decisions the next time.

Bland paused with his hand on the handle of the car door. His mind was on his wife, and why he should take the partnership, if not for himself, definitely for her. They married a year after he graduated from college. Later, after the birth of their son, Devin, at Bland's request, she put her career as a professor of journalism on hold to become a stay-at-home mom. Even though she never complained, Bland felt he owed her more than what he had given her. He rationalized the partnership would be the ticket that would eventually allow his family more time together.

Bland was snapped from his thoughts when John Scott, his loud,

elderly and nosy neighbor sauntered across the driveway. He suddenly disappeared from view of the side mirror. Bland stepped out of the SUV and made his way to the back of the utility vehicle where he saw John inspecting the rear lights.

"You know you have a rear light out?"

"Really?"

"Yep, the right-side brake light is out. I noticed it when you pulled in the driveway last night. Bring it to my shop and my boys will fix it up for you. By the way, when are you going to bring your wife's sedan down to get that starter fixed?"

"I haven't had the time, John. I've been so swamped at the publishing house."

"Well, hurry up and bring it down. Her car wakes me up every morning with that constant clicking of the starter. I am an old man, and I like waking up to my own clock. I'm not the rooster I used to be," he laughed with a wink of the eye.

Bland was relieved when John left his driveway and casually waved while walking down the sidewalk. Then Bland's thoughts turned back to the partnership and whether he should disclose the information to his wife. He feared that telling her could set her up for eventual disappointment.

He stepped away from the vehicle and proceeded up the walkway that led to the front entrance of the house. Somewhere along the way he would tell her about the partnership and discuss if he had done the right thing by considering it. He knew she would be upset if she were not part of the decision-making process. Nevertheless, she would tell him the truth—she never sugarcoated the truth, even if it meant disappointing him. She would often say, "If you're going to experience pain, it's better to experience it during the short term. To put pain off for the long term meant more pain to deal with later." He accepted all her crazy sayings because they were a part of her being her.

As he approached the front door of the house, Bland's concerns transcended into excitement. Carefully, he turned the doorknob and walked quietly through the foyer. Without warning, he felt a quick jab to his side. He dropped to one knee and shrieked.

She teased, “How many times do I have to tell you that you can’t sneak up on me? I’m a southern girl.”

He dropped his satchel on the floor. “More than I can recall, you being southern, that is. I think it’s the country girl in you.”

She leaned over to give him a warm kiss, then said, “More than you want to recall.” She looked toward the window. “What did John want?”

“He’s complaining about your car waking him up every morning.”

“That’s not true. I’m here most of the day. That old man,” she shook her head, “why was he looking at your car?”

“He pointed out to me that my rear light is out. He offered to take care of it, but I told him I will fix it.”

“Like you fixed the door handle to the guest bathroom? Or like you fixed the light fixture in the dining room? Or like you plan on fixing the phone in the bedroom, which I remind you has to be put on speaker to talk to anyone?” She paused, “Bland, I have been complaining to you about fixing up this house for years. All you keep saying is—”

Bland interrupted her, “I will get to it.”

“Yes, as you keep saying. Which reminds me of something else you keep doing or should I say, not doing,” she offered him a serious look. “I need you to stop disappointing your son.”

“How did I do that?”

“You promised to read to him last night, but you didn’t.”

“Honey, I stayed at the office longer than I expected.”

“I know, but that doesn’t matter to a six-year-old. Bland, I keep telling you that promises matter. Don’t make them if you can’t keep them.”

“You’re right.”

“So tonight, Devin is expecting you to read him his favorite bedtime story.”

Bland playfully frowned. “*The Big Bad Wolf*?”

“Is that a story?” Dakota chided.

“I meant to say *The Three Little Pigs*.”

“That’s not his favorite story, honey.” She continued, “The Big Bad Wolf is the antagonist in the story about *The Three Little Pigs*.”

Bland wrapped his arms around her waist. “He is also the villain in *Red Riding Hood*.” He pretended to bite her across her shoulder. “The

Big Bad Wolf is hungry." After he gave her a soft kiss on her lips, she was free again.

She stood with both hands resting on her hips and shaking her head. "*Little Red Riding Hood*," she corrected him and emphasized each word, "isn't his favorite story either."

"Oh yeah, I know that." Bland began to climb to his feet. "Can I get some help?"

"Oh sure, honey." She grabbed his satchel off the floor and handed it to him.

He got to his feet. "I think you hurt me this time."

"I won't tell Louis you screamed like a girl."

"When did you talk to Lou?"

"He called. That's how I knew you were on your way home."

"How did he know?" Bland stood upright.

"He tried to call your cell, but you didn't answer. He texted you, and you didn't answer that either. Then he called your office, and Paige told him you had already left for the day."

"Remind me to fire her when I get back to work, but first I need to fire my cell phone provider. I'm always having calls dropped or not getting calls at all. And, I never get my text messages."

"Darling, do you even know how to text?" she laughed.

He would never admit what she already knew—that he was not technologically savvy. He was traditional. As much as he hated to agree with the twins, they were right about him being conservative.

"What brings you home early?"

"I came home to see my beautiful wife and child, whom I adore, whom I missed all day, and whom I love very, very much." He paused to reiterate, "Did I tell you how much I love you and Devin?"

"Yes, and we love you, too." She smiled.

"So, what have you been up to today?"

"Besides cleaning this house, I have been taking care of your son." Before turning to head back to the kitchen, she added, "I fixed the Big Bad Wolf some chicken and mashed potatoes. I'm also preparing a fresh garden salad."

"That's perfect! I'll grab some wine from the cellar."

"Before I forget, Lou wants you to call him."

"Had he been drinking?" Bland asked, but he already knew the answer.

"You know, I couldn't tell."

"Well, let me call him before he drives over here."

Louis Nelson was an alcoholic and a starving jazz musician who picked up gigs in Georgetown and Adams Morgan on the weekends. Bland met Lou sixteen years ago, when Bland first arrived in the District of Columbia. Bland was walking on Seventh Street at the time. Coming from a nearby club was the beautiful sound of a soprano saxophone. He went to poke his head in for a second but ended up staying all night. Lou had a gift that all musicians sought, but alcohol restricted him from his full potential. You would not know it unless you knew Lou, and to know Lou meant knowing him only for a brief moment. His alcoholism ruined his welcome in many of the prestigious clubs in and around D.C. Bland had taken his number and booked him for many of the publishing house's black-tie dinners. The rest, you can say, was history.

Although Bland hated to admit it, Lou was his only friend. He had long ago given up keeping in touch with high school and college cronies. He was never one to have many people around him. That, too, made him a welcome friend to Lou, who had just as few friends as Bland. Lou cut down on his drinking and worked very hard to keep their friendship intact, especially after Bland refused to see him after he had been drinking. Attending any Alcoholics Anonymous meeting was never an option for Lou; he often regarded the people who went to such meetings as drunks with no self-control—the only difference between him and them.

After so many years of knowing him, Bland couldn't drop him as a friend. He looked forward to seeing him at their scheduled golf outings and hearing Lou play twice a month.

He walked over to the phone and picked up the receiver. His fingers pressed the number without his even looking. Bland knew Lou and a bottle of whiskey would be sitting at Lou's kitchen table when his phone rang.

Lou fumbled the receiver in his hand. “Hello,” he barked, “who is it?”

“Lou, it’s me, Bland.”

“Bland, how are you?” he said with a slight slur. “I tried calling you today.”

“Well, something came up, Lou.”

“Are you still coming tomorrow?”

“Will you be drinking?” Bland questioned.

“No, not at all,” he slurred.

“Then I don’t see why not. Where do you have to play?”

“Some new club next to St. Paul’s,” he tried recalling the name. “Rena’s, Rendell’s, something with an R.”

“Lou, it doesn’t matter; I’m sure I can find it. I’ll see you around seven o’clock.”

After hanging up the phone, Bland dropped his bag by the hall table, loosened his tie, unbuttoned the first two buttons on his shirt, and walked into the kitchen. He stepped closer to his wife while he marveled at how good she looked in her yoga pants and ponytail.

“Did you get a yoga class in today?”

“No, but I am hoping to get a run in later.”

“I see. Where is Devin?” he asked.

“In the back yard. Your son pulled three of the tulips from my flower garden today.”

“Oh! Now he’s only my son?” he asked, sarcastically.

“I think it would be good if Devin had a playmate.” She hinted at a subject she knew he didn’t want to talk about.

“We discussed that, Dakota. At this time our finances can’t support another child.”

She countered in a bitter tone. “If I decided to have another kid, I guess you would have to love it.”

“Don’t do that, Dakota. Another child will complicate things. Plus, I have too much on my plate as it is.” He was referring to the sacrifice it would take to write the book if he accepted the junior partnership. He also knew he could no longer use money as his argument for not wanting another child.

Dakota decided to drop the conversation because she was sure it was

going to lead them into an argument. She maneuvered around Bland to place a bowl on the countertop. She started cleaning the fresh vegetables in the sink, then stopped suddenly. As though an afterthought, she turned to the kitchen table and grabbed some papers and handed them to Bland.

"What's this?" he asked.

"They're the bank statements for this month. We are overdrawn $9,600.00."

"This can't be an accurate statement," he exclaimed. "I have my check directly deposited into our account. That would have taken care of this." He frowned at the names at the top of the statement, "Bland Benthall and Dakota Benthall." He knew there was no mistake.

"Bland, last month we were in the negative for double that amount, so your check went toward paying charges. Where are we going to get the money to take care of these overdrawn charges?"

"It's not the money, it's this bank. I already told you that we needed to join a new bank. They are robbing us blind. Even when you are a dollar over, they charge you. What banks do that?"

"All banks do that, Bland," her voice carried. "We need to manage our money better. Your quick schemes to riches aren't working and steadily driving us into additional debt."

"Listen, Dakota, I'm closing this account tomorrow."

"No, Bland. From here out I will handle the disbursement of the money; otherwise we're destined to be homeless. Tomorrow I will start searching for a new bank."

Bland saw his opening. "I've been offered junior partner at S&W."

She turned slowly as if she had heard some puzzling news.

"What?" She paused to let what he had said register. "When? Why?" He cut her off.

"Calm down, the partnership has a contingency."

"What is the contingency?"

"My writing another novel or, in their words, 'a bestseller.' "

A frown formed on her face because she knew he suffered from writer's block. She had assumed it would be a matter of time before he snapped out of it, but that was three years ago. He kept a hundred or so

ideas for stories locked in a desk in the basement. Surely, she figured, he could transform one of them into a bestseller. She had witnessed it before, and with more at stake, why not again? Although she didn't want to push him to write, she knew he needed to write again for the sake of the family.

Her frown turned into a smile. "There's nothing you can't do when you put your mind to it."

Her comment was meant to encourage him, but his mind had long been absent from writing his own stories. Still the excitement began to turn the ends of her mouth upward and elevated her eyebrows. Once he saw this, he knew he couldn't reject the twins' offer.

With excitement, she moved from the sink to give Bland a big, loving hug and kiss. With her arms still around his neck, she said, "I love you, honey."

When her excitement receded, Bland broke into a confession. "I'm wondering if I did the right thing by accepting the partnership."

Her eyes twinkled. "So, you had already accepted the partnership before discussing it with me?" She paused. "I do have one concern. Does it mean I'll see less of you than I already do? If it does, then you're making a terrible mistake, especially since you didn't discuss it with me first." She gave that look that showed her displeasure that he didn't wait to discuss it with her, but not enough displeasure that she would stay upset longer than a few minutes.

"I'm sorry, honey, I should have waited."

"Yeah, yeah, yeah, tell me anything," her frown turned into a laugh. She playfully balled her fist at him. "Let it happen again and see what will happen."

He clutched her by the waist. "Something is telling me I should pass on the opportunity."

"Honey, I'm not one to argue with a man's gut feeling, but Bland, we need this. Do I need to remind you of our enormous outstanding debt? Now, if you don't want to take it, then let me go back to work."

Bland didn't like the idea of her working and Devin being left in the hands of strangers.

"We talked about this before, and you know where I stand on that

issue. We're doing just fine without you having to work, and we will continue to do fine." He paused and held her tighter. "I'll tell you what," he said.

"Tell me," she inched closer to his chest.

"Let's try it. My adoptive mother had a saying, 'nothing ventured, nothing gained.' "

A few days later, Bland entered the office with vigor. He was unaware that the contract for junior partner had been on his desk for a few days awaiting his perusal. As he scanned the contract, his eyes grew wide when he saw the actual amount of his new salary. The generous seven figure deal also giving him vacation perks and a percentage of company revenue and bonuses was shocking. Nothing could be sweeter, he thought. He continued reading each stipulation. It was no secret the twins were smart businessmen. So, it wasn't a surprise to Bland that they put a clause in the contract that prohibited him from selling his novel to another publishing house. He considered taking it to a lawyer, but then shrugged his shoulders at giving a lawyer thousands of dollars to advise him. He understood that once he signed the contract, he was legally bound to all its terms.

Later that afternoon, Smith and Wilkins visited his office to retrieve the contract and congratulate him. Wilkins squeezed through the tight doorway of Bland's small office.

"Well, Bland, the contract has been in your possession for a few days. I am certain you got your lawyers to look it over. Did you get a chance to sign it?" Smith asked.

"Yes, I did." Bland smiled, knowing very well no lawyer was consulted.

"Then congratulations, Bland. I'm very excited about this. You truly have the ability to take this publishing house to the next level. At first, we were apprehensive about offering you a partnership. We didn't want to jeopardize the house with someone who wouldn't be diligent. But, as we said, Bland, you are family."

"So, don't make us regret it," Wilkins added in his powerful voice.

Bland was relaxed and somewhat confident about his new task, but after their statements, he didn't know how to respond.

"Don't worry, gentlemen. I'll do my best to make sure this publishing house competes with the largest publishing houses in the country."

"And those around the world," Wilkins added. "Remember, it's not about how small we are, just as long as we are heard."

"So, when do you plan on getting started on the novel?" Smith asked.

"I was thinking about today."

"Well then, let us get out of your way, so you can start writing your greatest work ever." Smith grinned as he grabbed the contract off Bland's desk and then turned to walk out of the office.

"Bland, keep us posted on the story," Wilkins ordered, as he put a cigar in his mouth.

Bland walked with the men to the elevator and waited for the door to close before his chin collapsed to his upper chest.

Paige noticed. "Is everything okay, Mr. Benthall?"

"Ask me again in several months."

Bland returned to his office and sat back in his recliner and turned to face the window. His view lacked the luster of the penthouse. He pondered on different ideas for a story. There were times when he used parts of a real story to set the basis for a fictional story line. He leaned forward in the chair to hit the intercom on his desk.

"Paige."

"Yes, Mr. Benthall."

"I want you to search the Internet for any interesting articles."

"Any particular articles you have in mind?" she asked, before pulling out a notepad.

"Interesting," Bland repeated slowly, hoping this time his request would make sense. "I'm looking for those stories that aren't ordinary. Come on, you can handle this."

"Yes sir," she said, and then remembering, "Oh, Mr. Benthall, before I forget, there is some paperwork at the front that needs your John Hancock."

"Okay, bring the papers back." Bland relaxed in the recliner and stared at the ceiling when a knock on his office door broke his gaze.

"It must be nice to be able to sleep on the job and still have one," voiced Larry Peterson from the doorway.

"You should try it sometime and see what happens," Bland hatefully replied. He lowered his eyes from the ceiling to Larry and from Larry to his desk. "I guess I'll do some work now."

Larry tossed a few papers across Bland's desk. "Here, you can start by signing these, so I can do my job. It puzzles me why the partners continue to keep you around."

"Because partners can do whatever partners want to do," said Bland, knowing Larry didn't make the connection to his sarcasm.

"Bland, let me give you a piece of advice. I think you should be careful before you're out of here altogether."

"Thanks, Larry. I'll keep that in mind."

Seconds later, Paige grunted as a means to get past Larry. She handed Bland a set of papers while wrestling with a few others. Quickly, Bland took the papers and signed them before Larry's eyes could decipher any words. He handed the papers back with a quick swap of the other papers.

"So, what did you find?" asked Bland, while spreading the other set of papers across his desk.

Paige tucked the first set of papers under her arm.

"Some are funny, while with others I just couldn't believe people actually committed such heinous acts of violence."

"Believe it, because stuff like this occurs every day." Bland looked at Larry. "It can even happen here. A nice and humble editor overworked and tired of insults comes to work one day and begins chopping his new senior editor into small parts."

Paige giggled, but Larry didn't find the comment amusing, as he turned from the doorway.

"When you are done, can you please put the papers in my box?" Larry frowned, then walked away.

Paige lowered her voice, "If you ask me, he is the one I am worried about slaying everyone." She giggled. "He is so weird. You might want to warn your wife."

"My wife?"

"I saw the two of them talking in the bank."

"The bank?"

She observed his confused expression.

"The bank near the publishing house."

"Oh, the bank," his voice carried. Then suddenly he remembered Dakota's defiant statement to manage the money, and his recommendation that they join a new bank.

"We were all standing in line waiting for the teller. Sometimes you are forced to talk to people. Glad it was her and not me."

Bland laughed, "I am sure she would have disagreed."

Bland began to focus on the different articles on his desk. Of the ten she gave him, only a few caught his attention; in particular, a story concerning a schizophrenic killing his entire family. Bland considered the article and what other elements would be needed to give the story that certain flair that's found in all of his books. He took the potential leads that Paige had given him and went to the local public library. It had been a while since he utilized such a resource and returning to his roots one last time might produce that bestseller he needed.

Bland looked up schizophrenia on the computer and a list of books on the subject directed him to the fifth floor of the library. He pulled the books from their various shelves and took a seat at a corner table away from the main thoroughfare of the library. He jotted down various notes on the disease, occasionally daydreaming about the characters and how the story should be structured. One thing Bland knew was that he didn't want to rush the story. A good story had to take its own shape.

By the end of the week, Bland was mentally exhausted. He had forgotten the amount of mental energy that went into writing a novel. The challenge, however, motivated him. In the next week, Bland researched as much as he could on schizophrenia. When he felt he had enough information, he thought about the different possibilities of a story.

After one long exhausting day, Bland arrived home late to find that Dakota had put Devin to bed and prepared a hot bath for him.

"My little man fell asleep?"

"He waited up as long as he could. For the past few weeks, even I haven't had much of a chance to see you. Either you're gone before I get up, or I'm asleep when you get home."

"I know, honey, but I told you it would be like this for a few months or more," he said, while sinking into the soothing water.

"I know, but that doesn't mean I have to like it. So, have you started writing?"

"No, I finished a lot of research and now I'm starting to bring the ideas together. I do have a good feeling about the direction of the story."

"That's good, honey." She took the sponge and squeezed it across his neck. "There is no rain in the forecast for the weekend, so I was thinking maybe we could take a drive to the parkway. I'm sure it's beautiful, and we'll have a lot of fun. What do you say?"

She dipped the sponge in the water to saturate it and again squeezed hot water over his neck and shoulders.

"Honey, the faster I can finish this book, the faster we can relax and have time for each other. I promise. We'll go another time." When he felt the sponge stop moving, he quickly defended his position. "Remember, this is what we agreed to do."

"I know, Bland, but I have to get used to you writing again. I don't mean to be selfish, but why do you have to write at the office. With modern technology, you can write from here or from the parkway. After all the books you've written, I think you could at least give yourself that much freedom. Plus, it doesn't appear to be mandatory for other writers to sit all day at the office and write."

"I'm an editor who became an author while writing at work. It just so happens that's where I wrote all my books. To the twins, that's the formula for my bestselling books."

"Bland, that's some crazy superstition they're holding over you."

"I don't care, as long as they get their book and I get my partnership. If they like, they can stand outside my office door the entire eight hours I am at work."

Dakota laughed aloud, then regained her composure. Bland slapped some water in her face before pulling her into the tub.

Eventually, the story would drive Bland to put in long days and weekends at the publishing house, that's if he wished to have the book completed by Christmas. Already he had written seven chapters. By the

end of each day, he was physically tired and mentally depleted. Today was no exception as he gathered his belongings and headed out of the office. The floor was empty as everyone had already left for the evening. As usual, darkness had sneaked up on him.

Bland stood in the reception area of his suite waiting for the elevator when he noticed how the moon's glow lit everything up. The office floor unexpectedly went dark when a drifting cloud shielded the moon's light. The floor was replaced with a dark and murky presence. Bland rushed into the elevator when it opened and instantly pressed a button for the main lobby.

When the door opened, Bland rushed out onto the basement floor before realizing where he was. When he realized he had pressed the wrong button he quickly tried to stop the elevator doors from closing and leaving. To no avail. The door closed, and the elevator proceeded upward. He angrily hit the button on the wall and waited for the elevator to return.

Bland looked up the tunnel-like hallway and considered how many years it had been since he visited the eerie basement. When he began feeling like he was in some thriller and trapped in a basement, he poked the button for the elevator again. Seconds later, emanating from down the dim hall were sounds of rumbling and drawers being opened and slammed closed.

Maybe it was years of writing suspense novels that tempted Bland to investigate. As he recalled, most of the rooms on the floor were empty so he considered it to be the security staff working. Nevertheless, he felt compelled to walk the dismal hall toward the sounds coming from the final room off the hall. The closer he got to the door, the louder the sounds from the room became.

A thought flooded his mind, Do I really want to open this door?

Bland paused momentarily when he heard the elevator ding and the doors open and close. He slowly turned the doorknob. He poked his head in first, then allowed his body to follow. On second thought, maybe this wasn't such a good idea after all. The instant the hall light pierced the ceiling of the file room, the rumbling stopped. The light allowed Bland to scan a few cabinet tops, but still a majority of the room

was dark. He looked to the side of the wall and spotted a light switch. When he flipped the switch, the room stayed dark, except for the light that came from the hallway.

To go further into the room meant completely closing the door. He stared into the darkness for a few moments before fully stepping into the room. The heavy door closed hard behind him. The red light from the exit sign partially lit the dark room. About a minute later, far in the back of the large room, the closing of file cabinets continued. His shoes could be heard echoing off the concrete floor. The rumbling stopped once more. Bland stood for a moment in the deafening silence. Suddenly, he was startled by quick movements around the file cabinets. He figured something or someone was heading to the door, so he turned on his heels to head back the way he had come. He tried to move swiftly through the corridor of file cabinets. Unexpectedly, a shadow darted in front of the red light. In the red glow of the light, Bland saw a fist before he felt a hard blow across the side of his head. He fell into a cabinet before falling to his knees. He reached up and grabbed the assailant's jacket. Then there was another sharp blow across his back, followed by a hard kick to his ribs and a fist connecting to his chin. Bland rolled over on his back. He was able to grab the man's foot, but the man jerked loose to position himself directly over Bland. In the blurry red glow, Bland looked up at the man before passing out.

When Bland regained consciousness, Jesse, the night custodian, was kneeling beside him with a wet cloth. Bland squinted to keep the bright lights from his eyes. Jesse tried mumbling some words, which were unintelligible to Bland. He could tell from his facial expression and difficult grunts that Jesse was worried about his welfare.

"I'm okay, Jesse, but did you get the license plate on the truck that hit me?" Although Bland knew his assailant wasn't a truck, he quickly equated the blow to be something of equal force.

Jesse pulled a pen and small pad from his shirt pocket. His hand shook as he scribbled on the pad. Bland repeated aloud what he wrote.

"What truck? Oh, Jesse, I didn't mean it literally." He looked at Jesse who still looked confused. He added, "Never mind."

Jesse chuckled before helping Bland to his feet. "Jesse, did you see

anyone leaving the building in a hurry?"

Jesse shook his head no.

"How did you get the lights to work?" asked Bland.

Jesse scribbled on the pad. The light switch has a short.

"Tell me about it." Bland grabbed at his forehead. It had started to swell.

Jesse began to write again on the pad.

"Check the pad at the security desk." Bland read verbatim.

From the confused glare in Bland's eyes, he didn't seem to understand what Jesse wrote. He waited for Jesse to hand him the pad to read.

After hours, you got to sign pad, the scribble read.

"That's right, in order to gain access to the floors after hours, you have to sign the log-in sheet."

Jesse smiled like a child. He had fought in the Vietnam War and lost the ability to talk when a grenade was tossed into his bunker. As a brave soldier, Jesse reacted by shielding his commanding officer from the subsequent blast. The result was that the officer lived injury free, but Jesse suffered mentally from sporadic flashbacks of the war, and physically from the inability to speak. The commanding officer that Jesse saved was Smith's and Wilkins's father. Out of gratitude, Smith Wilkins Stump III hired Jesse when Mr. Stump first started the business. Before Mr. Stump passed away, the men promised their father to keep Jesse on the payroll as long as he wanted to work, with the condition that Jesse keep to his mandatory psychiatric treatments. They didn't want him having any sudden combat flashes while he worked at the publishing house.

Bland didn't want to get Jesse too excited, so he tried walking on his own. He witnessed the concern on Jesse's face. It was obvious that Jesse didn't want anyone to think he hurt Bland. Given his mental condition, it would automatically mean losing his job.

"Don't worry yourself, Jesse; if anyone asks, you had nothing to do with this incident."

Immediately, a sense of relief spread across Jesse's face. As they headed back to the elevator, Jesse scribbled again on the pad, inquiring about Bland's injuries. Again, Bland assured him that everything was

okay.

Do you remember anything? wrote Jesse.

"A large shadow."

Maybe that's what knocked you out, Jesse wrote, then laughed.

"I don't doubt it."

As Bland drove home, he decided to stop by the hospital. The pain in his rib cage was excruciating. To the touch, his ribs felt broken, and Bland expected the emergency room doctor to confirm his suspicions; however, his ribs were only bruised. He called Dakota from the hospital. Rather than telling her the truth and having her worry about his safety, he created a story about running into a file cabinet when rushing to leave the file room of the publishing house.

On the way home from the hospital, questions concerning who attacked him bombarded Bland. However, he had no answers. He didn't want to notify Smith and Wilkins that someone was rummaging through the file cabinets in their file room. They would automatically halt access to all floors after hours. Then again, maybe that wouldn't be such a bad idea. He would get home earlier, he thought.

When he pulled into the driveway, Dakota was waiting at the door. She rushed to the car to grab his briefcase and threw her arm around his waist. Bland winced and took the opportunity to favor the injury.

"Honey, I know it hurts, but I'll take care of it. You know I have caring hands. If you had stayed home, none of this would have happened," Dakota said.

"Why is that?" he asked, as she struggled to get him through the front door.

"Because we would have stayed in bed all day," she flirted. "It wouldn't have been your ribs that got injured."

He laughed with the pain, "You're so crass."

4

THE NEXT MORNING, DAKOTA PLEADED FOR BLAND TO stay home from work. He assured her that everything was fine. All night he thought about why someone would break into the file room. He arrived at the office early enough to walk past an empty security desk in the main entrance of the building. He noticed the security log from last night lying on the desk. A thought compelled him to check the log to see if anyone signed in after hours last night. After perusing it, and seeing no other name on the after-hours log-in sheet, he scanned the galleria before deciding to return to the file room in hopes of finding a reason why someone would want to break in.

Now that it was daytime and other people were in the building gave Bland a level of comfort as he turned the knob to the file room. He stepped into the room where he had been attacked hours earlier. He hit the light switch with his finger. When the lights didn't come on, he instinctively hit the switch again. The lights flickered several times before fully illuminating. The room was now more visible and less threatening in the light. Bland scanned the room before he went any further. He had no idea there were so many rows of file cabinets stored in the room. He walked to the area where he was attacked. An object was partially visible

under the file cabinet. Bland dropped to one knee and reached for the object. It was a book of matches. He assumed the matches must have fallen from the assailant's pocket during their struggle. On the cover of the matchbook were the initials "HH" and the word "bar" behind the initials. He put the book of matches in his pocket.

Bland stood and began walking further back between the rows of cabinets to the general area where he had heard the drawers snapping shut. He read the identification tag on each cabinet. Not knowing what he was looking for, he hoped something would stand out. At the bottom row of one of the file cabinets, a drawer was slightly ajar. The tag on the cabinet read "printing jobs." Bland read the bottom row tag "A-E."

When Bland pulled the half-opened drawer completely open, it was empty. He frowned, then proceeded to open the drawer below it. It, too, was empty. Quickly, he stood to yank the silver handled drawer of another file cabinet. The inside of the drawer was empty, just like the drawers of the other cabinet. He dashed to another row of cabinets. Soon Bland realized that all the drawers of each file cabinet were empty. Why would someone want to break into an empty file room? Why would the publishing house keep so many file cabinets with nothing in them? It isn't making any sense, he mused. As he closed another drawer, he heard the sounds of hard sole shoes approaching. He peered over the cabinet to see who was coming.

"Bland!" Penelope called when she saw his face emerge from behind a cabinet.

Penelope, a tall attractive red head, worked in the accounting department on the fifth floor. She stood over Bland and stared with attractive invitations.

"Hi, Penelope," Bland grunted as he straightened his upper torso to give himself additional height.

"It's a surprise seeing you. What are you doing back here?" she asked.

He thought to tell her the truth but then reconsidered. "I was looking for a file, but I can't find it."

"Well, you won't find it here."

Bland's eyebrows rose with curiosity. "Why not?" he responded, as he leaned against the cabinet.

"Because the only thing back here are empty file cabinets. We used to keep old printing invoices back here. As you can see, we had rows and rows of them filled with years and years of printing jobs, some dating all the way back to the beginning of the company. The twins are old school; they only believe in paper. They don't care for technology, especially after a computer virus destroyed all of the most recent files."

Bland wouldn't agree with Penelope; he was just as conservative and old fashioned as the old men.

"If you ask me, it's another way for them to have complete control over everything."

Bland nodded and agreed with Penelope about the twins' controlling style of management. "So, what happened to all the files?"

"For the last two months, we've been shipping them out to a records management warehouse."

"Is there not enough space here to house them all?"

"Look around, Bland; we have plenty of space. It just so happens that there's a fitness club above us that the twins own. These two brilliant individuals decided to put the file room directly underneath the fitness pool, which leaks a lot. A number of files have been destroyed as a result of it."

"Even with the cabinets securing the files?"

"Water has been known to run and it will find a crack and ruin everything in its path. The old men are probably thinking it's just a matter of time before the pool itself comes caving through the ceiling."

"Why not drain the pool and repair it? That appears to be more feasible."

"Bland, as long as I have worked here, those men are more along the lines of preventive maintenance; that's more cost effective to them."

"Repairing is preventive maintenance."

"But not cost effective. Moving the files is more cost effective and in their realm of preventive maintenance."

"Preventive maintenance," he echoed. "So, what brings you down here?"

"As I said, it's hard getting those traditional men to change anything, even if it means saving me time and stress, they won't do it. So, I took

it upon myself to rescan all the printing jobs that were affected by the virus, which mainly consists of invoices less than a year old. I come down here to get the paper copies, and these are the last of them. This helps me when it's time for auditing because I don't want to be down in this cellar pulling files," she sighed.

She glanced around the room, and suddenly moved closer to Bland. She placed her hand on one of the file cabinets. He could smell her perfume.

Bland took a slight step back and said, "Can you do me a favor?"

"Sure, but a favor begets a favor."

"I'll remember that," Bland replied.

"But are you good for it?" she flirtatiously asked.

Bland smiled, "Depending on what it is."

She flirted on, "Well, I guess it depends on what your favor is."

She twisted one of her long red locks playfully around her finger.

Bland stood tall again. "Tell me if you come across anything out of the ordinary."

"Out of the ordinary? What do you mean?" she paused, then continued, "what are you actually looking for, Bland?"

"That's just it, I don't know. If you find anything out of the ordinary, can you let me know?"

"I'll do what I can, but don't forget you owe me."

Bland cleverly maneuvered around Penelope's flirtatious posture to head to the exit and shook his head in amusement. Once on the elevator, he again pondered why someone would break into an empty file room.

As soon as he stepped onto the editorial floor, the twins summoned him to the penthouse. He saw it as an opportunity to update them on the progress of the book, so he printed one chapter of the draft to take with him to the meeting.

On the elevator, Bland contemplated returning to his office and printing out the first few chapters, but when the door to the elevator opened, it was too late. As usual, the twins were waiting to greet him. He followed them to the study.

"Have a seat, Bland," Wilkins insisted. Bland took his usual seat.

Wilkins grumbled before saying, "Let's get down to business. How far are you on the book?"

"I found a topic, and I have been conducting some research on it."

"Something of true interest, I hope," Smith commented, as he sat in a chair across from Bland.

"Well, something promising."

"Good, good," Wilkins growled, as he shifted his weight from one side of the adjustable seat to the other.

Bland still couldn't understand why the twins had to know his every move when it came to the book. He figured they should be more concerned with the business of publishing than the immediate progress of the book.

"Well, what is it that has caught your attention?" Smith inquired.

"Schizophrenia," Bland said, as he handed Smith the first chapter of his draft.

"Schizophrenia," Wilkins repeated.

The two old men glared at each other. Wilkins stood and came from behind the large desk. He walked to the front of the desk to sit while resting one leg on the edge of the desk. He crossed his arms across his large stomach while Smith began to read the chapter.

"What are your plans for schizophrenia?" Wilkins asked with a rare calmness in his voice.

"I have a few directions I can go with the subject. I'm in the process of brainstorming some articles I've been researching. I just have to make a connection with some other ideas." Bland thought he would have them sweat a bit before letting them know how far along he had really gotten on the book.

From Smith's facial reaction, the idea didn't present itself as promising to him. After reading a few pages, Smith handed the pages to Wilkins for his perusal.

"I don't understand. I was expecting some type of malice at the hands of a schizophrenic," said Smith.

"It's only the first chapter of a draft. All the suspense, blood, and gore will come later."

"In the past, it only took the first few pages to grab my attention,"

Smith said.

"It's a new approach," Bland replied.

Wilkins looked up from the pages, "I think you need to work on your new approach."

"How can you knock it? It's only the first chapter of the draft."

"We're not knocking it, Bland; it just didn't grab our attention like your previous novels. However, if you're comfortable with the subject matter, then continue with it," Smith suggested.

"That doesn't mean to take forever before you have something else for us," Wilkins snarled.

Bland knew it was Wilkins's disposition not to be satisfied about anything, but it irritated him that Wilkins would try to rush him. In a defiant move, Bland struck back. "Mr. Wilkins, I've never been a writer who wrote because I had to finish by a deadline. Frankly speaking, gentlemen, if I'm to write this, I can't rush it; the story has to come to me. Nothing is set in clay. As I said, I'm brainstorming other ideas as I write. Trust me, the story has to have a way of telling itself."

After their pointed doubts about the first chapter, his plan to reveal subsequent chapters of the book was now no longer an option.

"Hmm," murmured Smith. Then he spoke, "There isn't enough time to let a story tell itself; maybe it's time for you to tell the story."

"I wish it were that simple," blurted Bland. Then he thought how he needed a break and badly. Suddenly, a thought came to him; it was worth a try. What the hell, he would use what iota of leverage he had to his benefit.

"Let us not get too discouraged over one chapter of a draft. It's just a draft and drafts are meant to be changed. Remember, I'm dusting off the writing cobwebs, so to speak. I have collected a lot of research material on my topic, and once I perfect the plot, the book is sure to be a success. However, I'm going to need some relaxation to bring my research and ideas together, especially knowing your apprehension about the first chapter."

"Bland, are you asking for a break already? You just started," Wilkins attacked.

"I'm asking for you to understand my position in trying to deliver on

what you want. I need to be away from here to organize my thoughts and ideas." Abruptly, he recalled their superstitious behaviors and elected to use it as a means to help get what he wanted. "I always took time for myself before all my novels. It's kind of a superstition I have."

"Superstition," Wilkins growled. "You're asking for a vacation? What balls!"

"I've been working for weeks, practically nonstop."

"On one chapter?" Wilkins raved.

"On hours and hours of research and writing," Bland countered with an elevated tone of voice.

Smith's easy tone slipped right under their loud voices. "Calm down, gentlemen. This may not be a bad idea after all. We don't want him to go against his established rituals." Smith's gesture caught Wilkins's attention. "As Bland said, it will give him time to organize his ideas and for us to organize our ideas. It's not like we don't have enough to manage around here."

"So, it's settled. I get the vacation?" Bland waited with high brows.

"I thought we were discussing you getting some rest," Wilkins barked.

Bland smiled, "Yes, that, too."

"Okay," Smith said, then glanced over in Wilkins's direction. Wilkins's menacing expression showed disagreement, while begrudgingly nodding yes. "Bland, you can have your relaxation, but—"

"A week expense paid rest," interrupted Bland.

"When did that become part of your rest?" Wilkins frowned.

"Today, sir," Bland replied.

"The hell it is! He can have the rest, but I'm not paying for it." It was obvious he resented ever dealing with Bland. He walked over to the cigar box and retrieved a cigar.

Smith glanced over to Wilkins, who gave a head nod. "Okay, an all-expense paid vacation. Bland, all I can say is that this book better be the best you have ever written." Smith grinned.

A victory smile stretched across Bland's face. "Thank you, gentlemen. You won't be disappointed."

Bland had a momentary thought to tell the twins about his attack in the file room, but then he remembered Jesse. The twins would want

every inch of detail, and Bland didn't want to get Jesse in any trouble.

As large as Wilkins was, he had managed to slip past Bland during his conversation with Smith. When his voice came from behind him, Bland spun around.

"Bland, you take your trip, but wisely use that time to work on the book. We will be expecting something when you return. And do a better job at keeping us posted."

Smith walked to the doors of the study. Bland watched as Wilkins walked toward the elevator. He knew that his time was up so, routinely, he followed. His thoughts ran with uncertainty as he watched the men start back toward the study. The doors to the study closed just as the door to the elevator opened.

As Bland rode the elevator down, he was slightly disturbed that the men were already condemning the book before they had a chance to read the other chapters. It was like they wanted him to fail. He tried to erase the negative thoughts and convert that energy to some positive thinking.

Bland couldn't help smiling. He couldn't believe he was successful in getting the twins to give him a trip. "Not just any trip," he said aloud, "an all-expense paid vacation. It doesn't get any better than this." He smiled again before he thought about the junior partnership. "I guess it can get better," he whispered.

The excitement carried over as he drove home. He couldn't wait to tell Dakota the great news. He called her cell phone but didn't get an answer. Automatically, he figured she was at the house doing something creative. He dialed the house number, but the phone just rang. When the answering machine didn't click, an instant frustration set in on him.

As soon as he entered the foyer of his home, he made his way to the answering machine. A red light blinked the word "full." Bland pressed the play button and listened for a brief second before erasing each message. Once he finished, he called for Dakota.

"I'm in the kitchen."

He walked into the kitchen to find her watering a few potted plants.

"Dakota, I don't want to beat a dead horse to death."

"That's an awful cliché," she laughed. "How do you beat a horse to death that is already dead?"

"You know what I mean. Anyway, can you please erase the answering machine once it's full?"

She stopped him. "I know, Bland. I haven't had a chance to listen to the messages."

"That's the point. There is nothing to listen to except you yapping away with your mother. You need to start locking your phone. You're butt dialing the house phone and the answering machine is recording your entire conversation. You know my cell phone isn't accepting messages."

"Bland, news flash, these days most people send text messages."

"I'm not getting them either. That's why, I am giving out the house phone number for people to leave messages on the answering machine. However, that is impossible if all the recording space is used up."

"Bland, I just forget. I have an idea, why don't you get a new cell phone?" she laughed. "A phone that allows people like me to leave a message. I know you will never do that, so why not buy a new answering machine, one that will stop recording after thirty seconds? That should alleviate the problem." She smiled sarcastically.

He refused to let her get the last word. "It stops recording after two minutes, but do you have to talk that long about nothing?"

"You're so antiquated and cheap, and you don't like change."

"Just start locking your phone, Dakota," he responded.

"Ah, Bland, stop fussing and get the patio door for me." She grabbed two of the potted plants as Bland rushed over to the door. "Can you grab that other pot?" He did as was instructed and followed her to the flower garden. "Just set that on the ground," she said. She looked at him. "From now on, I will make sure my phone is locked, so you won't miss any of your important messages. Truth be told, you need to get rid of that old house phone anyway. They're becoming obsolete now that smart phones have taken over. I would love to have one someday, hint, hint. Anyway, you're only mad because you couldn't reach me," she laughed.

"Ah! I get it. It's a means to your end. You're doing this to irritate me, so I will buy you a new cell phone, too."

"I sure do love my husband." She blew him a kiss. "Maybe you can

buy me a smart phone with a touch screen."

"Nothing is wrong with the phone you have, and I hate contracts."

"Bland, my phone is two levels up from a flip phone. You need to step out of the Stone Age. Smart phones do so much more. They have apps that allow you to navigate, to talk face to face, or you can leave a video message. You'll like that, since you're always complaining about not getting your messages. And, the Internet is a lot faster than that old computer in the basement." She smiled, "I just got another brilliant idea."

"What?"

"Why don't you get rid of that old computer, these antiquated phones, and our home phone service? It's just an extra bill, Bland. As I said, no one has house phones these days."

"I do."

"Baby, remember I said this, one day you will wish you had one of those smart phones."

Bland could tell by her movement that she was happy again. Just knowing the possibility of the partnership and the money it would bring into the house was reassuring to her.

Bland looked around the lawn. "Wow! The landscaping looks great," he admitted. "It's always good to know you have another interest. That's if hard times really hit us." He laughed, but she didn't.

Bland was quick to plop into one of the lawn chairs. No sooner than he was comfortable, Dakota dove on top of him.

"I'm not sure you'll let me do that," she kissed him on the lips. "So, what's all this yelling about? What pissed you off today?"

"You think you know me?" he smiled.

"After all these years, I should. Now come on and tell me. What happened?"

"I gave Smith and Wilkins a chapter of the draft today."

Her head lifted with interest. "What did they think?"

"Because I used schizophrenia as a theme for the story, they assumed some horrific scene should have taken place in the first few pages. So, when it didn't, they were quite upset with me. You should have seen Wilkins, snarling and biting at me. Thinking about it now, it was kind

of funny."

"Bland, just give them what they want. They are giving you a partnership."

"Dakota, that's not the type of writer I am, and you know that. I have to do it my way."

"It wouldn't be bad if you centered schizophrenia on some component of romance, mystery, and secrecy."

"Romance and mystery," he regurgitated. "I understand the element of romance, but what would be the connection to mystery?"

"Bland, people by nature are curious."

He grabbed her butt. "What secrets do you have?"

"You first," she playfully laughed. "I'm sure there are some things you haven't disclosed."

"I don't know of anything that would interest you," he replied with a serious face.

She gave him a suspicious glare. "I bet."

He quickly moved the conversation along. "I don't know. I've already written a number of chapters, and that would mean doing some rewrites. I'll have to wait and see where the story takes me."

"Well, you are the writer." She kissed him again. "I'm sure you will figure it out."

"Oh, you're not going to believe what Smith and Wilkins agreed to give me." He thought about his efforts for making the trip happen. "Actually, what I negotiated for us."

"Honey, not too much can surprise me, especially after they offered you the partnership."

"You know that vacation we've been planning for the last three years?"

She corrected him, "Four years."

"Okay, four years. Well, the twins agreed to give me a one-week vacation. And the best part, it's on them."

"They're going to pay for it?" she repeated. "Bland, I don't understand. Why would they do that?"

"They recognized how important I am. I mentioned how I needed some time to gather my ideas. Then, I reminded them that they want a

bestseller. Well, in order for that to happen, I needed a few things."

She felt his chest lift hers as he bragged.

"Bland, you didn't?"

"It worked. Plus, we deserve some relaxation time. These last few weeks I have been putting in a lot of hours at the publishing house. I need to rest, Dakota."

She smiled and agreed with a kiss. "Yes, you have been working really hard, honey. But there are some things around the house that you have been promising to fix. This is your opportunity to finish that "to do" list. Plus, there are some things I've been meaning to get to, and now I have the muscles to help me," she said as she stroked his arm.

"I said rest, Dakota, not work. Let's discuss what we plan on doing this coming week. It's paid."

"I want to travel," she smiled and slid underneath his arm. "You know, Bland, we haven't taken a good trip in some time."

"Okay, so how about Paris?"

"Why Paris?" she asked with a glum voice.

"If they are paying, we might as well make them feel it in their pockets. And you know what they say about Paris in the spring."

"Paris," she wondered aloud. "I don't know. I was hoping somewhere smaller, peaceful, and definitely away from the city. Not traveling across some big ocean just to be cooped up in a bigger city."

It was obvious Dakota wanted to return to her hometown outside of Greenville, South Carolina, where the people were friendly, and everyone knew each other. Never did it dawn on her that she would miss the country life until spending so many years in a bedroom community outside of Washington, D.C. The city and its fast pace had worn her down. Traffic was unbearable even on the weekends, and she had long believed that simplicity didn't exist in big cities.

How she longed to go back and experience the simple life—enjoying a peaceful afternoon where swinging in a tire from a tree was the best fun; drinking lemonade from a rim jar had long been a simple pleasure taken for granted; swimming in the nearby river always offering the best bath; lying about in long green grass to watch the daylight drift while the crickets chime into darkness; dozing off under a blanket of stars;

and dreaming morning couldn't come soon enough just to do it all over again.

She smiled with the thought of going back home to see her family and friends. Even though Bland was also from a small town, he was comfortable with the big city. Ever since he was a kid, he looked forward to escaping such a small place where futures and dreams seemed to get pigeonholed. His adoptive father had often told him as a youngster to aim for the stars. So he determined that complacency was never for him. After his adoptive parents died, he never wanted to return to that small town and she, knowing such things, didn't ask.

"Paris is away from D.C. It's just a more beautiful city, if you ask me," he added.

"Well, I guess you're right. I will call the travel agent tomorrow." She pulled away from his grip to stand.

He heard the disappointment in her comment. With gentleness, he reached for her hand. "What is it?" Before she could respond, he answered for her. "You really don't want to go to Paris."

She turned back to face him, "Not really."

"So how about we visit your folks?"

"Really?" she asked with a tentative smile.

"I think it will be great. You haven't been home in…" he paused to think.

"Four years," she said.

"It's been that long?"

"Yes, you know Mother loves the big city. That's why she thinks of every reason to visit us."

"Just think, all these years I thought they visited because they enjoyed my company."

"Daddy prefers the simple life, and he wouldn't care if he never left the country as long as he has a beer, a fishing rod, and a lake to fish in. That's what he calls home."

"I always said your daddy was easy to please." He laughed and continued, "It's settled."

"Except for our means of transportation," she abruptly said.

"Fly, of course," he said as he stretched back in the lawn chair.

5

MARGIE AND THOMAS GATES LIVED APPROXIMATELY twenty-five miles outside the city limits of Greenville, South Carolina, in a quiet and secluded area. A long dirt-laced driveway led from the edge of the road, then disappeared behind two tall willow trees before reappearing in front of a large country house. Off in the distance was a sprinkle of cows grazing in a wide field.

Bland scrutinized the old house as the setting of a mystery novel but erased the idea from his mind. He knew writing a story from this perspective required more visits. Frankly, he wished he was leaving the moment he stepped off the plane. There was even more regret when the cab entered the driveway as he remembered his summer nemesis that every countryside seemed to possess: mosquitoes.

Soon Thomas's voice broke through his thoughts.

"Bland, I need for you to help me pull a stump from the ground. The damn thing's giving me a terrible time, but maybe with some young muscle pulling, it will come right on up."

I didn't come for manual labor, Bland thought.

"Go on and change; I will meet you in twenty minutes."

"Sure," Bland grunted.

Dakota stared out the kitchen window into the back yard at the two men struggling to pull the deeply embedded roots from the earth.

"It's good to have you home," Margie admitted.

Dakota turned her attention from Bland and her father to her mother's wide smile.

"While you're standing there, why don't you clean those green beans for me?" Margie asked. "I figured I would fix those along with some sweet potatoes and baked chicken."

"Well, Bland will love you even more if you made it fried chicken." Dakota went back to staring out of the kitchen window.

"As hard as he is working out there, then fried chicken it is."

Dakota turned from the window to Devin in the next room.

Margie turned from the window to ask, "Well, how are things in the big city? I was shocked when you called to say you were coming to visit." Margie retrieved a bag of flour from the cabinet, "I don't want to pry, but is everything okay?"

"Why do you ask?"

"Because it's been a long time since you came home."

"Mother, everything is great. It couldn't be better." She turned completely around to face Margie. "Bland has been offered a partnership in the publishing house."

"That's great, Dakota!"

"It's not effective until he writes another novel."

"That shouldn't be too hard for him. That is what he does."

Dakota hoped the novel wouldn't be as hard as Bland predicted. She hadn't told her mother that Bland had stopped writing to edit.

"Hopefully, this mini vacation will clear his head, and he can come up with a story."

"Then he shouldn't be out there working like a dog. He should be resting. Let me call him." She moved toward the back door.

"No, Mother, he's okay. Anyway, Daddy will be the first to say a little work isn't going to hurt him."

"That's true," Margie laughed. "But a little work isn't what your father has on his mind."

The two women laughed. As their laughter settled, slowly Dakota turned back to the window with a fixed stare into the field. Margie paused from cleaning the chicken to look up at her daughter.

"What else is on your mind, Dakota?"

She turned from the window. "Does it show that much?"

"I am your mother. It doesn't matter if it shows or not. I can feel something is wrong. Does it have to do with Bland and this partnership?"

"Yes, Mother."

"Well, what's bothering you?"

"Mother," she was hesitant to talk about her personal affairs, "this partnership will help us so much financially."

"You need money?" She completely stopped washing the chicken to wipe her hands.

"That's an understatement," Dakota blurted with a shallow laugh. "Mother, don't get me wrong; Bland is a good man and a great provider. He just doesn't know how to manage money. We're in debt up to our ears."

"Have you considered your career again? Devin is older now."

"Bland doesn't want me to work. He's afraid of what it will look like for a man of his stature to have his wife working."

"I always assumed that with the income of the books you all were doing well. You never complained."

"Advances," Dakota said, as she moved away from the window. "That's how they get you. They give you large advances to lock you down for your next book deal. S&W gave Bland extremely large advances. As long as he's producing books everything is fine, but Bland has not written in some time."

"Well, what happened to all the money?"

"Besides the million-dollar homes, lavish jewelry, expensive cars, and a boat, the rest was squandered on bad investments and who knows what else. It's frustrating because he had the audacity to contemplate not taking this partnership." Her anger showed and increased with the inflection of her tone. "To avoid bankruptcy, we had to sell everything except the house we're living in. Now the bank is threatening to take that since he has gone and gotten us into more debt. And I found out that

Bland cashed out all the insurance policies. We need this partnership. If Bland is truly considering never writing again, then this partnership is the best thing for our family."

"You've always been optimistic and resourceful, so calm down, Dakota; it's going to be okay."

"Mother, you don't understand. Bland hasn't written a book in three years," hoping now her mother would grasp the seriousness of the situation.

Her mother's eyes showed surprise and concern.

"Why hasn't he been writing?"

"He's going through some long-term writer's block," she said with serious sarcasm. "Honestly, I don't think he has it in him to write another novel."

"Dakota, stay positive, don't give up on your husband too soon. He's provided for you since he married you, and he will find a way. If I left your father every time we were in a rut, you probably wouldn't be here. So, in saying that, stand by him, not against him. Most of all, let a man be a man."

"Mother, I am not against my husband. I just want him to make a good decision, and taking this partnership is a good decision. Heaven knows we can't afford another bad one."

After dinner, Bland retired to the swing on the front porch. He was amazed how the crickets' whine did not disturb the peacefulness around him. He had forgotten how much brighter the stars were in the country than in the city.

Soon his thoughts drifted back to the partnership and the security it would eventually offer. It wasn't long before Dakota joined him on the porch.

"Is there room for another?" she asked.

"Sure," he said, smiling and sliding to one side of the swing. "Where is Devin?"

"Fast asleep," she replied.

"And your parents?"

"In their room."

"I guess we are all alone," said Bland with some accentuation.

"That's if you're not taking into account what's out there watching." She looked toward the woods.

Bland noticed the serious look on her face. He turned his body toward hers.

"You're concerned about the book?"

"That and other things," her expression was unchanging. "Bland, have you decided on what you're going to do?"

"I thought I had decided."

"No, you haven't. You're not sure if you even want to finish this book."

"What do you suggest that I do?"

She paused to say what she knew she shouldn't. "Do we have a choice, given our problems?"

"Our problems?" he frowned.

"Bland," she said loudly, then lowering her voice to a whisper. "We are in so much debt." She didn't want to go into detail of the tremendous amount of debt that Bland had gotten them into after more bad investments. "We had to sell everything we own and take a second mortgage on the house just to keep it. Now we are back in the same position."

Bland countered, "No, we are not in the same position."

"Bland, the bank is threatening to foreclose on the house again. I've been contemplating borrowing money from my father to pay the mortgage."

"No, I won't allow it!"

"Then what do you expect us to do? We don't have a choice."

"We will get by. We have before." He added a cold stare to accentuate his stern words.

She looked at Bland with concerned eyes. "We're not bringing in enough money, Bland, to even get by. Don't forget the advances you still owe the publishing house. I hate to say it, honey, but Smith and Wilkins bought you cheap. They will never pay you what you are worth because of what you owe them. We can no longer survive with one income. If you don't take this partnership, we'll have no choice but to entertain me getting a job, or we will lose everything again."

"No, that's not an option."

"Then what is an option, Bland?" she asked in a state of frustration. "You don't want to believe it, but we're broke."

"We're not broke. Dakota, be honest with yourself, you never liked working, so is that something you honestly want to consider?"

"Is that what you really think? Bland, I gave up my career for us, and I would return to my career for us. There isn't anything I wouldn't do for my family, so how dare you say that to me."

Bland looked into her earnest eyes. He felt ashamed that he made such a hurtful remark. The last thing he wanted to do was hurt his wife. "I'm sorry, honey. You and Devin mean everything to me, and the last thing I want to do is hurt you or him." He hoped his next comment would ease the tension between them. "Okay, I will finish the book but, Dakota, I am going to need your full support and sacrifice."

Her eyes and the weight on her shoulders eased as she relaxed into his arms.

"Bland, you know I will sacrifice everything for my family, and there has never been a time when you didn't have my total support. This time will be no different. I understand you haven't written in years. I am here for you. Whatever you need me to do."

"I'm going to need you to be understanding. This book is going to take everything I have and everything you can give to make it successful."

"I know you're going to need your space, Bland. I won't pressure you."

He murmured under his breath, "You don't call this pressure?"

She looked up from his chest, "What did you say?" He dared not repeat it, after seeing her limp smile brighten.

"Bland," she called in a soft voice.

"Yes."

"I love you." Again, she pressed into his chest.

"I love you, too, honey."

"I was thinking," she said.

"Does that happen often?"

"Stop," she said with an innocent whine. Then she sat upright to see his face in the moon's light. "As much as I want you to take the partnership, I would rather for you to want it more for yourself. I know

writing is your life, but I also know that it hasn't been the easiest thing for you lately."

Through dim light, her eyes searched for his before connecting and continuing. "I know we have our problems, but through it all, I will be here by your side. You have provided me with everything my heart desired."

By pressing his finger against her lips, he stopped the flow of her words. "Shhh, you deserve what this partnership can offer us as much as I do. I realize you put your career on hold to raise our son. I recognize your sacrifice. And, yes, I don't want you to work. When I married you, I obligated myself to give you the best. I haven't forgotten my promise."

"Bland, you have given me the best."

"And more than you bargained for, like these financial problems that I got us into. But it's going to be okay." An assuring smile came across his face followed by a bold expression. "Plus, I've worked hard for this publishing house. I deserve to be a partner. You are right, the extra income will be good for us."

"Just let me manage the money from now on," she laughed.

He tightly hugged her shapely waist. "That wouldn't be a bad idea," he chuckled. "What would I do without you?"

Her eyes looked to the stars. She took a second to consider how much work it actually took to produce a bestseller. And that was when writing came easy to Bland. Now, given his lack of interest in writing, there was still that speck of doubt that maybe he didn't have it anymore. But she would never throw that in his face. Like a kitten, she cuddled more into his chest in an attempt to embrace the security he had just given her.

Her head and eyes turned upward toward his face.

"Well," she asked, "do you need your space right now?"

"What about your parents?" he asked while grabbing the small of her back.

"They're asleep by now."

"What about what's watching out there in the woods?" he asked.

"Let them watch."

She straddled him and began kissing him. She felt for his zipper and he pulled at her dress. Once inside her, the moonlight highlighted the

silhouette of their bodies—how they moved in unison with the swing, climaxed with the chirping of the crickets and faded with the passing clouds. Her body soon slumped over his in satisfaction. Life was good.

The week went by quickly, and before they all knew, it was time to leave. Bland had mapped out in his mind an itinerary: Saturday was dedicated for traveling, Sunday was set aside to spend with his family once they returned home, and Monday he would start making those changes in the draft. Even though Bland had not come up with any ideas for a new story, the entire stay was a much-needed rest. He would leave with those dreaded mosquito bites and new energy to put toward the novel. Bland finished packing the Gates's car and was ready to leave for the airport.

"All right, let's go," Thomas ordered, since he was driving them to the airport.

"How long is your flight?" Margie asked. She sat in the front passenger seat of the vehicle.

Dakota pulled the airline tickets from her purse, "Um, two hours and forty minutes. We have a layover in Charlotte, so it shouldn't be too bad."

"I never understood why the airline has to fly you out of your way rather than straight to your destination," complained Thomas.

"Daddy, we couldn't get a direct flight from your airport, so we have to go to a bigger airport for a connection."

"Well, I still don't understand it," Thomas replied with equal contempt as before.

Margie pulled down her sun visor to utilize her mirror as a way to stop Dakota from any further explanations. Margie knew that Thomas had a sore spot for airlines after one lost his fishing rods five years ago. They reached the airport in good time for Margie to pick up Devin and quickly flood him with kisses.

"Ah, Grandma," he squealed.

"Stop all that fuss," she said, as she kissed him again. "Grandmas are supposed to get as much sugar as they can." She took a moment to look at Bland. "Don't wait so long before bringing my babies back to see me."

"Yes, ma'am."

Thomas caught hold of Bland's arm. "Son, do you know of any good sport stores up there?"

"A few."

"See if you can find me a good fishing rod. I would be much appreciative. You can bring it the next time you come."

Bland knew Thomas needed another fishing rod like a dog needed another flea. It was Thomas's way of committing him to another visit, a visit Bland knew would have to come sooner rather than later.

6

FLIGHT 2189 WAS LATE ARRIVING IN GREENVILLE, AND its late departure jeopardized them making their connecting flight in Charlotte. After the plane landed in Charlotte, Bland looked at his watch. They had only ten minutes to make it across the terminal to the other gate. He grabbed the first available attendant he saw.

"Excuse me. Our plane just arrived. Where is gate E-15?"

"Concourse E," the attendant corrected, "down this corridor and make a right, go down the long hall to the escalator, then you will go down another long hall before you arrive at Gate E. You will see it."

"How long will it take to get there?"

"If you were to run, approximately fifteen minutes, sir..."

He quickly waved down an airport taxi to take them to the escalator. Once at the escalator, Bland ran ahead of Dakota and Devin in an effort to hold up the plane. The run took him over ten minutes. He arrived at the gate out of breath.

"Has flight 2189 left?" he asked, while taking deep breaths.

"No sir, but the doors are about to close. Let me call and tell them to hold the plane." The gate attendant picked up the phone, "We have one coming."

Bland corrected her immediately, "Two more plus me."

She looked and not seeing the other two passengers said, "Three more coming." After she hung up the phone she asked, "Sir, where are the other two passengers?"

Before Bland could say a word, Dakota and Devin came trotting down the hall. Perspiration glossed Dakota's face, and her heavy breathing overpowered Bland's voice. The attendant took their tickets, and they walked down the long chute to board the plane. Other passengers appeared perturbed because of their late arrival. Once seated, Bland inhaled and let out an exhausted sigh of relief. The plane moved away from the docking station and on its way to the runway when suddenly it stopped.

After twenty minutes of being in the same place, passengers, including Bland, became agitated. Every few minutes the captain announced on the intercom that the runway was backed up. When the runway still wasn't clear after forty minutes, passengers became even more restless, some slightly combative toward the flight crew.

Finally, the plane pulled back into the docking station. One of the flight attendants compounded the situation when he informed the passengers that the airport grounded all flights. Bland stopped a passing flight attendant to ask why.

"All we know, sir, is that all flights have been restricted until further notice."

"So, are we to sit on this hot plane until we know something?"

"No sir, we are about to let everyone off."

Bland looked frustrated. "Can we take a later flight?"

"I don't know, sir, you'll have to get that information from the gate attendant."

After all the passengers had deplaned, they congregated around the gate attendant to listen to their options. Bland didn't like any of the options.

"This is unacceptable," he paused long enough to read the gate attendant's name tag. "Nancy, am I understanding you correctly that we can't get a hotel or the option to get another means of transportation until after the last scheduled flight?"

"That's ridiculous," a voice shouted from the crowd.

Nancy lifted her voice so everyone in the area could hear her announcement. "Because of the situation, we're not sure when the flights will go back online. It is procedure to wait until the last scheduled flight before offering any kind of voucher. It is possible that passengers can make that flight."

"Given the flights go back online," another voice shouted.

"So, we're supposed to sit in this airport until then?" Bland questioned.

From the other passengers' grunts and groans, it was obvious that they agreed with Bland.

"Folks, it's not the airline's fault. The airport is the one that halted all flights," a frustrated Nancy responded.

There was a loud uproar of angry comments as a result of the attendant's true but insensitive statement.

"We apologize for the inconvenience this is causing you and your families, but again I say to you that it is not the airline's doing. We, however, are committed to doing everything we can to make this uncomfortable experience as comfortable as possible for all of our customers."

"This is it? Having us wait with no accommodations," snarled a woman in the crowd.

Nancy shrugged her shoulders, and one by one the passengers began to disperse.

Bland turned from the counter to take a seat beside Devin. Dakota moved from the counter to talk to Bland.

"Well, what do you want to do?"

Devin looked up at Dakota, "Mommy, I'm hungry."

"Let's get something to eat. Hopefully, the flights will be back online by the time we return."

Bland stood from his seat, "Is it safe to get something to eat?"

Dakota headed back to the counter to ask more politely, "Since all we are doing is waiting, is it possible to get something to eat without jeopardizing our flight?"

"Sure, you can go and eat, and if the flights go back online, I will send someone to notify you. Do you know where you are dining?"

"Not really."

"May I suggest a good restaurant around the corner?" Nancy said.

After two hours of dining and waiting an additional two more hours in the gate area, Bland had had enough. It was his opinion that the planes weren't going back online. He headed to the counter with renewed anger.

"My family has been here since five o'clock this evening, patiently waiting for the planes to go back online or for the last scheduled flight, whichever comes first. I have a small son and a wife who are exhausted. Frankly, enough is enough."

"Sir, all of our passengers have been waiting just as long as you," Nancy remarked before stealing a glance at Devin, who was fast asleep in his mother's arms. She cracked no smile, but immediately began typing out a voucher on the computer.

She looked around and then whispered, "Sir, it is your choice to have a voucher for a hotel and then catch a plane in the morning. There is a chance the flights may still be grounded tomorrow."

"Still grounded?" he questioned. "What's actually going on? I spoke with a few ground workers who say the airport is conducting a security test, but does a security test take this long?"

"Normally no; however, we are living in post-9/11 times, and you can never be too safe."

"Come on, I need to be back in D.C. as soon as possible. If I'm basing my decision to stay overnight on information I don't have, then that's going to put me in an uncomfortable position with my bosses. So, what's actually happening?"

Nancy swallowed, looked around, and slightly leaned over the counter.

"A few destination airports received bomb threats. Your destination airport was one of the airports that received a bomb threat. Our airport officials don't know how serious it is, but given how long we've been offline, it appears serious. As a precaution, our airport is conducting several safety measures. I don't think the situation is going to change by tomorrow, so I suggest you take another method of travel."

"Thank you," Bland whispered. "What's the next thing leaving town?"

"You have the option of getting a rental car or I can call and book you on Greyhound, whichever you prefer."

"What time is the next Greyhound leaving for D.C.?" Bland hastily asked.

"If you'll give me a minute, I can get that information."

In the meantime, he stepped away from the counter to inform Dakota of their new options.

"It's about a nine-hour drive from here to Maryland. If we left now it would put us home around six, maybe seven the next morning."

"Bland, I personally don't want to be on the road that late with Devin. Suppose we get a flat tire or something?" She thought about it to herself again. "No, Bland, I don't feel comfortable with driving."

When Bland could no longer hear the attendant's voice, he turned to step back to the counter, hoping that the bus was still an option.

"Sir, the last bus just left for Washington, D.C."

Dakota whispered softly to the attendant from her seat, "Does the train go through this area?"

Immediately, the attendant's eyes brightened. "You know, I think we do have an arrangement with the train company. I might be able to get you on it, that's if it hasn't left. Give me a minute to look up that information." Her fingers started tapping on the keys. "Oh, great," she said with enthusiasm. "The last train leaves within an hour, but it won't get you into Union Station until the next morning." The attendant stopped to look at her notes on the monitor of the computer, "9:00 a.m. the next morning."

"That's a long time on the train," Bland complained.

"Frankly, the train is excellent, and the airline has committed to paying for whatever accommodation will satisfy your traveling needs. Why not get a bed car? That way you can sleep on the train."

Dakota turned to Bland, "I don't want to sit in this airport any longer. Let's take the train."

"What about our luggage?"

"A driver from our airline will deliver your bags once they arrive at Reagan International Airport," Nancy replied.

"We checked four bags," Bland replied.

"We will be sure to get every bag you checked."

Bland thought about Thomas's fishing rods getting lost. "Unfortunately, that's not going to work," he said, not hiding his disappointment. Bland looked at Dakota, "What if the bags get lost?"

"Bland, I don't care. I don't want to be in this airport another minute."

"You should really hurry so you won't miss that train," said Nancy.

"Okay," Bland conceded.

"I'll call an airport taxi to help you with your carry-on luggage."

The moment the taxi pulled in front of the train station, Bland spotted the steel monster on the rails. A slight chill ran across his neck.

7

THE TRAIN HAD ALREADY STARTED TO BOARD PASSENGERS when they arrived at the station.

"Sir, I'm going to get someone to drive you right to the tracks because you won't make it if you go into the station."

"What about our tickets?" Bland asked.

"Don't worry. I've taken many airline passengers to this train. More than likely, the airline has taken care of everything. All you need is your ID."

The sight of the iron doors, the boxcar's cushion seats, and narrow aisle took Bland's mind back to the night of his first train ride. What he had thought he had buried deep enough was all coming back.

The porter broke into his thoughts, "Sir, this is your bed car."

Dakota looked to the porter, "Can you please lower the beds?"

Somewhere along their travels to the train, Devin had fallen asleep again. Carefully, Bland took off Devin's clothes and laid him in the bed. Dakota undressed and lay beside him.

"Are you coming to bed?" she asked.

"I have too much energy, honey. I need to wind down, so I'm going to sit over here and read a bit before retiring."

He gave her a kiss and within minutes he heard her muffled snores. She only snores when she's extremely tired, he thought. To keep his mind from wandering to old memories, he took a magazine from his carrying case and began flipping through the pages for an interesting article. Occasionally, he stared out the window at the porters who loaded the train. Helplessly, his mind drifted to years before when he had dodged the porters as he headed to the train. He caught himself and pulled his mind and eyes back to the magazine and continued flipping through the pages.

When the engine tugged on the link of cars, it startled Bland. He noticed that all the traffic had disappeared. The station appeared deserted like the old train station in his hometown. He thought of what the old train station might look like today. From a distance, he saw a ticket agent carrying a tote bag and running toward the train. Behind the agent, a woman struggled to keep up.

No way were they going to make it, Bland believed. The train was starting to move at a steady pace. Seconds later, the agent ran past the window. A slight breeze had begun to stir in the trees. As the woman approached Bland's window, her hat blew from her head. She contemplated chasing the hat, but to chase the hat meant missing the train. Instead, she watched the hat bounce along the landing. When she turned to run, in slow motion, the magazine slipped from Bland's hand, and she from his sight. Bland thought he must be confused about who he had just seen. Maybe his vivid imagination played tricks on him. An increasing anxiety pressed against his chest, causing perspiration to form across his forehead.

Thirty minutes had elapsed from the time Bland saw the woman. After all these years, it just wasn't possible that she would be here, at this exact moment in time. Maybe it is her. No, it just isn't possible, he thought. He erased each feasible thought with an even more visible head nod. He believed his mind and its constant illusions fabricated Grey. He wasn't sure if she even made the train, but curiosity of her identity raced through his thoughts to find out. But each time he attempted to leave the car, doubt and fear made him return to his seat.

He tried picking up the magazine again but found himself spending

less time reading and more time consciously weighing the entire situation over and over. According to his watch, an hour had now passed since he spotted the woman, and still he had neither committed himself to leaving the car nor permanently dedicated himself to staying.

Dakota's snores broke his wandering thoughts. A sense of conviction settled upon him. There his beautiful wife and son lay in the bed, yet he was totally consumed with finding some woman that he had fallen in love with twenty years before. There were moments when rational thoughts favored searching for the stranger. What's the harm in finding out; it would only take a few minutes to walk the train. He would be back before she awoke, he deliberated. As his mind kept hammering, he kept resisting the urge to leave. When he could resist no longer, he pulled a note pad and pen from his bag. The words, 'I'll be back in 5 minutes', were written on the pad. He carefully tore the paper from the note pad and stuck it to the window. He was certain Dakota, if awakened, would see the note and not panic when not seeing him. Being even more careful not to wake her, he slowly slid open the door of the bed car. Once he was outside, he breathed easily, that is before guilt assaulted him. He could not retrace his steps now, he thought. He had committed himself to at least five minutes and needed to relieve his mind of any doubts about the woman's identity. At least that is what he persuaded himself to believe.

A burst of excitement shot through his body as he walked the aisle of each car in search of Grey. If it were her, what would he say? He glared at his watch; two minutes had elapsed since he left the bed car. Bland's mind flashed back to the words the conductor uttered years ago, "You only have five minutes," so his pace quickened as his mind continued to flash back—younger and thinner. Expressions of fear and sweat cloaked his face as he ran up the aisle of the train in search of Grey. As he struggled against the train's force, its pull and turns sent him staggering from seat to seat. He gazed quickly at passengers as he went from one car to another.

Time was running out, and he felt like he was going to lose her again. Like before, panic took over. Bland hurried through the lounge area, dining area, and many of the passenger cars and still no Grey.

He stopped a conductor heading his way.

"Excuse me, how many seat cars are left in that direction?" he asked, pointing toward the engine.

"Two more, then cargo cars."

After inspecting each person in the last passenger cars, a feeling of deep disappointment gnawed in his chest. He displayed a changeable temperament. With disappointment, he thought the stranger he spotted must not have been Grey—or may not have made the train.

Slowly, Bland turned on his heels to head back to his bed car. He figured he had made a spectacle of himself by running from one car to the next without having an idea of what Grey actually looked like after twenty years. From the window of the bed car, she appeared ageless. To think of her as ageless now seemed ridiculous to him. He paused to study his appearance in one of the windows. A full, trim beard and rimmed glasses hid his once young and vibrant complexion by adding a more mature demeanor to his appearance.

"Ageless," he laughed.

Bland moved on from the window through the dining car and on to the lounge area. Momentarily, he stopped at the bar for a drink and succumbed to the idea of Grey not ever being on the train; that is, until he heard a laugh. Quickly, he turned to look, inadvertently spilling the tonic on the surface of the bar. Was it possible? he thought, as he glanced at the woman. It had to be her in the flesh. He began to stare. Maybe a little aged, but to his satisfaction, he thought. He wasn't sure because her face was at an angle. He wondered how he missed her before. Frankly, it didn't matter. He listened to her voice, a little heavier, he considered. Her movements were still as stunningly graceful as before. To him, the entire scene was surreal. Despite the last twenty years, in his heart he longed with a strong desire for it to be her. No longer concerned about his five minutes, his thoughts were now completely consumed with Grey and whether this was her.

Bland listened as a younger gentleman drowned the woman in compliments. She, on the other hand, flirted back with intellectual conversation that at times seemed to lose the fellow. To Bland, she appeared to be the perfect picture of the past. The way she caught the attention of all in the area was amazing. Bland believed the man's youth

held her attention, yet Bland's curiosity lured him to their table.

What he was about to do was uncharacteristic of Bland's behavior. Without delay, he interrupted their banter, looked into her eyes and asked, "Excuse me, I was wondering if you believe in fate?"

The remark took the woman and the younger man by surprise.

"I beg your pardon," the young man said.

Quickly, Bland gathered his thoughts, "I mean would fate have it that two people could reunite after twenty years?"

The woman replied by offering a bewildered stare. The younger gentleman rose to his feet to confront Bland.

Bland confessed, "I'm sorry; that just came out."

"Do we know you?" the man questioned, while still standing.

Bland turned to the man, "I think I know her."

The woman didn't answer. Bland waited for her to recognize him, but her silence remained in her bewildered gaze.

The man was quick to protect the woman, "I'm sorry, sir, but I think you've confused this lady with someone else."

After an uncomfortable silence, Bland thought it would be best to leave before further embarrassing himself. He took one last opportunity to scan over the strangely familiar face before saying, "I have been mistaken; please forgive my sudden intrusion."

"No harm done," the young man answered, then returned to his seat.

Before Bland completely backed away from the table, he noticed the woman staring warily into his face. Bland tried to convince himself that the moment he saw the woman, and how she resembled Grey, his mind had adopted a mania to create her into Grey. As he walked away from the table, humiliation etched deep across his face. How did he even allow himself to get to that point? He hurried out of the lounge car, refusing to look back. Like his first train experience, this incident would also go to the deepest part of his subconscious, but he was so sure it was her.

As soon as Bland disappeared from the lounge area, the young man turned back to the woman.

"Didn't I tell you, Brind, only crazy people ride the train?"

"So, what does that say about us?" the woman asked.

"What do you mean?" he asked.

"Are we not also riding the train?"

The young man smiled, "Now, there are some exceptions."

She focused her attention outside the window, concentrating to remember the past. She concentrated even harder on Bland's words to the point it sparked a remembrance of her words twenty years prior.

"If fate will have it, then you will still be here when I return," she said softly.

Overheard by the young man, "What did you say?"

"Bland!" she muttered.

Instantly, she lifted herself from the seat, then excused herself from the young man's company.

"Where are you going?" he asked when she stood. His voice quivered, "Please don't go, stay," he begged as she walked away.

Her eyes and mind were at discord with one another. As she sought to find Bland, discrepancy lay with her rationality of the entire ordeal. She was vexed at not speaking up when he first approached her. She recognized a familiarity about him. What if I don't find him, she contemplated. She raced up the aisle in the direction he went.

All the excitement had made Bland dizzy. He stepped into one of the passenger car's bathrooms to splash some cold water on his face.

Grey rapidly approached the end of another car when unexpectedly the bathroom door opened, and Bland stepped out. Grey slammed into him.

"I am so sorry," he apologized, before knowing who it was that nearly ran over him. He pulled Grey up to his chest and tried to brace her from falling. He could hardly breathe when he realized it was her.

"Bland," she gasped.

"Grey," he whispered.

"Jane?" Jane's eyes lifted from the pages of the book upon hearing Constance's voice.

"I'm back. Did you miss me?"

Before she received an answer, Constance started opening blinds.

"Open these blinds so some light can get in here." Suddenly, the

room lit up. "Um, that's better," Constance smiled. "I see you're back to reading again. Is the dark better on your eyes?"

Jane offered a head nod. Constance picked up the book to inspect its pages.

"You've read ninety-three pages since I've been gone. Any more headaches?" she asked.

Jane was fearful of telling the truth, knowing Constance would equate the headaches to the book and take it from her. Since the book was starting to interest her, she shook her head. You could tell from Constance's doubtful facial expressions that she suspected the headaches were still occurring. She wasn't sure if reading was causing the headaches. Nonetheless, she knew that was the only entertainment Jane had and taking that away would probably send her into depression.

"So, are you enjoying the book?"

A twinkle in her eyes was acknowledgment enough, and Constance answered aloud for Jane.

"You like it that much? Maybe I will take it with me on vacation; of course, that's if you're done with it. Are you feeling any other pains?" Constance asked, as Jane stood from the chair to stretch.

Jane shook her head no, and on her pad she roughly scribbled the words, "bad dream."

"You had a bad dream? When?" She answered for Jane, "Last night?"

Yes, Jane nodded.

"Is this the first one?" She waited for Jane to respond. "So, you've had more than one? I'll be sure to let Dr. Stewart know."

Jane moved her head from left to right.

"You don't want me to tell him? Why not? These dreams could be the key to your past."

Again, she shook her head before holding up the book.

"You think he's going to stop you from reading because of the dreams?"

With her bandaged hands pressed together, she pleaded.

"Okay, Jane. But promise me that if you have another, you will tell me."

Jane nodded her head. Abruptly, she started pretending to scratch

her arms and legs.

"You're itching, too? Jane, you're going to do a lot of itching. Now you understand why Dr. Stewart is leaving your fingers covered. Don't worry, it too will pass."

Constance took a few gauze wraps from a drawer and tossed them on the bed.

Jane's eyes seemed to grimace.

"There are some complementary therapies such as massages, which can help reduce the pain and itching. However, with your burns, I'll have to clear it with Dr. Stewart. He does not want the burns to be disturbed. He's coming to change your bandages so he can examine your skin. Maybe we can ask him then."

With disguised excitement, Jane touched the bandages on her face as a way of asking.

"Yes, he's planning on looking at your face as well, but I'm not saying he's going to leave off the bandages. It will depend on how the grafts are healing."

Constance noticed the collapse of Jane's enthusiasm.

"No, you shouldn't feel that way, Jane. When it's time, I'm sure Dr. Stewart will not hesitate to leave them off." She moved closer to Jane's side. "Don't get frustrated."

Dr. Stewart entered the room with his chart and a serious frown. Jane looked up and waved. Right away, Constance informed him of Jane's headaches. Jane's eyes widened.

When Dr. Stewart walked over to the sink to get a pair of latex gloves, Constance whispered to Jane, "I never said I wouldn't mention the headaches."

"You're having headaches?" he turned from the sink and pointed toward his head.

Jane was reluctant to answer for fear he would take the book away, but slowly she nodded yes. She looked at Constance. She expected Constance to reveal her suspicions that the source of the headaches was caused by the book, but Constance kept quiet.

The doctor offered an explanation, "Unfortunately, the migraines are

going to come and go for a while. It could very well be a side effect from the medicine you've been taking, or a lingering effect of the coma. Keep me and the nurses aware of them, okay? If they get any worse, I will order some more tests to make sure nothing abnormal is occurring."

He paused to reach for the scope light on the tray. "Okay, let's take a look at your throat." His eyes squinted. "When you swallow, are you experiencing much pain?"

She shook her head. She became agitated with anxiety, hoping when the bandages came off, he would leave them off.

"That's good. Sit still so I can look at your face and hands."

He peeled the bandages off layer by layer until her face was fully exposed to the cool air coming through the vents. Jane closed her eyes and allowed the air to float across her skin. It felt even more soothing when the doctor caressed ointment over the wounds.

"You're healing well." He smiled.

Jane's eyes gleamed before looking toward the bathroom. She wanted to look in the mirror. The doctor shook his head.

"Not yet, Jane, there's still a lot of redness and swelling in the face and around the stitches. I want to make sure it has nothing to do with infection."

Jane noticed her badly burned fingers.

Dr. Stewart followed her eyes. "Trust me, I had the country's top burn specialist work on you. There's no need to worry. I'm more than confident you will look as beautiful as you did before the accident."

Her disappointment showed on her face, not because she was going to look beautiful, but because he wouldn't allow her to see her face. The doctor moved aside to let Constance put fresh dressings on Jane's hands and face.

"Jane, I heard you went to see the voice specialist and had some physical therapy. It wasn't all that bad, right?"

"You didn't tell me that, Jane. Not that you could, since you can't talk," Constance laughed.

"Don't worry. As the weeks pass, therapy will get easier. I'll tell the physical therapist to get you a walker." Dr. Stewart stepped back from the chair, "I'll see you later during the week."

"But I'll be here to assist you every day," Constance smiled, then remembering, "Dr. Stewart, Jane is experiencing an extreme amount of itching. Do you suggest massages to help reduce the itching?"

"Let's give her several more weeks before any massaging."

When Constance saw the doctor about to leave the room, she stopped wrapping. "Excuse me, Jane, I have to ask the doctor something before he leaves." As Dr. Stewart reached for the handle to the door, Constance grabbed his arm and whispered, "Dr. Stewart, when do you think we should tell Jane about the baby?"

Dr. Stewart glanced back at Jane. "It's important to remember her mind is very fragile. If we tell her about the baby too soon, that could be devasting. In a few weeks I am going to have Jane meet with the psychiatrist, Dr. Westfall. I want to wait on the doctor's recommendation."

Once the doctor left, Constance expressed her opinion about Jane wanting to see her appearance.

"You can't say I didn't ask. Now about you wanting to see your face. He's right, Jane. Maybe I shouldn't say this, but I believe in being honest with people. Now is not the time for you to see your face."

Unable to clearly speak but unwilling to remain silent, her voice barely whispered, "Why?"

"Because you wouldn't see the beauty beyond the burns, the swelling, the cuts, and the stitches; you may think that's an awful thing to say, but…"

Jane slowly lifted her hand and placed it on Constance's hand. Jane knew her words were never malicious.

"Okay, I'm done," Constance smiled while gathering the old bandages. Suddenly, Constance's hospital cell phone buzzed. She glanced at the text scrolling across the screen. "Well, I have to go; patients are waiting."

Jane looked up in a panic as Constance approached the door. Constance abruptly stopped.

"Your book, I almost forgot that I slipped it in my pocket." She pulled the book from her jacket and tossed it on the bed. "If I get a minute, I'll stop in later. Hit the call light if you need me."

Jane took the book and quickly sifted through the pages until she found the place where Bland whispered Grey's name. Her eyes scanned along the words before commencing to read.

After Grey heard her name, she caught her breath and immediately began explaining. "I didn't realize it was you until I thought about what you said about fate being the impetus of two people reconnecting. It's been so long, Bland."

"For a moment I thought I was going crazy. I saw you rush onto the train, but I couldn't find you. I found myself panicking all over again, as if history had repeated itself just to remind me of what I lost."

"What do you mean?"

"I was afraid I lost you again." He saw her awkward expression, so he tried to explain further. "That morning when you left to take a shower, I tried looking for you, but I couldn't find you. When I refused to get off the train, I was thrown off."

"All these years, I thought you were disappointed because I didn't have sex with you."

"No way. I respected you for that. For two years I searched for you. I even tracked you all the way to Miami, Florida. But then you disappeared."

Bland looked around and spotted two empty seats.

"Come sit down." Bland led her to the seat.

"You have no idea how I felt when I returned, and you weren't there. I would have never suspected such a thing because I felt we connected."

"I felt the same, Grey."

"Bland, there were many times when I wondered if I would ever see you again. Then I often asked myself our purpose for meeting?"

Bland shook his head. "I don't know. It had to be something. Now, the two of us meeting again after so many years is beyond coincidence."

"More like fate or destiny, if you ask me," she smiled shyly.

"Call it what you want. I'm just happy to see you again."

"That night was so perfect," she confessed.

"And so was the conversation," Bland remembered.

"You remembered that conversation?" she asked as her eyelids lifted.

"I'll never forget it. We were discussing the idea of love at first sight."

Grey sat back in the seat, and Bland watched her laugh.

"Well, I have a question for you." He hesitated before continuing, "Do you think love at first sight could happen twice with the same person?"

Suppressed in Bland's mind was his latent love for Grey. She had become akin to a small crack in a dam, although, from afar in his mind, it could be ruptured by the smallest pebble.

Her laughter came to a slow halt, "If it was truly love, why not?" She knew the question referred to them. "The question is should it be left up to fate to determine such a thing again?"

Bland chuckled, "That's a very good question."

He cautiously clutched her hand. When he noticed the wedding ring gleaming on her finger, he offered a puzzled glance and pulled back.

His reaction was enough for her to notice and reply, "I'm divorced."

"How long have you been divorced?" he asked, wondering why she would still be wearing the ring. "I apologize, I didn't—" He tried to explain before she cut him off.

"No, it's okay," she smiled. "The divorce was sudden and still fresh. I'm not comfortable not wearing it."

"Wouldn't you have to stop wearing it to get comfortable not wearing it?"

"Let's not turn this into another debate," Grey laughed.

"If I may get personal, why did you get divorced?"

Grey's sights dropped on her ring. Sometimes it's hard to forget what happened and even harder talking about it. She drifted along a memory and recalled it out loud.

"About ten years ago, my company sent me to Brazil to research an area of interest for a client. There I met my husband, Don. He was a kind man, and he offered to show me around, even though he was there on business. I didn't tell him that I had visited the area many times. Long story short, I ended up showing him around. A year later, we got married and decided to have a child." She paused for a second to think and then continued. "During my pregnancy, I began having complications. I lost the baby. The doctor told me that I would be at high risk for having kids, and another pregnancy could be fatal. But Don wanted a child so badly, and it devastated him to know that the woman he married couldn't provide him with one. Soon I stopped existing in his eyes. I was

nothing, and eventually his attention went to someone else."

Her eyes glazed before watering. A tear slowly crept from the corner of one eye. Bland gently brushed the tear away.

"I'm so sorry. You must think I am some emotional basket case."

He thought about Devin; he didn't want to think about not having him.

"No, I don't. It must have been hard going through it alone. If you need to let it out, go ahead. I don't mind."

"Thank you, but I'm okay. I hate crying," she said. "Especially in front of people."

It took a few minutes before she regained her composure. Bland made an additional attempt to probe.

"Are you in the same type of work?" he asked.

She handed Bland's handkerchief back to him. "Sort of. I mean, I am doing the same thing, but I work for myself."

"And what does that consist of?"

"I consult for large corporations that are interested in relocating their operations to a new city. I mainly go into these communities and analyze a company's growth potential in that area. My client then reviews my recommendations to move forward or reject the area of interest."

"Wow, sounds like you are a very important person. How long does it take for you to assess an area?"

"It varies, depending on the area and its physical and technological infrastructure, the size of the company, and the urgency of the company's interest to relocate. With the economy changing as much as it does today, my assessment can range from a year to two years. And with technology progressing the way it has, a company can move overnight. It's the research that takes the time."

Bland laughed as he thought about the twins. They have no concept when it comes to the amount of research that goes into writing something substantial.

"Why did you laugh?" she asked.

"It's nothing. Please finish telling me about your job."

"Well, a few weeks ago, I was contacted by a private company out of Alexandria, Virginia."

"Alexandria?" He lifted himself in the seat. "I live in Montgomery County, Maryland. Alexandria isn't that far away. Wow! Another coincidence, right?" Bland grinned.

"I am meeting with the owners to discuss their interest and my possible employment. They seemed to have a pressing interest to relocate to the District of Columbia, but they wanted to be sure before making such a risky investment."

"The real estate there is really expensive," informed Bland.

"I know, but as for now, nothing is set in stone. If they don't accept the terms of my contract, then I will be off to Houston for another prospective client."

"That's a great area, but nothing like the District. I hope you get the contract," he said with hopefulness that it all would work out in her favor.

"So do I," her seductive smile insinuated getting something other than a job opportunity.

"I like to stay optimistic. I'm sure you'll get it."

"That's such a nice thing to say," she shifted her weight in the seat. "So, Mr. Bland Benthall, tell me about you, and what it is that you do."

"Well, what's it to know?"

"This isn't an interview, Bland, so tell me what you've been doing for the last two decades."

"That sounds so long ago," he said softly.

She ran off a series of questions. "Wasn't it? Anyway, I recall you being interested in English literature. Is teaching your current profession?"

"Impressive that you remembered. But no, well, that's not totally true. I made an attempt at teaching, but it never settled as a profession. I currently work in D.C. near the Capitol."

Bland stopped before divulging his occupation. He felt like a high school kid thinking of what he should say or not say that would gain him extra favor. Up until now, it had been customary to never tell what he really did for a living, especially being an author, but he had an overwhelming urge to disclose it to her.

"I work as an editor for S&W Publishing House."

"I've heard of that publishing house. What type of books do you edit?"

"A gamut of trade books and paperbacks. I specialize in suspense fiction."

"My favorite genre," she smiled while consciously placing her hand over the top of his. "Who are some of the authors you have edited for?"

"Have you heard of Richard Norman who wrote *Deadly Deeds* or *Love Suspense* by Karen Oberts?"

"No, I don't think I have. How about you, Bland? The urge to write never pinched you?"

"Have you ever read anything by Canis Lupis?"

Her mouth fell open, then she uttered, "Are you Canis Lupis?" She pointed at him. "You wrote *Black Pond Road,"* she paused only to gather in her mind a few more of his titles. "*Next Left*, and the *Graham Ford series*, but of all your books my favorite is '.... *at First Sight*." Again, she paused to inhale.

Bland thought about the title and the impetus behind it.

"How you allow the narrator to discover as the reader discovers. The roller-coaster ride that you tend to put you reader on is traumatizing, Bland."

"As a fictional writer, the author has the license to be creative, to be dramatic and, to some extent, lead the reader down a path without knowing where that path will take them both."

"I love it," she interjected. "I can't believe you wrote all those books." She gave an exhaling laugh. "How many books are there?"

"Twelve," he quickly replied.

She shook her head. "That's impressive."

"There are many writers that have many more titles than that," he admitted.

"I am sure there are, but I enjoy your style of writing. He, I mean, you are my favorite writer," she said and added, "all-time writer."

"Thank you for your very polite words and for buying so many books. I am sure S&W Publishing thanks you as well."

"That's where I've seen the words S&W Publishing. Now it makes sense!"

"What makes sense?"

"Why there was never a photo of you in the back of your books."

He started to chuckle, "I had to stay...."

"Anonymous. I get it, Bland. You are going to think what I am about to say is so crazy, but I realize now that you and I have been connected since we separated that morning on the train."

"In what way?"

"After my parents died, I wanted to disappear from everyone and the pain. I heard about this remote village. When I met you on the train, I was on my way there to begin a new life. Years later, I would meet you there. I mean a novel by Canis Lupis."

"Where did you go?"

"Honduras."

"Honduras," he repeated. He found himself in awe and slight disbelief. "How did one of my books find such a place?"

"I am sure it was left by one of the missionaries or volunteer workers that came and went every year. Little did I know it was you."

Bland was certain that Greysen believed it was fate that had brought them together, and that the presence of fate continued to connect them through the years and reconnected them again at this present time and place.

When he considered his thoughts, he also considered how unbelievable it sounded.

She tried to lighten the mood. "Bland, I am curious. Why didn't you use your own name?"

"Well, I thought of using my real name, but circumstances prevented me."

"So how did you come up with Canis Lupis?"

Bland smiled, "Isn't it obvious? I used the Latin name for grey wolf."

"If I am Grey, what is the significance of the wolf?" she murmured, then smiled. "Like I said, we were connected. I'm sorry, you were saying?"

Bland laughed, "I was saying that I truly have an admiration for wolves. I am drawn into everything about them. Over the years, I have come to see myself in them: shy, loving, fearful, yet very protective of family."

"But you spell it differently."

"Yeah, I use 'i' instead of 'u' because *I* am Canis Lupis, not *you*." He laughed. "That's not true. I was young and thought if I used the Latin rendition, I was sure to get sued."

"I like the creativity, Bland. But the books stopped coming. What happened?"

"The industry calls it writer's block. I like to call it burned-out."

"I'm sorry, Bland," she mumbled. She was still taken aback by the fact she was sitting beside a renowned author. She chose to move the conversation along, "So, of the books you've written, which is your best work?"

"I don't think I've written it."

"So, you will pursue writing again?" She smiled. "I'm looking forward to reading it."

The question struck him awkwardly, "Who knows, maybe one day."

She shook her head in astonishment before replying, "Bland, you're too good to be true."

"What do you mean?"

"Look at you. You're a prominent author who seems to be truly humble. Not to mention that you are extremely attractive. Honestly, men like you are hard to find." She offered a defiant expression, "I know!"

Bland laughed, "I hate to ask how you know."

"Honestly, it is kind of embarrassing, but I did put it out there."

"Yes, you did," he concurred.

"But don't judge me," she pointed. "My circle is very, very small. I have been to a lot of cities and picked up only a few friends. We like to keep in touch through our social media sites. They're always trying to set me up. One suggested I try an online dating site. I did. And, I will be the first to admit, my experiences were awful."

"I'm sorry to hear that."

"Don't be," she smiled. "I'm still single."

"Given your job I'm sure you have to stay technologically abreast, but frankly, I can't stand it. People put too much of their business on those sites for everyone to see. And don't get me started on cell phones. My—" he immediately stopped his thought in mid-sentence, for he was about to say *my wife*.

"Something wrong, Bland?"

"I thought I felt the train stop."

She glanced out the window. "No, it appears to be slowing down. But you were saying?"

"I am a dinosaur living in a fast, modern technical era." Bland pulled out his cell phone.

Instantly, Grey roared in laughter. "No way! That's a flip phone."

"You say it like it's prehistoric."

"Isn't it?" she laughed.

"Let's just say I like holding onto things."

"Well that's good to know." She covered her mouth to conceal her laughter. "It appears you have held on for some time."

"Go ahead and laugh."

"Bland, you definitely need to embrace this era. The world is changing so fast, and if you don't keep up, you will surely get left behind."

"So I've been told."

"My phone is my lifeline. I use it for so much," Grey admitted.

Just as she made her last comment, a conductor approached. "Tickets, please."

Immediately, Grey turned her phone toward the conductor so that he could swipe the phone with the mobile ticket scanner.

"Like I said, I use it for everything."

"You can use your phone as your ticket?" Bland asked.

"I downloaded the app that allowed me to purchase the ticket through my phone. You need to get a phone that will allow you to download apps that will help you to become more functional in today's technological society."

Bland shook his head. "Amazing!"

The conductor stood over Bland, silently waiting.

"Bland, she is waiting for your ticket," Grey said, as Bland looked up at the conductor.

"Oh." Bland dug into his front pocket to retrieve his ticket, but then remembered the airline purchased the tickets.

"I came over from the airline, and I was told the airline would take care of everything."

“What is your name, sir?”

“Bland Benthall.”

The conductor used the scanner keypad to type Bland’s name. Bland was certain the conductor would ask about Dakota and Devin. To his amazement, she didn’t.

As soon as the conductor exited the car, Grey asked, “You came over from the airport?”

“Yeah, all the planes were grounded because of security issues.” He elected not to go into the details.

“Fortunate for me,” she responded, then allowing her eyes to gaze into his. She redirected her attention back to Bland’s cell phone and laughed. “Bland, you really have to get an up-to-date phone.” Once her laughter ended, she introduced a more serious question. “How come you’re not married?” He noticed how her eyes settled on his ring finger. Instantly, she corrected her assumption with another assumption, “Well, I’m sure you have a girlfriend.”

“No,” his answer was for her latter question, but she was quick to accept it for both of her inquiries.

He knew she misunderstood him, and he wanted to correct any assumption by offering a simple explanation. It had been a long time since he wore his ring due to the constant swelling it caused to his finger; however, her talking over him gave him an excuse to think about divulging that information later, or not at all.

“It’s like all this was meant to happen, Bland. Why else would we be meeting again?”

Bland found himself caught in the throes of uncertainty as to what he wanted to happen, and what he knew should not happen. Nonetheless, it didn’t stop him from entertaining the thoughts of what might have been if the two of them had stayed in touch.

Dakota awoke from one of the train’s frequent jerks. She looked across the small room and saw that Bland wasn’t there.

“Now where is he?” she muttered. She glanced at her phone. “7:00 a.m.”

She brushed the window curtains back. The bright morning light

blinded her, and she didn't spot the yellow sticky note. Her mind wandered. Again, she looked out the window. This time the sticky note came into focus. Her eyes adjusted as she reached to retrieve the note.

"Be back in five minutes," she mimicked. "Not likely," she smirked. She dialed his number. When his phone rang in the seat below, she murmured, "He would leave his phone.. Well, I guess I can take a long shower before he gets back." Carefully, she rolled out of the bed and stepped into the bathroom.

Consumed in conversation, Bland had abandoned his original plan, which was to locate and identify the woman to satisfy his curiosity. He had been gone for nearly seven hours, and he figured the train wasn't too far from D.C. Sporadically, he would glance toward the end of the car to make sure Dakota wasn't coming.

If only he had known that his wife had showered and dressed, and her curiosity was compelling her to search him out, he might have returned to his sleeping quarters. Fortunately for Bland, Devin hadn't awakened, and Dakota refused to disturb his sleep. Instead, she took a seat in front of the window and waited.

Meanwhile, as Bland stared into Grey's face, a sudden whim to ask her out came over him. When he established enough nerve to ask the question, the conductor distracted her.

"Lady, we'll be pulling into Alexandria in about thirty minutes. This would be a good time to return to your seat."

"Already? Wow, where did the time go?" she asked, while looking at Bland.

"On good conversation," Bland replied.

"Yes, I agree, and I enjoyed every bit of our conversation. We must do it again."

"I was hoping you would say that. Not to sound too aggressive, but the sooner the better." He smiled as he stood.

"Maybe you can show me around your city."

Bland offered a doubtful look. "Are you sure you don't already know the city?"

"Even if I did, I am sure you know the better places to go." She moved into the aisle. "My seat is in that direction," she pointed.

"Please, allow me to escort you."

"Bland, you don't have to do that."

His pleading overpowered her lackluster refusal, "Please, it would be my pleasure."

"Well, thank you," she smiled. They made their way to her seat, which happened to be in the direction of Bland's sleeping car.

Dakota felt the train slowing. She looked up at the digital message over the entrance that suddenly glared with red letters.

"Arriving in Alexandria, Virginia, in ten minutes," read the message. Dakota then realized the next stop after Alexandria was Washington, D.C., their stop. The approximate time before the train reached D.C. was thirty-five minutes. Deciding that Devin had slept long enough, she was about to tap his shoulder when he rolled over.

"Good morning," she cooed.

"Hi, Mommy."

"Are you hungry, baby?"

"Yes," he rubbed his eyes.

"Then, let's wash your face so we can get something to eat."

Again, he rubbed his eyes, then looked around to ask, "Mommy, where is Daddy?"

She paused to look at him, "He's waiting for us, so come on, rise and shine."

Grey's seat car was six cars away from Bland's sleeping car, and the moment Bland realized in what direction he was heading, he knew he had been gone for some time. He needed to know if Dakota had called. Bland patted his pockets for his cell phone only to discover he left it in the sleeping car. He looked at his watch to count the hours he had been gone. Surely Dakota is awake by now, he contemplated. As he followed Grey up the aisles from one car to the other, anxiety showed up again. He stared into the small glass in the door, trying to see what figure was coming toward them.

"How much further do we have to go?" he inquired, knowing he was

getting closer to his sleeping car.

"It's the next car. Is everything okay?" she asked.

"Oh, I was just wondering because the train has stopped."

She responded, "Yes, it has, and I hadn't paid much attention. Well, here we are, Bland."

Bland reached up and grabbed her luggage from the top rack. Again, he glanced toward the end of the car in the direction of his sleeping car. Through the small window, a figure could be seen racing toward him. Suddenly, he felt panicky while waiting to see who would enter the passenger car. When the door to the car opened, two porters and a conductor quickly trotted up the aisle. Bland's fear slowly eased, and he breathed a heavy sigh of relief. The conductor stopped temporarily to give Grey direction on where to disembark.

"Miss, we will be unloading at the end of this car."

"Bland, you don't mind, do you?" She gestured for him to take the luggage to the end of the car.

"Not at all," he said, as he continued to head in the direction of his sleeping car. Once again he felt that uneasiness creep along his spine.

Dakota closed the door to their bed car. She and Devin headed up the narrow aisle. She walked through the next two sleeping cars with her mind convinced that Bland was in the lounge area gabbing. But more hope lingered on her mind that Bland was somewhere brainstorming an idea to write about, an idea for a story that would surely catapult him to partnership status.

Bland waited with nervous energy for the porters to open the door of the train. He looked through the window of the connecting passenger car. There were a few passengers talking and a few sleeping. He turned toward the hatch when he heard the porter pull the handle to the door.

Dakota was only a car away from Bland. As she moved up the aisle, from the small window of the passenger car she could make out a figure that looked like Bland. Her pace quickened. When Bland turned to the side, she was positive it was him. However, he didn't notice her coming up the aisle. He went on to step off the train to hand Grey her luggage. A sense of safety soon replaced what little concern he felt lurking within him.

She placed the luggage on the ground. He placed his hand on her hand.

"Grey, I can't explain what seeing you again meant to me. I just hope we can do it again and soon."

"I'll be waiting for your call," she said and stepped toward him.

Dakota was coming upon the disembarking area. She could no longer see Bland. She walked faster. Her eyes fixated on the last place she had seen him.

Bland turned to shake Grey's hand when she pulled him into a long, much needed hug. When she pulled back from the hug, their cheeks touched. Grey saw an opportunity to kiss him. He was apprehensive until he felt the softness of her lips.

—

Before Constance barged into the room, Jane's eyes couldn't move fast enough to read if Dakota would catch her husband with this other woman. Jane's mouth dropped open and her eyes frowned with discontent for Bland's actions.

Constance noticed her sudden reaction and asked, "What's that look you're giving me? I just came back to say goodnight."

Jane's eyes widened as she tapped the book.

"It's that good?"

Jane watched Constance as she maneuvered around the bed.

"I came to tell you that I have to go for additional training."

Jane tried hard to make a sound, but nothing came out.

"I know, I know. I just got back, but this is mandatory and part of my job description. You never know what will happen, so it's better to be prepared. I promise I will be back sooner than you know."

Jane clutched the book to her chest.

"Oh, don't worry, I won't take it. Like I could really pry it from your hands, or should I say bandages." Constance paused to wait for her next thought. "I'll miss you while I'm gone."

When Jane's eyes frowned, Constance became sad, like she was leaving a longtime friend. Jane leaned forward to give Constance a hug. Her scratchy voice somehow let out a bye, while Constance's eyes watered.

"I'll see you soon." Constance looked at her watch, "I have to go, Jane. I don't want to be late for my second job. Sometimes the less fortunate have to moonlight in order to afford the finer things in life; don't expect to get it on a nurse's salary. Nothing to worry yourself about; you will be in good hands while I'm gone. I found out you're assigned to a good nurse, so don't give her a hard time, okay? Dr. Stewart will also be around to check on your day-to-day progress."

Jane's eyes followed Constance as she moved back from the bed and walked to the door. Constance smiled, turned, and walked out of the room. Jane watched the door for several long seconds before her attention was drawn back to the book. As she started to read, she heard Constance's voice from down the hall.

"And, Jane, don't bother those bandages. You have to be patient."

—

"What the hell?" Dakota asked angrily as she pushed her weight forward through the crowd of passengers trying to disembark.

"Be patient," an aggressive voice said. "You're not the only one trying to get off the train."

"That's right; you planning on running over all of us?" grunted another voice.

Dakota tried to peer out the window since she could no longer move forward. For a second, she thought she saw Bland standing on the platform outside the train.

What seemed like a long intense kiss had only lasted a few seconds. "You have my card, Bland, so give me a call," Grey whispered in his ear.

Bland smiled as she backed away from his embrace. There was a thought to hold her just a little longer, but he didn't want to appear anxious. Instead, he intently watched her as she grabbed her luggage and turned to leave him.

Dakota finally arrived at the exit. From her position, she could only see those passengers right in front of her. She would have to get off the train if she wanted to be certain it was Bland who had gotten off the train. Impatiently, she waited with Devin for her turn to proceed down

the narrow steps. When they reached the bottom step, off to the right of the train was Bland.

"Bland!" Dakota called. With a new sense of panic, Bland turned quickly.

Dakota stood at the bottom of the steps with a curious stare. Quickly, she asked, "What are you doing? Why are you off the train?"

Bland looked from his wife then into the crowd of people that walked past. When he felt Grey had long disappeared, he gave more attention to his wife's questions.

"You've been gone for a long time, Bland." She pulled Devin close to her side.

"Didn't you get my note?" he asked as he approached her and Devin. He pulled Devin into his arms.

"Yes, I saw your note, but you have been gone for nearly two hours. Maybe, you should have taken your phone, it could have been an emergency," she said sarcastically.

Bland's timeline worked perfectly. The timeline allowed him to respond with a reasonable explanation.

"When I realized I didn't have it, I was on my way back to the car. Then, I happened to run into an old friend." Dakota looked around for that friend. "We began reminiscing and before we knew it, time had flown by. I didn't mean to have you worried."

Dakota felt guilty, so immediately she began to apologize. "I woke up and didn't see you. I'm sorry, honey."

"You must have awakened the moment I left the car." He rubbed the palm of his hand across her cheek. "I couldn't sleep, so I went to the lounge car." He kissed her on the cheek.

She turned and proceeded up the stairs of the train as Bland followed. Playfully, he tossed Devin in the air. "Are you hungry, little man?"

"Yes, Daddy."

"I know where there are some pancakes with your name on them. Come on, let's go and get them."

—

Highly disappointed with Bland, Jane closed the book.

8

IN THE FOLLOWING WEEKS, JANE'S VOICE RETURNED, BUT a slight depression befell her. There were times when the nurses found her sitting at the window for hours. She had lost her appetite for food, conversation, and the novel. When the nurses tried to make small talk, Jane chose to isolate herself. Yet, she couldn't isolate the headaches and dreams. She became consumed with trying to figure them out. She reread her journal entries about her dreams. Her eyes scanned over redundant words. She thought about the words and the dreams having some pattern, some possibility of the dreams showing her things about her life that she could no longer remember. Frustrated, she closed the notebook of journal entries. Her hands touched the bandages on her face. That added additional frustration because she had temporarily forgotten the bandages were there. She grabbed her walker and made her way to the bathroom. She stared for a long time in the mirror. She wondered what her eyes could tell her about the face hidden behind the bandages. After all, some say the eyes are the windows to the soul. Suddenly there was a twitch in her eyes, and a notion to remove the wraps came over her.

She began wrestling with the pin that was designed to prevent her from taking off the bandages. She pulled more aggressively at the snap

at the back of her head. When her attempts failed, she angrily knocked items off the sink, threw her walker into the other room, and smacked at her face. Then, she dropped to the floor and sobbed.

As another week passed, she began to believe her headaches were a direct result of the dreams, as she had stopped reading the book. Since Constance's absence, she had been having more of each, two, and sometimes, three times a week.

The nurses updated Dr. Stewart on Jane's behavior. He held firm that Jane had symptoms of depression. Her depression, he alluded, had less to do with the absence of Constance and more to do with Jane's long-term physical and emotional distress. For the next few weeks, he kept Jane extremely busy with her voice specialist and physical therapist. When there weren't any specialists or therapists to visit, Jane would sit for hours and stare out the window at the cars that passed the hospital. One evening, while staring out the window, something caught her eye on the bottom shelf of her nightstand. Jane had forgotten about the book. Suddenly, a bit of excitement returned when remembering what she had read. Before she could open the book, Dr. Stewart entered the room.

"Hello, Jane," he said, as he prepared to perform the normal tests. He flipped open her chart.

"Dr. Stewart, I'm so tired of tests and therapy. When can I go outside and get some fresh air?"

"Jane, we have to take one day at a time." He looked to the corner of her room. "I see you have received your walker. I hope you've been using it."

"It tires me. I don't have enough strength."

Dr. Stewart looked frustrated. "Jane, you are tired because you're learning how to walk again. That's the purpose of the physical therapy. The burns severely damaged your muscles and tendons and their ability to contract, which altered the range of motion of your joints. So you are going to be tired. You need that walker, so keep using it. Now, open wide and say Ah." He flicked on the scope light to check her throat. "Great, Jane. Your voice sounds a bit stronger? That's good. Try not to tire it out," he said teasingly.

"Well, doctor?" She waited.

"What?" he asked.

"The fresh air?" her voice whimpered.

"I'm concerned about the air causing more damage to your voice box."

"Why does my voice sound like this?" she asked.

"You mean hoarse?"

"Yes," she growled, then closed her mouth.

"Jane, there was severe damage to your larynx. That's the vocal cord that allows tone and sound to escape."

"Is it going to get any better?" She moved her head to the left so the doctor could inspect her ear.

"Only time has the answers."

"So, I am going to sound like a frog forever?" She had a frightened expression in her eyes. "And what if I look like a frog, too?" She frowned with her eyes.

"Then you'll have to find yourself a prince charming so he can give you a kiss and turn you back into the princess you are."

"Stop picking, Dr. Stewart. I'll just be a princess with a frog's voice."

There was a long chuckle from Dr. Stewart.

"Let's not react so fast. I'll continue to send you to the throat specialist on a regular basis. I spoke with the physical therapist, and he says you're doing well. I suspect with your use of the walker, you will only need to go a few more times. Have your bandages been changed today?"

"No."

"Well, since I'm here, I'll change them. It's been a few days since I've looked at your skin."

"It's been two weeks," she exaggerated with a serious tone.

He changed the subject. "So how are you feeling?"

"I've been better," she admitted. "I just need to get out of this room. Seeing these same walls every day will eventually get to anyone."

"This isn't what you want to hear, but you do have the window."

He began to unwrap the bandages from her hands and arms.

"That makes it worse. It's like you are in the desert, and someone places a glass of water in front of you, but you are told not to drink it.

Eventually, it's going to have an effect on you. Every day, I stare out this window to see cars coming and going. I can't help but wonder where they're going. I wish I was in that car, or any of those cars, leaving with them."

Though he sensed her frustration, he chose not to respond.

"Plus, I'm tired of looking at the same scenery every day," she admitted.

After taking the bandages off her hands, the doctor inspected her skin to see if it was healing to his satisfaction.

"No infection, and your hands are looking better, so we'll leave the bandages off." He looked up from her hands. "That should make you happy. As for some of the other full-thickness grafts such as on your legs and arms, they require a longer period of time for new blood vessels and soft tissue to form."

"How much time, Dr. Stewart?"

"Scar tissues sometimes need a year or more to fully heal and achieve maximum improved appearance."

"I have to keep these bandages on for a year?"

"I'm talking about the scars, not the bandages, Jane. And no, I don't expect them to be on that long. That's if you don't disturb the wounds. Now let me take a look at your back."

"Why my back?"

"That's the donor site for the skin graft. That's where we took healthy skin and replaced the damaged skin on your legs, arms, and hands."

"Is that where the skin on my face came from?" She had a grave concern that the skin on her face was worse than Dr. Stewart wanted her to believe.

"A small portion came from the back, but most of the new skin came from your upper chest. A section on your chest was selected because it better matched the color of your face. As for the donor sites, we're going to keep them covered with a sterile non-adherent dressing to protect from infection. Sit still so I can look at your face."

While he unwrapped the bandages from her face, she listened to his ambiguous, professional jargon. When Dr. Stewart didn't let her see in a mirror, she knew.

"Not yet ready?" she asked, obviously disappointed.

"Not yet."

"But why not? You're leaving the bandages off my hands, why not off my face?"

"Sometimes different scars require different treatments. Severe burns that destroy large sections of skin cause the skin to heal in a puckered way. As the wound heals, we're doing all we can to prevent the skin from overproducing collagen, and possibly causing the skin to scar."

"What does that mean?" she asked in a serious voice.

"Honestly, Jane, it could mean more surgery on the face as well as on other parts of your body. But let's not be too hasty. Your physical therapy will increase joint movement and hopefully eliminate any additional surgery. The skin may heal reasonably well on the face where we would only need to apply some cosmetics."

After he finished inspecting her face, he rewrapped it and then tossed the old bandages on the rolling tray.

She took his comment with a grain of salt. She didn't want to put any more attention on the skin or the face, so she purposely switched the subject.

"When is Nurse Connie returning?" she asked.

"Soon, but I hear you're still not eating. You do know that doesn't help our cause?"

Dr. Stewart touched on another subject that she didn't care to discuss.

"And what's our cause, doctor?" she asked with a level of annoyance.

"Getting you healthy with a proper nutritional diet, which will help to promote wound healing. Once your skin heals, I can take off these bandages so we can find out who you are. Since you can't remember, your face is the only thing we have."

"Why is it that I don't remember? Do I have amnesia?"

"Yes and no. What I mean is that simple amnesia involves a loss of information from the memory, usually as the result of disease or injury to the brain. I conducted various diagnostic tests—such as X-rays and blood tests—to rule out physical illness or medication side effects as the cause of your memory loss. After speaking with the hospital's psychiatrist, I think you are experiencing something called dissociative amnesia."

"Dissociative amnesia," she repeated.

"Certain conditions, including head injuries, can lead to symptoms similar to those of dissociative disorders, including amnesia. With dissociative amnesia, the memories still exist but are deeply buried within the person's mind and cannot be recalled. However, the memories might resurface on their own, or after being triggered by something in your surroundings."

"Can my appearance trigger my memory?" she asked with hopeful anxiety.

"Jane, I need you to be healthy so your wounds can heal. I don't want to feed you false hope. I spoke with the psychiatrist, and she says there's a chance your appearance won't trigger your memory. She says this disorder can be linked to a number of things. In particular, traumatic events that result in overwhelming stress."

"What kind of traumatic events?"

"Events like wars, accidents, or some other disaster. Listen, I took the liberty to schedule an appointment for you to see the hospital's psychiatrist."

"The hospital has a psychiatrist?"

"Our hospital specializes in dealing with people who have experienced or witnessed traumatic events and depression, which I think you are also experiencing."

"I'm not depressed, doctor; it's this place. I keep telling you all I need is some fresh air. I'm tired of this hospital and these bandages. I'm tired of being wrapped from head to toe like a mummy. I really believe some fresh air would do wonders for me."

Out of frustration, Dr. Stewart rubbed his hand through his grey hair. "You do know you're giving me more grey hairs? Okay, I'll tell you what. I will allow you to get some fresh air if you promise to stop missing meals."

"I promise," she said quickly.

"There's a small gazebo at the back of the hospital. You'll find it very relaxing. Only stay for an hour a day, okay? I don't want you exposed to the sun for too long." He smiled, "Take the patient transport elevator to the basement. Proceed straight, and you will see the loading dock. Keep

moving toward the loading dock, and the courtyard is to the left. Don't go right, or you will end up in the boiler room."

A sigh of relief exhaled from her chest, "Thank you, Dr. Stewart."

"But you're still scheduled to see the psychiatrist. Now, is there anything else you want to talk about before I leave?"

She shook her head from left to right. He gave her a weird look.

"What's that look, Dr. Stewart?"

"I hear you've been having some bad dreams."

She sighed, suspecting Constance had told him before she left. "How did you know?" she asked.

"Your attending nurse told me. How long have you been having these dreams?"

"About three weeks now. At first, I would get one, maybe two a week. Now, I get them all the time, but I don't understand them."

"There can be a number of reasons for these dreams, another reason to see this psychiatrist. I'm sure she can help with interpreting them. I need you to jot down as much as you remember about them."

"I've been keeping a journal."

"That's good. Where is your journal?"

She pulled the journal from her drawer and handed it to the doctor.

"I will give this to Dr. Westfall, the psychiatrist."

Jane's eyes turned sad. "I sound like a lunatic," she said while turning to look out the window. She wanted to hide her tears from the doctor.

"Hey, I thought you wanted some fresh air. It's a really nice day, so why don't you get that air? Use your walker and take that book you're always reading."

It was refreshing to be outside. The fresh air was liberating as she stood in the courtyard enjoying the flowers and the rooftops across from the hospital. Finally, she settled down to rest amongst the assorted sounds of the big city. She opened her book and soon was transitioned from her surroundings to words that reminded her of what had previously taken place on the train.

9

SINCE BLAND'S REUNION WITH GREY, HE COULDN'T GET her out of his thoughts. It was time to return to the office, if to do nothing but show his face. At times he considered the novel, and what it would take to make it better, but he couldn't get his mind off Grey. He wanted to call her, yet every time he picked up his office phone, he would hang up the receiver. His head slowly collapsed on his desk. He managed to turn on the computer, only to watch a blinking cursor on a blank screen. If he didn't hurry up and get Grey off his mind, there was a possibility the novel would never get written.

As he sat there daydreaming, he wondered why Smith and Wilkins hadn't broken down his door for the revised pages or for the idea of the new story.

Suddenly, a small envelope flashed at the top corner of his computer screen.

"You've got mail," the message read.

Bland clicked on the envelope and, to his dismay, the message was from Larry Peterson.

"Surprise, surprise! I heard about your promotion. Congrats, that's if you can get through your writer's block."

Bland felt that Larry was being facetious sending him an email. He was annoyed he had even opened it. He closed the email and pulled up his manuscript. Slowly, he read over the first chapter. It needs some work, he thought. His head dropped because he really didn't want to devote any more time to research. But he would have to in order to make the other six chapters connect. The door to his office opened. Thinking it was his secretary, Paige, he didn't bother to lift his head.

"What is it, Paige? If it's the twins, tell them I shot myself."

"We hope not," Wilkins replied, before shoving the door into the wall. His large size required the extra room to get into Bland's office.

The moment Bland heard the voice, he moved back from his desk.

"Mr. Smith, Mr. Wilkins."

"I'm assuming one week of vacation, and paid vacation, might I add, was enough time to rest and come up with some creative ideas for the story," Wilkins snapped.

Bland knew he couldn't further the lie of having written new chapters; however, he knew he couldn't be totally honest and say he didn't have a new direction for the story. Of course, that would be disastrous for him.

"It's coming."

"It's coming?" Wilkins repeated. "What does that mean?"

"It means the story is developing."

Smith looked at his brother. "Along the lines of the first chapter or something different?"

Bland waved his hand back and forth. "Let's say, I came up with some new discoveries, along the lines of what you want."

Smith smiled. "Great. That's what we wanted to hear. Come on, share a little with us."

Bland shook his head.

"You know we are making a large investment in you." He paused, "Okay, Bland. We can tell you don't want to let us in on it. But we are expecting to see something soon," said Smith. Without offering any goodbyes, the two old men turned and walked out of the office.

Bland waited until the elevator door closed with them in it before allowing his head to crash to the desk again. Right away, Paige poked her head into his office.

"I am so sorry, Mr. Benthall; I had no time to warn you."

"That's okay. Any stimulus that motivates me to write isn't all that bad."

Hopefully, it would motivate him to be more creative with the story. Paige handed him his messages and went back to her desk. Soon his thoughts were interrupted again when he started daydreaming about Grey. The urge to call her had returned. If for no other reason, he figured it would be polite to see if she received the contract, and if she still wanted that tour of the city. He knew it was just an excuse to see her.

A quick glance at the phone, and he turned back to the computer. From the corner of his eye, he spotted the picture of Dakota and him on Cliff's Peak. At once, guilt weighed on his decision to call. Never before had he considered being with another woman. Yet, he rationalized his thoughts that Grey wasn't another woman, but rather an old friend. But he knew better than that. She wasn't his wife, and that made it wrong, he told himself. Nonetheless, Bland pulled his wallet from his back pocket. Not yet acquiesced to the notion of not calling Grey, he rolled his fingers along her business card. His body relaxed in the recliner while contemplating. Deep down in his heart, he couldn't bring himself to call. After all, he loved his wife, and any relationship with Grey, platonic or not, he felt would jeopardize his marriage. So instead of calling her, he ripped the card down the middle and tossed it in the wastebasket. He felt an immediate sense of relief as he rolled his shoulders back and forth. A wavering doubt still hung over him. Nevertheless, he knew he had to keep his distance from Greysen Brindle.

"Paige, I'm leaving for the day. My cell phone is still acting up, so if my wife calls, let her know I'll be at the public library on 9th and G Street."

"Okay, Mr. Benthall."

The quiet atmosphere and solitude of the library was quite different from the office and his home. The library, he felt, was a great way to be alone, away from Dakota and her housework, and the twins constantly checking up on him. He would hide in his usual corner where he received most of his ideas for stories.

He laughed to himself when he realized he had just as many superstitions as the twins. Again, he thought about the first chapter of his first draft. Maybe the first chapter was a little slow. A rewrite to make it connect better with the other chapters might not be a bad idea, he thought to himself. He hoped that he didn't have to destroy any of the other chapters and start over.

Bland smiled as he jotted down an idea on paper. From his satchel, he pulled out his thin tape recorder and made a few remarks on it. Then he began to write out a new outline. After hours of concentrating on the first chapter, he didn't hear his name being called.

"Bland, is that you?" a voice asked from behind him.

He snapped his head around, "Grey."

She was absolutely stunning, and her captivating voice created stillness within him. He didn't question this impromptu meeting between Grey and himself; rather, he embraced it as an opportunity not initiated by him.

"I heard your voice. Did I startle you?" she asked.

"Just a little," he grinned.

"How are you?"

"Besides talking to myself, fine. Just working hard," a partial lie, he thought. "I've been sitting in this corner for so long, I kind of forgot where I was. Anyway, how are you?" He knew the rest of the day's work would be blown off. "What brings you to the library?"

"I got the contract," she said with a smile.

"Congratulations."

"I am doing some research on the particulars of the city," she explained.

"That's so good to hear. Can I be of assistance? At least we can enjoy some of this beautiful spring weather."

She was hesitant before saying, "Like you were supposed to call me so you could show me around the city?"

He didn't hesitate to reply. "I misplaced your number." Then he thought about the trash can.

"I guess it didn't mean much to you."

"No, it did. That's why I spent days looking for it. I haven't a clue

where it could be."

She reached into her purse and retrieved another card to give to him.

"Here is my card with my cell number. Maybe you won't lose this one," she said, then walked away.

Quickly, Bland gathered his notes and shoved them into his satchel and with haste he gave chase. He caught up with her just as she was exiting the library.

He gently grabbed her by the arm, "Grey, you made your point. Let me make it up to you."

She listened, all the while knowing she was planning to give him another chance to make it up to her.

"Please, Grey."

"I suppose you can make it up by taking me to dinner. Is tonight too soon?"

"Yes, I mean, I would love to, but why wait until later. I'm hungry now," he replied.

She blushed, "Sure."

Bland took Grey to a small restaurant on the Virginia side of the Potomac River. Flickering candles throughout the small eatery set a romantic ambiance.

"When I didn't receive your call, I thought time had repeated itself. And again I felt stupid."

"Why?" Bland asked before sipping his wine.

"The two times we met, I ended up sharing some personal parts of myself with you. I haven't shared many things with many people. When I think it's good to reveal myself to you, you disappear."

"That happened years ago, so don't think like that. You can always be open with me."

"Bland," she said softly while candlelight shadows flickered across her face, "I have had enough disappointments, and I don't need anymore."

The entangled lies had gotten more tangled, and instead of Bland revealing his truth, he chose to be silent.

"I understand," Bland dropped the conversation.

"Well, I must admit I'm having a wonderful time now." She tilted her

head slightly while her eyes grew soft.

Bland didn't say anything at first. He just watched her expressions and slight movements and thought how beautiful she was.

"Let's do it again sometime." He admitted to himself that he would love to see her again. But he knew he couldn't call her, so he hoped fate would again intervene and bring the two of them together. At least that allowed his conscience to be free from any guilt that he was the instigator of such a meeting.

She gazed at him. "You have my number. Give me a call. Well, that's if you don't lose it again."

"I'll make sure to put it in a safe place," he smiled before taking another sip of wine.

He didn't want to tempt himself any more than he already had. He knew her business card would eventually end up in the trash. After dinner, he drove her back to her car that was parked in front of the library.

"Bye, Mr. Benthall," she said and then leaned over to give him a soft kiss on his cheek before exiting the car.

That night, Bland purposely slept in the guest room, and the next morning he dressed and left the house before Dakota awoke. It was an uncharacteristic behavior meant to keep his wife from seeing his face. His countenance might reveal that he had spent the evening entertaining another woman.

When he arrived at work, he decided to stay clear of Smith and Wilkins. Being berated about the story was something Bland felt he could do without today. As he approached Paige, she gave him a signal that the coast was clear.

"They left about twenty minutes ago, and they asked their usual questions: Have you been in? When will you be back? Did you happen to leave any pages of the new book? And I lied, as usual."

"Thanks, Paige. I owe you one." So much for the freedom they promised, he thought.

"Oh, your wife called."

"Can you get her on the line for me?"

Bland entered his office thinking about some of the new ideas he had

for the introduction of the story. Soon Paige's cheerful voice sounded through the speakerphone.

"She's on line one, Mr. Benthall."

Bland grabbed the receiver, "Hey, you."

"Good morning. Are you busy?" her voice was very controlled and soft as she asked.

"Well, not so busy that I can't spare some time for my beautiful wife."

"That's reassuring because I didn't hear you come home last night. Or hear you leave this morning. So, are you sure you have time for little ol' me?"

"Honey, I'm sorry. It was a late night. The house was dark when I arrived, and I didn't want to disturb you, so I slept in the guest room."

"Bland, you know I don't care if you wake me. But I hate it when you don't wake me to say goodbye. Now, promise it will never happen again."

"You have my solemn oath that I will wake you before I leave."

"Bland, stop patronizing me."

He chuckled, then responded, "Well, let me get back to work; I have a partnership to acquire. Oh, this evening Lou is playing at Rendall's on the Water Front. I plan on sneaking by to check him out. Would you like to meet me there?"

"I can't, honey; Devin seems to be coming down with a fever. I want to keep an eye on him. You two boys have your fun. Tell Louis I will catch his next one." She paused, "I called you for something else," then remembered, "when you come in tonight, I need you to sign the new bank papers. I will put them on the kitchen table."

"So you took care of it?"

"I said I would, but they need both of our signatures. That way, any money taken out would need the approval of both of us."

Bland leaned forward with the phone. "I love you," he said before hanging up.

He returned to studying his notes. He picked up his satchel to get the tape recorder. As he fingered through the compartments in search of the recorder, he came across Grey's business card. He studied the card with various thoughts. Accidentally running into Grey was definitely different from purposely calling her to see if she would accompany

him to an evening of jazz. It would be only a friendly gesture between friends, he rationalized. He flipped the card between his fingers as he contemplated calling her. If he called, he had a strong feeling their meeting would lead to an adulterous act. The thought weighed heavily upon his mind. As before, he gave the card a long consideration. Unlike before, he didn't drop the card in the waste container; rather, he dialed the number. As the phone rang, Bland fought himself not to hang up. When Grey answered the phone, Bland stalled on his words.

"Hello, hello," she called.

"Umm, hello, is this Greysen?"

"Is that you, Bland?"

"Yes" he laughed lightly, then he leaned back into the recliner.

"What a pleasant surprise. I didn't expect to hear from you so soon."

"Well, I was thinking about you. Realizing how I owed you, I was wondering if you would like to accompany me to a jazz set tonight."

"A jazz set," her soft voice repeated with excitement.

"I'm sorry. I automatically assumed you knew what I was talking about."

"Bland, I'm familiar with jazz sets and, yes, I would love to hear some jazz this evening."

"Great, the musician is a friend of mine," he went rambling on, not sure what else to say.

"Where exactly is this friend of yours playing?"

"He's playing at a lounge in Georgetown. It's called Rendall's on the Water Front. He goes on at seven sharp. How about I wait for you outside of the restaurant?" He felt like a vibrant young man again when she agreed.

After hanging up the phone, he went back to sorting through his notes and trying to listen to the recorder. Gradually, he shut off the recorder and stopped making notes. His head tilted back, and his eyes closed. Surely he knew what he was doing, but he couldn't shut out the desire of wanting more than a gentle pursuit of Grey. He persuaded himself it wouldn't lead to any immoral acts that would jeopardize his marriage. He tried to shake off all thoughts of Grey, but to no avail. Immediately, his eyes opened, and he leaned forward in his chair. He stared into the open air. It hadn't

dawned on him until now. How was he going to explain Grey to Lou? Lou loved Dakota like a sister. Bringing Grey to one of his sets would put Lou in an uncomfortable position, so he contemplated cancelling his evening with Grey. Given, she sounded so excited about hearing Lou play, he thought, how can I cancel now when I initiated the invite?

When Grey arrived, Bland was standing in front of the restaurant and lounge.

"Have you been in?" she asked, as she approached him.

"No, I waited for you." He led her by the hand into the restaurant.

Grey and Bland were approached by an unfamiliar, thin man who seated them at a table near the stage. That's when Lou spotted Bland and rushed over.

"Hey, Old Timer. I guess we're just in time," Bland smiled.

"We have a few minutes before we go on, but who are you calling Old Timer? I may be old, but I'm still better looking."

"That you are," Bland laughed, then remembering to introduce Grey. "I'm sorry, Lou, this is Greysen Brindle."

"How did a pretty lady manage to find such bad company?"

"If he's too bad, I know how to handle him," she replied.

"Now that's a woman," smiled Lou. "Drinks are on me, so pick your poison."

"Lou, that's not necessary. I've got it," said Bland.

"Save your money."

"Then I'll take a Cosmopolitan," responded Grey.

"And you want the normal, Bland?" Lou stopped a passing server, "One Cosmopolitan and Cognac on the rocks for my friend." Lou then took a seat. "So where did you meet this guy?"

"On a train."

"Interesting place to meet someone," he cocked a smile toward Bland. "Are you from the area?"

"No."

"I take it you like jazz?"

"Love it. It's my favorite genre of music," she admitted. "I love the drums."

The server placed the drinks on the table. “Put it on my tab,” Lou ordered.

“Lou,” Bland still tried to dig in his pocket for his wallet.

“Bland, it’s already done. I want you and this pretty lady to have fun and enjoy the music.” His attention fell back on Grey. “So, you love the drums?”

“I’ve played occasionally,” she flirted playfully.

“You play?” Bland looked shocked.

“Well, I’m not a professional, but I used to play when I was younger.”

Lou took her by the hand, “It’s like riding a bike. It may get a little rusty, but it still rolls. Come up with me for one song.”

“No, I can’t.” She looked at Bland to be rescued. Instead, Bland nodded his head for her to go.

As she rose from her seat, Lou quickly leaned over and whispered to Bland, “She reminds me of someone else we know. She even resembles her, that’s if you disregard the hair color and style. Is she as assertive as your wife?”

Bland laughed, “Assertive is a nice way of putting it but we don’t have to worry about any of that, because it’s nothing.”

“I take it Dakota doesn’t know anything about this, nothing?”

Bland just looked at him and directed his attention to his band, “They’re waiting on you to start the set.”

Grey took a seat behind the drums and waited for her cue. She was impressive, and the crowd raved as she did a drum roll. Watching her and the vibes she gave off made Bland want her even more.

When she returned to the table Bland looked surprised, “I guess there are some things I still don’t know about you.”

“I guess you’re right,” she laughed as she sat down. “I used to play with a local teenage girl band. We thought we would be the next big sensation, but nothing came of it.”

“Well, I am truly impressed,” he placed his hand over hers and refocused on the band.

At the end of the night, Grey was caught in conversation with the regular drummer. Bland pulled Lou over to a quiet spot.

"What's up?"

"Um, this is between you and me, right?"

"Hey, man, how long have I known you?"

"You've known my wife the same amount of time and, although it looks bad, it's really platonic."

"Then why explain?"

"Well, the way it looks."

"Hey, it's okay; it's platonic, remember?" Lou laughed, then drank the entire contents in the glass.

"You're drinking again. I thought you stopped," Bland said.

"It's cool. A sip shouldn't hurt me," Lou answered with a slight smirk. "So what about the weekend, are we on for some golf?"

"I'll be tied up with this book for the next several months, but after that I should be free."

The two men let their voices die down as Grey approached.

"What are you two whispering about?"

"Your skills," Lou blurted, then leaned over to give her a hug. "Next time I expect you to do a full set, okay?"

"Sure, I'm up for it."

Lou joked, "Anything else you can do? Can you play chess too, because this guy here sucks?"

"I am familiar with the game," she smiled.

"Now, she really reminds me of someone we know." Lou blurted.

"Oh, yeah, who is that Bland?"

Bland shook his head, "Nobody, he likes to hear himself talk."

Lou turned back to Bland, "Bland, I'll see you later." Then he hugged him and whispered in his ear, "Be sure of the decisions you make. You may never get another chance to correct them."

After the jazz set, Bland and Grey took a walk along the streets of Georgetown.

"So, what are we doing, Mr. Benthall?"

"We're taking a stroll."

"I know that, but what are we doing? Where is this going?" She was blunt with her questions. She didn't want to waste any more of her life

on things that didn't materialize.

"If I had the answers, I would tell you, but I don't, Grey. Honestly, I don't know where this is going. I am not sure if this can go any further than this walk along these chaotic streets."

"What's restricting us from going further?" she led Bland into the perfect opportunity to disclose his marriage. Yet, in the same breath she took it away. "I apologize because I can only imagine you must think I am some desperate woman searching for a man."

For a moment, Bland didn't know how he was going to answer her question.

"You don't sound desperate, just cautious. And I can respect that."

"I don't want to move too fast, but I do want to move toward something special. I want more for myself and for my mate. Not saying that you will be my mate." She tried to explain further, but Bland interrupted her.

"No need to explain. I understand."

"Do you? Because I can't afford to make another bad choice in my life."

He recalled Lou's last comment. In that moment, Bland decided to go home to his wife and put this, whatever it was with Grey, to rest. After strolling a few more blocks, he walked Grey to her car.

"Bland, thanks for inviting me tonight. I really had an awesome time."

"Thank you for coming on such short notice."

She sat in the car, then rolled down her window. She laughed lightly, "I can't figure you out."

"What do you mean?"

"I wasn't expecting your call. But it was a good surprise, Bland. So, when will I hear from you again?"

"I think I'll keep you guessing." And he left it at that. He bent down and gave her a kiss on the cheek.

Bland watched as her car turned on Key Bridge and disappeared into the traffic. It was official, at least to him. He would not see Grey again. A sense of relief came over him. Not because he wouldn't see her, but because he had fulfilled what little commitment he had made to her. Clearly, he understood his weakness, and she was it.

When he arrived home slightly intoxicated, he remembered to do as his wife asked. He signed the papers, then made sure he slept in their bed. That morning he made love to his wife, but with Grey still lingering on his mind.

Hoping to forget about his evening with Grey, Bland worked diligently on the book for the remainder of the week. Going into the weekend, he decided to dedicate his time to the book. On Monday morning, Bland was back at it, rewriting parts of the first chapter and adding more chapters to the first draft. To his satisfaction, the story began to come together. He smiled with his thoughts of knowing soon he would be a junior partner in one of most prestigious publishing houses in the country. He sat back in his chair to think about what that meant to him and to his family. All their debt would be expunged, and Dakota could erase those financial worries that had caused her to be on edge lately. After making a few more tweaks to the draft, he considered submitting the chapters he had completed. However, it was tradition to finish the book, then let his wife read it. She would give him the nod if the novel was ready. He shook his head and decided he wouldn't let the twins see it until it was due.

He stood. He smiled. He stretched. "Time for a coffee break," he said aloud.

He was about to turn off the computer when he was distracted. The office phone began ringing. Bland reached for the receiver.

"Mr. Benthall?" Paige said.

"Paige, I was about to call you. I just sent to the printer several chapters of a draft. I need those collated and bound. Can you have that ready for me by the end of the day?"

"I'll get right on it, Mr. Benthall, but I called to warn you that the twins are heading down. And they are looking for you."

"What did you tell them?"

"Nothing."

"Good." He hit the off button on the speaker and scooted from behind his desk, through his office door, and into the hall.

"It's close to lunch, Paige, you want something from downstairs?"

Paige lifted her head from her desk when she heard Bland's voice resonate from down the hall.

"No thank you, Mr. Benthall. I'm good. But what do you want me to tell the twins?"

"Tell them I stepped out for lunch."

Quickly, Bland turned on his heels and started toward the rear of the office to the exit staircase. By taking the stairs, he was sure not to run into the twins. He did, however, run into Rudy, the security guard, as he exited the stairwell to the main lobby.

"Mr. Benthall, how are you?"

Bland took notice of Rudy. "Fine, Rudy. And you?"

"Great, just working hard. By the way, I heard about you being attacked."

"I didn't report the incident, so how did you know?"

"Word gets around, Mr. Benthall."

More like Jesse telling him as a means to protect his hide, thought Bland.

"I feel bad because we weren't there to help you."

"Yeah, how about that?" Bland said, and the two men laughed simultaneously. "Well, have you found out anything about my attacker?" Bland leaned against the railing on the staircase.

"Nothing as of yet."

"How about the security cameras? I am sure the cameras got something."

"Our cameras stay down more than they are working. And that night, the cameras on that floor weren't working."

"Are you serious?"

"Yup, take it up with the old men because we have made our complaints, but they have gone on deaf ears. I just left the file room and didn't see a thing. I looked at the logbook, and there weren't any log-ins to any floors after 9:00 p.m."

"So how did the person gain access to the floors?"

"Mr. Benthall, there are other ways to get on these floors besides walking through the main lobby and catching an elevator. Lately, we've been understaffed, so some of the floors go unchecked. During the

morning and afternoon hours, we have three people, but during the evening there is less traffic, so there's only one person on duty. I can't be at two places at one time."

"What do you mean?"

"I mean, I can't inspect the floors and man the desk at the same time."

"How come you're understaffed? Why not hire more help? Or at least tell someone there are security issues concerning safety."

"We did that, and we got these." Rudy referred to the mace on the side of his holster. Here, I have an extra canister. Just in case you run across him again."

"Now that's some serious firing power," joked Bland, then smirked sarcastically before saying, "Since I can never find a security guard when I need one, this might come in handy."

Rudy, noticing Bland's sarcasm, laughed, "We deserved that one. Hey, if it doesn't bother management that we're understaffed, then it doesn't bother me. I do my job, and I go home."

"People are doing some crazy things these days. It's a responsibility to secure safety, so Rudy, you should continue to press this issue."

"I don't know, Mr. Benthall. It's not like they're going to hire more people. Come on, we're talking about those old men upstairs."

"If they're not going to hire more people, they can at least equip you all with some firearms."

"This is an in-house security agency, run by the old men. Having firearms would mean purchasing a higher insurance policy. The old men don't consider this to be a dangerous job, at least not one that causes them to purchase firearms for all their security guards." He paused and lowered his voice, "Let me be honest, they're not giving ex-cons like me guns. I am fortunate to have this job and suggesting to them to get firearms would have me in the unemployment line. Mr. Benthall, I can't afford to lose this job. I have children to feed, so I like to keep my opinions to myself.

"Don't get me wrong, Mr. Benthall, I know safety is important, but keeping my mouth closed so I can keep a job is more important. They don't ask much of me. And occasionally for pulling some overtime, my supervisor gets me free tickets to the Wizards' games. So, in all, I'm fine

with that. They leave me alone, so I leave them alone. It seems to work out for everyone."

Somehow Bland understood the quandary that Rudy faced, and how his having employment superseded his own concerns about adequate safety.

Rudy raised his voice to its normal level, "Do you want to file an incident report?"

"That's okay."

"Well, be more careful next time." Rudy started up the stairway, then stopped suddenly. He turned to ask, "Mr. Benthall, do you own a gun?"

"No, Rudy, I never thought I needed one."

"As you said earlier, there are some crazy people in the world. Since you keep late hours maybe you should get one and keep it in your car. You never know when you might need it."

Bland processed the information. Rudy's advice wasn't a bad idea given how crime was spreading to the suburbs.

"Rudy, I will have to take that under advisement."

Rudy laughed, "I like that word, 'advisement'. You do that, Mr. Benthall. By the way, why were you on the records floor so late?"

"I accidentally hit the wrong button on the elevator, and it took me to the basement floor. That's when I heard all the commotion coming from the file room."

"I'm glad you weren't seriously hurt," Rudy said.

"No more than some bruised ribs, but I'll be okay."

A slight sense of accountability came over Rudy. "Mr. Benthall, I will mention to the evening shift to keep a keen eye on suspicious characters and report anything out of the ordinary."

"I'd appreciate that, Rudy. Thanks."

Bland entered the main corridor of the building to a horde of people coming and going. He chose to eat in a well-hidden spot in the eatery, a spot where he could see, rather than be seen. He ate his meal while watching people shop in the various stores. He thought about each person's personal life. That's until he spotted Penelope sauntering through the corridor. He stood to be noticed, then waved her over.

"Hello, Bland. You're finally asking a girl out for lunch?"

"I would have asked earlier, but I couldn't seem to catch up with you."

"Right," she said.

"Are you hungry?"

She shook her head, "No, I'm doing my daily stroll. I need to shed a few pounds."

Bland looked her over. "Where are the pounds?"

"Very charming, Mr. Benthall; now I know why I find you so adorable. I don't want my heart rate to drop, so would you like to join me?"

At once, Bland discarded his trash into the waste container. "I can do for a little exercise."

As they walked, Bland revisited the favor he asked of Penelope in the file room and asked her whether she found anything out of the ordinary.

"As a matter of fact, I did look, but I found nothing out of the ordinary."

"Nothing?" Bland echoed.

"Nothing, Bland. Even though I found nothing, you still owe me for looking. How do you plan on paying your debt?"

Bland brushed off Penelope's comment. After realizing Penelope didn't have any interesting information to share, he quickly said his goodbyes and looked for the nearest stairway. He figured the twins wouldn't wait around for his return. The moment Bland stepped onto his floor, Paige began to wave toward him to stop. Hastily, she grabbed the receiver of her phone and held it in the air. Like a confused puppy, Bland tilted his head to the side. Then he heard a ringing coming from Larry's office.

Paige pointed at the phone with her index finger for Bland to pick up Larry's phone. Finally, Bland caught on. He softly knocked on Larry's door before turning the knob. He peeped his head into the office. It was empty. Then Bland slipped into the room and made his way to the phone.

"What's going on, Paige?"

"Mr. Benthall!" her voice was excited. "Where have you been? I called your cell phone and searched everywhere for you. I even sent you a text."

Bland glanced at his phone but saw no incoming text.

"What's the urgency, Paige?"

"Smith and Wilkins are still in your office."

"Still in my office?" he uttered. Bland ran off a few questions: "How long have they been there? Do you have any idea what they are doing?"

"They have been in there since you left, and they closed the blinds so I wouldn't know what they were doing. But I do know they used your phone because your line stayed lit for at least ten minutes."

After a moment of silence, Paige asked, "Bland, what are you going to do?"

"Sometimes, Paige, you have to face the music," he said and then hung up the phone. He took additional seconds to ponder why the twins would hang around in his office, just to use the phone. It wasn't making any sense.

As he pondered, his eyes settled on a picture of Larry on his desk. Larry was in the center of the picture surrounded by adults and children. When Bland couldn't identify any of the individuals, his eyes dropped down to the inscription on the brass plate located at the bottom of the frame. His eyebrows lifted after learning that Larry served in the Peace Corps.

"I wouldn't have guessed in a million years," Bland uttered as he placed the frame back on the desk. He skimmed the documents scattered on the desk. One of the documents particularly caught his attention, so he picked it up and read it. He placed it back on the desk and then picked up a manuscript. It was the beginning of a novel, but what held his attention was the author's name. Was this some type of safety net by the twins? It appeared Larry was considering becoming an author.

As Bland skimmed through a few more scattered papers he heard the doorknob turn. Immediately, the papers dropped from his hand as he moved away from the desk.

"What are you doing in my office?" Larry asked, as he looked at the papers on his desk. He entered the office and closed the door behind him. Bland searched through his mind for a good excuse. He had a good idea that Larry was the pipeline that funneled information to the twins, so the last thing he needed was for Larry to know he was dodging them.

"I needed to borrow a staple remover."

"A staple remover?" Larry repeated.

"Yes, Paige couldn't find hers. I didn't have one, so we figured you wouldn't mind if I checked in your office for one. I mean, you being the good humanitarian." Hoping to ease the awkward tension by being in Larry's office, Bland referred to the picture of Larry and his friends.

Larry didn't reply.

Bland noticed Larry's disapproving frown. He clearly rejected Bland engaging in small talk while being in his office uninvited.

"Well, I see you don't have a staple remover either."

The two men maneuvered around each other. Bland moved toward the door and Larry to the desk. Larry opened the top drawer and pulled out the staple remover. From Larry's facial expression, it was obvious he was doubtful of Bland's reasoning for being in his office. He tossed the staple remover to Bland.

"Next time, don't enter my office for any reason."

"Advice well taken."

Larry snorted, "You can leave my staple remover with Paige."

Bland closed the door to Larry's office and headed up the hall to his office. As he passed the window to his office, he noticed the blinds still closed. He looked up toward the receptionist's desk and Paige was heading toward him.

"Mr. Benthall, I have that draft you wanted printed. I have collated the chapters and bound it."

"Thanks, Paige."

As Paige walked away, Bland paused in front of the door before deciding to enter the office. He folded the draft and stuffed it under his armpit. He knew without a doubt that it must be something extremely important to make the old men wait.

Cautiously, Bland pushed open the office door. He felt like a scared school kid. Before he could enter the room, Smith began to whine, "Come on in, Bland, and sit down."

Bland did as instructed. He watched quietly as Wilkins comfortably reclined in his chair while Smith stood. Suddenly, it came to Bland

why the men were still in his office. Bland had forgotten to turn off his computer. And he figured the men had read his draft. His eyes dropped to the floor, then back on the men.

"I see you got a chance to read some of the new manuscript."

The twins greeted Bland with frowns and an onslaught of questions.

"Bland, what is this?" Wilkins pointed to the manuscript on the computer.

Smith moved closer to the chair but didn't sit. "Bland, did we not make it clear that the partnership is contingent on a bestseller?"

Bland was not expecting the twins' intrusion or their dissatisfaction of the book. Immediately, he began to make excuses for their concerns.

"You know I've been doing a lot of rewriting, so I wouldn't pass judgment on the book, at least not before reading it all." When the men didn't respond, Bland continued defending his work. "Gentlemen, I know the plot is a little rough, but I'm certain you will like it once the book is complete. I just need more time."

"Bland, it was our understanding that was the purpose of the vacation," Wilkins growled. "So what's this you 'need more time'?" By now the story should flow. Sure, you changed the first chapter, but it still doesn't connect."

When it appeared the men were not buying the direction of the book, Bland became agitated.

"You have no idea the amount of pressure I am under trying to finish this book and knowing it has to be a bestseller."

"Pressure?" Smith repeated.

"Yes, pressure. Every day I'm here writing, and every day I'm being scrutinized and micromanaged on the progress of the book. I have adopted your conditions, and I am doing my best to adhere to all of your demands. If you're having some issues with the book, then credit it to that." Bland wanted to clear himself of any responsibilities as to why the book wasn't meeting their expectations.

"Is that the problem?" Wilkins blurted. "Because if it is, you can write the book wherever you want. Hell, you can write it on the moon, just as long as I get it by December."

"You're missing the point. I am working diligently to give you a prized

possession, but it's not going to happen overnight, and it's definitely not going to happen under these working conditions."

Smith began to shake his head, "Bland, it's not the environment that makes this book awful."

His choice of words delivered a sharp blow to Bland's pride. He chose to listen and not challenge the men as they voiced additional concerns about the story.

Smith continued, "It's what's missing in the book that makes this book dull. You changed your style of writing. Son, every good suspense novel has an edge, a sense of surprise, a bit of deception, and an element of tragedy. Where is it?" He pointed to the monitor, "Because it's definitely not here."

"I changed my style a little," Bland said, apprehensively.

"Your formula for success has been simple. That's what got you twelve bestsellers, so why on earth would you change now?" Wilkins spoke out of frustration.

"Yes, why change when that is your signature mark?" questioned Smith.

"I took your earlier suggestions and adapted the first chapter to a quicker urgency."

"You call that urgency?" cried Wilkins. "There's nothing urgent in the draft. It's still slow and predictable."

"He's right, Bland, nothing surprising at all. I thought you were going to change the opening of the book."

"As I said before, I wanted to make this book special, since it is my last."

Wilkins spoke bluntly, "Don't reinvent the wheel; if something works, stick to it. There was a time I could read the first chapter and know your book was a bestseller. Unlike your other bestsellers, this book lacks substance."

"Give it a chance, Mr. Wilkins. I'm including a creative twist. I think you will like it in the end."

"I have given it a chance and believe me it needs more than a twist," Wilkins snapped. "As my brother said, 'don't change your signature mark.' "

Bland was at a loss for words. There was no way possible, he thought, that he could deliver under their expectations. His contempt transcended into anger at the mere fact they had made such awful remarks without waiting for him to submit the final chapters.

Out of pure irritation, Bland bit back at the men. "What signature mark?" he raved. An insidious expression came across his face. "If you want a bestselling novel, then why don't you try writing it yourselves? You will see it's not that easy."

The old men looked at each other. Smith patted the palms of his hands toward the floor. "Okay, calm down, Bland. We know you're under some duress, so here's what we're going to do. Why don't you make some additional changes, do your rewrites? Better yet, you can start fresh with a new story. Whatever you decide, you have plenty of time to get the book to us."

Of the choices given to Bland, he had a feeling it was the last option they hoped he committed to.

"You want me to start over after I've put in countless hours on this novel?"

"We want you to be happy with what you write, but more importantly, we want to be satisfied with what we read. That way everyone gets what they want," Smith remarked.

Wilkins made sure he would get the last word, "We all put in countless hours, and that's what it takes to become a partner. Remember, Bland, no one is forcing you to do this. If you want to stop, then stop, but don't make excuses because that's a sign of weakness. Of course, weakness leads to failure."

Bland knew Wilkins would just love for him to fail. A deep part of Bland felt Wilkins's comment was motivated by their safety net, Larry Peterson. In fact, both Wilkins and Larry would love the pleasure of seeing him fail.

Smith walked out the office door without adding to Wilkins's remarks. When the door closed, Bland felt his anger rise. The nerve of the men to violate his privacy by reading the book without asking. He slammed the keyboard down, then kicked the chair out of his path. After pacing around his desk several times, he reached for the phone to call home.

Immediately, Dakota noticed the uneasiness in his voice. "Bland, what's wrong?"

He gathered his belongings and stuffed the printed draft into his satchel. "I'm on my way home. I'll tell you when I get there."

10

THAT EVENING BLAND AND DAKOTA SAT IN THE SITTING room discussing his confrontation with the twins. Normally her presence would calm him, but not this time.

"I'm so angry," he said, without pausing to take a breath. "They had the audacity to enter my office, unwelcome I remind you, and read the novel. The entire ordeal still pisses me off. You know, I have a good mind to say the hell with the partnership. It isn't worth the damn stress. As a matter of fact, the hell with ever writing another word again."

Bland figured he might as well toss that option out in case he got fired. At least he could save some dignity by resigning, he believed.

"Bland, try calming down. Everything is going to be all right. You're upset. And you're under an extreme amount of stress."

"You're right. I am under a lot of pressure, and that pressure just amplified."

"I figure it's their way of bringing the best out of you."

Dakota had yet to read the book, and she figured after the twins berated him, for certain, Bland wasn't going to let her read it. She felt all she could do was to stay positive. She trusted Bland to make the necessary changes that would make it an exceptional novel.

Her eyes probed, "Don't look at it as being negative, Bland. Let their scathing words inspire you to greatness."

"Greatness," he mocked her. "Well, they want their greatness to be written in the next six months."

"Is it possible?"

He looked at her strangely. "To write a book is possible, but to write a bestseller in that time is impossible, at least to my standards. It takes a lot of research and rewrites." To give his comment additional gravity, he added, "And more research and rewrites." His anger resurfaced. "If they could get the book now, they would. I believe, I would've had the book finished by December. But now they want me to write a new story. I will need a good two years or longer. That way I can really dedicate myself to some good research that would generate a great story. They want a bestseller. Need I remind them that none of my bestsellers were written in less than twenty-four months? I'm not some overnight writer who I can just crank out page after page."

She allowed him to vent before telling him something he must have forgotten.

"Then tell me, how were you able to write twelve bestsellers in such a small amount of time?"

Bland's voice elevated, "And what did that get me?" He answered for her. "Burnout. It got me burned out! The arrogance of them to think I can just keep cranking out page after page," his words slowed. "And the audacity of them criticizing my work. Did they forget the time constraints they put me under?" he fumed.

"Forget what they say. How do you like the book, Bland?"

"I don't know because I can't stop thinking how much is riding on this book. I can't fail—" Bland immediately cut his words because he didn't want Dakota to know about his previous failed attempts to produce a book. "Actually, the book is not even finished." He noticed her concerned stare and thought he should say something positive about the book. "Given what has been written, I think the book has the potential of being a bestseller."

Again, Dakota thought about asking for the draft to judge it on its merits. Again, she elected to leave the decision to Bland. If he wanted her

to read it, he would have given it to her to read, like he always had. She didn't want to stress him anymore than he already was, so she dropped the thought.

"What are your plans?" she asked.

"What choice do I have? If I want the partnership, I'll have to write what they want, and how they want it." He scowled at the thought of having to do it according to their terms.

"Bland, the partnership idea is great, but if you're going to be this stressed, then I can just go back to work. We can make it work, honey."

Their discussion concerning her returning to work always brought about an argument. She never seemed to win, yet they continued to find themselves in deeper debt with no resolutions.

"No," he said firmly. "We already discussed it. I'm going to have to write the book." She noticed his perturbed expression, and it didn't offer her any comfort. "I personally think the story is good the way it is." He paused to ask, "Where is Devin?"

She stood and helped pull him up from the sofa. "Devin ate and is already in bed. I want you to take a long, hot shower while I make us some dinner. Tomorrow, I want you to play hooky from work so we can wander to the mountains. That will help you clear your head."

Bland didn't disagree. When on his feet, he rotated his slumped shoulders, then climbed the staircase. Meanwhile, Dakota prepared a pitcher of iced tea and a fresh salad with chicken for dinner.

As she went to move his satchel off the kitchen table when she noticed the wrinkled draft in the side compartment. Fearing it would upset him, she considered not reading it. She knew he was no longer comfortable with the story because of the twins' remarks about it. Desperately, Dakota wanted to know for herself, but the only way to know was to take a chance and read the story. Curiosity compelled her to remove the draft from his bag, slide it across the table, and turn the first page. She hoped Bland wouldn't mind if she read a few pages. Maybe she could offer him a better perspective about the book. By the time he finished his shower, dressed, and decided to rejoin her in the kitchen, she had completed several chapters.

When he walked into the kitchen, she jumped like someone had just

caught her doing something wrong.

"I hope you didn't mind," she confessed with remorseful expressions.

She could tell from his acute glare that he did mind. He looked at her, then at the manuscript on the kitchen table. He poured himself a glass of iced tea before answering, "No, not at all."

She knew he was agitated about her reading the pages without his approval. Silently, she hoped her reading the book would spark constructive criticism that wouldn't lead into an argument.

He stood with his lower back resting against the edge of the countertop. He waited for her to respond, since she did read it. As Dakota put the manuscript on the table, she stole a half glance in Bland's direction. They both knew the procedure if she liked a book he had written. She would set the manuscript down then look at him with one of those satisfied smiles that comes after having good sex. Then she would say it was a bestseller.

Without her saying a word, Bland knew she didn't like it. Or maybe she felt guilty for reading it caused her not to respond.

He put off the inevitable. "So, what do you think?"

"Interesting," she said without an expression.

"Interesting," he repeated as he walked to the table to take a seat. "That's it. Just interesting?"

"I'm confused with the plot of the story. There are things that don't make sense, in particular, a schizophrenic hitchhiker. The concept of schizophrenia has been overused. Usually, the element of romance is present in all your books, but it is missing in this book. Your previous books had a way of keeping you guessing what was going to happen. Your books made you want to turn the page."

Bland snapped, "I see you turned the pages."

"I turned the pages, hoping it would get better. Frankly, I agree with Smith and Wilkins. It's missing a lot of what made your books great."

Just hearing her voice say those words sent a chill up his spine, which angered him even more. How could she agree with them, he thought? After dealing with the twins' harsh criticism, his emotions were still raw, and he wasn't prepared for her candidness about the book. He responded with defensive rebuttals.

“Are you just saying that because you want it to be better than all the others?”

“No.” She slurped the iced tea.

“Please, could you not slurp your tea? It’s not hot.” Taking a quick sniff, he refocused his attention back to the novel. “I know it’s different,” he admitted. “I thought I should take a different approach from the other books. You can’t expect me to take the same approach, knowing what’s at stake.”

Dakota didn’t say a word but waited for her chance to speak when he was finished protecting his story. Finally, his rage spent, he grew silent. Dakota knew then it was an opportunity to voice her comments.

“Bland, please don’t take my critique the wrong way. Sure, you are putting in the time because they require you to be there but, honey, you can tell from the narrative that it isn’t you. The tone of the characters is wrong. The plot is predictable and, more importantly, Bland, the book doesn’t have any personality.”

Suddenly, his voice rose again in defense of the book, “I’ve only had a short time to research the topic. Not to mention I am at that office from sunup to sundown. Now tell me, who can write anything under those conditions?”

“Honey, there is no need to shout. I understand what you’re going through.”

“Then why are you taking sides? Where is the support you pledged to me?”

“Bland, that’s not fair. You know I will do anything to make sure you are successful. And I mean anything.”

“By sitting at home?” he sharply remarked.

“How dare you!” she shot back. “It was your idea that I stay at home and raise Devin. Don’t you dare throw that in my face.”

It was a low blow, and one he wished he could retract, but the damage was done. He could tell from her bitter tone that she wasn’t finished.

“And I will say this. This book lacks the potential of being a bestseller. Not because you can’t write it but because you refuse to commit yourself to this project. Face it, you’re terrified of failing.”

“That’s ridiculous.” He waved a hand in the air.

"Is it, Bland?" she asked, to make him consider her words.

"I have twelve bestsellers, so why would I be scared of failure when I've had nothing but success?"

"Success," she screeched. "Your last two books published were anything but successful. Maybe that's why they weren't published in your pseudonym. Your last project was so awful that the publishing house didn't invest the money to publish it."

It hurt to hear her say such malicious but truthful words. From Bland's sudden loss of words, it was obvious he didn't know she knew about any of his failed books. As far as S&W not publishing his last novel, he didn't have the nerve to tell her.

"How did you know?"

"It's not important how I know. What is for certain is that you didn't share it with me. Bland, I could have helped you through that time."

Bland took her words as a stain of betrayal. Aggressively, he pushed back from the table, stood, grabbed his unfinished manuscript, shoved it into the counter drawer, and exited the room. Dakota didn't attempt to stop him. What would be the use? she thought.

That night he lay restless with a bitter glare on his face. Dakota sensed his inability to fall asleep. Still, she refused to add more fuel to his fire. The only way to smooth such flames was to let them burn out.

The next morning, Bland deliberately made no attempt to dress quietly. Dakota rolled over and watched in silence as he slipped on his shoes. She noticed him favoring his bruised ribs.

"You're grimacing. Are your ribs still hurting?"

When Bland didn't answer her, she sat upright in the bed.

"Where are you going?" Dakota asked. "I thought we had plans for today."

"I have plans. I have plans to work. Hopefully, I can make the story better," he remarked bitterly. "That's what you want, right? That's what the twins have been pressing me about, a bestseller," he sarcastically said before swinging his jacket over his shoulder.

No longer was Bland confident about the story. Over the years, there

seemed to be some consistency between his wife and the twins' opinion concerning his books. If one rejected the book, the other wasn't likely to accept it either.

Again, he began to rationalize the reasons for the book's weak story line—time constraints and the pressures of becoming a partner being the greater factors. During his long drive to the office, there was a moment he considered returning home and apologizing for his rudeness; however, his pride and anger chased the thought off.

Normally, a drive from the house to the office took thirty minutes, but this time it took over an hour. When he arrived at his floor, his disposition was still one of a bad mood. Paige sensed the disenchantment in his quick greeting.

"Paige, if anyone calls, I am out of the office."

He walked past her into his office. Larry's loud "good morning" boomed across the lobby.

"Not today, Larry," Bland shook his head. Thankfully, his blinds were still shut, so he didn't have to waste the energy to close them.

Bland contemplated if the partnership was worth the aggravation. The way things were starting out with the twins and Dakota were not good signs. He considered how Dakota knew about his previous books not being published. He pulled his chair up to his computer and began to consider their doubts concerning the novel. He felt the story line had a relevance to psychological diseases, which gave the novel great potential. It just needs to be connected better, he told himself. Reluctantly, he considered that an element of romance might be needed. Adding that would at least make Dakota feel better, he believed, but only a new story could make the twins happy. He would dedicate himself for the next several hours to make the book better.

After hours of nonstop work on the novel, even with the new additions, he wasn't sure if he made the book any better, at least to meet their expectations. Although he hadn't come to the inevitability of trashing the book, he did contemplate writing a letter of resignation.

The top drawer to his desk harbored all the pens, so he slid the drawer open. Lying on top of the pens was Grey's business card. He held the card in his hand before again flipping the card along his fingers.

He agonized whether to call. Suddenly, his discontent reverted back to Dakota as he recalled her scathing words about his novel and his failures. What infuriated him the most, besides her agreeing with the twins, was her knowing his pressures with writing.

Out of spite, Bland dialed the number. Grey's voice lifted when she heard Bland on the other end of the phone.

"What did I do to deserve this?"

"What do you mean?"

"I mean, it's not hard to know when someone isn't interested."

"Why would you say that?"

"Because of how long it took for you to call me after our evening of jazz."

"Trust me, Grey, it definitely isn't that. Lately, I've been under a lot of stress. I'm writing a new novel." Then he stopped. He elected not to go into great details about it.

"That's great, Bland."

"Yeah," he sighed.

After Bland's remark, Grey's tone of voice changed from jubilation to concern.

"Are you okay, Bland?"

"Honestly, I called because I need to hear a friend's voice. I just want to disappear, and I was hoping you would join me on a train ride through the countryside."

She figured the invitation was innocent enough, and it wouldn't hurt to get away from her number crunching for a few hours.

"Okay, Bland, but first I have a few business ends to tie up."

"Great! In the middle of the main hall of Union Station is the Center Café. You can't miss it. Let's meet there, say around three this afternoon."

"See you at three."

After Bland hung up the phone, he looked at his watch. He had a few hours to spare. He tried redirecting his attention back to the book. No need, he figured. Surely, the twins or his wife weren't going to like anything he wrote. He sat back in his chair and reclined with his thoughts about seeing Grey. He tried not to give too much thought to Dakota, since anxiety ran through his body over being alone with Grey.

After a while, he came out of his office with an expression more pleasant than earlier. Always perceptive, Paige noticed the mood change.

"Mr. Benthall, it's about time you came out of that den. I thought you were ready to hibernate for the winter."

"I apologize if I was brusque this morning."

"No need to apologize. My mother told me if you live long enough, you'll have those mornings."

"And she's right, so I am leaving for the day." Bland hit the elevator button.

Bland noticed how good it felt to be out of the office. He didn't want to give another thought about the book. That was before he spotted the twins walking along the crowded corridor. Quickly, he slipped into a gentlemen's apparel store and waited for them to pass.

When Bland arrived at Union Station, Grey was sitting at the station's bar enjoying an espresso. Grey looked up and saw him approaching with one arm swinging and the other in his front pants pocket. With a slight smirk, she checked out his walk.

"You know, Mr. Benthall, you have a sexy walk. And, I like your blazer as well."

"You do? Thanks," he said, as he took a seat. "Have you been waiting long?" he asked.

"Long enough to finish an espresso, but it's okay. What time does the train leave?"

He looked at his watch, "Three-thirty, so that gives us thirty minutes."

"Great, you can sit down and have a drink with me." She took him by the arm and led him to the bar stool.

Bewilderedly, he replied, "A little late to be drinking espresso?"

"On the contrary, there is a little more in this cup than coffee."

"Okay, then give me a double cognac on the rocks. Did you handle all your business?" he asked.

"I sure did," she smiled before sipping the espresso. "Bland, I am so excited."

"About?"

"This trip with you." Her eyes gleamed with delight. "Frankly, it's

been so long since I've traveled for anything other than work."

"I feel I should be taking you somewhere more glamorous than on a train ride through the countryside."

"It doesn't matter. It's somewhere, and I am glad it's not work." Her voice lowered and soft words rolled off her tongue. "I'm glad it's somewhere with you. Thanks for inviting me."

He felt her sincerity as they sat silently staring at each other.

Bland interrupted their precious moment, "Hey, we have ten minutes, so let's head to the train." He finished his drink and took her by the hand.

When they arrived at the train, his mind immediately reflected to when the two of them sat in the lounge car practically all night.

Bland smiled.

She noticed, "What is it?"

"I had a thought about the night we met. I'm sure you remember that night?"

"Sure I do. Is the entire night going to be a repeat?"

"I took the liberty to schedule a bed car in case we get tired of sitting in the lounge area."

A delightful smile stretched across her face. "A little overzealous, would you say?"

"Now, Ms. Brindle, do you think I am trying to take advantage of you?" He didn't allow her to answer, "I want to make sure you are comfortable." He silently vowed to behave. He didn't want to violate Dakota; however, he knew he wanted some quality time with Grey.

They both laughed.

It was like twenty years earlier. A sense of nostalgia filled the atmosphere as they sat in the lounge area drinking and reminiscing about the people they met on the train that night. They shared more stories and laughed at each one. Suddenly, the train came to a squealing stop. Passengers in the lounge car began investigating by peering out the windows. All Bland could see were fields of tall grass.

"I wonder what's going on," a stranger said, as he leaned across Bland's and Grey's table to look out the window.

Bland looked around the man's body to catch Grey's eyes. His facial

expression was: Can you believe this guy? She offered a smile in return. Bland sat back in his seat and waited for the man to finish probing. A surge of porters with unpleasant stares rushed through the lounge area. Bland managed to grab the last porter by the arm.

"Is everything okay?"

"We're probably going to be delayed, something with the engine." The porter tried to free his arm from Bland's grasp.

"How long do you estimate the delay?" Bland asked, with no intent of having to be somewhere. He found it kind of romantic to add more history to their short album of memories.

"I don't know, but the engineer is going to announce it in a minute," the porter said, so that Bland would let go of his arm.

Bland had forgotten he still clutched the young man's arm. Finally, the porter pulled away from Bland's grip and continued trotting down the aisle. As the porter promised, seconds later, the voice of the engineer came over the speaker.

"Sorry folks, we have engine failure. There is no need going into technical jargon of what broke in the engine. Unfortunately, we will be delayed for two hours or more. The needed part has to be flown to our location. Until then you can sit tight, but as fortune will have it, a small town is having its local festival just over the hill. For those who want to pass the time at the festival, local transportation is available to the fairgrounds. Again, I am sorry for the inconvenience this has caused. Thank you."

After the announcement, the intercom clicked off.

Grey's natural disposition wanted to take advantage of this opportunity to have some fun. She grabbed Bland by the arm. "Come, Bland, let's go to the festival. It'll be fun."

Although Bland initially displayed unwillingness for the spontaneous venture, with prodding from Grey, he soon changed his attitude.

"You're right, it will be fun," he smiled, while embracing the thought that no one he knew would run into him this far out from the city.

As they enjoyed the festival, one could see the genuine joy that Grey received from the rides and even more joy just being with Bland. Something spurred Grey to want a picture to observe the occasion.

Of course, Bland was a little apprehensive about the picture, given his marital status.

"Come on, honey, take a picture with me."

Grey's choice of the word "honey" registered in Bland's mind. A slight uncomfortableness showed in his expression and heightened when Grey entered the little picture booth. Bland stood outside the booth hoping she would sense his discomfort and end her plea.

She poked her head from behind the curtain. "Well, are you coming?" Bland didn't budge. "Oh, come on, Bland. Please? I don't want to take a picture by myself," she seductively whined.

She climbed out of the booth, grabbed his hand, and pulled him with her into the booth. The curtain fell in place, and a moment later from within the booth quick lights illuminated. After the picture had been taken, they took advantage of the semi-privacy to share a passionate kiss.

Grey pulled back from the kiss to look at the two pictures that spilled out from the machine.

"I thought there were supposed to be four pictures in a group," she complained.

Bland sat silently. He couldn't believe he allowed her to lure him into taking a picture.

She pulled a pen from her purse and scribbled the words, "my soul mate" on the back of the pictures.

"Here, you keep this one of us." She handed him the picture. "And, I will keep this one of me."

Bland's eyes widened with uneasiness. Hesitantly, he took the picture of them, slid it into the inside pocket of his blazer, and she put the other one in her purse.

The blast of the engine's horn announced that the train was ready to pull out. The time had passed without them even realizing. Once on the train, Bland sought more privacy for them.

"You want to head back to the sleeping car?" he asked.

"Sure, that would be fine. I can do with taking off these heels."

"Would you like a foot massage?"

She smiled, "After all that walking that would be nice. I didn't know you were into feet."

His voice dropped to a seductive tone, "There are a lot of things I'm into."

"Are you planning to reveal such things to me?"

"That was my intention. I wanted to reveal them twenty years ago, but we know how that turned out." Bland gave no further thought to his promise to himself to be faithful.

She laughed, "I'm sure you did, Mr. Benthall. You might get the opportunity to show me some secrets tonight," she smiled. "I hope the wait will be worth it."

As they entered their sleeping quarters, Bland's short smile temporarily reminded him that not all secrets would be revealed tonight. Certainly not the secrets that involved Dakota and his son.

The moment Bland closed the door to the sleeping car, he began to undo his trousers. She smiled when she saw his boxers.

"Wow, those are sexy. Let me see the rest."

At once, Bland attacked Grey with an onslaught of kisses. He had waited twenty years to have her alone. And he couldn't control himself. Straightaway, he went to unbutton his shirt, when Grey put her hands on his to stop him. There was a slight anxiety that overcame him.

"I don't plan to disappear, or no one is coming to throw you off the train, so there is no need to rush, Bland. You have me, and I am not going anywhere. Let us relish in every second of the moment."

Slowly, he moved her against the door. Unlike before, he gave her a slow, long, and intense kiss. Smelling her sweet fragrance seemed to arouse him more. His hands slid along her sides to her hips. His tongue caressed along her neck, then to her breasts. Her breasts exposed to the train's cool air made her nipples firm and delicate to the touch of his lips. As she dragged her fingers through his hair, she kissed him along his ear.

He did as he was told and took his time to indulge in her. His hand dropped between her thighs. His touch widened her eyes with anticipation of what was to come. She could feel him inside of her. Her bottom lip quivered, then curled between her teeth. Her grip tightened

on his hair. When he lifted her off her feet, her legs wrapped around his waist. She released her grip from his hair and aggressively kissed him while quickly undoing the buttons on his shirt. She wanted all of him, right then, right now.

11

IN THE EARLY MORNING HOURS, THE TRAIN PULLED BACK into the station. Grey and Bland said their goodbyes after agreeing to contact each other in a few days.

During Bland's drive home, there was a sense of guilt eating at his stomach. How could he sleep with another woman? What would Dakota say or do if she found out? That guilt began to find its way up his throat. Quickly, Bland pulled the car over, jumped out, and threw up on the side of the road. He spat several more times in hopes of removing any additional shame of what he did. As he continued home, he began contemplating explanations for arriving home at such an hour. Quietly, he pulled the SUV into the driveway and turned off the engine. Before exiting the car, he pondered a few other ideas about where he had been all night. As he walked to the front door, the inside of the house appeared dark and desolate. They must be asleep, he thought.

Slowly, he put the key into the lock and turned it. Softly, he pushed the door open, trying hard not to be heard. He was relieved that he took a shower on the train. Surely, he thought that taking a shower at such an hour would wake his wife and have her suspicion antennas detecting anything out of the ordinary. He set his satchel down by the door, then

quietly slipped off his shoes and began to walk with a feeling of greater relief. As he passed the opening to the dining room, a sharp jab landed near his kidney area.

"Ouch!" he groaned, then dropped to a knee. "My ribs," he cried.

Dakota hit the light switch. She stood over him like a mean nun. "Long night?" she asked.

"Long enough," he moaned, while clutching his sore ribs. "My ribs will never heal if you keep hitting them."

"Maybe not, if you can't call home or answer your phone."

"You called me?" he asked, still holding his side.

"Did you call me?" she snappily asked. "So what kept you out all night?"

"Honey," suddenly his mind reverted back to Grey calling him honey. Quickly, he shook the thought and continued, "I can't get any service on this old cell phone."

"Then I suggest you get a new cell phone or a new service. One that will let you call, text, and even email to let your wife know you are okay."

He looked up at her from the floor. "I know you're sore about me running out earlier and not calling. I didn't mean," he groaned as he rose to his feet, still holding his ribs, "to worry you."

"You didn't worry me," she said, while heading to the sitting room. She flopped on the sofa.

He stood in the foyer watching, not sure what to say. When he had a clear look at her eyes, shame attacked him. He looked down, hoping that his infidelity wouldn't be detected.

"Dakota, I apologize for my behavior last night," he said, his head still in a downward position.

"Bland," she said in a soft, caring voice, "Look at me." Slowly, Bland lifted his eyes to hers. "I love you, and I shouldn't have come at you that way. I know you are feeling a lot of stress, and the last thing you need is me coming at you. I am your support; however, I refuse to have you not respect me. I will not have you speaking to me any kind of way, and not calling home to say when you will be arriving is unacceptable."

"I don't have a problem telling you where I was," he lied.

"I trust you, Bland, but I don't think you should leave me sitting here

worried all night."

"I thought you weren't worried," he tried to smile.

"Bland, I'm not playing." She gave him a stony look. "We already discussed how the book is going to have you putting in late hours, but I still would like a call. Regardless of our disagreements, I still deserve a call."

All Bland could muster from his guilty demeanor was a head nod.

"And yes, I was worried, a little," she looked at him and called him over with her finger.

"What? You're looking to assault me again?" Bland asked, as he closed the distance between them.

"I promise, I will keep my hands to myself," she whispered with a coy expression.

He rested his head in her lap. She saw the opportunity to stroke her hands through his hair. As he started to drift to sleep, to their surprise, the television came on.

"How did that happen?" Bland lifted himself. "Oh, I'm lying on the remote." Dakota moved tight against his body when Bland laughed, "That couldn't have scared you. Not the way you punch."

The channel happened to be on an adult program. Bland laughed again, "There's nothing ever on television."

"What's wrong with this?" she asked bluntly with seduction in the tone of her voice. There was a slight kiss on his cheek, and it caught his attention.

"You're not keeping your hands to yourself," he reminded her.

"I said nothing about my lips."

She began to kiss him compulsively. She wanted very much to make love to her husband, so she maneuvered herself to where he was between her thighs. While underneath him, she pulled at his trousers. Then she noticed the distant look in Bland's eyes.

"What's wrong?"

The plot was thickening. The thought of making love to his wife weighed upon him. How could he, when knowing just hours earlier he slept with another woman? Already, he had to live with the guilt of knowing he violated her and his vows of marriage. If he didn't sleep with

his wife, surely her intuition alone would set off the alarm of adultery. There was no choice in the matter; therefore, he would make love to his wife, more out of obligation than to his vows.

"Nothing's wrong," he replied. He pulled her by the waist. "Hold up," Bland reached for the remote and clicked the off button.

That morning, the two of them slept on the sitting room floor with only a thin blanket covering them. Dakota rolled her body toward his. Bland awoke to her staring at him.

"Something wrong?" he asked, as his eyes brought her into focus.

"Absolutely nothing," she paused, "Well, yes there is something." Bland's heart began beating rapidly. "What came over you last night?"

"What do you mean?" he asked, still worried.

"You haven't made love to me like that since," she hesitated, "since our first time in college. It was so intense, so fulfilling."

"Stop it," he smiled. Bland thought of the impetus behind his performance. And his smiled disappeared.

"I'm serious, Bland. It was—"

Before Dakota could say another word, at full speed, Devin ran and jumped on their pile. As Devin began to wrestle on top of the blanket, underneath the blanket Bland wrestled to put on his boxers. Dakota tried rolling over to regain her comfort, but when Bland and Devin began to pull and tug at each other, she managed to wrap the blanket around her, without exposing herself.

"What do you guys want to eat?"

Bland looked up, the feeling of guilt still fresh on his face. "Just coffee for me," he answered.

"I want pancakes, Mommy."

"After I shower, then coffee and pancakes it is," she smiled.

Bland decided to call off for the remainder of the week. He spent an enormous amount of time at home with Dakota and Devin. A sense of remorse could rest as an argument for such behavior, and Bland dared not disagree. He even went so far as adopting household duties. He helped plant flowers in the flowerbed, hung new draperies in the living

room, and created animal designs to go around the perimeter of the ceiling in Devin's room. Any other time, he would have never performed such chores. It was his way of showing his loyalty and solidarity, less to his wife and more to himself. He told himself his adultery was a onetime thing; it would never happen again.

Bland was in the kitchen applying a second coat of mauve paint over the cabinets when Dakota sneaked behind him.

"You scared me."

"I must admit, I can really get used to you being home," she stated, then planted a kiss on the back of his neck.

Bland considered the kiss and smiled. He sensed from her body language there was something more that she wanted to discuss.

He waited a second before replying. "Being home has been fun, well except for the washing duties. I think I will leave the dishes and laundry to you." He smirked, turned back to the cabinet, and made a series of strokes with his paint brush along the grain of the wood.

She laughed, "I'm going to fix some lunch. Are you hungry?"

"I can do for a sandwich, since I'm working so diligently."

"Yes, you are. Now you can go upstairs and pry your son off that video game."

"An impossible task, but I think I have the solution." He climbed the stairs and turned into the first doorway. For several minutes, he stood watching Devin maneuver the controller with such accuracy. Finally, Bland tapped the side of the wall. Devin spoke without turning his sights from the game.

"Hey, Daddy, I knew you were there."

Bland looked down on the floor, then around the room, before asking, "How?"

"Because I see you in the television."

"You could see me with the TV on?"

"Yep, I saw your reflection, Daddy."

"Well, how come you didn't say something?"

"How come you didn't say something?"

"How old are you again?" Bland asked with humor.

"Daddy, you're so silly."

Bland went to take a seat.

"Daddy, you can't sit there."

"I can't sit down?"

"Daddy, that's Dookie Luke's seat," referring to a spotted, stuffed puppy with ears so long they brushed the ground.

"Okay, okay," Bland's head scoped around the room for a new seat. "Is it safe to sit on the bed?"

"Yes, I just sleep there."

Bland didn't realize he had gotten pulled into watching Devin play the video game until Devin noticed Dakota's reflection in the television.

"Hi, Mommy."

"You have the perfect solution, huh?" she smiled.

"Honey, I got so caught up watching him play this game. He's awesome. It's fascinating what they have done with technology."

"Yes, it is, so why do we still have that antique answering machine and that antique phone in the bedroom?" she asked, then laughed. "I hope you find it equally fascinating what I have done to these sandwiches, so come on you two. I want to be as appreciated as that game."

"Mommy, can I bring Dookie Luke?"

"Yes, you may bring Dookie Luke."

After lunch, Dakota wiped the table. Bland moved from his seat at the table so that Dakota wouldn't have to maneuver around him.

Something was weighing on her mind, but she said nothing as she watched Bland mosey to the kitchen counter to return to his painting. She spotted Devin dragging the spotted puppy across the kitchen floor. "Devin, I don't need Dookie Luke to clean my floors for me, so please take him back upstairs."

She rinsed the dishcloth in the sink before making her way to Bland's side. Silently, she stood with her back against the counter watching him stir paint with a wooden stick.

Bland stopped stirring the paint. "Don't worry, I plan on fixing the phone in the bedroom. If that is what's bothering, you."

"Though, I definitely want it fixed, that isn't what's on my mind."

"What is it?"

Cautiously, she moved into the conversation. "Have you decided what your plans are for the book?"

His lips curled. "Honestly," he turned completely toward her, "I don't know. A part of me wants to quit and say the hell with it."

"Bland, once you've started something, I've never known you to quit."

"I know, that's why this is so hard." He stared blankly into the opposite wall. "I know we need this financially, but I'm not sure if I can deliver. I think I need more time," he groaned.

"Lately, Bland, I know my actions and my words have been contradictory. I said I would support you, but I have been pressuring you about spending more time at home. That was selfish of me, and I am so sorry, honey. Do what you have to do to finish this book. Just promise me one thing."

Bland smiled, "Promise you what?"

"When you're finished with this story, share it with me first."

"Recently, it seems everyone wants to sneak a peek before the book is even done."

She cocked her eye at him and frowned.

"I know the comment wasn't necessary, but yes, you will be the first to read the novel." Hopefully, I can write the book they want, he thought to himself.

"Remember, I am here if you need me."

"If I need you," he repeated. "Imagine me not needing you." He smiled and hugged her tightly.

After spending an entire week in the house, and seeing Dakota's growing list of household chores, Bland was eager to get to the office on Monday morning so he could start working on the book. He wanted to tell her of his decision. He rolled out of the bed and made his way to the bedroom closet where he found her organizing her shoe boxes.

Bland's voice startled her when he commented, "You're up early this Sunday morning."

"Yeah, I need to rearrange this closet so I will have room for my shoes."

He took a long look at her collection of shoes. "You really need to donate some of these shoes to the homeless shelter."

"What would really be great is you getting down here and helping me."

"Oh no, not me, not in here. This is your domain," he retorted.

"It's our domain, since your clothes are in here, too."

Bland stood in the bedroom doorway in his boxers watching quietly as Dakota went about her systematic process of flipping open the shoe boxes, shuffling the shoes, then stacking one box on another box that laced the closet wall. When Dakota looked up from the shoe boxes, she noticed the boxers Bland wore and their stylish design.

"You look cute in boxers," she confessed. "You normally don't wear that kind of underwear."

He wouldn't dare disclose his reason for wearing them, but still he acknowledged her comment with a thank you.

"You know, I'm always setting a trend," he teased.

Her head popped up from the shoe boxes. "You a trend setter?" She laughed, then went back to her work, still talking. "Bland, you hate trends."

"I never said I hated trends. I feel some things aren't trendy. Take for instance, that suede coat of yours that's been hanging in this closet for years."

She interrupted his comment, "I'll have you know that coat is vintage. It will never go out of style."

"Let me bring you to a realization, honey. That coat resembles a dog with a nappy fur and a bad case of worms. That is not trendy." He moseyed deeper into the closet to find the coat to prove his point.

"I have a lot of people staring at me when I wear that coat. I am always asked where I purchased such a fine piece of clothing." She couldn't hold in her laughter.

"Vintage," Bland replied while holding up the jacket. The two of them burst into laughter. "You need to throw this thing out."

"What needs to be thrown out is that blue blazer I keep hanging up every time you leave it downstairs."

She stood to inspect the blazer. When she pulled it off the hanger, his eyes widened. He immediately remembered it was the blazer he wore while accompanying Grey on the train. She started to inspect it, then she slipped it on.

"I'm surprised you still have this old thing. She noticed the stitching to the lining coming loose. "What happened to the lining in the jacket?" She began to feel around the inside pockets.

Bland frowned with an increasing panic, remembering what was in the inside pocket. He tried to pull the jacket off her shoulders, but she was quick to dash playfully into the bedroom.

A slight perspiration formed on Bland's forehead as he watched her dig into the inside pocket.

"All right, you had your laugh. Give me my old jacket."

"Why don't you come and get it," she said in an enticing voice. "I feel something in here," she said suddenly and with a wide grin. "Is there something you don't want me to see?" she asked as she maneuvered away from Bland's reaching hands.

Nervous energy shadowed Bland as he managed to corner her at the head of the bed. He tried to grab her and the blazer.

"I almost have it in my hand," she said excitedly.

Bland held his breath as Dakota dug her hand deeper into the inside pocket. When Dakota exposed her hand, she pulled out the inside lining of the pocket as well. "Now, what is it that I found," she said while laughing and poking her fingers through a large hole. "I found a big hole. Look at this. This is what you were hiding from me."

Bland closed his eyes and dropped his head. He let off a big sigh of relief.

"And you have the nerve to call my jacket raggedy," she said as she took off the blazer and handed it to him. As she walked back into the closet, Bland rammed his hand into the side pocket in search of the photo of Grey. He searched between the inside lining and the material of the jacket. Much to his surprise, it wasn't there. He looked down at the floor but didn't see anything. He headed back to the closet thinking the photo had fallen on the closet floor. Slowly, his eyes scanned the floor of the closet. Still he didn't spot it. Hopefully, it fell out of his

pocket while on the train.

He watched as Dakota returned to her system of opening the shoe boxes, when suddenly her demeanor changed. His eyes widened and she gasped when she saw what lay on the inside of one of her shoeboxes.

"Bland, what is this?"

He made his way further into the closet to see what she was referring to. Was it the photo of Grey?

"Give me that," he ordered. His mind was now off the photo and on what was in her hand.

"I asked a question, Bland. Who does this belong to?"

Bland was anxious as she retrieved the 9-millimeter from the box and handed it to him. After speaking with Rudy about the attack in the publishing house and all the things that can go wrong, Bland had decided to take a weekend concealed weapon course and purchase a gun.

"It belongs to me. Give me the shoe box," he ordered again.

"Why do you have this? And how long has it been in this house?" Bland replaced the gun in the box and stored it on the top storage rack in the closet. "Bland, Devin could have gotten to that gun, and I don't want to think about what could have happened."

"It's okay. The gun was on safety."

"Bland," she said with a frightened glare of concern.

"Dakota, I purchased the gun for protection. I thought I told you about it." He knew he didn't tell her. Because he knew how she felt about guns, he wasn't certain if he was ever going to tell her.

"No, Bland, you never told me about it. And with Devin in the house, you should have told me. That's so careless of you." She stood up to face Bland.

"I know, I should have told you. With the increasing violence spreading to the suburbs, I need to protect my family. Since I'm spending more late hours at the publishing house, you need to know where it is in case you need to use it."

"You've had years of late nights at the office, so why now?"

He thought about his attack at the office and his conversation with Rudy that persuaded him to get a gun. "Because the world has changed,

and I feel more comfortable that this is in the house."

She released a heavy frustration from her nostrils. Bland grabbed her and kissed her on the forehead. He wanted to give her a sense of comfort.

"We probably won't have to use it, but it does give me comfort to know it is here."

"I don't feel comfortable with it being around Devin."

"I know, and that's why it will be on this top rack from now on."

Defiant, she said, "Bland, I don't feel comfortable with it being in the house."

He hugged her tighter as a way of reassuring her that it would be okay. She lifted her head to see his eyes. In her eyes, the issue of the gun wasn't settled.

"Trust me, it's going to be okay," he reassured her. Then he felt that announcing his intentions to work on the book would lighten the mood. "I figured I would return to the publishing house tomorrow. I'm more than sure the twins think I've gone AWOL."

When her response was less of the excitement he had expected, he repeated his comment.

"Did you hear me? I'm returning to work."

"That's good, Bland." Her mind was still on the gun. "Have you called to tell them you were returning, so they'll know you didn't abandon them?"

"I called Paige and told her, but not the twins. Speaking of the twins, they haven't called or tried to get in touch with me. I might not have a job when I return."

"I'm sure you will have a job, Bland. They need you as much as you need them," she said without any emotion.

"Yeah, you're always right."

"And, I am right about the gun, Bland."

He wanted to avoid any additional conversation about the gun, so he blurted, "How about we go out tonight? There's a new restaurant that just opened on Wisconsin Avenue. It will be fun." He attempted to make amends for the gun, but also for the remnants of guilt that often resurfaced to remind him of his infidelity.

"Sure, that will be good." Still, lackluster excitement coupled with

disappointment accompanied her reply.

He grabbed her by the shoulders and gave her a secure hug. The embrace lasted for several seconds. He pulled back from her arms.

"Listen, since you feel that uncomfortable about the gun, I will get rid of it."

"You promise?"

"I will ask Mr. Scott if he knows of anyone looking to purchase one."

"Thanks, honey." She paused as though having to remember something important. "Bland, see if Mr. and Mrs. Scott can watch Devin for a few hours while we go out tonight. Speaking of Mr. Scott, he came by early this morning. He wants me to bring my car to his shop so he can fix the starter."

"I told him I will bring it down," snapped Bland.

"I know, but he keeps complaining that the thing is annoying him every time I try starting it."

"I'll drop it off tomorrow on my way to work. That way I can talk to him about the gun." He paused, "That means I'll have to catch the metro from his shop into work."

"I don't mind following you or even coming to get you from work."

"No," he said, "I plan on hearing Lou play tomorrow night. He can bring me home."

"Where is he playing?"

"I'm not sure. I'll have to call him."

"Is there any room for me to tag along?" she asked, hoping he would say yes.

"Always," he smiled. "We will have to get another babysitter for tomorrow night."

"I will take care of it, honey." She pulled closer to his body to drag her finger down his chest. "Since you're not doing anything, why don't you help me finish the closet?"

"I have no problem with that, but first I'm going back to sleep."

She pushed him away and returned to the closet.

After dinner that evening, Bland and Dakota decided to take a stroll along the boardwalk on the Potomac River. After a rather long walk

they took a seat on an empty bench. Bland pulled her close and wrapped his arms around her shoulders. Dakota embraced the light breeze that passed as she peered at the bright stars in the night sky.

Bland caught her stares and expressed a confession that suddenly came upon him.

"You mean everything to me. The possibility of losing you would be the same as the sky losing a star."

"With so many stars, what would it matter? It's just a star," she said, wanting to see what he would say.

"It's not just a star, it is part of a cluster of stars, each adding its dynamic appeal to the universe. You are my star, Dakota, you bring brightness and happiness to my cluster, to my entire being."

Dakota turned to look into his eyes to reflect what she saw in him. It was no secret why she married Bland. He was charming, sincere, and had a tenacity to succeed. She really loved him. Though at times he could be stubborn and selfish, she couldn't abandon him during their hard times. As his wife, she knew she wanted to be by his side and aid him in any way possible.

"I love you, too, Bland," she said, then lay her head against his chest.

The next morning, a surprise summer breeze brushed his face as he rushed out of the house to his car. Then remembering that he had to drop Dakota's car at Mr. Scott's garage, which was a hassle, he now wished he had never agreed to do it. He glanced at his watch. He was running late, and he desperately wanted to get to his office in the event the twins showed up. It would at least appear he was serious about putting in the hours to finish the book, so he could become a partner.

"I need to get to work," he murmured under his breath. "It will have to wait." He climbed into his SUV and backed out of the driveway.

When Bland stepped off the elevator of the publishing house, Paige greeted him with a big smile.

"Bland," she cried out with an excited squeal. She came from behind the desk to give him a hug.

"Wow, maybe I should stay away more often," he joked.

"By the way, you have a visitor."

"A visitor," disbelief accompanied his tone of voice "This early?"

"It's almost eleven and she—" Paige replied, then Bland interrupted her.

"She," his eyes roamed in the direction of his office.

"Is something wrong, Mr. Benthall?"

"Nothing," then he regained his focus. "Did this 'she' give you a name?"

"I didn't ask."

He offered Paige an unpleasant stare before starting toward his office. He could barely make out the woman's appearance through the mini blinds. When he opened the door to his office, sitting in front of his desk was Grey. Given his wide eyes, she could tell he was surprised to see her.

"Grey," Bland sighed, then walked around to the front of his desk. He immediately spotted Dakota's picture; fortunately, it was turned out of Grey's line of sight. Still, he couldn't be certain if she saw it during her inspection of the office, which he assumed she did.

How did she know where I worked? he asked himself, with a sense of dread. Then he recalled disclosing that information to her. After gathering his thoughts, Bland walked cautiously over to close the door and shut the mini blinds to the gossiping eyes of Larry Peterson. He then turned back to Grey. She stood to greet him. He embraced her, so he could hide Dakota's photo under some loose papers.

Grey noticed some uncomfortableness in his posture. "Is this a bad time, Bland?"

"Not at all. This is a pleasant surprise, so what brings you by?"

"You," she said, without smiling. "This morning I had a meeting a few blocks away. I didn't realize how close I was until I looked up and saw the big S&W name on the building. I thought I'd take a chance and drop by, given the fact that I hadn't heard from you since we took our spontaneous trip. Let's just say it's my way of making sure you were okay."

"I meant to call you, and I know it seems like I deserted you after…" he stalled.

"I would be lying if I said I didn't think that. You gave me no other choice but to think that. And I had no other alternative but to drop by

and ask if that's the case. I don't want you to think I'm only good for one thing."

"No, no, nothing like that, Grey. I've been extremely busy. I figured you would be the same, busy, that is."

"Bland, I know what this must look like to you. I mean showing up at your place of employment uninvited. You probably think I went through all your stuff, which I didn't. I am not that type of woman."

Bland was relieved. "What type of woman would that be?" he explored.

"Bland, I don't want to appear as a stalker, or even worse, someone desperate to find a man."

He smiled and released her from his grip. "No such thought came to my mind. Well, maybe a little." He laughed.

"Honestly, Bland, I hope I'm not intruding in your space."

Bland sat on the edge of his desk, "No intrusion. What you're witnessing is my expression of flattery. You're taking the time out of your busy schedule to see me. I'm truly flattered." Anxiety occasionally had Bland looking up at the door. "So, the meeting you had this morning, was it about your contract?"

"Yes," she nodded and continued. "I had to meet with the executives this morning to discuss some minor details."

"All is well, I hope."

"Everything is fine. We're all in one accord." When she sensed him flinch, her speech slowed, "Are your ribs still sore?"

"Today, they are extremely tender," he answered.

"Is there anything I can do?"

"Well," he paused, and the guilt resurfaced to his chest. He didn't want another incident of him pulling off to the side of the road. "No, it will be okay."

"Maybe some warm healing hands would do the trick," she pressed on.

That grabbed his attention. "You're certified in massage therapy?"

"I'm not going to say all that. I just wanted to know if I could help. I hate to see a man in pain. And I promise you'll be safe in my hands."

"Is that right?" Bland smiled, then thought about his wife. He tried

not to think about Dakota. Then, with a blank face, he looked at Grey and felt what he was doing to her was just as unfair. A part of him wanted to reveal the truth to her. He wanted to at least give her the choice to decide what she wanted, but deep inside, he knew she would never continue in such a love triangle.

She noticed his inattentiveness. "Bland, what's on your mind?"

"What do you mean?"

"One minute you were talking about your side, and then you were consumed in thought."

"It's nothing," he shrugged his shoulders.

"Well, I was thinking a single man like you probably misses out on a lot of home-cooked meals. How about coming to my place for dinner?"

"That would be awesome, and very tempting; however, I must first share something with you."

She sat down and patiently waited for what seemed to be a struggle for him to say something.

Abruptly the telephone intercom buzzed. "Mr. Benthall?"

Bland reached for the receiver, "What is it, Paige?"

"I wanted to give you a heads up, the twins are heading down."

"What did they want?"

"They asked if you had showed up for work. Also, they made the comment that maybe you were taking this week off too."

"What did you tell them?"

"As always, I told them nothing."

"Thank you, Paige." He hit the off button on the speaker.

Grey stood from her seat. "That sounds serious, so I guess I should be going."

"Can we finish this conversation later?" he asked.

"Sure we can."

He escorted her to the elevator. "It's close to lunch; how about you give me a minute, and we can walk together to the Aerospace Smithsonian. You'll love their cafeteria. That's if you have time to eat."

"Sure," she beamed. "I guess I can keep myself occupied with all the beautiful boutiques and shops downstairs."

"I won't be long," he smiled.

When the elevator door opened, Smith and Wilkins walked off.

"Glad to see you're back, Bland," Smith said, before noticing Grey standing to his right. "I'm sorry, Bland, are we interrupting?"

"No, she was just leaving."

"Well, please, don't be so rude. Give us a formal introduction," remarked Wilkins, as he held out his hand to greet Grey.

The king of being rude is asking me not to be rude, thought Bland. When have the twins ever been so interested in whom I associated?

"Gentlemen, this is Ms. Brindle. Ms. Brindle, this is Mr. Wilkins Stump and Mr. Smith Stump. They happen to own this beautiful building you've fallen in love with. Not to mention, they are my bosses."

"Not for long," Wilkins blurted. Then his eyes refocused on Grey, "It was a pleasure meeting you."

Bland knew Wilkins's kindness could only last for so long.

"Yes, it was a pleasure," Smith agreed.

Grey smiled at the two men, "Likewise."

The two old men glanced at each other before making their way to Bland's office.

"Let me get in there before they start going through my desk."

"Why would they do that?"

"It's a long story."

Bland waited for the elevator door to close before returning to his office. When he entered, Smith and Wilkins stood on opposite sides of the room. They didn't inquire about the woman, just the novel.

"Three strikes and you're out, Bland," exclaimed Wilkins. "And two of those strikes have already been used, so I hope you've gotten your issues straight."

"What do you mean, issues?"

"Never mind that," Smith said as he moved between the two of them. "Bland, it's obvious that you don't possess the love you once had for writing, so how about this? You stay on as an editor; however, Larry will remain senior executive editor."

As the old men left his office, Bland stood, thinking about what he

should do. He watched as they stepped into the elevator.

Rushing out of the office, Bland shouted, “Wait.” The elevator was held. “Okay,” Bland said, “I’m ready to finish this book. I want to finish this book. And I’ll do it your way.”

The men turned toward him, “Bland, are you sure? You don’t have to do this, not to yourself or your family.”

“I am sure.”

“You are?” Wilkins frowned. “Then it would be in your best interest to show up to work every day and before eleven. At least then it will increase your chances of finishing the book before the deadline, which I remind you is steadily approaching.”

Bland brushed off Wilkins’s comment, even though it was interesting that Wilkins knew what time he arrived at the office.

“You will have it,” Bland said with confidence.

12

When Bland spotted Grey, she was leaving a boutique. He looked around before waving her toward him.

"Your meeting didn't take long," she said, as she approached him.

He noticed the bag in her hand. "I see you found the boutique?"

"Yes. I was able to find me a little something," she seductively remarked.

He grinned, "Are you ready to eat?"

Once at the cafeteria, they took a spot that overlooked the Washington Mall. During every quiet moment of the conversation, Bland stared into Grey's eyes. Her beauty was captivating. Except for his wife, he had never seen a woman so beautiful. It was humorous to some degree, he thought, how his strength was intact when Grey wasn't around, but once in her presence, his strength faded. He sat there in silence, wondering if he wanted this to go further than their one impromptu sexual encounter. He never meant to cheat on Dakota, but being with Grey had him again contemplating such a thought. He didn't have to wonder if Grey felt the same way; her eyes revealed the truth.

Held within Grey was a sense of uncertainty. She knew what pain

felt like, and at one point Bland, too, had contributed his share. After trusting him a second time and not receiving a call after the train ride in the countryside, it made her reconsider his explanation for disappearing years ago.

"Why did you just laugh?" asked Bland.

She had learned to channel unpleasant thoughts with laughter.

"I had an awkward thought." She chuckled again.

"Would you like to share it?"

"Maybe later; anyway, how is the writing? I was curious to know what actually went into a book."

"Words," he laughed.

"That's not what I meant. I mean what goes into writing a good book?"

"Well, to be frank, a lot of energy. There are times I write all night." Bland hadn't pulled an all-nighter in many years, but it was an opportunity to boast, so why not. "To me the most taxing thing about writing is the research."

"Research?" she questioned, with an awkward expression behind her words. "I assumed research was done more for nonfiction works."

"Both nonfiction and fiction require a certain level of research. I want to be accurate with the setting, the plot and the conclusion. Once the research is done, I then concentrate on the characters. It is then that I disappear into the story." That was before the writer's block, he thought.

"It's good to have somewhere you can disappear," she admitted.

"Everyone has a place where they can escape. My place is my writing."

"I don't know, Bland. Maybe I do, but I haven't found it yet."

"I am sure it's there. Better yet, I know it's there and waiting for you to discover it or maybe even *him*."

She picked up on his invitation that he could be that place where she could disappear. "You say that like you really mean it."

Not sure if he meant it himself, he continued with the invite to see where it would lead. "Why wouldn't I?"

"Bland, I told you already. I can't take any more words that people think I want to hear. And I definitely don't need to feel any more pain."

"Tell me something, Grey, what happened?"

"What do you mean?"

"When did you lose sight of love?"

"I haven't lost sight, Bland. I want to be told less that I am loved and be shown more that I am loved. I gave my all to my ex-husband. I love hard, Bland. My love stopped being reciprocated the instant he found out I couldn't bear him any children. What happened to unconditional love? What happened to honoring our vows? Shouldn't I have been enough?"

He didn't know how to answer her.

"In his eyes, I wasn't a woman. I began believing that I wasn't a woman because I was told a real woman can bear children."

Bland couldn't help but feel the pain she carried in her heart. He wanted to comfort her, but not knowing how she would react compelled him to hold to his slight hesitation.

"Do you know for certain you can't have children? Maybe there is a medical procedure that can help."

"I have a chronic disease called endometriosis."

"Endometriosis?" he questioned.

"I have bad menstrual cycles and severe cramps that sometimes hurt so badly I can't walk. Over five million women suffer from it. It's a progressive disease that gets worse over time."

Bland looked blankly at her sad face and slumped over posture. He didn't hesitate this time. It no longer mattered what she might think or how she perceived his actions. He rose up from the table and walked around to her seat. He knelt down to wrap his arms around her. The moment he embraced her, an uncontrollable flow of tears that had been mired for some time drained from her eyes.

After her moment of purging, he reached for a napkin to dry her eyes. He understood what those tears represented: A lifetime of disappointment compounded with the fact she may never be able to bear children. He wanted to say something to comfort her; however, all he could think of was his own child and how fortunate he was to have him in his life. Ironically, the thought made him clinch Grey tighter.

Immediately, she covered her eyes with her hands, not wanting him

to see her resolve falter.

"It's okay," he whispered.

She adjusted herself in the seat and leaned back so she could see his face.

"In the last four years, I have had eight surgeries. They want to take my uterus, but I can't let them do it. Not before I have a baby. I know I can have one, even though they keep telling me it's highly improbable. I just want one, that's all. There are people having children who don't want them, why can't I have one?"

Bland knew her question was rhetorical. Nonetheless, her words were strong as the tears once again flowed. Bland sensed her plea wasn't for him to hear, but to a higher being.

"Grey, it's okay," he softly repeated because he didn't know what else to say at such a moment.

"Bland, you will never understand the pain a mother carries after losing a child." She suddenly smirked, "Look at me." Then she let out that laugh that suppressed all emotions. "I'm sitting here crying all over your expensive shirt."

"I can buy another shirt but not another chance to be a friend."

"That's sweet, Bland. You've always had a way with words. I guess that's why you are a writer."

Suddenly, her words stopped when she saw what Bland held in his hand while on his knee.

"Bland, you didn't," she stated in disbelief.

"Yes, I did. I kept it all these years because I knew in my heart I would see you again. He leaned forward and placed the necklace around her neck. She let her fingers slide down to the locket, then to Bland's chin.

"You are truly amazing. I thought I lost it in the shower or some other place on the train. You had it all these years." Her eyes filled with tears when she opened the locket and discovered the picture of her parents was still there.

She smiled and Bland noticed. She looked at the empty picture slot and thought of him as her soul mate.

"What's with the smile?"

"For now, I'll keep it to myself."

"Okay, suit yourself," he said, returning her smile. "Come on, let's go," he reached for her hand.

After Bland paid the bill, he refused to let her leave in such an emotional state. Down the road was a quiet park, and this was a perfect time to visit. As they sauntered along the rock pebbles that stretched the length of the National Mall, Bland felt a completeness overcome him. He walked with Grey into a small garden area adjacent to the mall. For a long time, the two of them sat in comfortable silence.

"Bland, you are so beautiful, like those leaves." She surprised him with her remark. Surprisingly, a series of whys flashed in his mind: Why was this happening? Why was this woman having such an effect on him? Why did she reappear in his life at this particular time? Why did he want to pursue her and jeopardize his family?

"That's comforting," he replied.

"Plus, your spirit is beautiful and being around you is so pleasant. It's like we've been a part of each other's lives forever. It's like we never parted after the first time we met. I know it sounds crazy."

"Strangely, I feel the same way. So now what are we supposed to do?" He was hoping she would give him a way out because he had no strength to say no to her.

"I don't know. What does your heart tell you?"

He hadn't intended on their stroll turning into a proposal of his love for her. Without reservation, he knew what he should do. However, what he should do and what he would do were two different things. Instead, he was silent.

"Are you okay?" she asked, as he stared off into open space.

His head jerked with a sudden reply, "Just thinking about the direction my heart is taking me."

"I want to see you again, Bland," she blurted, while grabbing his hand to display the sincerity of her words.

"You do?"

"Yes, that's if you feel the same."

He wanted to see her again. He had already violated his marriage vows and he tried to fight the temptation to want her again.

"I do want to see you, but I don't know if it's a good idea."

Desperately, he clung to a thin thread of his marriage. That thin thread was starting to give way.

"I understand. You don't see me the way I see you, and it's okay." Grey felt rejected.

"No, Grey," he gently touched her on the upper arm. "I don't want what happened on the train between us to appear trivial. You entrusted a part of yourself to me. I'm afraid I won't live up to your expectation. Sure, I'd love to see you again. I've being waiting twenty years to see you," he paused. "Frankly, I haven't stopped seeing you since the first time we met. Often, I saw you in my dreams and I longed to hold you and kiss you. The fact of knowing I couldn't, or wouldn't, get the opportunity to have that pleasure again tormented me. And when I saw you again, in the flesh, I...." He had a loss for words. "Believe me, Grey, when I say it's not you that stops me."

"Then what is it, Bland? What's stopping us from getting to know us again, more than something physical?"

"I don't know. Maybe I'm not the man you think I am." He hoped she would hear his plea for help, but instead she only listened to her heart for companionship and love.

"Bland, you are everything I want in a man, and truth be told, maybe I am not woman enough."

"Regardless of what you may think or how another man has made you feel about yourself, the thought never entered my mind. You are woman enough for any man and let no one make you feel that way again." He gently brushed his thumb along her cheek and kissed her forehead.

13

INSTEAD OF PULLING BACK FROM GREY DURING THE upcoming months, Bland spent more time with her. Soon their rendezvous began to expand from the local area to other cities. Bland was in disbelief that he couldn't say no to Grey. Slowly, she was becoming an addiction, and the more time he spent with her, the less time he spent with his wife and even less time working on the book.

The cab pulled around to the neoclassical façade of the faux Roman Arches Constantine of Union Station. Bland paid the driver, then bolted inside the main corridor of the station. Grey sat on one of the many long benches admiring the grand central interior of the station. She saw Bland approaching and went to greet him with a hug and a kiss.

"Wait here. I have to purchase a ticket for a private sleeping car."

When he returned, he grabbed her bag, and they proceeded toward the train.

After an escapade of passionate lovemaking until morning, Grey fell asleep in his arms. The morning sun crept upon her crimson lips and then upon his resting face.

"What time is it?" she asked.

"Seven-thirty."

Bland used his fingers to stroke her hair.

"You want breakfast?"

"That would be nice," she smiled.

"I'll get breakfast while you continue to relax."

"Okay, but don't be too long. I want you beside me." She turned her body around to give him a long, intense kiss.

Bland dressed and then headed to the dining car. He maneuvered the turns of the narrow halls like a skilled passenger, and suddenly he had a flashback of him walking behind Harry, the conductor, years before. Bland remembered having difficulty keeping his balance and occasionally falling into the seats and walls of the trains. Now, like the old man, his movement was rhythmic as he made his way up the aisle. When he reached the dining car, he placed his order, then sat at an empty table while the food was being prepared. Unexpectedly, he heard someone call his name. A sudden sense of panic latched onto Bland. His heart slowed its fluttering when he saw it was Rudy, the security guard at the publishing house.

"Mr. Benthall?" he called with excitement. Then Rudy ran off some questions, "What are you doing here? How are your ribs?"

Bland had totally forgotten about the incident in the file room. Hopefully, he could answer the latter question and escape the former question of why he was on the train.

"Oh, they're fine. That reminds me about the break-in, were there any arrests?"

"Not yet. So where are you headed?" asked Rudy, who seemed to be happy he saw someone he knew. Before Bland could attempt to answer Rudy's question, Rudy was already telling him his destination.

"I'm on my way to Cleveland to see the Wizards whip up on them Cavs," giggled Rudy.

"The season started already?"

"It's a preseason game, but we still plan on blowing the Cavs off the court."

"Cleveland is pretty good. Are you sure your guys can handle that

type of pressure?"

Rudy started nodding his head, "They don't call us the Wizards for nothing, and we have the perfect magic trick that will put Cleveland's back against the wall."

"You traveling all the way to Cleveland must mean you're a committed fan. Do you catch a lot of games?"

"I don't get to many away games, but whenever they have a home game, and it's on a Friday, I am there."

"I'm surprised you get the time off, since you're so understaffed."

Rudy smiled, "Substitution shifts."

"What are substitution shifts?"

"Either you get another guard to swap shifts with you or you call on favors from other security guards outside the company."

"The twins pay other security guards from outside agencies to take your shift?" questioned Bland.

"No, they don't pay anything because they don't know."

"They don't know?"

Rudy shook his head. "We've been so understaffed that if you really need to get time off, sometimes you call on favors. We all do it, from the supervisor down. The trick is getting an outside security guard who doesn't have a life and doesn't mind making an extra under-the-table buck or two. It's the informal part of the publishing house that allows things to get done on the lower level, since these old men refused to hire extra manpower."

"So basically you guys are mall cops hiring other mall cops without anyone's knowledge. No wonder people are getting attacked."

"That's funny," Rudy said, but didn't laugh. He went back to his original thought, "So where are you going, Mr. Benthall?"

Bland smiled, "I'm also heading to Cleveland."

"You're going to the game too? I didn't know you were a fan."

"I am a fan, but unfortunately this is a business trip."

Rudy sighed, "Well, if you ever need tickets, I'm your man. I have crazy connections."

"Yes, I'll remember that."

Bland was only creating small talk until his food came. Abruptly, he

said, "I must get going, Rudy. My food is here."

Rudy noticed all the food. "Are you with your wife?"

Bland paused and his eyes glanced toward the direction of his car. "Not this time. I came by myself."

Again, Rudy looked at all the food. "Man, you have a big appetite. Lucky you, my wife keeps me under close surveillance."

Rudely, Bland ended the conversation.

"Well, I'll see you back at the publishing house," Rudy said.

Rudy watched as Bland headed up the aisle with his food and disappeared behind the sliding doors of the dining car. Quickly, Bland made his way back to the sleeping car.

"I hope you like your eggs sunny-side up," he said, as he entered the sleeping car.

"That's fine," Grey said, while pulling the table out from the wall. "But I'd rather have you." She smiled.

Bland made sure that the two of them stayed in the sleeping car until the train's engineer announced their arrival in Cleveland.

"Okay, this is our stop." He pulled the bags from the top storage compartment.

"Cleveland?" she announced with sudden excitement.

"What do you know about Cleveland?"

"Only that it's a great sports town. I have some predictions. Do you want to hear them?"

He lightly chuckled, "I'm eager to hear them."

"I predict the Browns will make the playoffs this year."

"Wait, the Browns?" he laughed hard. "You are talking about the Cleveland Browns making the playoffs? The Browns haven't made the playoffs in the last—"

She interrupted. "I am aware of that. Can I finish?"

"By all means."

She smiled flirtatiously. "As I was saying, the Browns will make it to the playoffs because the Browns had a good draft this year and made some good acquisitions to improve the team. As for the Indians this year, I predict the Indians will win the World Series with great pitching and big hitters. Of course, the Cavaliers, my favorite sports team, will

have another rebuilding year. You can't lose the greatest player in the world and not," she laughed. "And those are my predictions." She smiled.

Bland shook his head as she smiled as if having won a prize.

"You never cease to amaze me. I will admit those are some bold predictions, to say the least," he shook his head. "I think you're being a bit overenthusiastic. You do know we're talking about Cleveland teams?"

"Laugh now, but bow later," she followed her remarks with a wink of the eye. "I always wanted to visit Cleveland. Thank you so much for bringing me."

"I hope you like it just as much as Chicago."

"You are here with me. Of course, I will. Maybe we can catch a Cavs, Indians, or Browns game, or maybe all three." She gave Bland a wide grin.

He was amazed. "You are a big sports fan?"

"My ex-husband was a sports fanatic, so I guess it rubbed off on me."

Bland leaned forward to look out his window at the passengers when Rudy came trotting down the walking path. Bland dropped the curtains quickly so he wouldn't be seen.

"Cleveland is a beautiful city," he said, as he turned to Grey. "There are other things to do besides going to a game. I figured we will do some sightseeing. We can visit the Rock & Roll Hall of Fame, the Great Lakes Science Museum."

"Isn't the Football Hall of Fame close by?"

"As a matter-of-fact it is."

"Maybe we can go there as well after we catch one sports game?" she pleaded.

Bland was skeptical about attending any professional games, especially a Cavs' Game. He didn't want to chance running into Rudy with Grey attached to his arm. He believed it would be hard to explain why he was accompanying a beautiful woman that wasn't his wife. "Let's play it by ear."

Monday morning, Bland and Grey flew back to Washington, D.C. They kissed and, like always, agreed to see each other in a day or two.

Instead of going home, Bland caught a cab from Reagan International Airport to the publishing house. It was his way of prolonging the inevitable—seeing Dakota. Not to mention, he had nothing prepared for the twins, so he thought he would try putting something together in case he ran into them.

When he stepped into the lobby, Paige's eyes bulged as if she was about to explode with information.

"Mr. Benthall, where have you been? Your wife has been calling all morning and afternoon. She sounds really upset. I tried calling you, but your phone was giving some weird buzzing sounds."

"Did she say about what?" he asked, as if he didn't know.

"No, but if I were you, I would call home as soon as possible. Also, the twins said for me to send you up whenever you arrive."

"Tell them you haven't seen me."

"Can't."

"Why?"

Her head and eyes pointed upward toward the small camera that recently had been mounted in the corner of the ceiling.

"They're probably looking at you right now."

"Shit," he replied. "They'll do anything to micromanage this project."

"Not too loud," she whispered. "Who knows? They may have surround sound, too," she said, without looking to see. "I'm told the camera is for security purposes."

"Are any more of those up?"

"I have seen some along the galleria. However, as for the other departments of the publishing house, I don't think so."

Bland took the elevator to the penthouse and as usual the twins were there waiting when the elevator door opened. There were no facial expressions, just orders to follow them to their study. Bland glanced at his seat and was heading for it when Smith stopped him.

"No need to sit, Bland, this won't take long."

Bland stopped his forward motion and went into a civilian's parade rest.

"Bland," growled Wilkins. "We have given you everything you asked

for, but still we haven't seen an iota from you. Nothing. I don't believe in wasting good money for nothing."

Smith took up the sentence where Wilkins stopped. "Nobody likes to lose money, Bland. We've been patient, so exactly what stage is the book in now?"

Bland was calm as the two men waited for an explanation.

"Gentlemen, you gave me until December, did you not?"

"Bland, your months are running out," Wilkins uttered.

"But you did give me a deadline, so there is no need to continue micromanaging me. You said you wanted a novel by a certain date, and you will have your novel in exchange for the partnership. I mean junior partnership. Don't forget, I am doing the impossible, at least when it comes to my standard of writing. Frankly, gentlemen, this will probably end up being my best work ever." He added a little extra to soothe their anger for not having the rewrites completed for their review.

"Are we in for a surprise?" Wilkins asked.

"Believe me, if the book keeps developing like it has, you will be in for the biggest surprise of your life."

"Away from the direction of what we previously read?"

Bland nodded, "A complete rewrite."

Immediately, after saying those words, he bit down on his teeth with regret. A rewrite meant a new direction, more research, and more writing—things he was less committed to than with the first draft.

Wilkins gave Bland a skeptical stare and then said, "You were fighting so hard not to do the rewrite, why the sudden change of heart?"

Bland was willing to tell the men anything at this stage to get them off his back.

"I found a new motivation that has shown me the book was lacking a level of romance, cruelty, morality, and perfidy of the world."

Bland knew what the men wanted to hear, and he was delighted to see them glance at each other before smiling.

"Good, that's what I like to hear!" Smith responded.

Bland wanted to address the men about the camera, but when he saw them move in the direction of the elevator, he didn't want to engage them in another drawn out conversation.

The two old men walked Bland to the elevator and kept their stares on him until the elevator door closed.

Dakota wanted to be supportive of her husband and allow him to finish the book before the deadline, even if that meant tolerating his erratic schedule. Yet, her tolerance of his late nights at the office, perfume scented shirts, and lengthy trips to conduct research had taken their toll on her. She tried taking it all with a grain of salt because she convinced herself it came with obtaining the partnership. What Dakota couldn't understand was why her husband started neglecting her physically. She wanted to believe that he wasn't being unfaithful. She wanted to believe it was the work, the book, and the pressure of working late to get the novel finished that made her appear less desirable. That's what she made herself believe for months. However, sometimes love makes a person overlook the obvious to thwart the pain of the truth.

Bland was only to be gone for an overnight trip to Cleveland; however, Dakota hadn't heard from him all weekend. She had left countless text messages and voice messages on his cell phone, office phone, and with his administrative assistant for him to return her calls.

After Bland left the twins' office, he felt somewhat relieved to have the twins temporarily off his back. However, there was a new problem, and he knew it wasn't going to be as easy to get Dakota off his back. He wasn't ready for what was coming, but he knew he couldn't avoid her. He dialed his house number, hoping Dakota wouldn't pick up.

When Dakota heard the phone, she answered it on the first ring. "I've been calling the office, Bland. How come you haven't been returning my calls?"

Bland didn't have time to answer.

"Where have you been?"

"You know where I've been."

"You said you would return on Saturday. It's Monday, Bland."

"My research extended through the weekend," he tried to explain, but she interrupted.

"You promised you would call if your plans changed."

"I tried."

"Bland, come on. Do you think I am that naïve? I didn't get a call from you."

"Once again the answering machine isn't picking up. I am surprised you answered this time. How many times do I have to tell you to lock your phone, so your phone will stop inadvertently calling the answering machine?" he asked in a sharp tone.

She shot back with equal tone, "Then get us both up to date phones, one where locking the phone or not won't be an issue for me and especially one that will allow you to answer a call and call home."

He ignored her remarks. He knew that something was bothering her, something other than him staying a few extra nights in Cleveland. Nonetheless, they both agreed to the sacrifices it would take to finish the novel. And now it pissed him off that she would be so upset.

"If what's bothering you is me not being at home, then I will be there in a few hours," he said angrily.

"You're missing the point, Bland. Even when you do come home, you make it your business to sleep in the guest room. I can't help but think you are avoiding me." Dakota's voice cracked, and she coughed while continuing, "I don't want to make a big deal out of it. I know you're working hard on the novel, but I feel you've been putting me off. When you worked on other projects, you always spared some time for little ol' me, especially for our anniversary."

"Our anniversary," he gasped, then feeling like an idiot. "I am so sorry. I've been so busy I completely forgot our anniversary was Saturday. Why didn't you say something?" he asked in a more pleasant tone.

"What could I say, Bland? I can never seem to get in touch with you. It's impossible for anyone to reach you, not even your administrative assistant can reach you. Lately, you've been doing your own thing. Plus, I figured you would've remembered since we celebrate it every year." She stopped and lowered her voice to a dejected tone. "It's not like you to forget."

Bland dropped his face on his office desk. He felt so ashamed.

"I'm so sorry, honey. Trust me, I am not avoiding you. It's just that so many things are on my mind." His voice stalled. "Listen, I want to do

something really special for you. Can I do that?"

"I don't know." She tried to hold onto her anger but saw it slipping. "It depends on what you have in mind."

"The best," he sounded anxious.

"I can do for the best right now," she admitted. A tear ran down her cheek. She had longed for him to show her some attention.

"You deserve nothing less than the best. Can you call the Scotts and see if they mind watching Devin? I will be home around six."

"Do I get picked up like a high school sweetheart?"

"I said the best, so I will be there to pick you up at six on the dot."

"Well, you have to get my father's permission," she joked lightly only to introduce a sensitive request.

And he responded in kind. "Do I have to make another visit to South Carolina, or can I do it by phone?"

"I'll let you slide with a phone call. By the way, Mother wants to know if we are coming down for the Thanksgiving holiday."

"I can't say for certain. I'm supposed to have the manuscript turned in by December. Frankly, it depends on how much of the book I have completed, but Thanksgiving is a-ways off, so we'll see. As for now, you need to get yourself ready, honey."

She hung the phone up with a spreading smile and a new glow of hope that Bland felt her loneliness enough to change his uncharacteristic behaviors.

After he heard the dial tone, Bland began kicking himself for not remembering their anniversary. He told himself he was losing it and becoming reckless. He shook his head. Suddenly his cell phone buzzed.

"Hello."

"Hi, Bland."

"Hey!" Bland recognized Grey's voice.

"I was sitting here thinking about our evening of nonstop dancing last night. I'm sad it had to end."

"Well, I'm glad you had fun."

"I had an awesome time. Thank you for taking me to the Cavs' game. It is official that Cleveland is now one of my favorite cities. Oh, Bland, I can't wait to do it again," she said excitedly. "Frankly, I want you right now."

He laughed, “I just left you.”

“I know, I am being selfish, but it’s your fault. You spoil me too much, and I love it.”

“Well, I have another surprise I want to give you.”

“Then surprise me by not telling me,” she said seductively. “But really, Bland, it’s my time to spoil you. I was thinking dinner on me.

“Figuratively or literally?” he laughed.

“Bland, stop it. I am trying to be serious. Can I take you out for dinner? My way of saying thank you for inviting me to Cleveland?”

Bland smiled, “You want to take me out?”

“A woman can’t take a man out?”

“Well, I never had a chance to get used to that, but I suppose it’s acceptable.” He leaned back in his chair and twirled around while staring at the ceiling.

“I am glad you will allow me to, so let’s say seven this evening.”

Bland was about to agree before he remembered, “No, not seven, I can’t do it at seven.”

“If the time is bad, we can do it another day,” Grey suggested.

Despite his dinner date with his wife, Bland couldn’t bring himself to say no to Grey.

“I’ll figure out something and call you later.” He closed his cell phone and immediately dialed Paige’s extension from the office phone. “Paige,” he called through the intercom. “I need for you to do two things for me. First, I ordered something from one of the shops downstairs. I received a text that it just arrived, so when you get a chance, I will appreciate it if you could pick it up for me. I have the order slip.”

“It’s a surprise, Paige, and I am sure it’s the right package. Just grab it for me before it’s sent back.”

“Does your package need to be gift wrapped?”

“You know, Paige, that would be a good idea. Yes, get it wrapped.”

“And your second request, sir?”

“I also need you to make reservations for two at Carlylés, seven o’clock.”

“Carlylés, wow that sounds serious. I wish my fiancé thought I was special enough to take me somewhere as elegant as Carlylés.”

"Give him some time. I am sure he will take you there one day."

As planned, Bland arrived at the house at six sharp to pick up his wife. He noticed the Scotts exiting his house when he pulled up. Devin somehow scampered between the two to get to his father's car. Before Bland could get out of the car, Devin was climbing into his arms.

"How's my boy today?"

"Fine, Daddy."

"What did you do today?"

Devin hunched his shoulders, "Not much."

The Scotts walked over. "Hello, John and Keri, thanks for watching Devin tonight."

"Anytime."

"Is Dakota ready?"

Keri smiled brightly, "Yes, she is."

Dakota came out the door wearing a stunning fitted blue dress accessorized with a colorful shawl over her shoulders. It had been a long time since Bland had noticed her beauty. He handed Devin through the open window to his neighbor and climbed from behind the steering wheel of his vehicle.

"I feel overdressed," she said with a concerned facial expression.

"No way, you're beautiful. Just splendid for where we are dining this evening. I should be the one concerned."

He kissed her.

"Well, there seems to be a storm approaching," noticed John. "You two best be getting along before you get caught in it." As Bland escorted Dakota to the passenger door of his SUV, John began to complain about Dakota's sedan. "Bland, when are you planning to bring your wife's car to the shop so that I can replace that starter?"

"I'll do it first thing next week."

"That's what you said months ago," John sparked.

"John, leave Bland alone so they can go."

Keri looked on with approving eyes as Bland backed out of the driveway. "Doesn't she look lovely, John?" They watched as Bland drove slowly up the street.

"So where is my husband taking me this evening?"

"I thought I would take this very special lady to Carlylés for dinner."

"Carlylés?"

"You're worth that and much more," Bland confessed as he briefly looked in her eyes. Momentarily, he thought about Grey and was surprised that the guilt didn't attack him like the times before. He was starting to become immune to the guilt that attaches itself to cheaters.

All through dinner, Dakota noticed how Bland was constantly checking his watch. Eventually, he politely excused himself from the table to find the restroom. Once there, he searched for an empty stall to call Grey.

"Hey."

"Hello, Bland, I didn't think you were going to call."

"I couldn't wait to call you," his voice echoed off the walls.

"I'm sorry, I can barely hear you. It sounds like you're in a tunnel."

"I'm in the restroom, so maybe that's the reason for the echo."

"Are we still on?" she asked.

There was an indecisive pause. "Change of plans."

"Okay," she waited and hoped she would be a part of the new plan.

"Instead of you taking me out, how about a nightcap at your place?"

He could hear the excitement in her voice. "Sounds like a plan."

"Good. I'll see you tonight."

Her soft voice whispered, "I'll be waiting with nothing on, so please don't make me wait too long. You know how badly I hate waiting. The key is under the flowerpot. Oh, Bland, be sure to lock the door behind you."

Bland knew this would put him in a situation with Dakota, but a situation that could be resolved with a reasonable explanation.

Dakota had started on dessert while he was gone, a double layer chocolate cake.

She saw him approaching. "I thought we could share this," she said, smiling, with cake crumbs on her lips.

"Sure we can," he replied. He sat down with restless eyes. He knew

she would notice and ask if there was a problem.

"Umm, this cake is so good," she said, as she pulled the fork from her mouth. When Bland didn't respond, she paused to look at him. "Bland, I can tell something is wrong."

"I just got a call from Lou. I think he's in trouble."

"What kind of trouble?" Her posture and eyes perked up. She lowered her fork back to the plate.

"Frankly, I'm not sure, but it has to do with owing some bad people money. Lou gave me the impression that if the debt isn't paid, the penalty would be limbs breaking."

"Limbs breaking," she repeated in shock, paused, then asked, "like a finger?"

"Like a hand, an arm, or a leg," he was quick to point out.

Her upper torso tilted inward. Her eyes filled with both concern and fear for both Bland and Lou.

"Bland, why doesn't Louis just call the cops?"

"These aren't the type of people you call the cops on. That's if you want to live."

She knew that look when Bland already had decided to help Lou. This wouldn't be the first time, nor would it be the last, she thought.

"What are you planning?"

"What I have to do. Go to his rescue, as usual. I'm so sorry this had to happen on our make-up anniversary dinner."

"Okay, go help Louis, but please be careful. I want you to come back in one piece. How long will you be gone?"

"Well, that depends on how much trouble he's gotten into."

"It doesn't matter what time you call, just call me and let me know you guys are safe."

Bland demanded that Dakota take the car, and he catch a cab.

On his way to Grey's, Bland called Lou from his cell phone. He began to wonder if Lou had already hit the sack for the night. Not talking to Lou would spell disaster. The receiver clicked.

A groggy and intoxicated voice said, "What?"

"Lou?"

"Who is it?"

"It's Bland."

"Oh, Bland, hey? I was trying to reach you earlier." Lou's words tumbled over one another.

"Oh, no, Lou, you've been drinking?"

"That's why I called you. I needed to talk to someone, but you weren't there, man. A lot is going on, Bland." There was a belch and then another belch.

This made it very difficult; now he wished he'd never decided to use Lou. Using Lou put him in jeopardy of getting caught, but not to use him would prevent him from seeing Grey. Bland had no choice; he had to trust that Lou would remember what he would tell him.

Bland callously ignored Lou's issues and said, "Lou, I need you to listen carefully. I need for you to cover for me tonight."

"Cover for you?"

"Yeah, I have to take care of something, so I told Dakota I would be with you."

"We're not kids. We are grown men, so why would you say a thing like that, Bland?"

"Lou, I need to take care of some business, so can you cover for me?"

"This business, does she play drums?"

"Nothing like that, Lou. Trust me, this is business."

"Okay, business, I've heard that one before. All right, I'll cover for you."

"Better yet, don't answer your phone," Bland said quickly.

"Why?"

"Just don't answer it."

"Okay, I won't answer the phone. Now is there anything else I can do for you before I pass out?"

"No, Lou." Then the phone clicked.

The taxi pulled up to the front of Grey's apartment, which resembled a luxurious townhome. The key was right where she said it would be. Quietly, he entered the apartment, remembering to lock the door behind him. Bland followed the dim light from candles back to her bedroom.

He found her nude and on top of the covers. She lay on her stomach. On the wall, descriptive silhouettes showed his clothes coming off. He crawled on the bed, then up along her body. Gently, he kissed her in various spots as he moved slowly along the contour of her body. She felt his soft lips touch the back of her calf then up the back of her legs. Along her buttocks his tongue glided to the small of her back before sliding along the curvature of her spine to her neck. He rolled her over to her back. He commenced to kiss her softly on her lips, then down across her clavicle to her cleavage. He blew across her breast before starting down her stomach and stopped briefly to circumnavigate around her navel with his tongue. As he approached her pelvic bone, he lifted his head, filled his lungs with warm air and blew out the candles.

When Bland didn't call home or return home that evening, Dakota became worried and called Lou. Too inebriated to remember not to answer the phone, he growled, "Yeah."

"Louis?"

"Yeah," he replied as he rolled from his stomach to his back. "What?"

"Louis, it's Dakota. Are you okay? Bland said you were in some type of trouble."

"Trouble, why would I be in trouble?"

"That's what Bland said."

Lou coughed into the receiver of the phone, "Let me speak to Bland."

"Isn't he there with you?"

"No, I haven't seen Bland."

"Are you sure? I mean you have been drinking. Maybe he's in the other room."

"I may have been drinking, but I'm not drunk. And I sure as hell know who's in my house."

She didn't want to engage in an argument.

"I'm sorry, Louis. Sure you would. Anyway, do you know where Bland could be?"

"I have no idea. He's your husband." Then he hung up the phone.

She couldn't understand what was going on. Why would Bland fabricate such a story? Was something wrong at the publishing house

and he didn't want to alarm her? The faster she brushed a thought away, another one took its place. She called his cell, then the office phone, but no answer. She tried texting him, but no reply.

14

THE NEXT EVENING WHEN BLAND WALKED THROUGH the door of his house and saw Dakota standing in the foyer with her arms folded, he knew she had talked to Lou. He figured Lou had said something he wasn't supposed to say. Quickly, his thoughts began to race.

"Where have you been?" she asked immediately.

"At the office," he said calmly.

"You've been at the office for an entire night and day?" she questioned, her tense body language punctuating the question.

"I was with Lou and, after he passed out on the floor, I went to the office." From her attitude, it didn't take long to know from where her questions came.

"Bland," she glared, "I called the office."

"Honey, I was in the office asleep."

"I spoke with Louis. Louis said he hadn't seen you. Bland, what's going on? What you're telling me doesn't make sense."

"As drunk as Lou was when I found him, he wouldn't remember seeing anyone."

"I asked you to call and let me know the two of you were okay. I was up all night worrying. Even a text would have sufficed."

"Damnit, Dakota, I wasn't in a position to call you."

"What does that mean, wasn't in a position? What position was required that would have allowed you to notify your wife that your limbs weren't broken also?"

Her frustration grew when Bland didn't answer. "They made phones to prevent individuals from getting in such positions! That's supposed to be the reason Louis used his phone to call you," she sarcastically said.

"I thought they made phones so wives could annoy the hell out of their husbands. And I don't know how to text," he retorted sarcastically to annoy her.

"What did you just say?" she frowned.

He recognized his attitude and carefully moseyed toward her. He eased up along her body and to her cheek. Softly, he pressed his lips against her cheeks along with an apology.

"I'm sorry, honey. It's so damn complicated texting on my phone. I should have called, but it was so late I didn't want to disturb you. I agree that shouldn't be an excuse. I wasn't tired, so I figured going to the office to burn off some energy by working on the book would be a good thing. Not to mention, the partners upset me today, so my attitude stinks right about now. I didn't mean to take it out on you."

She accepted his kiss easier than his excuses. Dakota walked into the den and sank into the seat.

"You're giving me the same old explanation over and over, Bland."

"Now, Dakota, would you rather I lie to you? Come on, honey, you can't be mad."

"Should I not be mad? I've only been sitting here all night and all day waiting for my husband to call to let me know he's not injured. You can be so damn inconsiderate." She revisited her earlier question to answer it for him. "Yes, I am beyond mad. You keep asking me to tolerate a lot, and I have. Now, I'm tired, Bland. I'm so tired of this, this novel, this partnership, your late nights, your being gone for days, and you never having the time for your son or me."

"I know I messed up. You have every right to be pissed off. I promise it won't happen again. I'll do my best to set time aside with you and Devin."

He crawled up alongside her on the sofa and laid his head on her chest. He understood that was a weakness of hers. Unwilling to compromise, she pushed his head. Again, he placed it on her chest, and she began massaging through his hair.

"So, what ended up happening last night?"

"With what?"

She offered Bland a suspicious look. "With Louis, and the bad men wanting to break his limbs?"

"Lou was drunk. There weren't any bad men, just a bad and angry drunk."

Her suspicious stare gradually faded away.

"Bland, I've been thinking about this partnership. Instead of it providing us with more time, it has taken what little time we did have."

"Honey, I told you that is the way it starts out. You have to be willing to take the good with the bad, but the bad doesn't last forever. It's a small sacrifice for a large gain. Listen, I know you're tired, and I know my staying away for days at times may have you thinking crazy thoughts. You know when I write I put in long hours and a great amount of research. That sometimes requires me to be on the road. You know this."

"That doesn't mean I have to like it, Bland. There's the Internet. Why not use it to do your research? It will save us money and give us more time to share with each other."

"No real writer uses the Internet." He knew he used the Internet all the time, but he needed persuasive leverage for when he wanted to travel and be with Grey.

"I guess that's the one thing I didn't miss when you were writing full time." No longer angry, but out of pure spite for not calling, she pulled hard on a chunk of his hair.

He knew his next question was going to inflict guilt on her. "You want me to stop?"

"You know I would never ask you to do such a thing." She gave his hair another hard tug. "I just miss us and the time we used to share together. I'm tired of sharing you with the publishing house and your work. I feel like we are drifting apart, and I don't know what to do to stop it. I'm trying to be patient for our family, but I don't know how

much more I can take."

Even after discussing these new fears of hers, Bland decided to let her know that in the coming weeks he had to leave town again. He tried to break it to her as gently as possible, but it fell on deaf ears.

"You have to leave?" she repeated as if hearing something that didn't make much sense, especially after she disclosed the fact she was tired of him traveling and being away from home. "Did you not hear anything I just said?"

"I'm chasing the story, Dakota. That's what I do."

Her fuming went silent for a short minute, then she said, "Bland, I understand you have your own formula for writing your novels, and for years I have been committed to your journalist style of writing. You have to chase the story? This is more than a little excessive and extreme! Isn't there someone else you can send in your place?"

"No, it's my story. The partnership is only guaranteed if I have a bestseller." He emphasized the word "I."

"To hell with the partnership, Bland!" She angrily pushed his head from her chest.

He sat without responding.

She offered a solution. "Devin and I can come with you. It will give us a chance to spend time together as a family."

"That's the last thing I need," Bland blurted. Dakota looked stunned. "Not to sound insensitive, honey, but I wouldn't get any work done. I would feel guilty not spending the time with the two of you. I need to get this book finished. Plus, Devin shouldn't miss school."

Without a word, she stood and left the room. He puckered his eyebrow and thought fresh air would do him some good about now. He turned, walked back out the front door, climbed in his SUV, and pulled off. Dakota dashed to the window when she heard the engine start. It wasn't her intent to run him off. Her chin collapsed onto the top of her chest. She made her way to the sofa, rested her elbows on her thighs, and began to cry. Her tears subsided when she saw the red bow tied around a white box. She figured it had fallen out of Bland's pocket. She wiped her tears as she slowly untied the red bow. Her eyes lit up when she saw what Bland had bought her. He had finally purchased a smart phone for her.

Bland drove without any destination in mind. He needed to release some steam. As he approached the Interstate, a thought flashed in his mind to head to Grey's place. Quickly, he shook the idea. He needed to be more focused on the novel, he told himself. The deadline was approaching, and not a word had been written since the draft was rejected. He had been spending so much time with Grey that he had no desire to write, no desire to do anything except be with her. Even when he wasn't around her, she consumed all of his mental energy.

The exit to the publishing house was approaching. Bland could keep straight and end up at Grey's place, or he could take the exit to the publishing house and start on a new story or try salvaging as much of the old story as possible. He shook his head and decided to take the exit to the publishing house.

The chill in the air was perfect. He drove around the block to the parking garage, which he soon discovered required an access badge to enter. This is new, he thought, and then he remembered the surveillance camera in the reception area—maybe the old men are trying to make the place safer; maybe they replaced those old cameras.

He drove around in search of a parking space. He was skeptical about parking the car on the street; it might get towed or worse, stolen. Near the publishing house was a pay service parking lot with an attendant. Bland paid the parking attendant and began to walk the long block back to the publishing house. He breathed in the cool air and pulled his jacket tight against his chest. Quickly, he moved along the sidewalks of the empty streets of downtown and occasionally admired the pre-Halloween decorations on street poles. He considered the number of things that had taken place over the previous months: his promotion, his meeting Grey, his constant friction with his wife, and now his dead-end story.

Lingering in the night air was the aroma of fresh rotisserie. Across from the publishing house was a local park, and at the other end of the park he heard and saw people scampering into a small restaurant. He realized he could do for a bite to eat. He turned from his path to

the publishing house to head for the restaurant. Rather than make his journey quicker and cut through the deep, daunting park with its dark spots and scaling trees, Bland decided to walk around it. As he sauntered along the dark edges of the park, he recalled the attack in the file room and suddenly an uncomfortable feeling shadowed him. He looked around, but there was no one.

When Bland reached the restaurant, he noticed that a majority of the patrons were late night party hoppers looking for a quick meal before heading home. The warm temperature of the restaurant was welcoming. He worked his way through the horde of people to place his order and waited for one of the stools in front of a large viewing window to come open. As soon as one did, Bland was the first to claim it. As he waited for his order, he decided to call his wife.

"Hey," he said softly.

"Hello," her voice dragged.

Bland could tell by her dull reply that she was still upset. He couldn't blame her. If she knew what he was really engaged in, he would probably be divorced or dead. When it came to Dakota, Bland contemplated that death certainly could come before divorce. "Are you okay?"

"I'm okay, Bland. I'm just tired."

"Why don't you try lying down?"

"I am in the bed talking to you on the speaker phone," she replied, still with the same monotone.

"I just wanted to say I'm sorry. Lately, I haven't been very attentive to your needs or concerns, but I want you to know that I do appreciate you. I really plan on making up all this lost time to you and Devin."

"Bland, the only thing I've ever asked of you is never make me cry. I want you to become a partner, but your method of getting there—"

Bland interrupted, "My method..." There was a loud chatter inside the restaurant. He cuddled the phone tighter to his ear and turned to look out the window.

"Where are you?" she asked.

"I am in a restaurant near the publishing house. Now, you were saying something about my method?"

"Bland, the long hours at the publishing house, and the long weekend

trips that last longer than two days."

"Dakota, are we seriously having this conversation again?"

"Bland, I rarely get to see you. Your son doesn't get to spend any time with his father. I don't understand. With technology the way it is today, you don't have to take these trips. Everything is at the touch of your fingertips."

"If the twins and you didn't think the draft of the book sucked, I wouldn't have to put in late nights or chase stories that sometimes take me away from home. You know me. I am conventional. I have to do it my way. And since we are having this conversation again, I will say this again. You knew the sacrifice it was going to take from both of us. You knew this before you signed on for this. So, please, don't throw it back in my face like it's my fault."

"Bland, I have sacrificed," she blurted and continued, "How much more do I have to sacrifice?"

He could hear her strength falter through disappointing sighs. He felt he needed to say something that would calm her. "All of this will be over soon. The book will be finished, and this will be behind us." He hated to lie to her, but what else could he say that would make the situation better?

"Good for you, Bland," she cynically said. He sighed heavily enough for her to hear, "You're never satisfied. You can't have me home all day and expect me to do my job, too. They want me at the office. You know this, so why do you persist in putting more pressure and guilt over my head?" He ended the call before she could respond. He heard his name called. A man held up his order. Quickly, he grabbed the food and decided to take it back to the publishing house.

As he walked along the sidewalk, his body slumped over to trap in heat. Soon Bland was out of the light of the restaurant and approaching the dimly lit, deserted sidewalk circling the park.

After walking a few blocks, that same uneasy feeling he felt earlier draped over him like a heavy blanket. Occasionally, he scanned the perimeter. All was quiet, except for his hard-soled shoes scuffing the asphalt. Still he felt uneasy. With a sense of urgency driven by paranoia, Bland turned to look behind him. He looked down the sidewalk as far

as he could see. As his eyes focused, he noticed a fast-walking figure was approaching him. Bland turned his sights from the figure and continued to walk toward the publishing house, but with more purpose. When he heard the echo of the stranger's shoes and heavy breathing, Bland quickened his pace even more.

Once again, he glanced behind him. The silhouette had closed a large amount of the distance. Bland looked to the sky to find the skyline of the publishing house. The building was still a reasonable distance away. He reluctantly decided to shorten his travel time by cutting through the dark, unpopulated park. Certainly, the incident in the file room had something to do with his not wanting to detour, but the bull-breathing, quick-trotting person behind him gave him no choice. Bland abruptly took one of the park's trails to see if the figure would follow.

With each of Bland's quick steps, the skyline of the building drew closer and closer. As he went deeper into the park, the trees blocked out any view of the publishing house. He gave another look back into the darkness to see if he was followed. He saw no one. Perhaps no one is following me after all, he thought, convinced his newfound paranoia was playing tricks on him.

With relief, he took one more look behind him to be certain, when someone slammed into him, knocking the wind out of him. Both Bland and the figure fell to the ground. Bland caught his breath and jumped to his feet with flaring arms.

Quickly a voice yelled, "What are you doing?" The jogger began picking himself off the ground. "What is your problem, dude?"

"I'm sorry, I turned, and you were there. I thought—"

The jogger interrupted, "This is a public park. Of course, you're not the only person out here."

"You are right," Bland replied, as he extended his hand to help the man to his feet. "I am extremely sorry. Are you hurt?"

"No," the jogger curtly replied.

The angry-faced jogger brushed the dirt from his knees and long sleeve shirt. Bland handed the jogger his nightlight and running cap, who crudely jerked the light and cap from Bland. Obviously upset, the man took off running again.

Rather than find refuge in the publishing house, Bland decided to go to his car. The slightest excuse to procrastinate from writing was good for him. Still his shattered nerves ran through him like the cold night air through his hair.

His cold hands fumbled as he desperately searched his pockets for his keys. Once in the car, he felt safe. Everything was quiet. He shook his head. I'm going crazy, he thought.

Suddenly, a large hand smacked his driver's side window. Bland's reflexes shifted his body weight away from the window, and he looked up toward the hand.

Between the large hand and the window was a note. Bland's eyes focused on the words on the note. It read, Hello, Mr. Benthall. The hand retracted from the window, and Jesse stood grinning. He went scribbling on his pad. Why are you parked out here? Didn't you get a badge?

Bland slowly cracked the window to speak. His heavy breathing slowed his response. "No, Jesse, I didn't." He kept the window up as he talked to Jesse. "Why are you out here so late?" asked Bland, as Jesse was about to back away from the window.

I'm on third shift for the next few weeks. During my break, I do my PT, Jesse wrote.

"PT?"

Physical Training, the words on the pad read.

Bland studied Jesse's fitted shirt against his chiseled physique. He was impressed that a man of Jesse's age could still be in such good shape. Bland now wondered if the bull-breathing figure following him earlier was actually Jesse getting in his nightly regimen.

I have to stay in shape to answer the country's call to fight, the words on the pad read.

"Fight who, Jesse?" Bland was confused. He watched as Jesse scribbled more words on his notepad before pressing the pad against the window.

The terrorists, you have to be ready for whenever they try to attack us.

"It's good to know, Jesse, that you're here keeping us safe," replied Bland. He didn't know what else to say. "Well, thanks for coming over and saying hi to me."

I saw you getting in your car, so I came to say hi.

"Yes, and thank you for doing that," Bland responded.

How are your son and wife? Don't see much of them lately, the words read.

"Fine," remarked Bland, then continuing, "I will tell her you asked about her."

Inconspicuously, Bland checked his watch. Jesse turned the pad back to Bland for him to read.

I have to go. I have to clock back in before I'm late.

"Okay. Nice seeing you again, Jesse." Bland casually saluted the war veteran before pulling off.

As additional weeks passed, sporadically, it was apparent that Bland didn't care that he was spiraling out of control. Grey seemed to offer the support he felt he was missing during this crucial time in his life, and in return he offered her the love she was missing in hers. The more they met, the more the feeling of guilt vanished as an issue.

Dakota felt Bland's attention decrease for her, only to be replaced by an increased agitation toward her. His pattern had become apparent to her. Normally after he returned from a spontaneous trip, he took a week to hang out around the house, at first doing everything he could to make up for his disappearing acts. Eventually, a week for atonement dwindled to a few days. It was only a matter of time when eventually he didn't come home after a trip. When she asked, his first explanation centered on the book; after a while he didn't give her the courtesy of telling her anything.

Ultimately, Dakota saw Bland as a two-sided coin. There were days when he was sweet and affectionate, very much the man she had fallen in love with years ago. At other times, he was mean-spirited, selfish, and standoffish toward her. She was very aware of the distance he was putting between the two of them. Yet, as his wife, she needed her strength not to waiver, so she didn't falter when Bland rejected her physically, disregarded her emotionally, disappointed her personally, and abused her mentally until her euphoric spirit was on the verge of a nervous breakdown.

Where there was once laughter and joy hovering about them,

there were now arguments and resentments between the two. Dakota felt lonely in her world, isolated from his world, and betrayed by his promises. Bland had blinded himself to what he was putting her through, but Dakota was a fighter and she was raised believing that before you abandon someone, you exhaust all remedies to make things work. In her heart, she felt there was more she could do, so she tried tirelessly to prepare extra meals that Bland missed, to create romantic evenings that he had no desire to attend, and to accessorize her beautiful body that he neglected to see. Her swirling hopes had become a desperate wish that no longer seemed tangible. Bland and his lack of interest in her had sent her into a tailspin of hopelessness. She was tired of arguing and tired of fighting, so she began to pull herself into a shell, isolating herself from him, his behavior, and any interest in his novel. She also no longer had a yearning for Bland. She dressed herself with a cold façade. Her voice was weak and frail, her skin pale as she often listened to talk shows berating women as to the reasons for running their husbands away. As she wondered where she had failed in their marriage, it was apparent she had lost herself. And, for her own reasons, she blamed herself. She decided that what little strength she had left, she would preserve for her son, Devin.

15

AFTER HOURS OF SITTING IN THE COURTYARD READING, Jane closed the book with a heavy heart for Dakota. Dakota's pain caused Jane to weep, but her strength gave Jane hope that Dakota would prevail in her marriage. Given the anguish Bland was putting her through, Jane questioned in her mind if the marriage was worth saving. She sat there wondering what type of man knowingly would put a woman through such pain and have no sense of remorse and ownership or seek to relieve her of it.

It wasn't until the night draped the daylight did she return to her room. That night Jane's dreams took her to a different place with different faces. As she squirmed in the bed, occasionally her voice wailed out "no" or "stop." She kicked off the covers as her body fought to wake up.

"No!" she growled again in her sleep. The late shift nurse ran into the room. Jane clutched her own neck, choking herself. The nurse fought to pry her hands loose.

"Jane!" the nurse called.

Jane breathed heavily. Finally, she woke, crying. When she saw the nurse, she immediately buried her face into the woman's abdomen.

"It's a bad dream, Jane."

Jane pulled away from the nurse's abdomen. Her words skipped as her voice raced. "A bad dream," she repeated.

The nurse took Jane by the shoulders and gently laid her back on the pillow. "You're safe, Jane."

"I don't want you to leave, Connie," Jane pleaded.

"Don't worry, I'll be right here," the nurse responded.

Jane did not notice she wasn't Nurse Constance. The nurse pulled the covers over Jane and watched her eyes fight the sleep.

The next morning, a nurse's aide opened the blinds in Jane's room. Slowly, her eyes opened, then snapped shut when the sun's light hit them.

"I'm sorry. I didn't mean to wake you. I just thought the room was too dark."

Jane's eyes squinted, and her scratchy voice revived. "Do they train the nurses to pull the drapes back when someone is sleeping? Didn't you think that was going to wake me?" She was looking for an argument, but her throat was too sore to engage in one.

"Oh, I'm not a nurse. I'm a nurse's aide," the aide gently retorted.

"What time is it?" she snarled.

"It's almost noon."

Jane looked around the room.

"Are you hungry? Lunch is being served."

"Yes, I'm hungry." Jane rolled over in the bed.

"You had a long night?" the aide asked.

"I got caught up in this book."

"It must be a good book," the aide smiled cordially, then rinsed out Jane's water container. "What's it about?"

"How men take good women for granted," she complained, with awkward body movement.

The door opened and in walked Dr. Stewart, accompanied by a nurse.

The aide said to Jane, "I'm going to check on your lunch."

After the door closed, Dr. Stewart said to the nurse.

"Take her blood pressure."

The nurse strapped the blood pressure cuff around Jane's arm. Jane watched the red digital numbers on the machine change as the pressure

around her bicep increased. Soon the numbers stopped changing and displayed a series of numbers.

"So, did the fresh air help you sleep last night?" the doctor asked.

"I guess. Where is Nurse Connie?" Jane asked, while studying the nurse.

"She's still away," the doctor answered.

"Still away? I could have sworn she was here last night and woke me from my nightmare."

"You had another bad dream?"

"This one was worse than any of them." She started to explain but stopped when she noticed the nurse eavesdropping on their conversation. "I really don't feel like talking about it."

"Maybe you will feel like sharing it with Dr. Westfall today."

"Dr. Westfall?"

"She is the psychiatrist I told you about. She might be able to give you some clarity about your dreams. I gave her your journal and she's expecting you later today. Her office is in the adjacent building, and a nurse will return later this afternoon to escort you."

"I don't understand why I can't take myself. You have me using a walker that I really don't need anymore. My legs are strong, Dr. Stewart."

"All patients have to be transported from one building to another by wheelchair. Stop fussing. I'll tell her to roll you carefully to the building."

Jane smiled slightly. After everyone left the room, she took a sponge bath and prepared herself to see the psychiatrist. There were a number of questions she wanted the doctor to answer.

As Jane sat on the bed waiting for the nurse to come and escort her to the psychiatrist's office, she thought about what her life was before she arrived at the hospital. Was she married? Did she have kids, or was she in love? Her thoughts were interrupted when Constance burst through the door.

"Jane!"

Jane felt elated when she heard the voice. Quickly, she straightened her slumped body and stood from the bed.

"It's you!" Jane screamed in excitement. "I thought you quit and weren't coming back."

"Come on, me leave you?"

"You've been gone so long, I didn't know. When did you get back?"

"I got off the plane an hour ago. And I came straight here to see you."

They embraced each other for a long time, and then they sat on the side of the bed.

"Wow, it's nice to know I was actually missed. Anyway, listen to you. Your voice improved since I left, Jane."

"Right, who's going to take me out after I say hi? I sound like a deep baritone man."

"A man won't care as long as he can make you sing soprano. You know what I mean?"

They both laughed as Jane clutched Constance's hand.

"Did Dr. Stewart tell you?"

"Tell me what?"

"That you're scheduled to see Dr. Westfall."

"Yes, he told me."

"But did he tell you that I'll be escorting you to the doctor's office?"

"He didn't tell me that. He just said a nurse would do it." Jane pulled Constance into another hug.

Constance stood on her feet. "Get ready." Constance left the room and returned with a wheelchair.

"Oh, come on. Do I have to?" Jane complained.

She offered Jane an unyielding smile. Jane flopped her body in the seat. As Constance wheeled her along the hospital corridor to the patient transport elevator, she changed the conversation to a subject more serious.

"I heard you had a bad dream last night."

"Dr. Stewart told you?"

"No, the nurse you thought was me told me," smiled Constance. "Hopefully you'll get some answers about those dreams."

"Connie, I went over those dreams forward and backward and none of them make any sense."

"Something is triggering the dreams. That's why Dr. Stewart is having you see this psychiatrist."

"All I want to know is who I am."

"Jane, don't get frustrated, because answers come when they come."

Jane sighed, "I hope she can tell me something."

Once off the elevator, Constance pushed the wheelchair across the long sidewalk to the adjacent building. Jane closed her eyes as she smelled the air. She wished she could sit in the sun and enjoy more of the fresh air.

They entered the building and took the elevator to the fourth floor. Constance wheeled the chair down the corridor to the psychiatrist's office. She stopped at the door to offer Jane some last words of advice.

"Be strong, Jane, and don't worry. I hear that Dr. Westfall is pretty good at what she does. She's helped a lot of patients with head traumas."

"You mean diagnosing people who are crazy? That doesn't take a lot of experience."

"Give her a chance, Jane."

Jane stood from the wheelchair and gave Constance a big hug and then entered the doctor's office.

The secretary waved for Jane to take a seat.

"Dr. Westfall will be with you in a moment."

Jane sat quietly as she looked at the cover of magazines. Soon a side door opened, and a man and a woman stepped into the waiting area.

"Yes, I will see you in a week," Dr. Westfall said.

Jane looked at the doctor whose eyes were stuck on the paper the man held out. She tried to read it but couldn't.

Jane noticed the man said nothing, while Dr. Westfall occasionally commented.

Hastily, the man turned and stumbled over Jane's feet. He stopped within an inch of her bandaged face. He stared into her eyes and, as if seeing a ghost, he stumbled backward and then moved forward toward the door.

Jane turned to look as the man rushed down the hall.

"Oh, he'll be okay," Dr. Westfall waved. "So you must be Jane?" Dr. Westfall reached out to shake her hand.

"I guess, well, yes." In her heart, she really hoped that Dr. Westfall could help tap into her memory and tell her who she really was.

"It's good to meet you. Dr. Stewart told me about you." Dr. Westfall

held the door open for Jane.

"What, about my multiple illnesses?"

Dr. Westfall laughed, "No, about your sense of humor. Come on back and take a seat."

Jane rose and followed the doctor into an adjacent room. The room was softly lit with one lamp. Jane immediately noticed the leather sofa. The doctor walked around a chair, and Jane assumed that was Dr. Westfall's seat.

"Take a seat." She walked over to the sofa while the doctor talked. "Let me clean this up."

She referred to a miniature tape recorder that was sitting on the table beside the sofa. The doctor hit the eject button to retrieve the tape. She slid it in its tape container and walked to the far side of the room to put the container in a locked cabinet. Jane watched the doctor's every move as she retrieved another blank tape and then, from her desk drawer, Jane's book of journals.

Dr. Westfall returned with a full explanation for the purpose of the tape recorder.

"I hope you don't mind; I normally tape my sessions. I make an electronic copy and back that up with a hard copy." She pointed to the tape recorder. "The recordings are uploaded to my computer and the tapes never leave my office. Listening to the recordings outside of our sessions helps me with making my diagnoses." She added, "It's only for my records. Doctor-patient confidentiality. That's if you don't mind."

"I don't mind."

The doctor inserted a USB into the port on the tape recorder, then slid a tape into the front of the recorder and hit the red record button. Dr. Westfall's soft tone identified the session, Jane's name, the date, and the time.

The doctor sat in her chair as Jane sat on the sofa. Quietly, different emotions began surfacing within Jane. Maybe this wasn't a good idea, she thought.

"Jane, how are you?"

"Look at me, doctor; how do you think I am?" Jane recognized her rude sarcasm. "I'm sorry. I'm just frustrated. I mean, I don't have any

idea what I look like, or where I'm from. I know nothing about myself, except that something awful put me here."

"Jane, what makes you think it was something awful?"

"Look at me, doctor. I'm covered in bandages because I was severely burned. I don't think I got these burns from lying in the sun."

The doctor laughed. "Nonetheless, you do have them. How do the burns make you feel?"

"Angry and very afraid."

"Afraid?"

"I don't know who I am. I don't know what to expect when these bandages come off. I am afraid that the burns have scarred me mentally and physically for life."

"Jane, it's important that you know that burns are often accompanied by pain and anxiety, even during recovery. A person may also experience emotional distress if a burn alters his or her appearance. That could be why you're facing some frustrations. With very few exceptions, most people are self-conscious about their appearance. If something affects that appearance, such as scars, they are even more self-conscious. Such excessive anxiety and overwhelming stress have been known to increase certain levels of depression, which are symptoms of dissociative disorders."

"Dissociative disorders," she repeated. "Dr. Stewart mentioned something about my lack of memory having to do with amnesia."

"Dissociative disorders are mental illnesses that involve disruptions or breakdowns of memory, consciousness or awareness, identity, and perception—mental functions that normally operate smoothly and when disrupted can result in blocking out certain memories. With this disorder, Jane, the degree of memory loss goes beyond normal forgetfulness and includes gaps in memory for long periods of time. Dissociative amnesia is more common in women than in men."

"So there's no hope for me? I won't ever remember?" Jane asked, with a sense of fright in her tone.

"Well, Jane, there are suggested treatments aimed to help the person suffering from dissociative amnesia to safely express and process painful memories. One treatment in particular that I've found to be successful

with many of my patients is clinical hypnosis. This technique uses intense relaxation to achieve an altered state of consciousness, allowing you to explore thoughts and memories hidden from your conscious state of mind."

"Can it help explain why I am having these dreams?"

"Dreams can offer a pattern that allows passage into the mind. Memories may be playing out through your dreams." Dr. Westfall reached for the pad of journals and continued, "These dreams could be your subconscious playing scenes of your life, something similar to a short movie. You only get to see pieces of it, and it's up to you to put the puzzle together. Tell me something that you find consistent in all the dreams."

Jane spoke softly, "In the dreams I can never see my face. It's like it's distorted. Dr. Westfall, why can't I see my face?"

"I suspect your mind is still dealing with the imagery."

Jane looked confused.

"Your mind will present scenes like a movie. That seems to be what is happening and probably not in any particular order. Treat each dream like a scene or, better yet, like an image."

"An image?" Jane echoed, feeling puzzled.

Dr. Westfall used another analogy. "Like a film's negative. When the picture has good lighting, you eventually see an image. Likewise, it seems the mind needs to generate more light," she paused. "And that, I am afraid, comes with time and hopefully through some therapy. Whatever the traumatic experience is that traps the memory can sometimes release it as well."

Jane uttered, "Like a dream?"

"Exactly like a dream, better yet, through your dreams. It's up to us to start making cracks in it. Hypnosis is a proven method for making such cracks. I feel it's the safest treatment for exploring these dreams you've been having. I want to use your journal entries to help me find what lies beneath the dreams."

"Okay, so what do I do?"

"I need you to lie back on the sofa. I want you to make yourself comfortable. Allow your body to relax. Allow your breathing to relax.

Let your arms rest beside your body. Relax your knees and feet. Relax your toes and hands. Remove everything and everyone from your mind. Look at the wall in front of you. I want you to concentrate on my voice and the numbers I say. As the numbers decrease, you will return to your first dream. When I start calling numbers in ascending order, you will awake from your dream."

Jane lay still while concentrating on the doctor's voice. Dr. Westfall moved in closer to her body.

"Jane, your eyes are getting heavy. Six, five, four, now they're starting to close, three, two, and now they're closed, one. You're at the place in your first dream."

Jane's chest began to heave as her breathing became heavier.

"Tell me what's going on," the doctor said.

"I'm running," she gasped.

"Jane, are you running from or to someone or something?"

"I can't see."

"Jane, look behind you and tell me if someone or something is chasing you."

For a moment there was silence. Then suddenly, "Someone is chasing me," she said, shockingly.

"Can you see the face?" the doctor asked.

Jane's body began twisting on the sofa. "I can't see the face," her breathing still heavy. "There are people."

"Jane, I want you to slow down from running. There is no longer anyone behind you. Concentrate on the people. Tell me about the people."

"They're standing, waiting."

"What are they waiting for?"

"I don't know."

"Look around you, what else do you see?"

"Silver," Jane said, her breathing becoming slower.

"Silver?" the doctor repeated. "Is the silver in some form of object?"

"I can't tell what it is."

"Look into the silver, Jane, and tell me what you see."

"It's a blurry reflection of me." Jane's body turned with a sense of

compassion to her words.

"Can you make out anything?"

"No," she said, as she took a deep breath.

Dr. Westfall went to another journal entry.

"Jane, you're in a room, but there are no windows. In this room is a small door. What are you doing in the room?"

"I'm trapped, and I can't breathe."

"Can you make it to the door?"

"It's so far off." She began to cry.

"Go toward the door, Jane. I want you to make it to the door."

"I'm trying, but the room is closing around me, please help me. I'm going to die. Please help me." Jane's voice raced, and her breathing increased.

"Calm down, Jane," Dr. Westfall softly said, while referring to Jane's journal. "You're no longer there, Jane. You are in another place, another time. In this new place, you are sitting on a park bench. What do you see around you?"

"I see people walking and holding hands, and birds singing under a beautiful sky. There is a light breeze. Oh!" she suddenly said.

"What is it, Jane? What is it that you see?"

"A crow just swooped in and settled at my feet. It's so black and beautiful. Its eyes are watching me."

"How does that make you feel?"

"Uncomfortable."

"Why does it make you feel uncomfortable?"

"Because . . ." she paused, "the sky is changing with dark clouds stretching across it. The breeze is turning violent. People are running."

"And the crow, Jane, what is the crow doing?"

"It's still staring at me, but now with red eyes. The crow is flying away."

"Jane, will you encounter this crow in another dream?" the doctor asked.

"Yes, in the open I see a tree with no leaves. On each branch is a black crow. At the top of the tree there is a white crow. Its eyes are solid red with blood seeping from each eye. I'm caught looking. It's flying toward

me, and the other crows are following. The white crow settles on my head, while the black crows are all over my body. They're pecking at my flesh!" she screamed. "Please stop them! Stop them!"

"They're gone, Jane, and you're in another dream, another time. You are in a place where there is light flashing across a room. You are abruptly besieged by another woman. The two of you struggle. Now tell me what happens next."

"I see light flashing across her face. She's trying to strangle me, and I can't seem to stop her." Jane's voice stalled, then she choked.

"Jane, what happened next?"

"I am at a funeral. I see a fresh dug grave and casket. People are sobbing, but no one takes notice of me as I approach the casket."

When she becomes quiet, Dr. Westfall immediately explores.

"You're at the gravesite, Jane. There's a casket and people present. Do you recognize any of the people?"

"No."

"Move to the casket, Jane. Are you at the casket?"

"Yes."

"Jane, when I tell you to, I want you to open the casket. After you open it, I want you to tell me what you see." Dr. Westfall paused for a second, then continued. "Open the casket, Jane. Is the casket open?"

"Yes."

"What's in the casket, Jane?"

"No, no, no!" Jane screamed.

Her arms flailed in the air. Dr. Westfall began counting in ascending order.

"One, two, three, four, five, six."

Jane woke up. Her eyes focused on the ceiling fan. She lay in silence for several seconds, then she sat upright on the sofa.

"How do you feel, Jane?"

"I'm okay," she said.

"Would you like a glass of water?"

"No, thank you," Jane said, as she continued to gather herself. "So, how did I do?"

"Actually, you did very well. The dream entries in your journal

provided me with a good start."

Jane's eyes brightened, "Did I say who I am or what I looked like?"

"You couldn't tell me. That may have something to do with you wearing these bandages."

"I've been asking Dr. Stewart to remove them," Jane grumbled.

"I'm sure he has his reasons why he hasn't. Who knows? After several more sessions, hopefully we can remove all the bandages, those covering your body and those covering your memory. Maybe then we will know who you are."

"What did I say that could help me or rather help you find out who I am?"

"It's a process, Jane. There is a degree of patience that comes with unlocking the memory. When there is something to discuss I will let you know. As I said, hopefully, after a few more sessions, we will be closer to knowing your identity."

Jane sensed Dr. Westfall's unwillingness to discuss the session. "So there's hope for me?"

"There's hope for us all, Jane. I will speak with Dr. Stewart about scheduling you for another appointment. I'm also prescribing something for the headaches and something to help with the anxiety you're experiencing."

Jane stood from the sofa and started walking toward the door.

"Jane, there is a nurse waiting to take you back to your room."

After Jane had left the office, Dr. Westfall headed straight for the recorder to dictate the session she had with Jane.

"It appears the patient's fears have blanketed the patient. The patient's mind is protecting the patient from whatever she is running from. Take, for instance, journal two. The patient spoke of a door that's far off, and when the patient approached that door the patient began suffocating. That could very well be an exit point in the patient's mind. If the patient can make it through that door, the patient will most likely have a breakthrough. First, I have to get the patient to the door and then through the door.

"Other significant things the patient mentioned in her journals

were a crow, a casket, and her being strangled by a woman. This is a classic case of the conscious and subconscious entangled, one trying to suppress the other, while the other tries to free itself. Sometimes only one can survive. I believe that's the reason for the casket. However, I will not be certain until I probe deeper."

The doctor paused, took a seat at her desk and continued speaking into the recorder.

"In a few of the journals, a crow or crows were the focal point of the dreams. A crow symbolizes change in the patient's life, a change that sometimes can come abruptly. That could very well be the fear that traps her in her mind. And the thing chasing the patient could actually be the patient's past or the patient chasing herself. This also could be the reason why the patient couldn't see her reflection in any of the dreams."

Dr. Westfall hit the stop button of the recorder. She removed the tape from the recorder and wrote Jane's name on the front of it. She returned the tape to its case and slid from behind the desk. She stood silently before pulling the USB from the recorder to store it in the top drawer of her desk. She ejected the tape from the recorder and walked over to the cabinet and carefully stored it with the other tapes.

For the next hour after Jane returned from Dr. Westfall's office, she couldn't stop thinking about her session. She contemplated why Dr. Westfall didn't reveal her findings about the dreams. There was a knock on the door.

"Come in," Jane said. "Hey, Connie," she murmured. Jane pulled the cover back from the bed.

"Don't get out of bed. I just wanted to stop by to see how everything went today."

Constance stood beside the bed and listened to Jane whine about not discovering her identity.

"I thought the doctor was going to tell me something about myself. I don't know what I was expecting."

Constance began laughing. "What did Dr. Westfall have to say?"

"You mean what she didn't say."

"What do you mean?"

"She says that unlocking my memory is a process that requires patience."

"If that's what she said, Jane, then you have to be patient."

"I know. If only I didn't have these bandages, maybe I would have gotten some answers. As long as these wraps are on, I won't get them."

"Jane, Dr. Stewart isn't going to rush or jeopardize your health. When it's time for the bandages to come off, he will be the first to tell you. I know it is frustrating, but how many times are we going to go through this? Time is the only thing that is going to help you, so be patient, and everything will happen in due time."

Jane's eyes fell to the floor with added agitation, "Well, I hope you're right, I've been in here for…?"

She paused to wait for Constance to give her the answer.

"Almost eight months, Jane."

"Eight months! I'm sure I can handle what is under these bandages."

"When the time comes, then you can prove it."

Jane lay back in the bed about to submerge her face in a pillow. Constance watched as Jane held the pillow just inches away from her face and then interrupted her self-imposed suffocation.

"I'm sure of this. If you reopen any of those stitches, I promise you, it will be another eight months before Dr. Stewart lets you see your face. Come on, Jane. Sit up. I want to tell you something."

Slowly, Jane sat up in the bed, her posture dragging as low as her spirit. Constance noticed her demeanor. "Jane, if only you had an idea of your condition when you were found, you would be grateful that Dr. Stewart was able to save your life. You were broken up, Jane, and I do mean literally. Third-degree burns had damaged the bones and skin tissues in your legs, hands, and face. Not to mention, you suffered from a serious puncture wound and head injury and the—" Constance cut her words immediately.

"What? You were about to say something, Connie. What is it?"

Constance stalled on her words until she thought of something that could make sense without telling Jane the truth.

"I was…going to say…don't forget the infections you incurred and your voice box. The damage to your voice box was so severe that the

doctor wasn't able to save all of your vocal cords, and it appears you've forgotten the coma you were in that still has you requiring physical therapy." Constance paused and started again with a softer voice, "Jane, you have been through hell and survived, so stop being so hard on yourself and don't be so hard on Dr. Stewart." Constance turned her wrist to check the time. "I have to go."

After Constance left the room, Jane gave much thought to her comments. Instead of gratitude, a feeling of anger draped her spirit. If Dr. Stewart had let her die, then her suffering would have been limited to that moment and that moment only. Now, without her memory or identity, she felt her suffering would be for an eternity.

Early the next day, Jane awoke with the book on her mind. She sat up in her bed and began to read.

16

AFTER SPENDING AN ENTIRE WEEKEND IN ST. LOUIS playing rather than working, Bland and Grey arrived back in D.C. early Monday morning. Grey enjoyed her weekend, but she was slightly worried since she hadn't worked on the proposal she was presenting to the executives later that week. Bland, too, came to the realization that if he didn't have a novel by the deadline, the twins would ask for his resignation.

The moment Bland was out of Grey's presence he turned on his cell phone, and it immediately rang. The voice on the other end was accompanied with a sense of urgency.

"Mr. Benthall, can you hear me?"

"Yes, I can hear you."

"Mr. Benthall, you need to go to Memorial General immediately."

"Slow down. Is this Paige?"

"Yes, Mr. Benthall. I've been trying since Friday to reach you. I thought you would have gotten the message by now, but when the hospital called me again this morning, I got very concerned."

"Well, I'm okay. What's this about a hospital?"

"Your wife, she's in the hospital. All I know is that she's been there

since Friday. Unfortunately, I haven't been able to get any additional information."

Bland questioned Paige's facts. "Since Friday, Paige, are you sure?"

"Mr. Benthall, that's all I know. And Smith and Wilkins have been down my neck to find you. Mr. Benthall, I think you should get over there right away."

Bland didn't respond; he just ended the call. Was he that distant to not know that Dakota was having problems? He questioned several alternatives as he pushed his SUV to speeds of 80 to 85 miles per hour to the hospital. Once he parked, he rushed into the hospital.

"Excuse me."

"Yes sir, how can I help you?" asked one of the volunteers sitting at the information desk.

"I am looking for Dakota Benthall."

The woman rolled her chair over to a computer. "Sir, when was she admitted?"

"Sometime Friday."

"Okay, I found her. She's in the adjacent building."

"The adjacent?" he repeated.

"That's the Psych building."

"'Psych as in psychiatric?" Bland questioned.

"Yes sir. Take this hall to the end, then take a right. You will see two elevators with 'W' on them. Take either to the second floor."

Bland didn't hear the rest of the directions as he was already running down the hall. The woman yelled out the room number, "She's in room 2042."

When Bland reached the Psych Unit, he saw a security checkpoint off to the side of two double doors. The security guard was bent down behind the desk. Bland didn't wait to address the man. Instead, he quickly darted behind a doctor who had swiped his badge before entering the double doors.

When Bland tried to rush by the nurse's station, he was stopped by a nurse.

"Sir, this is a restricted floor. You have to have a badge to gain access."

"I'm here to see my wife," Bland said with much urgency.

"You have to get a badge at the security desk outside the doors."

Bland glanced down the hall for room 2042.

The nurse noticed and asked, "What is your wife's name, sir?"

"Dakota Benthall," Bland replied, as he continued to scan the room numbers.

"Do you have identification, sir?"

Bland didn't answer. His mind and eyes had fixated on the room numbers. He spotted the number 2042 and made a beeline for the room. The nurse called for him to come back.

When Bland reached the room, Mr. and Mrs. Scott were sitting in the room along with Devin. John Scott was first to get to his feet when he saw Bland.

"Bland, where have you been? We've been trying to reach you since Friday. No one knew how to contact you. I called your job and left messages," Mr. Scott said in a fatherly tone of voice.

Bland gave no answer to any of his questions. He first looked at Dakota who was asleep.

The door to the room abruptly opened and in rushed two security personnel and the psych nurse that stopped Bland earlier.

"Sir," spoke one of the security personnel. "We need to see your identification."

Bland looked at the men with irritation. Then he pulled his identification from his pocket and handed it to the nurse.

"As I said to you, this is my wife!"

"I understand what you said, but with all due respect, I don't personally know who you are or your relation to this woman."

Mr. Scott interjected, "Bland, they're only doing their jobs. It took the wife and me a time to get back here to see Dakota. We didn't have the proper identification, but we were able to show we were her neighbors. Not to mention, we brought her to the hospital."

The nurse perused the ID carefully and then handed it back to Bland.

"Thank you, sir. From now on, you have to check in at the desk." She and the security guards exited the room.

Bland focused his attention back on Dakota. "What is the doctor saying?"

Mrs. Scott began updating Bland. "I talked to the doctor briefly, but he's not giving us any information since we're not her immediate family. She's been asleep since we've been here." She paused, then added as she glanced over in her direction, "Poor baby."

Bland took his eyes from his wife to peer upon Devin who was asleep on a small bed cot. Uneasiness swooped in to rest upon his shoulders and heart. Looking at his wife in that hospital bed made him wonder what he was doing jeopardizing everything he claimed he loved. The more his eyes volleyed back and forth from Dakota to Devin, the more he knew he had to put an end to his affair with Grey. He always knew there were risks involved with seeing Grey, but seeing his wife lying lifeless wasn't one of them. That brought a new concern and reality to him; his relationship with Grey had to end immediately.

Mr. Scott's heavy voice finally broke through his deep thoughts. "Bland, come with me."

Bland followed him to a nearby waiting area. It was empty, so he felt free to speak.

"On Friday, Dakota let Devin come over to hang out with our grandson, Joey. When Keri took Devin home, Dakota didn't answer the door. Thank God my wife is as nosy as she is; otherwise, she wouldn't have entered the house or found Dakota passed out on the bathroom floor. She found an empty pill bottle beside her."

Bland interrupted, "Did Devin see her?"

"Don't worry, Devin was in his room. He didn't see a thing. I am assuming she took the pills. I'm sure the doctor had her stomach pumped." Mr. Scott removed his cap and wiped his forehead. "I hate to see her like this, Bland. Now, it's none of my business, but you have a beautiful wife and son in there who love you. I'm not one to tell a man how to run his house, but I know this much—"

Bland cut him off, "Then don't start now." Bland's guilt suddenly put him on the defensive. "I don't want to be rude, John, but there's a lot going on, and a lot you don't know, so I prefer that you don't comment at all. I do appreciate you and Keri helping out with Devin and making sure Dakota made it to the hospital."

Abruptly, the door to the waiting room opened and Bland's voice

dropped when he heard another voice. Mr. Scott recognized the doctor from earlier and decided to dismiss himself.

Dr. Robertson wasted no time introducing himself and updating Bland on Dakota's condition.

"Hello, Mr. Benthall. I am Dr. Robertson, the physician who's been caring for your wife since her arrival on Friday. I've been watching her closely, as it was reported that an empty pill bottle was found by her body."

"So, what are you implying?"

"I believe your wife is suffering from a mental disorder."

"A mental disorder? What mental disorder?" Bland aggressively asked.

"Depression."

"Depression!" Bland sounded off. "My wife isn't depressed."

"Mr. Benthall, depression isn't something to be taken lightly. Major depression affects a good percentage of middle-aged people. Those who experience major depression may become suicidal."

"You think my wife tried to take her life by taking some pills?"

"I don't know the answer to that, and she has not admitted that, but as a precaution, we went ahead and pumped her stomach and checked her blood. After getting your wife's blood work back, it was discovered that your wife is expecting."

Bland stared bewilderedly at the doctor. After his continuous blank expression, Dr. Robertson suspected that he had no knowledge of the pregnancy.

"Mr. Benthall, you didn't know your wife was pregnant?"

Bland shook his head, "As you said, it was just discovered, so why would I know?"

"You've misconstrued what I said. I just found out, but according to the ultrasound, she's about twenty-four weeks of gestation."

Bland calculated the time in his head. "Six months? Are you sure?"

"Yes, twenty-four weeks pregnant is our best guess based on the size of the fetus."

"No. Are you sure she knew, doctor?"

"Given the changes a woman's body goes through once she's pregnant, yes, I'm sure she would have known."

Bland didn't want to believe Dakota withheld such information from him.

"Mr. Benthall, I want to keep her for a few days to monitor her and the fetus. Also, I am recommending a therapist to sit down with the two of you once she recovers."

"A shrink," clarified Bland, already knowing the reason. Unlike his sudden attacks on Mr. Scott, Bland continued to listen to what Dr. Robertson had to say. Once finished voicing his concerns, Dr. Robertson turned on his heels and headed out of the waiting area. Seconds later, Bland went into deep thought. Now he knew that the circumstances were serious enough to warrant his removal from the affair with Grey. He pulled his cell phone from his pocket and quickly tapped his fingers over the keypad. The phone rang several times before Grey picked up.

"Hello."

Bland's voice stumbled. When he spoke, his voice was slow and quite different than when he normally greeted her.

"Hi, honey," she said.

His reply was even more sluggish, "Hey."

As usual, Grey gained control over the conversation and began running with it. She, too, had a concern that had been plaguing her for some time. She wasn't sure when the right moment would come to confront Bland, but to her no time was better than the present.

"Bland, I need to talk to you about something."

"Funny you should say that because there has been something I need to get off my mind as well."

She offered him the opportunity to share what was on his mind.

After knowing his wife was experiencing such pain, he knew without a doubt what he had to do. He would put off breaking Grey's heart a few more minutes. Instead of sharing what was on his mind, he volleyed the invitation back to Grey, and she took it.

"Are you sure?" she asked, then uttered, "Bland," her tone sounded serious. "We've been seeing each other for some time now, and a part of me feels you haven't been honest with me."

"What do you mean?"

"I don't want to make a big deal out of it, but whenever we're together I notice you turn off your phone. The majority of our meetings strangely enough are always on a train or at my apartment. Not to mention that you've never invited me to your home. I'm not insinuating that you are married, but I do need to know if there is someone else important in your life."

She had given Bland his opportunity to disclose his marriage, but he stalled. Given the latest circumstances concerning his wife, revealing the truth should have come easy for him; still he couldn't bring himself to tell her. Instead, he began to address her concerns by offering a dangerous invitation.

"What are you doing this evening?"

She hesitated, unsure where he was going with his line of questioning or what restaurant or on what train he wanted her to meet him next.

"I'll be unpacking from our Saint Louis trip." He heard her faint laugh, "I hadn't made any plans, but I do have to jump on this proposal before I lose my contract. So, I can't take any more spontaneous trips."

The door to the waiting area opened, and Bland said nothing. After the stranger sat a reasonable distance, he continued.

"I want to invite you to my house tonight."

—

"Your house!" screamed Jane, looking up from the book, then back to it.

—

"Your house?" His invitation caught Grey by surprise, but to a small degree it caught him off guard as well.

It was obvious he could only pull off such an outrageous stunt with Dakota being hospitalized. His conscience understood it was a callous act when he offered, but some part of him suppressed such scruples so that he could tell Grey face to face that he was married. At least, that's what he told himself.

"I mean that was one of your reservations, right?"

"Well, yes, but—"

"If it's a problem then maybe—."

"No, it's not a problem. I am at a loss for words. Anyway, yes, I would love to come over."

Jubilation seeped from Grey's excited voice. She regained her vigor as he agreed to pick her up from her apartment. She eagerly wanted to get off the phone just so she could have time to prepare. After hanging up the phone, Bland sat with a blank look on his face. He heard his name called, and it was Mr. Scott holding a cup of coffee. He pushed the Styrofoam cup in his direction.

Bland sat up to take the cup of coffee. "Thank you." Then he apologized for his earlier behavior.

"Say no more. I know it's frustrating working so hard. Having Dakota in the hospital isn't helping things. Son, have you thought about what's really important?" He took a seat beside Bland and went on explaining. "Bland, what does it mean if you work so hard to get ahead in life and when you get there, you lose the most important thing on the way?"

Bland attempted to respond to the question.

"Bland, the question was rhetorical."

Bland sensed where Mr. Scott was taking the conversation, and he wished he could disclose to him that the marriage was drowning not because of work but as a result of his infidelity.

"Mr. Scott, do you think you and your wife can keep Devin for a few days, just to give me some time to straighten up the house before Dakota comes home?"

"Sure we can."

"I don't want to over-impose. You've done a lot already."

"Bland, he's no bother. You need to take this time and get your house in order. That's what a man is supposed to do, son. By the way, this Friday night, we plan to take Joey to The Pizzeria."

Bland chimed in, "Is that the restaurant and video arcade located downtown?"

"Yes, that's it," confirmed John. "How about you drop Devin off at The Pizzeria. He can spend the night with my grandson, and we'll bring him home in the morning. That will give you more alone time with your wife."

Before leaving the hospital, Bland stopped by Dakota's room. She was still sleeping. He looked at the contour of her body and he still couldn't tell she was pregnant. While standing there, he remembered what Mr. Scott said earlier about losing the things you loved the most. He wasn't sure if he had lost his wife, but he was sure that he had fallen in love with another woman and, given his actions, losing Grey seemed to outweigh losing his wife.

He walked over to the side of the hospital bed and kissed her on the forehead, then over to Devin to kiss him on his cheek.

When Bland arrived at his house, he immediately started taking down all the family pictures. He was careful to store them behind the chair in the living room. He also hid any other artifacts that alluded to marriage or a child. After an hour of rummaging through the entire house removing pictures and other things, he climbed the ladder to the storage attic. In the attic, Bland had stored a duffel bag filled with youthful, college memoirs. He dragged the bag down the ladder and into the living room. Before unzipping the duffel bag, he settled himself and thought what he was doing was turning into something other than a confession. After several deep breaths, he unzipped the bag and pulled out a few pictures of himself. He dug back into the bag a few more times and came across a miniature wooden chest. Suddenly, Bland became emotional; he had forgotten about the chest that Dakota had given to him when they attended college together.

A lever on the side opened the hidden compartment on the chest. Inside the drawer were old newspaper articles that Bland had written during his college days and other artifacts, such as expensive writing pens and awards that he had accumulated while writing for the college paper. He gathered them up and began placing his old pictures on the mantel, various tables, and other places throughout the house. He placed the miniature chest on the nightstand in the bedroom. Bland made his way over to Dakota's dresser drawers to pull out any remaining items when he came across birth control prescriptions that hadn't been filled for months. He studied the date of each prescription to determine exactly when she stopped filling her prescription. Had she stopped taking her pills? Did she get pregnant intentionally?

After debating with himself on the matter, he stored the prescriptions underneath his clothes in one of his dresser drawers. Before leaving to pick up Grey, he was careful to take one last look around to make sure he hadn't forgotten to remove any feminine toiletries, perfumes, and jewelry. As he proceeded through the upstairs hallway, he was quick to close and lock Devin's bedroom door, partly to conceal the existence of his son, but especially since that's where he stored the majority of Dakota's wardrobe.

When they arrived back at the house, Grey entered the foyer with inquisitive eyes. As she roamed the downstairs portion of the house, she was taken aback by the décor of the home. She was extremely impressed with Bland's color schemes and his boldness as a man to use mauve and pink as a theme throughout the house. Most bachelors wouldn't jeopardize their masculinity to do such a thing, she figured. She made her way to the patio window and stared out. She was even more surprised to see a flowerbed in his back yard.

"Bland, I wouldn't have suspected you to have a green thumb."

"Only during the summer," he laughed. "But I do have to get out there soon and clean those old weeds out."

"Come on now, be honest. Who's your gardener? As a matter of fact, who's your interior decorator?"

He smiled.

"Well, I must admit, you are every woman's dream man."

"Why. Because I know how to color coordinate?" he smiled.

Bland walked over to the counter and then took the liberty of popping the cork to a bottle of Chardonnay. He poured the wine into two crystal wineglasses.

"Why, yes, that and because you are ambitious, sensitive, caring, intelligent, and good-looking. Like I said, every woman's dream man."

"You can tell all that from some colors?"

He handed her the glass of wine and headed to the sitting area of the house.

"You will be surprised what a person can tell from colors and the same goes for clothes."

"Interesting," he remarked, as he took a seat. He tapped the cushion

beside him, a blunt invitation for her to join him. That quickly, he abandoned telling her the truth about himself, the reason for her coming over.

"What's so interesting?" she asked while flirting with her eyes.

He took her glass and his and put them on the small table beside the sofa.

"You are." He leaned in to kiss her. The weight of his body pushed her against the arm of the sofa. The sofa's leather seemed to give and crack as the two of them kissed. It wasn't long before they were lying across his wife's bed, while his wife lay in a hospital bed. It seemed not to affect him that he was violating his wife, their vows, and their home.

His hands ran through Grey's soft hair. Wanting to savor the moment, she kissed him slowly. Bland could feel her nails dig into his shirt as she pulled it over his shoulders. Wildly, Bland ripped her shirt open and buttons went sailing across the room. He did the same thing to her bra. Her voice faltered as his hand maneuvered along the side of her neck, then to her breast. Her back arched when he squeezed her breast. She wrapped her legs around his waist then dug her fingernails deep into the comforter on the bed. Being at Bland's house was more than Grey ever could have expected it to be.

The next morning Bland jumped into the shower. The door to the bathroom was purposefully left open so he could sporadically keep an eye on Grey, who just so happened to be scanning the room. Her eyes stopped at the miniature wooden chest on the nightstand. She rolled over in a fetal position to study the fine craftsmanship on the chest and contemplated the time it took to complete such a beautiful piece of art.

With shaving cream masking much of his face, Bland poked his head around the door to check on Grey. He noticed her studying the wooden chest. He took a few seconds to tell Grey the history of the chest.

"Yeah," he said loudly in order to speak over the running water. "A good friend gave me that when I first started journalism." Purposely, he omitted the name of the person who gave him the chest.

He stepped back into the bathroom.

"It's so beautiful; it must have cost a lot of money."

"I guess." He stepped in the doorway of the bathroom. He used his finger to guide her to the lever on the side. "Hit that lever," he instructed.

When she did, the hidden doors on the chest opened. She went on to inspect the contents inside.

She looked over a few pictures of him and his college cronies. She even went so far to try on his high school class ring.

"All these old clippings you wrote?"

"Yep."

She looked up at him in surprise and laughed, "Bland, you are dripping shaving cream on the floor."

He darted back into the bathroom. He rinsed the razor under the water and quickly shaved one side of his face before returning back to the doorway.

"What's wrong?" she asked.

"What do you mean?"

"You're not shaving the other side?"

He touched his face with his hand, "Oh," and went back into the bathroom. "I guess you can say that chest contains a lot of important events in my life," he said, before finishing his shave.

"Is that right?" she smiled while fiddling with the locket around her neck. She maneuvered to her back to take the locket from around her neck. She dangled it in front of her before opening it. Grey had trimmed down the photo of her and Bland and placed it in the locket in the slot opposite her parents' photo. She closed it and turned over the locket. She rubbed her thumb along the engraving that she had put on it years before. She gave much thought to what he said about the chest harboring the important things in his life. She figured that's where he had kept her locket all those years. She frowned as she contemplated leaving the necklace and locket in the chest.

When Bland heard a snapping sound, he poked his head from the door again. He noticed she had sat up in the bed with her back against the headboard and her hands clinching the linen against her chest.

"What was that sound?" he asked, as he focused on the chest and its closed doors.

"What sound?" she playfully giggled.

The house phone suddenly rang. Bland thought not to answer it, but the answering machine would pick up. He didn't want to chance Grey overhearing who might be leaving a message.

He went over to the phone.

"Why don't you jump in the shower?" he offered her a seductive stare. "I will join you after I take this call."

"It would be my pleasure."

He waited for her to close the bathroom door before he picked up the receiver.

"Hello," said Margie.

Bland could hear Dakota's mother repeat "hello" several more times. Suddenly, he remembered to hit the speaker button on the phone in order for him to be heard. When Margie heard Bland's voice, she called his name louder through the speaker. Immediately, he turned the volume to the speaker down so the conversation would not be overheard by Grey.

"Bland, how are you? I've been calling Dakota's cell, but she isn't answering. Is she home?"

"No, Margie, she's..." suddenly Bland paused. He didn't want to alarm her by saying she was in the hospital. "She went to the store, but I'll tell her to give you a call."

"Thanksgiving is just around the corner, darling. We just wanted to know if y'all were coming to visit for the holiday."

Bland figured it would be good for Dakota to get away. "Well, that's the plan, Margie."

"Great, we will see y'all then."

As Bland hung up the phone, he heard Grey's voice call from the bathroom.

"Are you coming, or do I have to wash myself?"

"Here I come."

A few days later, Dr. Robertson released Dakota from the hospital. Bland was advised to watch her carefully and make sure she received plenty of rest. He even gave Bland the name of a psychologist in order to schedule a follow-up appointment with his wife and himself.

Before Bland arrived at the house with Dakota and Devin, he

diligently put every picture, cosmetic item, jewelry, and clothing in their rightful place.

Quickly, Devin bolted past the two of them to his room. Gradually, Dakota entered the house and looked around as though she hadn't been there in quite some time. She noticed a few out of place items and tilted pictures on the walls. While Bland went to retrieve her bags, she had made her way upstairs. She heard Bland call her name.

"In the bedroom," she answered.

She moseyed over to her closet and noticed that her suits and shoes were out of place. Maybe one or two wouldn't have caught her attention, but she could tell that everything in her wardrobe was no longer in sequence by designers and colors. Though her jewelry was in its right place, her makeup case was closed, and she never closed her makeup case. She commenced walking around the bed, now acting more as an inspector than a disillusioned, broken down housewife. Dakota noticed the miniature wooden chest on the nightstand. She hadn't seen the chest since college, and why Bland pulled it out now was beyond her. She went to pick up the chest when a pinkish oval button stood out beside the base of the nightstand. She bent down to get it when she noticed three more buttons. Her first inclination was maybe Bland had destroyed some of her clothes. Maybe that's the reason for the disorder in the closet, and after some level of guilt, he returned the clothes back to the closet.

The excuses she conjured were not satisfying enough to sway her intuition that another woman might have been in her home, in her bedroom, in her bed. She sat down on the bed and began to contemplate other reasons for the buttons and messy closet; that is, before she noticed the strong scent of flower perfume on the comforter—the same scent that remained on his shirts when he returned from out of town.

Quickly, she stood to her feet and pulled the comforter back. She bent down over the sheets and took several long sniffs, then immediately began pulling the comforter off the bed.

Bland happened to walk into the room at that very minute. He stood in the entrance of the room watching her pull the linen sheets with disgust.

"What are you doing?" he asked.

"What does it look like?" she softly said because she was too tired to shout or argue.

He moved to the middle of the room. "What are you doing with the sheets?"

Without giving Bland a look, again she said, "What does it look like?"

"I can see what it looks like, but why are you doing it?"

"Like you have to ask?" Abruptly, she stopped pulling and turned in his general direction. "If you're confused, Bland, then maybe you needed to read the directions."

"What are you talking about?"

She held up part of the sheet. "How to correctly cover things you want to cover up."

"Those are clean sheets. I washed them."

"Don't clean one without cleaning the other," she replied, as she grabbed the comforter off the floor. "This isn't my scent." She then threw the buttons at him. "These aren't mine, either."

Bland didn't try offering an explanation. An act of denial would only make the situation worse.

"This type of paranoia is what landed you in the hospital."

"No, your absenteeism, lies, and desertion are what landed me in the hospital," she yelled.

"I haven't deserted you. You tried to desert us. Aren't you the one who tried to commit suicide?"

"Is that what you think? I tried to kill myself?"

"Dakota, I don't know what to think anymore. You're keeping secrets. Why haven't you told me about the baby?" he shouted angrily, as if he weren't keeping his own secrets.

"Don't you dare yell at me and keep your voice down before Devin hears you."

"Did you purposely not take your birth control pills?"

She looked at him as if she were trying to look through him. "I might have missed taking a few. It doesn't matter if I didn't tell you about the baby. A baby wasn't going to keep you home, something or someone of more importance had your attention. You were too busy with work and

everything else you've been doing. I know you better than you know yourself. It's definite in your eyes that you don't love me the same. You don't hold me the same. I would be stupid to think it's work that has all your attention at this point—the trips out of state, never coming home, and your secretary and colleagues never knowing where you are. Sure, you may be putting in work, but it hasn't been with your book, and it sure as hell hasn't been with your wife."

"Are you accusing me of being unfaithful?"

His tone died the moment he heard Devin come out of his room.

He peeped around Bland's leg, "Are you okay, Mommy?"

"Mommy is fine, baby. Why don't you go downstairs and play, okay? Daddy and Mommy have to talk. But come here first." She grabbed him by both ears and, as always, she pulled up on them. "Mommy's little Mickey Mouse."

"No, I'm Spider-Man, Mommy," he said, then ran from the room.

She looked back at Bland. He could hear the hurt in her voice dissipate as she probed him for answers.

"Why are you doing this? Am I not enough woman? Do you need me to work? That's your son down there. He's seen you less than I have, and it doesn't seem to bother you any. What is it, Bland? What is going on? Is it me? Do you love someone else?"

"I love my wife," he responded quickly, without an admission to his guilt. "Remember, I am not doing this for me but for us. I asked if you wanted me to stop, but you said no. Ask yourself, Dakota, what happened to you? Look at you, running around smelling sheets like a crazy woman. And whenever I do get to see you," he paused, "you're moping around the house in the same old gown and with your hair out of place."

"My hair?" She was in disbelief that he could say such a thing. "I am the one who's cleaning and cooking and taking care of your son, while you're out doing who knows what and with whom."

When Bland started to walk out of the room, she grabbed him by the arm.

"No, Bland! You need to stop running every time the conversation isn't in your favor. Talk to me!"

"The doctor said it's important for the baby that you get rest."

He yanked his arm from her grasp and walked out of the bedroom.

She could hear the door to his SUV open, then close. Ironically, somehow the guilt of accusing him had laced her more than the guilt of infidelity had laced him.

17

BLAND DROVE TO A NEARBY BAR, THE CAVE. HE WASN'T there long before Lou tapped him on the shoulder.

"Don't drink too many of them or you might end up like me."

"And how is that?"

"An alcoholic."

"According to you, you're not an alcoholic."

"Well, Bland, it's like this, sometimes we can lie to everyone around us, but we can't lie to ourselves. At least I can't anymore."

"Lou, save the preaching, please. By the way, how did you know I was here?"

"Your wife, she called me all upset. Plus, this isn't your hideout. It used to be mine. Remember how many times you found me here in a drunken stupor trying to remove the pain of something?" Lou grabbed a seat at the bar beside Bland. "I'll have a soda and put it on his tab."

"You stopped drinking again?" Bland asked.

"I had a moment of weakness trying to stay sober by myself. I have to remind myself it's one meeting at a time. Bland, be honest with a friend. Does all this confusion have anything to do with that beautiful drummer?"

Bland was too ashamed to answer.

"What are you doing? I thought it was nothing, or at least controllable." Lou shook his head, then sipped his soda.

"I thought so, too, but I can't get her out of my system, Lou."

"I've known you for sixteen years. You've seen me do some dumb things, and you've given me some great advice. Well, here is sixteen years' worth of advice being repaid." He looked at Bland with a brazen face. "Many men go out looking for something they already have at home. Don't get sidetracked. Let the drummer go, Bland. I understand you care a lot about her, but you have something special waiting for you at home. Hell, I shouldn't have to tell you that; you should already know. Don't make the mistake I made. This alcohol has seduced me smoother than a woman's voice, and I've lost everything because of it. A woman is just as powerful as alcohol and even more persuasive, so don't let it lead you astray. Do the right thing."

"You're right, Lou."

"Give your wife a call."

Bland reached for his cell phone. "I have no service."

"Yeah, I have that problem in here as well. Here take these quarters; go and call your wife and apologize to her. And try doing something nice for her this weekend like bringing her to hear me play Friday night at the Winslow."

Bland rose from the stool, his mind now on a new agenda. Lou grabbed his hand. "Be nice."

Lou tapped his glass for another hit of soda. He swallowed the beverage with one quick gulp, then stood.

"Well, I have to go to the hospital to see my father."

"How's he doing?"

"Diabetes took his leg but, other than that, he's optimistic."

"Does he have insurance?"

"He's a veteran so the government takes care of its own. Actually, he's getting fitted for a prosthetic leg today."

"Send my regards and tell him I said get well because I plan on whipping him in chess."

"It's his leg that's gone, Bland, not his mind." Lou tapped Bland on his

shoulder, "So I'll see you and Dakota Friday night?"

"Yes, you will. You think you can give me a lift Friday morning and drop me off at the publishing house? That way Dakota can pick me up from the office. It will give us more time to spend together."

"No problem."

Bland headed to the pay phone to call home. Dakota sneezed and coughed into the phone as she answered. Her saddened voice touched his heart.

"Are you okay?" he asked.

"I'm tired, Bland. I don't want to argue."

"Neither do I. Dakota, I'm sorry for yelling the way I did and running out again. I'm not trying to hurt you. I never meant to hurt you. Truly, I want us to get past this."

"Bland, there is something weighing on my heart that I must ask." Dakota waited, sniffed, and then asked her question. "Bland, was there another woman in our house, in our bed?"

Dakota's shoulders slumped as she waited for his response. She made her way over to her vanity set. She sat, then turned her body to face the mirror. She didn't realize she held her breath while she waited for Bland to respond. In that breath was a prayer of hope that he hadn't violated her in such a way. If he did, she wondered if she could forgive him.

As much as Bland wanted to come forth with the truth, his knowledge of her pregnancy prevented him from disclosing it. There was no doubt in his mind that such devastating news would send her into a further tailspin of depression and despair. He didn't want to chance hurting the baby or having Dakota hurt herself.

"Dakota, there wasn't a woman. There is no other woman." There was a pause in Bland's voice. "I tell you what," said Bland. "How about dinner and going to hear Lou play Friday night?"

She turned away from the mirror as she heard Bland suggest doing something nice for her. "What about Devin?"

"Well, Friday evening, the Scotts are taking their grandson to The Pizzeria, it's a restaurant with a video arcade located inside of it. They wanted to know if Devin could attend. I figured why not. It's not too far from my office. We can drop him off. Afterwards, he'll sleep over at

their place. John said it would be good company for their grandson. Lou agreed to drop me off at work on Friday, so you and Devin can pick me up, and then we can drop Devin at The Pizzeria. How about it?"

"Just you and me, not the cell phone, not the publishing house or the book?"

"Just you and me having a great evening alone," he promised.

Friday evening, Dakota sat in front of her oval mirror, indifferent about her evening plans with Bland. Her misery could be seen on her face and in her puffy eyes. She knew that the evening could be promising, and she would have to give Bland a chance. At the same time, she didn't want to expose herself to being hurt again. No longer did she want to be a puppet on his string.

She mulled over the idea of getting back stronger and closer with her husband. She was somewhat willing to gather herself, refresh her appearance, and even muster the effort to make it all work. After all, Bland was the love of her life. She pulled out his favorite dress, her favorite shoes, and accessorized them with long patterned earrings and a diamond heart pendant. She laced her eyes with heavy eyeliner to divert attention from the bags that sagged under them. She meticulously blended her foundation to hide the discoloration and stress lines in her face. She arched her eyebrows and pulled up her hair to show off her long neck. Then, she took additional time in fine-tuning every small thing on her. She wanted to look absolutely stunning for Bland. After accessorizing herself with hope, courage, strength, and patience, she allowed them to dress her with a new confidence.

Before she knew it, she had somehow found a lost smile. Dakota felt good about herself. A ringing cell phone interrupted her solitude. She strolled over to the phone and answered with sexy sophistication. It totally confused Bland as to who he had called.

"Dakota?"

"Yes, Bland."

"You sound different."

"Are you sure it's not this new smart phone you bought me? I had the service switched over."

"Oh, so you finally opened your gift? I hope you like it."

"I love it, Bland. You really surprised me this time." Then Dakota's voice slowed as if to remind herself of something that had been lost. "I really needed this special surprise."

"I was wondering. It's been weeks since you had the phone, why didn't you say something?"

"Bland, like we've been in a good place to discuss anything?"

He chose not to incite an argument, so he went back to talking about the phone.

"That reminds me, the sales rep said for you to set up a password; otherwise, you will be butt dialing people. At least, now, someone can leave a message on the answering machine at the house."

She laughed softly, "Funny you should say that because I think my butt left a message on the answering machine."

Again, she laughed. She hoped Bland would notice her playful humor as a suggestion to move away from the negative place in which they found themselves to a more peaceful loving place.

"Wow," Bland said, as he listened to her go on about the phone and how excited she was to have it.

"I even used it to set up my own social page."

Bland's facial expression questioned, "A social page?"

The excitement spilled out of her mouth. "It's awesome. Mom and Dad can go online and look at Devin's new pictures. I can see old high school and college friends and their kids." She noticed his awkward response. "Bland, do you even know what a social page is?"

"Sure I do. And I know you had someone to help you set it up."

She roared out a long laugh. "Yeah, you're right. Sharon helped me set it up."

"Sharon, our neighbor, helped you set this up?"

"Yes."

"When did you see her?"

"Earlier today we took the boys to the park to play. I showed her my gift and she was nice enough to show me how to work the phone."

Bland chuckled, "She didn't have time to help you set up a password?"

"No, because I had to get ready for my husband."

Bland smiled, "You really sound amazing."

There was a subtle smile on her face as well. Maybe I should have fixed myself up a long time ago, she thought. She carried the soft seductive voice further, "You suppose it's not your imagination?"

"I am sure it's not that, but I am willing to see where I can take it later."

When Bland started flirting back with her, a tingle trickled down her spine. Feeling like a young woman, Dakota slid the tip of her tongue across her upper lip.

"All depends if you're trying to be a bad boy or a good boy."

"Whatever boy you need me to be."

"Well, let's wait and see if the boy is deserving of what I have to offer. I'll be there to pick you up in forty-five minutes."

"I have a meeting with the partners, but it won't be long. Instead of coming to my floor when you arrive, just go to the security desk, and someone at the desk will call and let me know that you are here. I'll come down and we can leave."

"Why not just call you on your phone as I get closer?"

"I don't have reliable phone service, so I might not get the call. This will be easier."

"You should have gotten yourself a smart phone, then you wouldn't have those problems," she ended with happy laughter.

"Well, I am a little old fashioned, so one thing at a time."

"A little old fashioned?" she laughed. "Okay, I will go to the security desk to let you know when I arrive."

Bland hung up the phone and gathered what he had of the old manuscript. He realized he hadn't given the novel any valuable attention that would please the partners; however, he did manage to write a new first chapter that centered on a new plot. He planned to give the twins the new chapter to read, but for added security, he stuffed the old manuscript in his satchel. Before he could get out of the office, his office phone rang.

"Hello," Bland answered. "Yes. Thanks for reminding me. I totally forgot. I'm coming in a minute. Did you get the balloons? Good, just wait for my cue," he said to the person on the other end of the phone.

He stood, grabbed the pages of the new first chapter and made his way to the door, and his cell phone rang. Bland sighed with frustration as he gasped before answering it.

"Yeah!"

"Hey, handsome, how is your day?"

After recognizing the voice, he softened his tone. "I've been writing. At this moment, I am about to go into a meeting."

"I don't want to hold you up. I just called to see if we're still on for tonight?"

"Tonight?" repeated Bland, puzzled.

"We made plans to take a ride to Ocean City, Maryland."

"I'm sorry, Grey," he said, remembering. He had been so wrapped up with Dakota and the idea of a new baby and the book, that he had totally shoved their plans to the back of his mind. "I have a meeting in five minutes. Can I call you after my meeting? I might have to get a rain check on our date, say tomorrow?"

Her voice grumbled with complaint. "I was looking forward to seeing you this evening. Maybe I can sneak by and see you after your meeting."

Bland panicked; he knew Dakota would be on her way to the publishing house, and he didn't need the two running into each other.

"No. I mean, I have no idea how long this meeting will last." He looked at his watch. "Frankly, I'm already late."

"Okay, okay, I don't want to pressure you. I'll just have to wait. Speaking of meetings, I'm looking at my calendar, and I have an appointment myself." Before Bland could ask, shocking words slipped out of Grey's mouth. "I love you, Mr. Benthall, and I will talk to you later."

Her comment definitely caught him by surprise. He just stood silent in the hall. Only when Paige called his name did he shake the thought. As he approached Paige's desk, Bland juggled the loose papers while trying to put away the cell phone.

"You know you're late?" she said, while she maneuvered her seat around a heater behind her desk.

"I know," he exclaimed, then noticing the heater. "Is that a propane heater?"

"I guess."

"What are you doing with that?"

"Keeping warm. It's always cold in here."

"Then tell the maintenance man to turn up the heat."

"I did, but they claim the heat in the entire building is on a seasonal timing system."

"A what?"

"The heat isn't activated to come on until the beginning of next month."

"Are you serious?" He thought it was ludicrous for such thinking, especially with the cold months already here.

"Until then, he brought me this heater," she stood to grab the mail. "Get going. You are late, and they are watching."

"I know, but I keep thinking I'm forgetting to do something."

"Is there something you need me to do while you're in the meeting?"

"As a matter of fact, there is something you can do."

"What would you like me to do, Mr. Benthall?" she chuckled before lifting her eyes from the envelopes.

"Take Monday and Tuesday off."

"Why?" she looked puzzled.

"That's my birthday present to you."

That was the cue before people came walking into the reception area. A large cake and black balloons saying OVER THE HILL were brought into the reception area. Paige, who was fully surprised, broke into tears. Bland smiled and gave her a hug.

He handed her a white envelope, then whispered in her ear, "Now you and your fiancé can enjoy Carlylés."

She screamed with excitement, "Thank you, Mr. Benthall." Her cheeks were slightly reddened. She went on thanking them all.

"You all," she cried, "got me!"

Bland looked up at the lobby camera. He was seriously late. He almost forgot. In a whisper, "Paige, my wife is on her way to pick me up. She's going to call from downstairs. Please send me a text when she arrives."

"Are you sure? I know it's hard for you to get text messages on that phone."

"If I don't respond then have a good reason for coming to get me."

"Your wife isn't a good enough reason?"

"Not according to them. It appears that only the book has that much power."

Bland backed away from the desk. He pivoted on his heels and moved toward the elevator.

Jane put the book down to rest her eyes. She considered how fortunate she was not to be Grey or Dakota. She offered Bland no compassion for the mess in which he'd gotten himself involved. What did he expect? she thought. Surely, they will find out about each other, she hoped.

The door squeaked, as Constance stuck her head in the room.

"Tell me, what's going on in the book?" Constance eyed the book on the bed. By this time, Constance had fully entered the room. "I'm sure you've been reading this morning."

Jane smiled, "I thought you didn't want me to tell you."

"Well, tell me if it's worth reading."

"So far so good," her voiced cracked, then she coughed through her unexpected laugh. "Started out slow, but it's gotten better. This man is truly caught between deceptions."

"Um, sounds like a typical man to me." They both fell into laughter.

"And he's real cunning, too. He—"

Abruptly, Constance interrupted, "Don't tell me because I plan on reading it."

"Next time don't ask me!"

Constance began with her daily duties of unwrapping the bandages. Slowly, she sponged warm water around Jane's face followed with some cocoa butter.

Jane moved in closer to whisper, "Connie, let me take a peek."

"No!" Constance said firmly, without stopping her circular rotation of applying cocoa butter.

"When do you think the doctor is going to let me see my face?"

"Jane, why do we go through this every time I take off your bandages?"

Jane didn't respond. Without warning, Dr. Stewart entered the room

and went about his normal routine. He flashed his small light in her mouth.

"Open wider and say, 'ah.' Okay. That's enough."

He then typed on the medical tablet his observations of her throat and the readings from the blood pressure machine.

"Is everything okay?" inquired Jane, after he finished looking down her throat. "Are you sure there is nothing I can do that will make my voice sound softer?"

"There's a chance it will sound softer. That's if you quit all the excessive talking you've been doing lately. I think I liked it better when you couldn't say a word." He laughed. "But there's also a chance your voice may never sound like it did. Like I said before, time is the only determinate, so continue to talk less and continue to read more. Now try being quiet so I can check the grafts and stitches."

Jane sat with apprehension as the doctor slowly scanned over her face. She fidgeted until Dr. Stewart became impatient.

"Jane, please."

"If that's really my name," she scornfully remarked.

"Well, it's the name your surrogate mother gave you," he said, glancing over at Constance.

Jane growled, "Thanks for the name, Mother."

Constance chuckled, "You're welcome."

Dr. Stewart continued with his observation of her hands, legs, back, and face. He made a few "uh-huhs," before telling Constance to redress the wounds.

Jane sat quietly until her curiosity compelled her to ask. "So what's the verdict, Dr. Stewart?"

"The donor skin is healing and so are the grafts. Everything continues to look good, and the swelling is gradually coming down in your face."

"So that means I can take them off, right?" she softly asked, not wanting to upset him.

"We're close to taking them off, Jane."

That wasn't the answer Jane expected.

"That's what you said weeks ago," she snapped.

He laughed only to reply, "And, we're a few weeks closer than we

were before. Now wouldn't you say that's progress?"

She sighed while her eyes showed frustration. "You don't want to know what I'd call it." The doctor didn't respond, so Jane tried to provoke him again. "Why did you send me to that psychiatrist? It didn't help."

"Dr. Westfall said the session went very well. You disclosed some very interesting things that may help in finding those answers you are seeking. Also, the ones I am seeking."

She exploded, "Why didn't Dr. Westfall share with me more details about the dreams?"

Dr. Stewart gave her a stern look. "Listen, Jane," he paused from inspecting her face to peer into her eyes. "We all want answers, but sometimes we don't know where to go to learn those answers. Dr. Westfall is trying to help you find that place, and neither she nor I will jeopardize your health in getting them any sooner. Okay?"

Briefly, they both went silent.

The doctor turned to leave. "Nurse, I'm done here so we can finish making our rounds."

With Dr. Stewart's back turned, Constance mouthed silently at Jane, "I told you."

Jane shrugged her shoulders.

Constance followed Dr. Stewart out of the room, momentarily peeking back over her shoulder and seeing Jane angrily grab the novel.

18

THE DOOR TO THE EXAMINING ROOM OPENED, A NURSE led Grey to the exam table.

"I am going to need a urine sample. You'll find the cups in the bathroom." She pointed to the restroom that was inside the examining room. "I'll return in a moment with the doctor."

Grey laid the thin hospital gown that was given to her across the back of a chair before heading into the bathroom. Minutes later, the door to the bathroom opened, and Grey walked to the center of the room.

As she undressed, her thoughts would address years of being vulnerable to the physical pain of severe cramps and bleeding and the emotional suffering of not being able to bear children. Though her body was bare, her soul was also exposed: she no longer wanted to be imprisoned by the disease of endometriosis. Grey put on the gown, then sat on the edge of the exam table contemplating her price for freedom.

The door opened and the doctor entered with a medical tablet and two nurses.

One of the nurses took the urine sample out of the bathroom and exited the room, while the other nurse stood to the side of the doctor.

"Hello. Ms. Greysen Brindle. I am Dr. Ford." Dr. Ford pulled a stool

to the front of the examining table. She looked at her medical tablet and read off the information that had been typed into the computer by the registration nurse. "You are here to get your annual gynecologic exam. It also notes that you've been experiencing back pains."

"Yes, I have."

"When is the last time you had a cervical exam?"

"It's been over a year."

The doctor studied the information on the tablet, then looked at Grey.

"You suffer from endometriosis. Have you had a long history of the disease?"

"Since my early twenties."

"I'm going to need your medical records from your previous doctor."

"I can get you that information."

"Have you been experiencing excessive bleeding?"

"Somewhat, but that also could be credited to my heavy menstrual. That is, when I have them."

"Are you experiencing a lot of pain?"

"Yes," she replied, "for years. Frankly, doctor, I am tired of the pain."

"There are options to deal with the pain caused by endometriosis. I see you've tried other options to reduce your pain. Have you entertained hysterectomy surgery? It is the most extreme option."

Grey's eyes darted to the floor, then back on the doctor, "I have."

Dr. Ford waited for her to continue, but when Grey didn't, she drew her own assumptions.

"I see that you disclosed you had a ruptured ectopic pregnancy and a pre-term birth. I will be honest with you, Ms. Brindle."

"Please, call me Greysen."

"Greysen, the likelihood of infertility is greater as the disease progresses. Because you have experienced an ectopic pregnancy and had previous tubal surgeries, you are at a higher risk for ectopic. Also, as you get older, your risk of miscarriage increases. I don't mean to discourage you, but you are a high-risk patient. If you are putting off a hysterectomy to consider childbirth, I will have to refer you to a reproductive endocrinologist who can recommend options such as

drug therapy to improve your chances of conceiving."

Her eyes settled on the doctor. "Dr. Ford, I am familiar with a lot of procedures and therapies." She paused, then continued, "I have endured numerous surgeries; I have done natural therapies to help balance my estrogen, and I have taken all types of medication to deal with the pain of trying to conceive. Because I believed that having a child would complete me as a woman, I have refused the option of removing my uterus. Up until recently, I would have continued to deal with the pain."

Dr. Ford interrupted with a question, "So what has changed your mind?"

"Someone special has shown me there is more to life even when you can't bear children."

"Have you and your partner considered in vitro fertilization." The doctor went on to explain, "IVF is a process where we take one of your eggs to be fertilized outside of your body. Then later, the egg will be implanted into your uterus or a surrogate's uterus. Both methods have become popular options these days for those wanting children."

Grey didn't respond.

Understanding, the doctor shook her head. "Okay, but first things first. Today, I want to administer the pap test in order to retrieve a sample of cells," she said and continued, "I also want to do a bimanual examination to get a feel for the size of your uterus and the size of your ovaries. After everything is completed, then we can discuss all the options that are available to you, including IVF, before we make any major decisions." The doctor smiled, then she stood from the stool. She handed the tablet to the nurse before moving toward the sink to wash her hands and put on a pair of latex gloves.

"Greysen, I'm going to need you to put your feet into the stirrups."

After the nurse assisted Grey with the stirrups, she slowly laid her back on the table. To conceal herself, the nurse allowed Grey's gown to fall between her legs until the doctor was ready to perform the exam.

During the bimanual exam, Dr. Ford took one hand and checked Grey's cervix. The other hand was placed over her abdomen. When Grey grimaced, the doctor's eyes suddenly looked to Grey.

"You felt that?"

"Yes."

"Has the pain always resonated in the abdomen area?"

"No, in my back also."

"Does it hurt when you urinate? You could have a bladder infection."

"Yes, it does."

"Have you seen any blood in your urine?" Dr. Ford asked, as she went back to examining Grey's cervix and abdomen. Abruptly, the doctor pulled away from Grey. The gown dropped down between her legs.

"I thought it was due to the endometriosis."

The doctor looked over to the nurse. "Have we gotten the results of her urine test?"

"It should be ready," said the nurse.

There was a knock on the door of the examination room, and another nurse entered with a folder. Immediately, the nurse in the room moved to the door to take the folder. Dr. Ford stood, then removed her gloves and washed her hands before taking the folder.

The nurse helped Grey remove her feet from the stirrups and then helped her sit up.

Dr. Ford studied the results of the test.

"Okay," said the doctor, without any expression on her face. She walked over to the bed to speak with Grey. "Greysen, the nurse is going to draw your blood. I want to run a few more tests on you."

Determined to be 100 percent free from physical pain and mental anguish, Grey took a deep breath and prepared herself for the inevitable.

"Doctor, I understand what you're doing, and I am thankful. I have come to grips that I will not have children, so we don't need to prolong the surgery with more tests. How soon can I have the hysterectomy?"

"Greysen, I don't think you understand."

"Is something wrong, doctor?"

"I guess you can say that, but first I want to get a blood test to measure HCG levels." She noticed Grey's blank stare. "It's a substance produced during pregnancy."

Grey frowned, "What?"

—

"WHAT!" Jane's head lifted from the book in slow motion. She was in a state of shock. "Is she pregnant?" Then quickly her eyes descended back to the novel.

—

Grey's eyes showed her confusion. "Pregnancy" she repeated with shock. "I can't be pregnant. Me? Are you sure?" she asked, while only believing bits and pieces of what the doctor said. "But I've been having my period."

"Yes, Greysen, I am serious. After my examination, I'm thinking you are further along in your pregnancy than I first thought. I've ordered a 3-D vaginal uterus scan to determine your baby's gestation. Since you're experiencing bleeding, the ultrasound will also help to determine the cause of the bleeding."

For a moment, Grey went speechless, "Doctor, I don't know whether to be excited or scared."

"It's best you stay practical, Greysen. Excessive bleeding can become serious and pose a risk to you and your baby. First, let's get some blood work, and get an ultrasound, then we'll know where we stand. A nurse will be in to draw your blood." Dr. Ford said, as she walked to the door.

"Dr. Ford, thank you," Grey said, displaying a bright smile.

Dr. Ford smiled back, "Get dressed. After your blood has been drawn, a nurse will take you to the ultrasound room."

Bland watched Smith pour himself a drink before glancing out the large window of the study. He noticed the gray sky and treetops beginning to sway from the force of the wind.

Wilkins rocked back in the large leather seat and puffed smoke circles toward the ceiling. The leather cracked as he occasionally turned right to left listening to Smith offer his opinions about the manuscript.

"I like what I'm reading, Bland. I even like the fact that you started from scratch. This new first chapter has all the mesmerizing elements to a great story—deceit, love, pain and misery."

Bland interrupted, "All of that and more. Let's just say that I took your advice."

"So, when can I read the rest of it?" Smith asked.

"Not until the deadline," Bland answered.

"You're willing to risk everything on this one submission?" Wilkins snorted. "You do remember our response to the last draft? If you had waited and submitted that at the deadline, we would have rejected it. And you would have lost everything." Once again, he wanted to make Bland aware of what was at stake.

"It's to your benefit, Bland, to let us read it now," acknowledged Smith. "If it goes off track, we can help bring it back."

Bland realized the men were cynical that he had more than one chapter finished of the new book, so to get their attention Bland pulled from his satchel the old manuscript. Immediately, Wilkins sat up in the chair.

Bland smiled, "I'll take my chances."

"Is that the finished draft?"

"All of it, except for the final chapter," Bland lied, feeling relief that he brought the manuscript along.

Slowly, the large frame of Wilkins resettled into the seat. He sighed and continued to puff on the cigar. Smith went to grab the manuscript, but Bland pulled the book from his reach.

"Remember, a book for a partnership. But not until the deadline will you get this."

Smith smiled and pulled back his hand. "You're playing hardball? Okay, that was the original deal, but—"

Wilkins blurted, "Contingent that you deliver a bestseller. We can trust you will keep your word?"

"We have a contract, Bland. Plus, the numbers won't lie. The sales will determine if it's a bestseller, not us," Smith stated.

"You don't have to sound so dramatic," Bland replied, as he settled deeper into the cushions of the seat, listening to the twins negotiate a read. Bland smiled and stole a peek at the clock on the wall. Dakota should be on her way, he thought.

Meanwhile, Dakota was snapping Devin into his booster seat. Once in the car, she checked her lipstick in the rearview mirror. She looked

beautiful, and Devin gave her confirmation in syllables.

"Mommy, you are beau-ti-ful."

"Thank you, baby."

She tried starting the cold car, but the starter began scratching. Again, she turned the switch, but this time with more force as if that should make the difference. After several tries, the car's motor turned over, and Devin screamed with joy. The motor shook, and the engine started to stall before catching a constant idle.

"You did it, Mommy! You're super, Mommy!"

She played along with him. "Able to start a car," she turned around to look at him, "and able to tickle a stomach with the blink of an eye and drive backwards." She put the car in reverse.

As Dakota's eyes peered into the rearview mirror at Devin's face, unbeknownst to her, Grey lay on the ultrasound table watching the monitor for an image of the fetus.

Dr. Ford watched as the tech maneuvered the transducer within Grey's abdomen until the image appeared on the monitor. A nurse turned the volume up on the ultrasound machine, so Grey could hear the baby's heartbeat, while the tech took the necessary measurement. Immediately, Grey became emotional. The entire situation was so surreal that she couldn't help but both laugh and cry. The tech printed out a few of the three-dimensional images for Grey to take with her. After the doctor reviewed the images, measurements, and readings from the machine, she settled Grey down for a serious discussion about the fetus and the pregnancy.

"Greysen, I've determined that you're nearing the end of your second trimester. Normally, a fetus in its second trimester is further developed, but your baby is SGA." Given the expression on Grey's face, the doctor went into a detailed explanation. "What I mean is your baby is unusually small for its gestational age. An underdeveloped fetus can develop many medical problems. For this reason, the amount of time a baby can spend in the womb will largely determine the types and severities of problems that it has at birth and beyond. Again, this can be very dangerous to you and the baby."

Grey listened attentively because she absolutely wanted to give the

baby a chance to survive, even if it meant her dying.

"It's important that you know the risk involved. I'm referring you to Dr. Dows, who is a perinatologist. He is the best high-risk doctor on the East Coast. I'll have the nurse call his office and set up an appointment for next week."

Dr. Ford could tell Grey's mind was preoccupied.

"Grey," she called.

Grey continuously looked at the images printed from the ultrasound machine. She reached for her purse to retrieve her cell phone, then realized she left it in the car.

"Dr. Ford, is there a phone I can use? I really want to call my boyfriend to tell him the good news."

She smiled, "I understand, but you can't dial out on these phones. Here, use my cell. We'll step out to give you some privacy."

She called Bland's cell phone, but there was no answer. She thought and then remembered he was in a meeting, so she attempted to call his office phone to find out how long the meeting would last. She didn't want to leave a message on his voicemail, so she hit the zero prompt for the operator. She needed to speak with a live person.

Paige answered. "S&W Publishing House, Editorial Department."

There was a tremendous amount of noise in the background, which made it difficult for Paige to hear.

"You want to speak to whom?" Paige yelled back into the receiver. "Oh, Mr. Benthall, I'm sorry but he's tied up for at least another forty minutes." Then the phone clicked. And all Grey heard was the dial tone. She sat quietly thinking how excited Bland would be. As a matter of fact, what was she thinking to tell him such news over the phone. Quickly, she dressed herself and drove to the publishing house.

The two women arrived at the publishing house a few minutes apart. Dakota parked her car in the parking garage across from the firm, and Grey parked on the street. Maybe it was the timing or where they parked that placed the two women in the lobby at the exact same moment. Dakota was close to the phone, and she had already been given instructions from Bland on what to do when she arrived at the

publishing house. Yet, she abandoned all of that when a mannequin in a boutique window caught her eye. The female mannequin wore soft pink slippers with matching lace lingerie.

Grey caught a glimpse of Dakota as Dakota walked past the security desk. Instead of placing the call, Dakota sauntered over to the boutique with Devin holding her hand.

Grey approached the security desk. Unknowingly, she would perform Dakota's instructions with perfection, and Paige, who thought it was Dakota, gave the reply that she would call Mr. Benthall, so he could leave his meeting and meet her in the lobby.

By this time, Dakota stood in front of the long mirror with the lingerie against her beautiful dress. She couldn't help but think this was the final piece to cap the evening. She felt a wave of energy come over her as she modeled in her mind how the piece of lingerie would look on her bare skin. She stared into that mirror as if seeing someone she'd never seen before. What she saw not only caught her attention, but it caught the attention of Grey, who watched Dakota from the security desk. To make use of the time until Bland arrived, Grey decided to visit the boutique.

Dakota became lost in her thoughts while she contemplated purchasing the lingerie.

"That will look so pretty on you," a voice said.

The comment pulled Dakota from her thoughts as she looked away from the mirror to settle her eyes on the stranger.

"Excuse me," Dakota answered with slight concern. She searched through her mind where she had met the woman. Dakota's nose twitched when it caught a familiar scent.

Respectfully, Grey continued, "I'm sorry, but you don't know me. I just happened to see you over here modeling that beautiful lingerie. It's gorgeous."

"I don't know if the color suits me."

"This color will look great on you," Grey admitted.

"A few months from now I won't be able to fit in this. My husband would say money going down the drain," Dakota confessed.

"We're about the same size and same frame. I purchased the exact

piece when I was last here, and I must say my man loves it on me and taking it off me," Grey laughed as Dakota offered an uncomfortable sigh.

"Hmm," replied Dakota. Given the stranger's candid response, Dakota's eyes returned momentarily to the mirror to give the lingerie one last consideration.

"Of course you will be able to wear this unless you were—" Grey stopped midsentence to scrutinize Dakota in the mirror. She broke out in a rather wide smile then asked, "I might be mistaken, but are you expecting?"

Dakota smiled with surprise, then replied, "Why, yes, I am expecting."

"Congratulations."

"Thank you." She looked at the stranger with a peculiar stare before asking, "How did you know?"

"At first, it was something you said. Then I looked at the contour of your body."

"You can tell all that just by looking at my frame?" Dakota's eyes dropped to her abdomen. "I can hardly tell myself."

"My doctor showed me how." Already overjoyed by her news, Grey began to use herself as an example. She opened her jacket and pulled her blouse down straight. "Now look."

A confused Dakota asked, "What am I looking for?" Then she grinned, "I see it. It's in the hips and in the midline. Wow."

"Is this your first child?" Grey asked.

"This will be my second." Her head whipped around the boutique. "My son is somewhere around here."

"Are you throwing in the towel after this one?"

"If I had my way, I would have four or five, but my husband is content with one." She looked at her stomach, "Well, soon to be two." Her head whipped around the room again in search of Devin, then back to Grey. "How about you? Your first?"

Grey smiled as she rubbed her stomach. "After years of complications and losing a baby, this will finally be my first, which is the reason for my excitement."

"Well, congratulations," smiled Dakota.

Grey went on to introduce herself. Dakota sensed how strange it was

that this woman felt comfortable discussing her personal business with her. At least more than what Dakota felt discussing with Grey.

“My name is Greysen, but my friends call me Grey.”

“What an interesting name. Well hello, Grey, it is a pleasure to meet you. My name is Dakota.”

“Your name is so strong.”

Dakota extended her neck to see over the clothes racks. She wanted to keep an eye on Devin.

“Well, thank you,” she said without taking her eyes off Devin.

“How did you acquire your name? Let me guess, you were born in North or South Dakota,” Grey smiled.

“No, I wasn’t. My father had a horse named Dakota. According to him the animal was so beautiful, but unexpectedly the horse died from some complications. Then I came along, and I inherited the name Dakota.”

Grey chuckled.

“It seems we both acquired our names from our fathers.”

“How funny,” laughed Dakota. “So, how many months are you?” Dakota asked as a way of extending polite conversation.

“I found out today that I am near the end of my second trimester.” Given her size, Grey saw the unbelieving stare Dakota wore on her face. She blurted before Dakota could ask. “I know I’m small, too. I have some personal issues going on,” she bashfully grinned. “That made it more difficult to detect that I was even pregnant.”

Quickly, Dakota thought, you and me both.

“That’s enough about me, so how about you?” She didn’t give Dakota time to respond before saying to her, “I would say you look to be three, maybe four months.”

“You would think, but no, I am also around six months.”

“What a coincidence,” Grey said excitedly, “the two of us being in the same stage.”

“Yes, what a coincidence,” Dakota said with a slight smile, while Grey’s smile beamed as she thought about Bland. “You have such a vibrant glow about you.”

“Thank you.”

"Do you know the sex of the baby?" Dakota asked, while steadily keeping her eye on Devin.

"No, but I don't care if it's a boy or girl. I just want the baby to be healthy."

"Have you considered any names?"

Grey smiled, "If it's a girl she would be named after me. If it's a boy, I would name him Grayden. Of course, the boy's name may change when my significant other finds out."

"Oh, he doesn't know?" Dakota asked.

"I plan on telling him today. I am so excited. I just can't wait to tell him. He is so wonderful, compassionate, and sensitive, yet strong. I get so excited thinking about him."

"Grayden? That's a nice name, and your significant other sounds like a wonderful man," Dakota said, but also thinking at one point that Bland had similar characteristics. "Where did you meet?"

"It is funny because we met years ago, but it's also amazing how fate can bring people back together. Surely he's my soul mate."

"That's so beautiful that you feel that way," Dakota smiled.

Grey happened to notice the sudden sad expression on Dakota's face. Dakota gave a look that signified she once knew that feeling, but all she felt lately was emptiness. Nonetheless, Grey's excitement was contagious. Maybe that was the reason for their meeting, Dakota thought. Soon Dakota's cheeks lifted, and she smiled with a sense of rebirth.

"You have a beautiful smile," Grey acknowledged. "Don't let it disappear."

"Thank you," Dakota replied, as her sense of smell drew keener to identify the familiar scent the woman wore. "While we have been talking, I have tried to remember where I have smelled that fragrance you are wearing."

"It's a bath gel. It was a warming gift given to me. You like it?"

"It's a very unique fragrance."

Suddenly, Grey had an idea. She reached for her purse, which was hanging off her shoulder. While Grey searched through her purse, Dakota took a few more sniffs before she scanned in Devin's direction.

Grey found what she was looking for, and then she swung her purse

back over her shoulder.

"This is my business card. My address and my number are on the card. I haven't been living here long, so I don't know many people. Anyway, if you want to get together sometime, maybe we can go shopping for baby stuff or perfumes."

Dakota thought the gesture was nice, but a little overzealous. Never had she been approached in such a manner. She laughed to herself as she looked over the information on the card.

Dakota lifted her head. "Yes, we should get together. That would be very nice." Dakota noticed Grey's locket as she responded. "That's pretty."

"Thank you."

Then Grey's eyes settled on something more extravagant. "Wow! You really have someone who loves you." Grey marveled at the five-carat, princess-cut diamond and sapphire ring on Dakota's finger.

Dakota modestly glanced at the wedding ring Bland had given her and gave a wry smile. Then she looked back at Grey. For the moment, the two women stared into the other's eyes in silence.

Bland kept looking at the clock on the wall and wondering why Paige hadn't texted him. Given the time, he was sure Dakota had arrived. When his phone did vibrate, Bland glanced at the text. It read, "Time to go." Finally, he thought. Right away, Bland tried to rush the conversation.

"Well, gentlemen, we can sit here and talk until the deadline, but then the final chapter will not get written." He turned to Wilkins, "So I must depart so I can secure my junior partnership."

Smith smiled, "That's the attitude, Bland. Yes, you do that."

In the few times he visited the penthouse, this was the first time he was not escorted to the elevator. Once the elevator door closed, Bland laughed that his plan worked. He held the old manuscript with its new cover page and new title in his hand. It got the partners off his back and bought him more time to figure out what he was planning on doing about the book.

When he walked off the elevator, he had to dodge balloons on the way to his office.

Paige stopped him the moment she saw it was him.

"What happened to you texting me back? I was about to head up to rescue you."

"Honestly, I was so anxious to get out of there I forgot."

After Bland's explanation, Paige informed him that his wife called and was downstairs waiting.

"Thanks, Paige."

He rushed into his office to collect his things. Once in his office he heard a knock on the door. He assumed it was Paige rushing him to not keep Dakota waiting any longer than he already had.

"Paige, I'm coming," he said with his body bent over his desk.

"I'm sorry, Bland, but Paige isn't enough woman to fill this body." Penelope batted a few of the balloons out of her way before moving her voluptuous frame into the doorway.

Bland swung his head around in her direction. "Penelope. I was just thinking about you."

"Sure you were, and what about because I haven't heard from you?"

"I know it's been some time since we last talked. But did you find anything out of the ordinary?"

"You're looking at her," she smiled.

"Well, anything other than yourself?"

She laughed heavily, "Bland, you're so funny? Where have you been?" she inquired while standing in his doorway with one hand on her hip and a slip of paper in the other hand.

"I've been around for weeks, and I've been looking for you," replied Bland.

"I hope you were looking to pay your debt and stop avoiding me." She paused, "Looking for me," she repeated again. "Mr. Bland Benthall, you know where to find me."

"Now what makes you think that I have been avoiding you?"

"Because I haven't seen you, and like I said, you have an outstanding debt."

Bland had forgotten the debt. Either way, Penelope had never said what he would owe for the additional information.

"Anyway, I came up to say happy birthday to Paige when I saw Mr.

Good Looking back here. Oh!" Something came to her mind suddenly, "I went through the scanned files, and I noticed some paperwork was out of place."

Bland uttered, "Well, that is out of the ordinary given how organized you guys are in that department. What type of paperwork?"

"Several recent invoices, Bland, but why worry yourself over it. Maybe an intern mixed up the paperwork when scanning into the computer, but I am going to look into it."

"Maybe you're right," Bland agreed.

"I am always right. Now, how about paying your debt?"

Bland looked past Penelope to the clock on the wall. "I have to meet my wife downstairs."

Bland headed to the elevator as Penelope whispered, "Excuses, excuses."

"Are you going down?" he asked, just as the elevator opened.

Penelope pulled at the string of another floating balloon. Aloud, she read the script on the balloon, "Over the hill, is she?"

With a slight smirk, she gawked, "Yes, I'm going down." There was a bitter sweetness to her voice.

"This is my floor. You're getting off?" Bland asked.

"I'm headed to the parking garage, Bland."

"Well, have a good weekend, Penelope."

The lobby was extremely busy with people scurrying in and out of shops. Bland dodged people as he walked toward the security desk. Dakota wasn't in sight. He flashed a smile at the security guard, whom he had never seen before. Nonetheless, Bland was happy to see another face with security.

He scanned various parents and their children, but still he couldn't spot his family. He turned and bumped against a few people. After a time of standing and looking, he became perturbed. Bland pulled out his phone to call Dakota but then stopped. He reminded himself that she had been waiting for him for nearly a half hour. He calmed himself and slowly looked through the horde of people. He turned toward the food court, thinking Devin might have been hungry. Then he saw Devin

crawling across the entrance floor of the lingerie boutique. He smiled because he should have known. Dakota loved sexy undergarments. As he walked to the boutique, a feeling of anticipation came over him. He was honestly looking forward to their evening together.

In the meantime, Dakota and Grey were laughing. Each gave the impression of enjoying the other's company.

Grey felt the lingerie that lay over Dakota's arm. "By the way, that is a stunning dress you are wearing," Grey admitted.

"My husband and I are having a date night."

"Ah, that is so wonderful. And you look so beautiful."

"Thank you."

"Someone is going to have some fun tonight. Hopefully, the lingerie will extend the date," Grey's eyebrows raised.

"Well, I know I can't get pregnant," Dakota giggled.

Grey joined with equal laughter. The two of them were unaware they touched hands like two women who've been friends for years.

Dakota, in the midst of her laughing, looked at the time. There was a realization that she had yet to notify Bland that she was there.

Her laughter faded. "I'm sorry, but I have to be going. The time has sneaked up on me. I've been here enjoying myself so much I totally forgot to tell my husband I had arrived. I will be sure to give you a call."

"It was a pleasure meeting you," Grey smiled.

"The pleasure was mine," countered Dakota.

While the two shook hands, Bland strolled into the boutique. He spotted Dakota in the far corner of the store, but she had yet to spot him. Bland stood there for a moment looking at her hand gestures and thinking how stunning she truly was. Wow, she's breathtaking, he thought. Where did he lose sight of her? He started thinking of what it was about Grey that could have him contemplating leaving the most caring woman he had ever known.

In Bland's immediate vicinity, he didn't notice the back of Grey's head. Maybe he was too busy daydreaming about his wife.

Dakota peered over Grey's shoulder and saw Bland. Her eyes smiled as he approached. When he was right upon Grey, Grey saw the

heightened expression and gleam in Dakota's eyes. She turned and fixed her eyes on Bland. In a split second, Bland went from smiling to blank face. He had no idea what to say because he had no idea what was said between the two women.

Both women wheeled through their minds what they wanted to say to him. Dakota thought about asking his opinion concerning the color of the lingerie, while Grey considered announcing that Bland was about to be a father. Neither, however, would receive the opportunity.

When Devin tugged on his father's jacket and called, "Daddy, Daddy," all eyes shifted to Devin.

Bland quickly looked down, then he turned his attention back to Grey whose smile disappeared from the sudden shock. Dakota didn't witness the sudden change of expression on Grey's face because Grey had turned to face Bland and Devin. Bland's eyes roamed back over to his wife, who gave a formal introduction.

"I'm sorry," Dakota paused to get her name correct. "Greysen, this is my husband, Bland, and my very rambunctious son."

Instantly there was sorrow in Grey's soul. It was like someone had kicked her in the stomach, and all her breath escaped at once. Grey gave Bland a long incredulous stare and momentarily squeezed back the pain and tears that wanted to gush out like a broken faucet. She couldn't decide whether to hit him, run out crying, or stand with dignity. She managed to maintain her composure and chose the latter.

It took every ounce of strength that Grey had to take her eyes off of Bland and place them back on Devin.

She squatted to Devin's level, "Hello there, young man and what's your name?"

"Devin," he answered bashfully.

"That's such a nice name, and you're so cute," she said, while holding back the tears. Quickly, she stood. She felt foolish not to have known and to have fallen twice to betrayal.

She purposely faced Dakota. Bland became anxious, wondering what she was going to say to Dakota. Though Grey was furious, heartbroken, and torn, the look on Dakota's innocent face made her wonder what it would benefit her to destroy Dakota and have both their insides culled out. For that reason, she abandoned a solemn pledge amongst women to

divulge when one's husband or partner was unfaithful.

She looked at Dakota and gently said, "Again, it was nice meeting you." She could barely look at Dakota for fear the tears would uncontrollably come and Dakota would know about her and her husband without Grey saying a word. She drew in her breath, turned, and gave Bland one last disdainful stare.

In that moment, Grey's expression told Bland everything she was feeling. He knew she was floored by this discovery. As soon as Grey exited the boutique, Bland probed about the familiar stranger. It was his way of determining what exactly transpired between the two.

"We're running late, and we have to drop Devin off with the Scotts. By the way, who was that woman?" Bland cautiously asked.

"I don't know. I just met her, but she was very pleasant."

"How did the two of you meet?"

"She approached me." Dakota paused with a faint laugh. "It's kind of funny."

Thinking the worst, Bland quickly inquired, "Funny as in?"

"She just walked up to me and said congratulations. She had been watching me from a distance. From the contour of my body and the way I favored certain movements she could tell I was pregnant."

"You told a stranger you were pregnant?"

"She told me I was pregnant, Bland. Plus, I didn't see the harm in that."

Dakota was about to tell Bland that the stranger revealed her own pregnancy but stopped when she spotted Devin outside the entrance of the boutique. She bolted past Bland to catch Devin before he ran off again.

—

Jane momentarily looked away from the book only to shake her head. Her disposition was one of anger as she uttered lightly, "I wish you would have been exposed as a two-timing snake."

—

19

When they arrived at the restaurant, Lou was waiting at a table for his guests. Like a gentleman, he took Dakota's coat and politely pulled out a chair for her.

"Wow! You look marvelous, Dakota." He looked at Bland, "You don't look bad yourself, buddy. Thanks for coming, guys. Dinner and drinks are on me tonight."

"We wouldn't have missed this for anything," smiled Bland, as he waited for Dakota to sit before taking his seat. Bland took a passing glance around the restaurant. "This is nice."

"Tell me about it. If I play well, who knows, this might become a regular gig."

"That's great, Louis," congratulated Dakota.

Lou glimpsed at his watch, "I have to go; bills need to be paid."

During dinner, Bland wondered what transpired hours earlier between his wife and Grey, but he thought if he kept asking questions, it would invite a level of suspicion. He tried hard to keep his mind off it and on the soft sounds of the saxophone, which had Dakota wrapped in the moment. It had been some time since she and Bland escaped to hear

Lou play. It had been even longer since the two of them had a beautiful, peaceful evening together. Occasionally, they gazed into the other's eyes as they listened to Lou play. Lou surprised Bland by playing his favorite jazz song. Instantly, the song took Bland back to the night of the train ride where he first heard the song playing from the old train station's speaker. That fast, his mind had drifted off to Grey and what she must be feeling.

As they ate, he noticed Dakota truly engaged in the moment. She inched her hand across the soft cotton tablecloth to clutch his fingers.

"Honey, have you decided if we're going south for Thanksgiving?"

Suddenly he remembered Margie's call concerning Thanksgiving. And he elected not to tell Dakota that she called.

"I've been giving so much attention to the book that I haven't given much thought to going." He looked at her face and knew it might not be a bad idea to go. "That's a few weeks from now. I'll have to finish up a few loose ends, so I don't see why not. Plus, I would hate for your dad to have to fly here. I would end up owing him another favor."

Her eyes lit up. With every slight breeze, the oil lamp flickered glimmers of light across her face. Dakota sat under the dim romantic light of the restaurant, scripting how she planned to seduce this handsome man sitting across from her. Bland tried to show some attention, but each time he glanced into Dakota's radiant eyes, he only thought about Grey and the candle lit dinner they enjoyed by the Potomac.

Nothing seemed to be working for him. On the one hand, he loved his wife and wanted to recover the fervor of their once true love. On the other hand, he fed off of Grey's presence and her zeal for life. Eventually, despite such a perfect evening, Dakota noticed his mind wandering. There seemed to be nothing she could do to hold his attention. By the end of dinner, Bland had barely touched his food. Toward the end of Lou's first set, Bland was desperate to leave.

"What's wrong, Bland?" she asked, while attempting to grab his hand again. "It's like you're lost in your mind."

He leaned forward into the misty light to whisper in her ear.

"I'm so ready for this book to be complete. That's all. I'm just thinking how I can improve the story. I apologize if I am ruining the evening."

"The evening is perfect, Bland." She caught his eyes before asking, "Can we go back to the way it used to be?"

Her eyes could only hold his for a second before guilt compelled him to glance away. Her gut instinct warned her there was more that Bland wasn't letting her know. By his blank stares and rushed movements, she could tell something was agitating him.

The waiter came to the table to present the dessert menu. "Did you leave room for something sweet?" asked the waiter.

"No, thank you," Bland waved.

Dakota gave a suspicious stare. When the waiter walked away, Bland leaned over the table again. "Are you ready?"

"Bland, why are you in such a rush to leave? We have the evening to ourselves. And we came to hear Louis play."

"Yes, we did."

Lou came by the table at the end of his first set to check on his guests.

"Are you two okay?"

"Wonderful," Dakota said, with a satisfying smile.

"How is the food?"

"Very good," replied Bland.

"You should try the Chardonnay, Dakota; it is excellent. If I can't drink, I can at least tell someone else about it. By the way, what are your plans for Thanksgiving? I want to invite you to a gig that night."

"We made plans to visit my parents."

"Okay, I guess you're not going to make the gig," Lou laughed. "It's fine though. Have a great time with the parents."

Lou noticed Bland's agitation and how Dakota's smile had all but disappeared. "What's wrong, Bland?"

"We're going to call it a night, Lou. I have a long day tomorrow, and the deadline for the book is only a few weeks away."

"Bland, tomorrow is Saturday. Surely you can rest for one day."

"I wish I could," he said, as he pushed away from the table. He grabbed Dakota's hand.

"Anyway, thanks for coming." Lou kissed Dakota on the cheek and escorted them to the front door of the restaurant.

"I'll call you, Bland."

The ride home was devoted to listening to the sounds emitted from the windshield wipers removing a mixture of rain and snow. As Dakota sat in silence, she wondered what happened to make the evening turn sour so quickly. Thoughts zigzagged across her mind like the snowflakes over the windshield of the car. As the snow came down more heavily, only to be scattered away by the wipers, so did her thoughts, only to be wiped away by her doubts. Still, Dakota wasn't willing to give up. There was the possibility that the evening could end on a happy note, she hoped. She agreed to take the doctor's orders and take things slow. Yet, her body most definitely needed to release some stressful energy.

Bland fought himself on the way home. He didn't want to end the evening on an awful note, but he couldn't take his mind off Grey. The only way to get his mind off Grey was to talk to her, and that wasn't going to happen while Dakota was around. He needed to explain to Grey that he had wanted to tell her, but the fear of not knowing how she would react had prevented him from disclosing his marriage.

Bland needed a plan to get away and, in his mind, he began to calculate ways of doing just that. He tuned out the snow and the sounds of the wipers so he could concentrate.

When Bland pulled into the driveway, the snow had abated. He parked next to his SUV. Silently, they walked to the door, barely acknowledging each other except for their politeness not to let the other slip and fall. She led the way into the house, slightly pausing at the bottom steps to see if he was joining her. He instead headed to the kitchen. She didn't want to take it as another rejection, so she went upstairs to run her bathwater, and laid the newly purchased negligee across the bed. She set the mood with soft music and soft light. While sitting at her vanity, she looked at herself stonily in the oval mirror, while the bathwater gushed hollow beats. She questioned where she had failed in her marriage. The sound of water overflowing brought her out of her self-induced trance. The tops of her legs smacked against the base of the vanity when she rushed to stand. She stared at the water spreading across the bathroom floor before an instinctive reaction took over and she tossed several towels on the floor to soak up the water.

After she turned off the spout, she heard the sound of soft chatter. Quietly, she walked to the top of the stairs and heard Bland talking in a low tone on the phone. She couldn't fathom why he would muzzle his voice. He's never done that before, she thought. She stood listening, trying to make out the muffled sounds. She headed back into the bedroom. Her movement was slow and calculating as she knelt down to the floor vent to better hear what was being said. Bland had put his antiquated cell phone on speaker, as he often did, in order to hear better. That's when she heard a female's voice faintly say, "No."

Silently, Dakota listened to Bland's pleas for the woman to meet him in thirty minutes. It was hard for her to make out the woman's response. A feeling of betrayal cloaked Dakota as she listened to Bland beg this woman for forgiveness. Forgiveness for what and to whom, Dakota sadly asked herself. She heard Bland hang up. As she stood, she now understood why Bland was so distant to her and Devin. She didn't want to believe her suspicions were true and she could only wonder what this other woman had over her. While her mind whirled back and forth with questions, the front door of the house closed. She rushed to the window. It had started to snow again, and the heavy snowfall blurred her view, but she was able to see Bland get into his SUV.

—

"Oh, hell no! Follow him!" Jane screamed as though Dakota could hear her fight for Dakota to expose Bland.

—

Maybe it was anger, maybe it was fear, or maybe it was pure contempt that drove Dakota to jump into her sedan. She turned the key, but the engine did not start. She shifted the key in and out of the ignition but there was still only a clicking sound.

She slammed her hands against the steering wheel with an utterance of profanity. "Start you damn car!"

The next desperate attempt at starting the vehicle was successful. The engine clicked once before starting. She hurriedly backed out the driveway. The back end scraped the asphalt as the front-end suspension

dragged the edge of the pavement, and red brake lights reflected against the white snow. There was an urgent shift through the gears, a hard pressure to the gas pedal, and a reckless skidding up the street.

When Dakota reached the beltway, she was uncertain of Bland's distance from her. She became lost in the rage of how he could cheat on her, and how dare he not respect her and their family? Thinking of such things, her speedometer slowly increased to speeds of 75 and 80 miles per hour. Nothing was making sense, but she had made up her mind that she going to get to the truth.

The snow began to fall heavily. As she reached to switch on the wipers, the car hydroplaned across two lanes of traffic. From her driver side window, she glimpsed cars passing her by and feared a sudden impact. Frightened, she tightly clutched the steering wheel before her instincts from driving the dirt roads in South Carolina kicked in. She turned the steering wheel in the direction of the backend slide, and the car straightened out. With hands trembling, she managed to catch her breath. She got the car under control. With force, she pressed on the pedal, and the engine hummed to accelerate. Within five minutes, she spotted a car with only one taillight and then remembered that the taillight of Bland's car was out.

Suddenly, she began to cry because the pain of being alone was more real now than ever before. She tried wiping her tears, but when she thought about Devin, the tears ran faster than she could catch them. In such low visibility, she had to stay fixated on the vehicle's nonworking taillight. When the car's brakes were activated, only one taillight lit up, then disappeared around a bend. When Dakota came around the bend, there were now two cars with opposite taillights not working. Because the snow was coming down so hard, she couldn't make out which vehicle was Bland's. Her only method for following the car was now being challenged. She was sure, she thought, it was the right taillight not working, that is, until this car shows up with the right taillight working. Suddenly, the vehicle with the right taillight working flashed its brake lights while the vehicle with the right taillight out broke for an exit. There was only a three-second window to follow the exiting vehicle or stay on the beltway and follow that vehicle. She had no idea where Bland

was going, so her making the right decision was crucial if she wanted to get to the truth.

She began to feel scared because she didn't know what to do. Any chance of exiting the beltway was about to close. She looked ahead to the other car, which was slowly getting out of sight. She pressed her foot hard against the gas. Within her peripheral, the car with the right taillight out whipped around the shoulder of the road to the off ramp. On gut reaction, she whipped the steering wheel right, hit the brakes hard, and the back end fishtailed left onto the berm of the road. The front end of the car lifted when the tires smacked against the small concrete barrier causing the car to go airborne for a few seconds then land into snow, mud and grass. Her body shot forward and whiplashed backwards as the car's front grill went through the snowy dirt and grass, then slid on the pavement of the off ramp, fishtailing several more times until she gained control.

While Dakota raced to catch up to the vehicle that was now out of sight, Bland was pulling his SUV around Union Circle in front of Union Station, looking for a parking space. He hurried his pace into the golden glare of one of the flanking archways, uncertain if Grey would even be there waiting. Sitting at a deserted bench in a rain jacket with an attached hood covering her hair and much of her face was Grey. She stood when she saw Bland approaching. He ungently grabbed her by the arm and walked her toward the long marble steps that led to the trains. Neither said a word.

Minutes later, Dakota's sedan skidded around M Street Circle. She didn't think about finding a parking space as the car slid down the drop off and pick up area of lane B of Union Station. She slammed the car into park and jumped out. She flipped off her heels, lifted her garment to her knees, and took off running through the large vaulted space doorway of the station. As she ran, her bare feet smacked against the marble floors of the main concourse to echo off the white granite walls.

As late as it was, there were still people traveling the large hallways. Dakota didn't care to think about the tears of mascara streaks that stained her face, or her hair that fell and lay wet across her face; all she thought was that she wanted to see for herself that Bland was with

another woman. Dakota had run to the center of the station and stopped because she had no idea where to look. Like a merry-go-round, she turned looking for Bland. There was an announcement of an outgoing train in less than three minutes, so she considered the departing deck.

"Where are the trains?" she asked a passing custodian.

"Down there," he pointed to a long flight of steps.

She rushed over to the terrace that overlooked the trains. Quickly, her eyes scanned over the many passengers that came and went. There, down by the fourth car, she spotted Bland in his two-piece tailored suit, with no tie, talking to a woman with a long raincoat that came to her ankles. She couldn't make out the woman's profile because of the rain bonnet. Momentarily, Dakota watched the two of them. Bland's mouth and hands gestured with a sense of panic, but the woman's neutral mannerisms were a rejection of his excuses.

The conductor stepped from within the train and yelled, "All abroad, outbound!"

Dakota turned sharply when she saw Bland escorting the woman onto the train. Gradually, the train began to move out of the station. Dakota went scampering down a flight of marble steps in the main hall of the station. Suddenly, her feet slipped from under her, her body slung backwards, and her focal point went from the train to the ceiling of the station. Those individuals in the surrounding area regarded her scream as if it were a whistle preceding a train's departure, while those close enough to her saw their space invaded by flailing arms and feet. These people knew the impact between Dakota and the solid marble steps could potentially fracture her bones.

Hearing the loud commotion, the conductor leaned from the open hatch of the train to see what had happened. He could only see a part of a woman wearing blue lying on the floor. He watched as people hovered over her before he stepped back into the train and pushed a button to close the hatch. Bland and Grey stood in the aisle of the train. They listened to the conductor tell a porter that it appeared a woman in a blue dress had just fallen down the steps.

Meanwhile, Dakota lay motionless with her eyes locked on the gold leaf that adorned the high ceiling, and the Roman statues that encircled

and guarded the main hall of the station. As pain vibrated throughout her body, a tear ran down the side of her face.

A man's voice asked, "Are you okay?"

His voice came from underneath her body. Her eyes shifted from the ceiling to the people standing around her, then downward to see the man's legs underneath hers. The stranger had managed to throw his body between her and the solid steps before the fall could cause serious damage. Fortunately for Dakota, she didn't absorb that fatal impact. The stranger urged her to try to move. She pushed the man's large stomach as a means for support, while two other men grabbed her upper arms and pulled Dakota to her feet.

The realization that Bland was more concerned about this other woman than her made her feel worthless. With her bruised body and defeated spirit, she managed to make it back home safely. Dakota experienced extreme anxiety as she went back to the bedroom to slip off her evening dress. On the bed was the negligee she had purchased at the boutique. She decided to put it on and wait by the bedroom phone for Bland to call.

If Bland had known those screams belonged to his wife, maybe he would have run to her aid. Instead, he assisted Grey down the aisle of the car to a seat. There was an urgency to explain and apologize for hurting her. But Grey was uninterested in hearing any explanations Bland could muster. Bland saw in her eyes how disappointed she was with him. She pulled from his grasp.

"What did you say?" she asked, stunned as if hearing him say something totally stupid.

"I know you're disappointed," he repeated.

"Is that what you think? You think I'm disappointed. Oh, I'm not disappointed. I'm furious at you. How could you, Bland?"

"I love you, Grey."

"How can you say that word? You betrayed love, and yet you stand there and say you love me with the same breath you tell me lies. What am I supposed to believe, Bland? Except that you are married with a child. When were you going to disclose that information?" She paused

for a second then screamed in anger, "Why didn't you tell me?"

Bland glanced around to see who heard her sudden outburst. He lowered his voice to a whisper.

"Believe me, Grey, I wanted to tell you so many times, but I didn't want to hurt you. I didn't want to hurt anyone."

"Bland, you are a hypocrite. Not only are you hurting me, but you're hurting your wife. I stood there and noticed the pain surface across her face when I spoke of my man and how wonderful he is. And how awful of me to throw my happiness in her face, not knowing the same man that was creating love for me was causing her pain. So, yes, I do have compassion for her."

"You don't understand, Grey."

"I don't know how you expect me to understand. I saw her eyes and now I can't help but feel her pain. Bland, I was once that other woman. You don't understand. I would have done anything for you, anything."

"I know... I know. And I will do anything for you."

"Except tell the truth, which you can't seem to do."

The voice of the engineer cracked from the train's speakers.

"Next stop is Alexandria, Virginia."

Seconds later the train began to slow its pace. Grey walked toward the car's door, and Bland tried seizing her. With force, she managed to jerk away. When the train came to a complete stop, unexpectedly Grey turned toward Bland.

"And to think I wanted to share something special with you, something that would have changed everything between us."

Then she turned and ran down the few steps of the boxcar. Bland watched as she ran toward a taxi. As the train pulled off, Bland couldn't help wondering what Grey meant. He could only imagine that she was referring to her devoted and unconditional love.

Bland didn't want to return home. He didn't know how to explain his sudden absence to Dakota, and he dared not use Lou as his alibi. So instead he went to the office. He assumed working on the novel would at least, if only temporarily, get both women off his mind. When he arrived at the office that evening, it was empty except for a few birthday balloons floating around the reception area.

20

THE NEXT DAY BLAND STILL HAD NOT CALLED HOME. John Scott waited in his truck with his grandson as his wife and Devin hurried through the snow for the front door of his house. Dakota's car was in the driveway and Mrs. Scott couldn't understand why she wasn't answering the door. She was afraid Dakota had tried to hurt herself again, and this time was successful. After several more attempts with the doorbell, Mrs. Scott cautiously turned the doorknob. The door opened. She called to Dakota from the foyer. When there was no answer, Mrs. Scott's nervousness increased with every step she made. She thought about calling Mr. Scott.

Dakota slid off the edge of the bed and headed into the bathroom. She tossed some cold water on her face and brushed her hair. She could hear Mrs. Scott and Devin making their way up the stairs. Quickly, she stepped out of the bathroom.

"Oh, there you are. We've been ringing that doorbell and calling you for some time."

"I'm sorry, Keri, I didn't hear the doorbell."

"Devin," Dakota called. He came charging into the room and straight into his mother's arms. "I love you," she said.

"I love you, too, Mommy. Can I go and play now?"

"Sure you can."

Mrs. Scott scrutinized her weary face. "Did you get any sleep last night?"

"Yes," Dakota lied, to stop any further interrogation.

"Well, if your skin is that pallid after getting a good night's sleep, maybe you need to get some sun," Mrs. Scott suggested. "You know the sun is a high source of Vitamin D or Vitamin K. I can't remember which one, but I do know it's good for you. You need to get out of this house. It's sunny and the snow is starting to melt."

"Is that so, Keri? Then I'll do my best to get some sun later."

"What do you have planned for today?"

"I don't know, maybe take Devin sled riding, so I can get some fresh air to go with that sun."

"That's good, but make sure he's wrapped up. It is kind of chilly. By the way, in case I didn't mention it, the circus will be in town on Monday. John and I are taking the grandchildren. Maybe Devin can go with us."

"Thanks, Devin would love that."

"So will John," Mrs. Scott laughed. "Last night, it felt like I was babysitting three kids."

"Thank you so much for watching mine."

"How did the evening turn out?" Keri asked.

"Great, a lot of dancing, eating, and…" she paused because she couldn't bring herself to tell another lie.

"You don't have to say it. The way you're walking all hunched over tells me he got the best of you," chuckled Mrs. Scott. "Well, we're getting ready to head to the flea market. Talk to you later." Her conversation stalled momentarily to inquire, "Speaking of Bland, where is he?"

"He had to run to the bank," she replied because that was the first thing that came to her mind.

She walked Mrs. Scott to the front door, then waited for her to get into the truck. As John backed out the driveway, Dakota gave him a pleasant smile. Once the truck had gotten far enough up the street, she dropped her head in defeat. Her walk up the stairs was slow, partly from the soreness in her legs and back from last night's fall, and from the pain

that had settled upon her heart.

Devin met her at the top of the stairs. It surprised her when he asked, "Mommy, are you sad?"

She refused to let Devin see her in such an emotional state, so she fought back her tears. She tossed her head to the side, "Everything is okay, baby. Mommy isn't feeling well."

"Is Daddy getting you some medicine?"

"Yes, baby."

"Okay, Mommy. I hope you feel better." He leaned forward to give her a hug.

She clutched him and squeezed him tightly, tighter than she ever had. With only an iota of strength left, she fought to hold herself together, at least for Devin.

She sniffed and asked, "Are you hungry, baby?"

"No, not yet," he turned and ran to his room.

She walked back into her room, leaving the door ajar. She made her way back to the side of her bed. There she started to consider Bland and his mistress and their personal encounters. Did he embrace his mistress like he embraced her? Were their kisses slow, meaningful, and passionate? Did he hold the small of her back like he did with her when they took long walks? Did he make love as passionately to her? Her hands and lips trembled the more she thought about what they might have done together.

It was after sunset when Bland called home. His voice was tired and scratchy.

"Hey," he called through the speaker.

Dakota was calm, her demeanor reserved like she had done this before.

"Yes," she answered.

"I tried to call you late last night, but my phone is still acting weird."

She coldly remarked, "So whose phone are you using now?"

"I'm in my office. I've been here since last night," he stated, hoping to lighten her anger. "Has Devin gotten home?"

"He's been here since one o'clock, and you're just calling at six o'clock

to find out."

"Okay," he paused, waiting for her to say something that would indicate how he needed to carry the conversation. Once he knew she wasn't going to bite, he pointed out his mistake for leaving without letting her know.

"You have a right to be upset," he admitted, as a hopeful overture.

She didn't want to play the game anymore and she blurted, "Bland, I want you to think about this before you respond. Is there something you want to tell me?"

He didn't know how to answer the question. He considered his disappearing might have been the motivation for such a question.

"Where did you go last night?" she asked, to see if he would confess.

He snorted, then pushed out a terrible fake cough. He thought about Lou, but again, he knew Lou wasn't an option. She, however, sat there waiting for him to lie about never rendezvousing with a woman.

"I had to meet a woman, Dakota."

"A woman?" She was shocked Bland was finally telling the truth.

She stared at the wooden chest, waiting for him to continue.

"It was a last-minute decision on my part, so I decided to meet with her at Union Station."

She couldn't believe what she was hearing, or she just didn't want to believe what she was hearing.

"Bland, who is this woman?"

Bland's voice became defensive. He didn't want to lie any longer nor disclose the entire truth. "Dakota, I think there are some things we need to talk about."

"This woman you met, was it for business or personal?"

"It was personal."

She went ahead and asked the inevitable question they both knew was coming.

"Are you having an affair with this woman, Bland?"

"I don't know how to tell you this, but just to say it. I am not happy, Dakota."

She wouldn't allow herself to believe that. "Not happy?" Her tone was bitter, "I don't believe that, Bland. I've been by your side through good

times and bad times, like a wife is supposed to be by her husband, so how can you say that to me? If anyone should claim not being happy, it's me."

"Can we talk without our voices rising?"

Again, she directed her attention back to the woman. "Bland, are you having an affair? That's all I want to know."

Still he didn't answer her.

"Why won't you answer me?" she screamed. "Who is she, Bland?"

"Does it matter, Dakota?"

"Tell me, then, do you want to be with her? Are you willing to lose your family for her?"

Her head began to ache, so she pressed the side of her left temple with her thumb and index finger.

"I don't want to discuss this over the phone," he blurted.

"Are you going to leave us?" she began to cry.

"Dakota, I don't want to discuss this right now."

"Then when do we talk about this, Bland? You're too busy running to stand still long enough to talk about anything. I need to know what my husband has been doing!" Her words stalled as she cried. "Was I not a good enough wife that you had to bring someone else into our marriage?"

Her voice continued to crack. Tears streamed down her face and under her chin. Before Bland could respond, he heard the dial tone. She drew her hand back to destroy the wooden chest but stopped when Devin abruptly barged into the room. She gathered her composure, then watched in a daze as he flew his model plane across the room. It swerved through the air for several seconds. She saw the airplane on a collision course with the wooden chest. She snapped from her trance to throw her hand forward to stop the collision. Inadvertently, her elbow smacked into the chest, causing it to fall to the floor. The handle of the chest snapped off and its contents spilled out.

"I'm sorry, Mommy," cried Devin, as Dakota sat on the bed and peered down at the mess. She shook her head and elected to pick it up later.

"Come on, let's feed my little man."

"Dakota, Dakota," called Bland. An echo bounced off the wall when he slammed the receiver of the phone. He sat behind his office desk with no desire to do anything. He thought about the decisions he had made, and the choices he had to consider.

How did I get in so deep? he thought. Then he wondered if he had lost Grey. An equally uneasy feeling draped him that maybe he had lost his wife also. He told her what he thought she needed to know. However, he wasn't totally committed to abandoning his family for Grey. In case he did, Dakota needed to know his unhappiness was a rationale for his decisions.

There was a sense of relief that the lie was out. He knew he loved his wife, but still he didn't have an answer as to why he was willing to jeopardize everything for Grey. There was a time when in Dakota's absence he craved her the most; now in her presence, Grey occupied his every thought. The debris of unfaithfulness, love, and soon the unthinkable cluttered his mind as he contemplated this new reality, this new destiny that may no longer include Dakota.

He closed his eyes and allowed the silence to absorb his rapid thoughts. *Everything is happening so fast,* he said to himself, as he gazed through the open blinds at the helium balloons floating around the reception area, then down the hall. Briefly, he cut his eyes to the camera mounted in the corner of the ceiling.

After Devin ate, he went into the living room to play his video games. Dakota went back upstairs. She had forgotten about the mess scattered on the floor. Slowly, she made her way to the floor to sit. She took her time looking through the numerous articles and artifacts that Bland had put aside. She remembered it was she who cut out the majority of them and put them in his chest years before. The thought brought more tears to her eyes. Maybe it wasn't too late to make it all work. She thought of her insecurities, ambition, and selfishness as reasons for chasing her husband into the arms of another woman. As she read the articles, she cried, smiled and even laughed. For a moment she forgot the unhappiness. Her spirit, slowly regaining its joy, lifted her slumped

shoulders and downturned mouth. She pulled to her knees, lifted the wooden chest, and slid it back onto the nightstand. She decided to forgive Bland, hoping that would free her from the pain that slowly suffocated the joy, hope, and strength from her. There was a confirming smile as she went to stand. With one knee heavily pressed into the carpet, she began to use the other knee as leverage to stand. A glossy shine caught her eye. She had missed something, she thought. How did it get all the way over here? she wondered, as she crawled to the closet door. She moved the door slightly back.

"Oh, what's this?"

She grabbed the photo that was somehow previously unnoticed. Her body slumped and she rested her back against the closet door.

She played with the photo before focusing in on it. Gradually, her eyes settled on the faces of the black and white picture. Her eyes glazed over Bland and his whimsical smile to the cheek of her face that lay against Bland's. Where did Bland get this picture of us? she pondered.

She moved the picture closer to her eyes. A new focus was placed on her pinned up hair in the picture. She turned the picture left then right for better lighting. When that wasn't sufficient, she got to her knees, then to her feet. She moved to where she could position the picture under the lampshade.

"Now I can see," she said softly, this time holding the picture well within the light.

Suddenly, Dakota frowned while blurting, "This isn't me."

She looked to the bathroom then went back to studying the picture of the female. She scrutinized the woman's face, her hairstyle, and her smile. Then it dawned on Dakota who the woman could be. This must be the woman Bland has been meeting. This picture is grainy, but I believe I've seen this woman. "Why do you look familiar?" she said aloud, hoping she could recall the time and place. Then she asked a more important question. How did this picture get in my house, in my bedroom? Did Bland bring this into our bedroom?

Dakota looked again at the picture, searching for a clue as to the woman's identity. She turned the picture over to see if there was a name on it. On the back there was a phrase that read "my soul mate."

I've heard or seen that phrase before. She took a second to think. Where did I hear that phrase? she asked herself. Suddenly fresh to her sense of smell was that eluding fragrance.

"There is that scent again," she whispered. "Where did I smell that scent? It was just recently."

She sniffed the air. The scent pulled her nose closer to the picture that she held in her hand. She leaned her nose forward to sniff.

That's odd, she told herself, as she sniffed the picture again. Why would that scent be on this picture?

Remembering something, instantly her questions began to line up. She rushed over to the dresser, grabbed her purse and began emptying the contents of the bag onto the bed. She rummaged through the items like a scavenger. Soon enough, she found in the clutter what she was trying to find. Dakota brought the business card back to eye level and then used her smart phone to look up the social media page that was on the card. She waited anxiously for the phone to pull up the page. Once it did, she was disappointed to find there wasn't a profile picture to go with the name, Greysen Brindle.

Dakota compared the picture on the nightstand to the few pictures that were displayed on the page. The hairstyle and makeup in many of the pictures were vastly different from the photo, which caused Dakota to doubt if Greysen was the woman in the photo. As she continued to peruse the page, one picture caught her attention. Dakota stared at a selfie of Grey sitting in a lingerie identical to what she purchased at the boutique. It was the selfie's backdrop that caused her anger to thunder out of nowhere. Grey lay with her back against the headboard of Dakota's bed. Her mind drifted back to the evening she returned from the hospital. The scent from the comforter came back as fresh as that day she met Grey in the boutique.

She looked at the picture repulsively. She wanted to throw up. This woman was toying with me, she thought scornfully. She slammed the side of Bland's wooden chest that went sailing into the wall. A thunderous sound resonated throughout the room. Then there were a series of events and people that flashed through her mind: Bland, Devin, her trip to South Carolina, the promotion, the twins, and Grey. Suddenly Dakota's

mind summoned up Grey's words, *"I'm also pregnant. The doctor says six months. This is my first child."* She paused to think. He was sleeping with her the same time he was sleeping with me. Then more of Grey's words were summoned up, *"It is funny how fate brings people back together. We met years ago. He is my soul mate."* Dakota commenced to toss the phone, jewelry, clothes and other items across the room. She paused to let Grey's words settle in deeper.

Dakota's face turned sideways. His soul mate? "I thought I was his soul mate," she yelled. Furiously, she tore the photo down its center, then ripped off the lingerie that she wore for Bland. Filled with heartache, she sat on the bed and began to sob. She recalled how Grey paraded about her pregnancy. It all made sense, thought Dakota, a stranger walking up to her and engaging in conversation about being pregnant. She couldn't believe it. She didn't want to believe it. Dakota grabbed the house phone, but there was no dial tone. She needed to find Devin a place to stay. She really didn't want to call on the Scotts; she didn't want them asking all sorts of questions. She had some serious business to attend to, and she wanted to stay focused. She grabbed her cell phone from the dresser to call Sharon. Maybe their children could entertain each other, she thought.

"Damn you, Bland, how could you do this to us?" she cursed, as she hit the prompt to dial Sharon's number. As Sharon's phone rang, Dakota cursed again, but it didn't relieve the pain that latched itself to her heart. She inhaled to embrace the realization of what was happening, and what she needed to do to stop it. After several more rings, Sharon's voicemail answered. "Soul mate," she echoed again. On those words, her face frowned inward. In an instant, her hands began to shake uncontrollably. The cell phone slipped from her hands and landed next to the nightstand. Dakota made her hands into tight fists. She wanted to squeeze out the pain she felt.

The house phone rang suddenly and snapped Dakota out of her rage. She regained control of herself and answered the phone by tapping the speaker button.

"Hello," Dakota said with an intense voice.

"Bland?" the voice asked through the speaker.

"This is his wife."

"Just the person I need to speak to," the voice said.

With all that had taken place, Bland knew he still had to deal with the novel. Yet, there was no way he could motivate himself now. He closed the laptop. He then looked at the desk top computer and its blue screen before he laid his head back in the recliner. Abruptly, the office phone rang so loudly it startled him. Immediately, he sat up to yank the receiver off its base.

Dakota screamed through the receiver in panic. It was something about Devin being sick and a hospital.

"Calm down," he said.

Her voice slowed down to catch her breath. "You have to come home."

"What's wrong?" he asked. To know it concerned Devin made him sit up in the chair.

Dakota wanted to expose Bland. She wanted to see his reactions and dare him to deny the unborn baby. She hadn't thoroughly thought her plan through; she just said the first thing that came to her mind that would get him home.

"It's Devin, he doesn't look that well. I want to take him to the hospital, but this damn car isn't starting."

"What's he doing now?"

"He's," she stalled, "he doesn't look so well, Bland, please hurry."

The hospital wasn't far from his office.

"Can you ask the Scotts to take you, and I will meet you at the hospital in a half hour?"

"The Scotts aren't home, Bland, so could you please come and see about your son?"

"See if Sharon is at home."

"Never mind, Bland, I don't know why I called."

"I'm on my way," he slammed the phone.

He grabbed his satchel and rushed out of the office. Once in his car, he sped through the half-lit parking garage and nearly slammed into Jesse's car, which was turning into the parking garage. As Jesse slammed on his brakes to prevent hitting Bland's SUV, the two men made eye

contact. Slowly Jesse pulled his car into the garage as Bland raced out.

After Bland hung up, Dakota looked at the cell phone. A calmness overcame her as she picked up Grey's business card to study the number and to contemplate her next move.

She wanted to reserve her resentment for Bland and her revenge for Grey. She stood in the center of the floor plotting. After several long intense minutes, she decided to call Grey. She tried using the cell, but the battery was dead. She picked up the house phone, then with urgency dialed the number on the card.

Grey answered, "Hello." There was a moment of silence before Grey said hello again.

"Ms. Brindle? This is—"

Grey recognized the voice. "I know who you are."

"I need to talk to you. Can we please meet?" asked Dakota.

Grey felt a sense of responsibility to meet with Dakota to explain her innocence. She couldn't imagine the pain Dakota felt after knowing her husband was having an affair and expecting a child by another woman. When she was faced with something similar, Grey didn't get the chance to meet with her ex-husband's lover. She decided to extend the courtesy to Dakota because she had nothing to hide. She wanted everything in the open.

Dakota suggested a meeting place.

"Okay, it will take me twenty-five minutes to get there."

As soon as she hung up, Dakota threw on some clothes and bolted down to the living room. "Devin, I'm taking you over to Sharon's house." Devin screamed with joy.

"Will Chad be there?"

"I think so, so put on your shoes and jacket so we can go."

Dakota then rushed back upstairs and into her bedroom closet to search for a pair of shoes. When her eyes bounced off the shoeboxes on the floor to the one shoebox stored on the top rack, her quick movements slowed. She wondered if Bland had gotten rid of the gun. She pulled the shoebox down, flipped off its lid. The 9-millimeter was still there. She studied the weapon with an evil eye. Her thoughts were consumed on

the gun, until Devin called from the doorway of the closet.

"Mommy, I'm ready." When Dakota didn't respond, Devin asked, "What are you doing, Mommy?"

Suddenly, his voice registered. "Just grabbing a jacket, baby," she said, while grabbing the first one she saw, which happened to be Bland's blue blazer. Then she slipped an object into the pocket of the blazer.

—

The book tilted forward in Jane's hand as she lay in the bed in disbelief. The fact that Bland was destroying one woman's family and another woman's hope of having one had her in awe and in anger. A man is blind as to what is important, she thought. She believed or rather hoped that Bland would come to his senses. Then again, maybe it was too late. Dakota did call Grey to meet with her. Dakota needs to know the truth, thought Jane. More importantly, Jane had to know what Dakota put into her pocket. If it was a weapon, did she plan to use it on Grey? And why Grey, when Jane felt it should be used on Bland. She brushed the thought away quickly so she could get back to the book.

21

THE SNOW HAD ABATED, BUT IT WAS STILL A WET AND windy evening as Bland drove with high speeds to his house. A lot of emotions were swarming around in his head. He had given his decision a lot of thought. There would be no more flip-flopping; he knew what he had to do. As soon as he had the chance, he would tell Dakota he should have been there when she found out about her pregnancy. More importantly, she should never have had a breakdown. He had to admit that everything was happening because of him.

As he drove home, Bland tried calling Dakota on her cell phone, it went straight to voice mail. He wondered if Dakota was lying about Devin's illness, although she had never done that before. But, given the circumstances, Bland had never put her in such a position. He dialed the house phone, but it was busy. He thought of the possibility that something serious had happened. Hopefully, she was able to reach the Scotts. He dialed the Scott's number, but received no answer. When Bland arrived home, he saw Dakota's car was not in the driveway.

He ran into the house and called out, "Devin! Dakota!" But there was no response. He took the steps two at a time straight into the main bedroom. The room was ransacked. On the bed were items from Dakota's purse. Bland stepped over the contents of his wooden chest to

pick up the receiver of the phone. Where are they, he thought?

Fright slung its ugly face over his already weighted shoulders to compound the guilt he lugged around. He spotted several of his precious items scattered across the hardwood floor. The scene multiplied his fears that something worse could have happened. Ironically, his thoughts considered his life being without Devin and Dakota. Immediately he felt a piercing pain in his chest. He grabbed the old phone book and called the local children's hospital. Nothing. Devin hadn't been admitted. He directed his focus back to the contents on the bed.

Dakota noticed the gate to S&W's parking garage was up, so she pulled in. She climbed from the car and scurried to the elevator. As she came off the elevator, she stared down the long corridor.

Through the long hall, Dakota walked, jogged, walked, and jogged until she was at the security desk. After business hours, all visitors had to report directly to the front security entrance for access to the upper level floors. "Hello," the security guard said. Dakota acknowledged the woman with a polite smile, then signed the register. She hurried over to the main elevator when Jesse noticed her. She looked at him with intense eyes before stepping into the elevator.

When she stepped off the elevator, inflated balloons floated in various directions. Radiant light beamed through the large transparent windows in the lobby.

Dakota's eyes darted to the blue glow that emanated from Bland's office. When she was closer to the office, she saw that the blue glow came from his computer screen. Then her eyes settled on his laptop that rested on top of the desk.

Minutes later, Grey quietly walked the corridor of the publishing house's lobby. Everything looked so different with the office empty. She felt a strange and cold presence as she approached the security desk. The security guard offered a pleasant smile when Grey walked up to the desk.

"Hello, I need to get to the editorial floor."

"That would be the sixth floor. We need all visitors to sign this

register and state the time and the floor they are visiting."

Before writing her name, she noticed Dakota had already signed the register. Hiding in the corner with his cleaning supplies was Jesse, who watched as usual. After Grey entered the elevator, Jesse followed the digital numbers over the elevator to see where it would stop.

—

"Jane," called Constance from a distance. Jane looked up from the book.

"Hey, Connie, how did you know to find me in the courtyard?"

"A little birdie told me."

"A little birdie," Jane laughed.

"I thought I'd give you a few days since you were so upset about not seeing your face. Are you okay?" She sat beside Jane on the bench.

"I've felt better. I know Dr. Stewart means well, and I didn't mean to upset him, but I don't think he understands how I feel."

"Trust me, Jane, Dr. Stewart understands. He's viewing your situation from a wider perspective that includes both far-sighted and near-sighted vision. Do you have any idea what might happen if he lets you see yourself prematurely? You could be further damaged, even go into shock or depression."

Jane whined, "That's not nice to say, and somewhat of an exaggeration."

"Not really. That's why it's pertinent that Dr. Westfall makes these connections in your mind." She moved in closer to Jane. "Jane, that's why everyone is taking their sweet time because you're too sweet to lose."

Jane smiled. Constance saw the opportunity to lighten the mood. "You carry that book everywhere you go?"

"Yeah, can't seem to put it down. Not to mention that this man is so stupid. He just upsets me."

"All men have a way of doing that and, trust me, you don't need a book to tell you that. Anyway, I just wanted to check on you."

"Thanks, Connie, you know it's always a pleasure seeing you." Suddenly, she asked, "Oh, what time is it?"

Constance looked at her watch, "Ten minutes to the hour."

"I'm supposed to be at Dr. Westfall's office."

"Come on, I'll roll you over there."

On their way, Constance asked, "Since your last session, have you had any more dreams?"

"Just the same recurring ones." Jane wanted to ask a question that had been on her mind for some time. "Connie, were you there the night I was found?"

Before Constance could answer, they had arrived at Dr. Westfall's office, and that was a great relief for Constance. "Jane, we're here." Constance gripped Jane by the shoulders. "Everything is going to be okay. Like I said, the doctor knows best, and these sessions will help."

Dr. Westfall led Jane back to her office. Immediately, the doctor turned down the light and took a seat in the lounge chair. Jane noticed the tape recorder on the table when she went to sit down.

"Jane, I had a chance to listen to the tape of our last session, and I think I want to try something that may help restore some of your memory. I want to explore beyond your dreams. I believe we should do this in incremental stages, so I'm going to attempt to go back to the point you were found at the hospital and work our way backward."

Jane looked with excitement because she too wondered how she managed to end up at the hospital.

"Are you okay with that?"

"Sure. I'm okay with it."

"I'd like for you to lie back on the sofa and try to relax."

This was the first time Jane felt comfortable and eager for the doctor to perform hypnosis on her. She believed her questions would finally get answered. She glanced at the clock on the wall, then focused on the ceiling fan to relax. She watched the wooden blades circulate until she woke up in a state of hysteria. Her breathing was rapid, and beads of sweat dripped from her forehead. Her hands trembled uncontrollably. The doctor tried to calm her by refocusing her on the ceiling fan.

"You're okay, Jane. You're safe," she added.

Jane's chest rapidly lifted and lowered as she tried to catch her breath.

When Jane was fully conscious, Dr. Westfall was leaning slightly

over her with a tissue in hand. She started wiping the sweat from Jane's forehead. She helped her sit up and positioned her against the back of the sofa. Finally, Jane's breathing slowed, and she regained control of herself.

Once Dr. Westfall knew Jane was okay, she removed the tape from its player and stored it in the cabinet on the far wall. She then returned to her seat.

"What happened, doctor? What did I say that has me so disoriented?"

"Jane, you were under but not for long. I had to bring you out." As she began to explain, the secretary rushed into the office.

"Dr. Westfall, we have an emergency."

Dr. Westfall bounced from her seat, "I'm sorry, Jane, but do you mind seeing your way out?"

"That's not a problem, doctor."

The doctor rushed out of the office and left Jane alone. Jane gathered herself, then looked up at the clock on the wall. Over thirty minutes had elapsed. That doesn't seem quick to me, said Jane to herself. She moved toward the door and noticed the cabinet which stored the tapes partially open. Consciously, she glanced at the front door, wondering if the doctor would reenter at any moment. Hesitantly, she did an about-face turn and moved toward the cabinet. There was something the doctor was keeping from her, she felt. Again, she peeped around the cabinet doors. Quickly, she scanned over the number of tapes stored. When she reached the middle section of the cabinet, she saw her name on the spine of a few tape cases. When she reached for the cases, tapes began to fall out of the cabinet. Afraid that Dr. Westfall might return at any minute, she began to panic. After grabbing tapes off the floor, she stuffed a few in her pockets that had her name on them and threw the others back into the cabinet. She then closed the cabinet doors and fled the office.

Chaos filled the hallways as Jane slipped through the horde of nurses and doctors trying to restrain an out-of-control patient. Jane didn't ask a nurse to wheel her back to her room; instead, she quickly walked the entire distance.

Once in her room, she thought about her actions. Guilt soon captured

her conscience and the consequences that might result from stealing the tapes. She contemplated returning the tapes and apologizing to the doctor for even committing the crime. She paced the floor before deciding to hide the tapes underneath her mattress. Minutes later, her curiosity provoked her to retrieve the tapes from their hidden spot. However, she still needed a recorder to listen to the tapes. She recalled one of the aides mentioning a recorder at the nurse's station. She rolled off the bed, crept to the door, and carefully peeked into the hallway. Jane felt extremely nervous. She didn't feel comfortable asking for a recorder, knowing she had just swiped the tapes from Dr. Westfall's office. Fortunately for Jane, the station appeared to be unmanned. She took the opportunity to dart up the hall. She looked around before making her way around the desk to search for the recorder.

"Hello there."

Jane snapped her head backwards when hearing the voice. She breathed a sigh of relief as she realized the voice came from a computer's screen saver. Her heart beat rapidly as there was an instant panic to move quickly before someone came. Hastily, she went rummaging through the drawers to find the recorder. It was hidden well in the back of a drawer. She grabbed it and rushed back to her room.

She placed the recorder on the table, grabbed a tape with her name on it, and shoved it into the player. Dr. Westfall's voice came through clearly. Jane sat back in the chair to listen. When she thought she heard someone at the door, she clicked the "off" button on the recorder and tucked it underneath her buttocks. She waited until it was safe to retrieve the player. If someone entered unexpectedly, it would look strange, she thought, her sitting at an empty table staring at the wall. She decided to pretend to read the book while she listened to the tape. That way, if someone barged into the room, she would stop the recorder and pretend to read.

Jane pulled the novel from the drawer and opened the book to where she had left off. She pushed the play button on the recorder. Nonchalantly, her eyes continued to gaze over the words while she listened to the tape. Unknowingly, Jane's mind fell into a trance and she didn't consciously

realize she was reading the book. Somehow, her mind placed the book and the recorder in sequence.

Dr. Westfall's voice bellowed from the recorder, "Jane, I want you to focus on the ceiling fan. The blades will start to spin slower and slower. The slower they get, the deeper you will fall asleep."

Jane sat upright in the chair to hear. From the recorder, she could hear Dr. Westfall shifting her weight in the leather chair. She continued to listen intently to Dr. Westfall's voice emitting through the recorder.

"Jane, I have returned you back to the night you were found in the bush outside the hospital."

Jane heard leather cracking, then a grimacing sound came through the recorder. Suddenly, from the recorder the doctor asked, "Tell me what is happening."

Jane listened to herself breath heavily before saying, "I'm in so much pain. My skin is on fire."

"It's okay, Jane, you're safe," Dr. Westfall's voice paused on the recorder. "Jane, I want you to take me back, before the pain, before the injuries. I want you to take me to that place where it all happened."

The sounds of the recorder drifted to the background of Jane's mind while the letters on the pages became the foreground of her visual. She began to read.

—

From the lobby floor, Jesse moved closer to the door to watch the digital numbers flash over the elevator. When the door opened on the editor's floor, floating balloons danced around Grey as she exited the elevator. Dakota was nowhere in sight. Cautiously, Grey moved away from the elevator. She jumped when the elevator door closed behind her. She proceeded to walk further into the dark reception lobby. Grey tried to adjust her eyes in the darkness, hoping she could make her way through the maze of balloons. Grey saw the room starting to brighten. The moon's light shined through the large windows in the reception area. Now that she could see, Grey walked quickly to Bland's office before another passing cloud blocked the light of the moon. When she made it to his office, it was dark and empty. She stood in the doorway

and called out. Her voice echoed off the walls of an empty hallway.

"Who's there?"

"Who's there?" came an echo.

She knew she wasn't alone, given that she saw Dakota's name on the register. Then she began to panic. What was the real reason Dakota wanted to see her? she wondered. Grey decided to turn back. She walked in the dim light toward the elevator. Slowly, as she made her way back to the reception area, the light she trailed disappeared. Grey stopped. She couldn't see anything.

—

The voice from the tape player soon regained Jane's attention. "Something is against my body. I feel it on both sides of me."

"What is it, Jane?" asked Dr. Westfall from the recorder.

"I don't know," replied Jane's voice. She returned to the book.

—

Grey stood still, waiting for the light to return before traveling any further up the dark hall. Occasionally, she heard balloons bumping the ceiling and the walls as they floated around the reception area. When a shadow fell upon her skin, she nervously jumped back. Grey hugged her chest with relief when she realized it was her shadow cast by the reappearance of the moon. When she made it to the reception area, she paused to look around the room. Once again, the light was starting to disappear. She looked over toward the elevator and moved in its direction when a pair of hands slammed against her chest and drove her hard into a wall. Briefly, Grey lost her breath from the impact. When she looked up, standing in front of her was Dakota.

—

From the recorder there seemed to be a violent struggle taking place.

"What is it, Jane? What is happening?" Dr. Westfall's voice asked.

"No!" screamed Jane's voice through the speaker.

—

Dakota's eyes were scary, while Grey's were contrite and concerned. Their faces were vivid in the moonlight.

"I know how you feel," Grey pleaded. She felt Dakota's grip around her arms tightening.

"How would you know? Are you married?" Dakota asked in a very calm voice.

"No, but—" Grey tried to explain, but Dakota cut her off.

"Then how can you possibly know how I feel? You have no idea what I feel."

Grey's voice became stronger. "I have been married, and I know what it feels like to be betrayed. My husband did it to me."

Dakota laughed, "So I guess that validates what you're doing."

"You're not listening to me. It's not like I stole him."

"You stole more than him. You stole my family, my happiness, my life. This wasn't supposed to happen. I was a good wife, a loyal and faithful wife. No, this wasn't supposed to happen, not to me."

"And it was supposed to happen to me?" Grey's voice rose. "I immersed myself into that man—body, soul, and spirit. I didn't know he was married."

Dakota gave a suspicious smile, "What is your motive? Why are you doing this?"

"What do you mean, my motive?"

"You know what I mean." Dakota's eyes shifted when Grey didn't respond to her question. "How did you meet my husband?"

"I told you. I knew him a long time ago."

"Yes, and fate brought the two of you back together? Let me guess, of all places on a train."

"I know my words are unusual, but that's the truth." Grey tried to free herself from Dakota's grasp.

"I'm sure your reunion with my husband had nothing to do with fate."

"What are you insinuating?" Grey cried. "I don't care what you believe. Believe what you want." Again, Grey tried to free her arms but was impeded by Dakota.

Dakota then looked at her with an angry face. "And you had the

audacity to congratulate me. That must have been your way of throwing it in my face that you're carrying my husband's bastard child? What were you thinking?"

"Get out of my way!" Grey shouted, while trying to break loose of Dakota's grip.

Dakota's physical adrenaline pushed Grey back into the wall. "Do you deny that it is his baby?" Dakota asked. Then she released her grip from Grey.

"It is, but he doesn't know."

"He doesn't know a lot of things, but I'm sure you told him that."

"No, I didn't."

"I saw the two of you at the train station." Dakota's eyes glared as she recalled the incident. "I saw how he held you, and how he led you on that train. I can only imagine how many times the two of you met and made love on trains, while I was at home taking care of his son."

"He wanted to meet me, but I didn't tell him about the baby, mainly because of the situation."

"The situation," Dakota remarked viciously.

"You may not believe this, but I can't be with Bland now," admitted Grey.

"You mean, not until I'm out of the way?"

Suddenly, Dakota dug into her coat pocket. She gripped her hand around the object she retrieved earlier. Slowly, she began to pull it out.

Grey began to push Dakota away from her. Dakota slammed Grey back into the wall. She moved her free hand up toward Grey's throat when she noticed the locket around her neck. Her eyes locked in on the back of the locket and what words she could make out in the dim light.

"Umm, I guess he was your soul mate." When Dakota tried snatching the locket, Grey quickly secured the locket in the palm of her hand.

Dakota leaned forward when she smelled that familiar fragrance radiating from Grey's body. She recalled the feminine scent from the boutique to be the same scent on her comforter. She thought about the picture she found in her bedroom, and the selfie of Grey in her bed in lingerie posted on social media for everyone to see. The thoughts and visual images of Bland and Grey together began to fuel the rage within

Dakota.

"It was you in my house, in my bed, between my sheets."

Grey didn't answer.

"Is that where you conceived? And you're telling me you didn't tell him about your baby? Do I look like a fool?"

"I won't lie to you. I never knew about you and, yes, I do love Bland. And, yes, Bland has given me something beautiful, but when we were on that train, I couldn't bring myself to tell him. I thought about you."

With a cynical sigh, Dakota commented, "This is my fault?"

"It's not your doing or mine. It is Bland's doing, so there is no need for us to be at odds with each other."

Dakota dropped her eyes to think, then she began to shake her head. "My mother always said, 'Don't open gates in your life that don't need opening'. But I didn't listen because I needed him to be—"

Grey interrupted and pleaded, "Listen to me, Bland deceived me as much as he deceived you."

Gradually, Grey noticed the room was getting darker, so she tried giving Dakota a nudge so she could pass. Dakota snatched her by the arm to pull her close.

"You know, it doesn't matter because you're not having that baby."

Grey stopped struggling, "What are you saying?"

"Why should you be happy, while I live in misery?"

"You're talking crazy. Move out of my way!" Grey demanded.

Dakota's voice was more serious. "You're not having his baby."

Anger replaced Grey's fear. "I said move!" This time, Grey removed her hand from the locket to force her way past Dakota. The force was strong enough to cause Dakota to bite her tongue.

Immediately, Dakota violently forced Grey's shoulders to the wall and repeated, "I said you're not having this bastard child!"

Grey knew in order to protect her unborn baby she had to remove herself from such a volatile situation.

Without warning and much to Grey's surprise, Dakota struck her in the stomach. Grey crouched over with a loud scream. She looked up at Dakota with fuming eyes. Grey punched Dakota in the face to escape her assault. Dakota responded by wrapping her hand around

Grey's neck and squeezing. In retaliation, Grey lashed out at Dakota's throat. From the exit door, a crack of light streaked across the ceiling. That's when Dakota drove Grey's head hard toward the wall. Her head flopped backward to smack the wall hard. Grey's nails slashed across Dakota's face and her hands latched to her neck. When Grey felt the locket snap from her neck, she released her grip from around Dakota's throat. As the two wrestled for the locket, Dakota's jacket managed to get pulled over her head. She slipped her arms from the sleeves to free herself from the jacket. When Dakota lifted her head, Grey hit her in the face a second time. The jacket fell to the floor. Dakota backed away to throw a punch that landed square on Grey's chin. Grey charged Dakota and grabbed her by the hair. The room was more than half dark. Soon the darkness blinded them. The two women wouldn't release their grip. Unexpectedly, the elevator door opened, and someone rushed onto the floor.

—

The voice on the recorder came back in sequence with the book. And Jane began to listen.

The voice on the tape recorder began to jump, "Someone else just entered the room. Help me, please. She has my hair. It's dark, very dark. I can't see." Quickly Jane's eyes sped over the words.

—

A woman's voice screamed in panic, "What are you doing with that? No, NO!"

Seconds later there was the sound of a loud firecracker followed by an explosion.

—

Jane heard a loud scream followed by several loud slaps. It sounded like someone's hand smacking against a leather sofa.

"Relax, Jane. Tell me what's going on."

She began to cough, "I can't breathe."

Jane listened to the tape as her voice screamed louder from the

speaker. She could hear Dr. Westfall telling her not to smack herself in the face and arms.

"I have to get out of here. Fire is everywhere," Jane said and coughed again.

More screams blasted from the recorder before the player abruptly clicked off.

Jane sat in silence, still unaware that she read the book in sequence with the tape recorder. Before she could give it much thought, there was a knock on her door. Jane scrambled to stuff the recorder and tape under the mattress.

"Come in," she sat upright in the chair.

The nurse's aide poked her head in the room, "Are you okay? I thought I heard screaming."

Before Jane could answer, the aide had entered the room.

Jane shook her head, "Probably me laughing." She held up the book so the aide could see it.

"Why were you leaning down by the bed?" asked the aide.

Jane stalled, "I dropped something."

"Let me get it for you."

"No, I'll get it later."

Seconds later, Constance ran into the room. "I got a text from the nurse's station that screaming was coming from your room."

"Nothing like that, just my emotions being let off." Again, Jane held up the book.

"If that book is causing those types of emotions, do I need to take it?"

"I'll use more restraint," Jane smiled.

Constance gave the nurse's aide the okay to leave the room.

Jane noticed the serious look on Constance's face.

"Is everything okay?" asked Jane.

"Dr. Westfall said she is missing some taped sessions from her cabinet. Would you happen to know anything about some missing tapes?"

Jane looked down and saw part of the tape showing. She turned her body to use the side of her leg to push it back under the mattress.

"No," Jane replied.

Constance looked at Jane suspiciously while Jane held to her innocent stare.

"You look so happy, Connie," Jane said, hoping to divert attention from herself and the missing tapes.

"Is that supposed to be a joke," Constance replied. She then lightened her mood with a smile. "I do have some good news to tell you."

"What? You found a man?" laughed Jane.

"You are full of jokes today."

Before she could start telling Jane the news, Dr. Stewart entered the room with a man they had never seen. Dr. Stewart, usually with stern facial expressions, offered a slight smile that immediately demanded Jane's attention.

"Hello, Jane."

"Hello, Dr. Stewart," she replied quickly, while sliding her body onto the bed.

Jane looked over to the stranger and his attire. No doctor's coat, just plain clothes, she thought. She considered him from her past. Maybe someone has come to claim his lost love. Maybe that's what Constance was trying to share with me, she wanted to believe. He is cute, maybe I should be on my best behavior. Who knows, I might just find a new home after all.

Constance stepped to the side to let Dr. Stewart pass.

"Jane, this is Dr. Moss."

There goes that idea, Jane thought.

"Dr. Moss is a plastic surgeon. He is one of the leading plastic surgeons in the country and a personal friend of mine. I am highly indebted to his services, since underneath those bandages is his work."

Jane looked baffled. "He did this?" She pointed to her face.

Dr. Moss approached Jane, "Hello, Jane."

"Hello."

"To answer your question, yes, I am the doctor who performed your surgeries. I've come by today to check on you. I hear you've been making great progress."

Dr. Moss moved into the bathroom to wash his hands. Meanwhile, Dr. Stewart reached into his pocket to retrieve a pair of scissors. He

handed the scissors to Dr. Moss, who began cutting through the bandages. Constance's neck shifted back and forth to witness the bright surprise in Jane's eyes.

Once the bandages were completely off, Jane felt the cool air floating across her face. She closed her eyes momentarily and embraced the feeling of forever being uncovered and unrestrained.

The room was quiet as Dr. Moss silently inspected the condition of her skin. He used his index finger to touch around her stitches. Dr. Moss's face was still and showed no expression, so Jane was unsure as to what he thought.

After he finished inspecting her, he nodded to Constance to redress her face.

"Just when I started to get used to the cool air," Jane blurted.

Dr. Moss smiled, "Don't worry, you'll get that cool air soon enough."

"How does it look? And please, be honest."

"Actually, I'm pleased with the healing. There may be some cosmetic work needed later. Other than that, the bones and the grafts seem to be healing very well."

Jane looked at her hands and the scars left by the grafts. Curious to know, she asked, "Will my face look like my hands?"

"Frankly, your jaw lines were badly burned, but the rest of your face wasn't burned as badly as the rest of your body. When dealing with skin grafts, it's important to look after them with great care, for they are very fragile and susceptible to infections, especially those burned areas that didn't need grafts. Those areas are considered open wounds and take much longer to heal, which was expected. There was some bone damage in your face, so some reconstruction was also necessary.

"As of now, I want to leave the dressing and bandages in place. I want you to avoid strenuous exertion and stretching of the area until the stitches are removed."

"Then will I be free from these bandages?"

"Let me talk with Dr. Stewart and see what I can do."

The two doctors exited the room. Constance waited for the door to close before showing her excitement.

"He's cute," Jane grinned.

Constance showed a wide smile, "I was thinking the same thing. Anyway, I think the bandages are coming off soon, Jane."

Jane's voice rose with added excitement. "For good or temporary?"

"I'm thinking after Dr. Moss does his touchup. I give it another three, maybe four weeks."

Jane grew silent.

"What's wrong, Jane? I thought you would be happy."

"Another three to four weeks. I was hoping another two or three days."

Constance laughed, "You're impossible to please."

"I believe seeing my face will help me remember who I am. What more pleasure can I receive than that?"

"That's not a guarantee, Jane. I already told you seeing your face could stimulate a negative reaction. There's an old adage, 'don't put the horse before the cart.' The bandages will come off when they come off, and your memory will come back when it comes back. What has Dr. Stewart been telling you for months now?"

"It will come when it comes, but shouldn't I remember something about that night?"

"It was a rough night for you, Jane."

"I tried talking to Dr. Stewart, but he refuses to talk about that night." The question that she wanted to ask Constance suddenly resurfaced. "You were there. I'm sure you can tell me about that night."

Constance was hesitant to answer Jane, afraid that if she admitted her presence that night, she might slip and reveal something that she shouldn't, such as the baby. Not to mention, Dr. Westfall made it clear to Constance that Jane was too mentally unstable to handle such news. Constance elected to deceive Jane about her location and involvement at the hospital that night.

"I only remember what I was told, Jane. I was not there to witness anything. I happened to be in another part of the hospital and about to go home."

"Well, what did you hear? Come on, Connie, tell me something. It's killing me not to know."

"Okay, Jane, that's enough," she said softly, purposely averting

anymore inquiries. "The doctor said you need to get some rest. You have a long day tomorrow. Are you going to be okay by yourself?"

"I'll be okay," Jane said.

"If you need me, I will be on the floor. Just use your buzzer to call the nurse's station, and they will page me."

Before the door completely closed behind Constance, and before Jane could again grab the tape, Dr. Stewart and Dr. Moss reentered the room. Quickly, Jane pulled her hand back from under the mattress.

"Jane, we have great news," Dr. Stewart said.

"In a week you will come to my office for cosmetic surgery," said Dr. Moss. "That's pretty much the last phase to this entire process. Cosmetic surgery will help with your overall appearance. I need you to be in good health, so please take care of yourself, eat right and get some rest."

The two men exited the room, and this time Jane felt apprehensive about listening to the tapes. She was afraid that Constance or Dr. Stewart might walk back in the room, so instead she picked up the book and resumed reading it with a smile on her face.

22

AFTER CALLING THE SCOTTS AND GETTING NO ANSWER, Bland sat on the top of the steps to think. He didn't have Sharon's number, so he went back into his ransacked bedroom to see if Dakota had written it down. He gazed over the sprawled merchandise on the floor, then to the bed. What was she doing? he asked himself. Bland jumped when the bedroom phone rang.

He grabbed the receiver but could hear nothing. "Hello," he answered impatiently. "Hello." Bland then remembered he could only hear and be heard through the speaker of the phone.

"Bland," Wilkins shouted through the speaker.

"Mr. Wilkins?" Bland said curiously. Why was Mr. Wilkins calling to the house at such an hour?

"Listen to me carefully. There has been an accident, and you need to get to the publishing house right away."

"Accident? What accident?"

"You will know more when you get to the publishing house," his voice softer than Bland could ever recall.

"I can't, Mr. Wilkins, my son is not feeling well, and I was supposed to meet my wife at the hospital, but she has yet to admit him. I think something may be wrong, so I think it is best I stay here until she returns."

"Bland—"

Bland interrupted, "I am so sorry Mr. Wilkins, but I can't."

"It involves your wife," his voice raised.

"What do you mean, my wife? I don't understand."

"That's all I can say, Bland."

Bland sensed alarm in Wilkins's tone. "What are you saying, Mr. Wilkins?"

"For you to get here as soon as possible."

The phone clicked. Bland stood in the middle of the bedroom floor with his mind spinning. What in the hell is going on? he asked himself. Why is my wife there?

He began to worry. When the constant buzzing from the phone registered, he stopped his thoughts to hang up the phone. His eyes glazed over the items spread across the bed. He leaned against the wall to collect his thoughts.

"What was she looking for?" His eyes moved around the entire room, then back to the sprawled mess on the bed.

In the pit of his belly, he had a feeling that something awful had happened. Searching for answers, he paid particular attention to the scattered contents from Dakota's purse. He fiddled with additional thoughts. Suspicions that he was seeing another woman clearly could have been the reason for the disarray in the room, he believed. Immediately, his assumption about the bedroom was confirmed when he saw the picture that he and Grey had taken at the fair was ripped in half. He searched through the debris for the other half of the picture that composed Grey's image but could not find it.

Bland rushed out of the bedroom then down the stairs. On his way out of the front door, the phone rang again. He rushed to the phone without hesitation, thinking it might be Dakota, and he managed to answer on the second ring.

"Dakota!" he called with hope in his voice.

"No." The spirit in Bland's voice was lost in the reply.

"Is this Bland?"

"Yes."

"Bland, this is Sharon, your neighbor. Is your wife home?"

"Actually, I'm looking for my wife and my son."

"Devin is hanging out with my son."

Surprised, he said, "Devin is at your house?"

"Yes, Dakota said she was going to the store to get a few things. She asked if I would watch him until she returned. Trust me, Devin is in no rush to go home." She continued. "He and Chad are having a good time. I only called because I missed Dakota's call and saw that she left me a voice message. I don't check my voice mail often. I assumed it was her telling me she had returned from the store."

"No, she hasn't."

"I keep calling her phone, but she doesn't answer. Is everything okay?"

Because he didn't know how to answer the question, he let the silence linger a few seconds longer.

"Bland," Sharon called.

"Sharon, do you mind if Devin stays with you awhile longer? Maybe he can spend the night?"

"Sure, he can stay."

"I can bring you his pajamas."

"No need, Bland. Devin and Chad are about the same size. He can wear a pair of Chad's pajamas. Are you sure everything is okay?" she asked again.

"I don't know," he replied honestly. "I have no idea where Dakota is. She is not answering her phone. I just received an urgent call to return back to my job."

"Bland," her voice sounded panicky.

Realizing he had frightened her, Bland changed his words. "Sharon, I'm sure everything is okay, no need to worry."

"Anything I can do?"

"You're doing enough. I really appreciate it."

He put the phone down and ran to his SUV. As he drove, he stared blankly at the road ahead. As he neared the publishing house, he saw flashing lights across the backdrop of the dark sky. Underneath the disorderly light show appeared to be an even more chaotic mass of

people moving in and out of the building trying to put out pocket fires.

Bland parked his car a block from the building, away from the multitude of fire trucks, emergency vehicles, and police cruisers. He approached the burning building and saw flames pouring out of windows. He stopped in front of several firemen struggling with long hoses and rescue workers that assisted people with air masks to various ambulances. Standing a reasonable distance away from the building were Smith and Wilkins, watching the remaining fires as they were extinguished. Bland hurried his steps toward the men as his eyes looked over the massive destruction to the building. Desperate to know what this had to do with him, he walked up to the twins.

Composed, Smith extended his small hand to greet Bland.

"I need to know what's going on," Bland exclaimed.

"And you will," murmured Smith and continued. "This is Fire Chief Ryan. He's going to bring you up to speed."

Bland looked at the discolored face of the fire chief. The fire chief glared back at Bland. From that look, Bland suspected the worst.

"Mr. Benthall, there was an explosion that took place on the sixth floor."

"That's my floor," Bland blurted.

Chief Ryan continued, "The cause of the explosion has yet to be determined."

The chief then pulled out the security register and perused it before asking, "Can you identify any names on this pad?"

Bland remained composed as he hesitantly took hold of the pad. He had no idea what he was supposed to see on the pad. His eyes scrolled down the white paper until his head lifted from the page like a deer in headlights. Dakota's name stood out immediately.

"What does this mean?" he asked.

The chief responded, "Can you finish looking, sir?"

Bland glanced over to the twins, whose faces displayed feelings of deep sorrow. Then he repositioned his eyes back on the paper and scanned a few more names until he came to Greysen Brindle. Bland gasped when he scrolled back up the pad to see the time Dakota had entered the publishing house.

"Seven forty-five," Bland muttered.

That was forty-five minutes after the time Dakota called concerning Devin. Bland wasn't certain, but he believed Dakota had somehow met with Grey. He became frustrated and redirected that frustration to the Fire Chief.

"Are you going to tell me what the hell is going on, or do I have to guess?"

"Again, Mr. Benthall, we don't know all the facts."

"Then, can you tell me what you do know?"

There was nothing that could have prepared Bland for what he was about to hear.

"Mr. Benthall, I understand you're frustrated, but what we do know is that there were three bodies found on the sixth floor. As you can see, your wife and Greysen Brindle logged your name as the person they were coming to see."

Bland's knees buckled before he became pale faced.

"What do you mean, bodies?"

"There was an explosion, Bland," Wilkins said. "We believe Dakota and this Brindle woman were on the floor at the time of the explosion."

In disbelief, Bland challenged the men's findings. "How do you know it was them? It could have been someone else."

Chief Ryan spoke up quickly, "That's what we don't know, Mr. Benthall. We have to wait for the medical examiner to determine that."

Bland looked confused, "I thought you said there were three bodies."

"Yes, it appears one of the women was pregnant. I'm assuming the blast might have sent the woman into premature labor, because we found the remains of a fetus. I am told your wife was pregnant. Is that information correct?"

Traumatized, Bland plunged his face in his trembling palms and quietly answered, "Yes."

"Again, Mr. Benthall, before we assume anything, let's wait for the medical examiner's report."

He lifted his head from his hands to ask, "Why is that? Aren't the bodies identifiable?"

"The bodies were so close to the initial blast that they were charred.

Heat and time can destroy teeth, so there may not be enough for dental identification."

"You don't know the cause of the fire?"

"An accurate determination concerning the cause will not be given until the arsonist investigator has inspected the site, which can take weeks."

"You can't tell me anything?" Bland spat hatefully.

"I assure you, Bland, there will be a full investigation," Smith replied in a concerned voice.

Bland was still in a state of denial when the bodies were wheeled out of the building. His entire body slumped over as he faced the grim reality that those bodies could be Grey, Dakota and his unborn child. Bland then collapsed to both knees, pain suffocating him as if it were smoke.

He didn't want to believe it, but somehow guilt managed to shadow him like a fast-fading sunset. He was crowned with the ultimate guilt that a man could place on himself, knowing his selfishness was the cause of their deaths.

Jane, too, suffocated on tears as the book dropped from her hands. She sobbed knowing that an innocent baby had died because of Bland's selfishness. Jane wasn't convinced who she thought might have died in the explosion, given the fact that someone did rush on the floor before the explosion. She took what the fire chief said about finding three dead bodies, and one of those bodies being a dead fetus. She knew both Dakota and Grey were six months pregnant. Furthermore, the chief never mentioned the other body found was pregnant. Jane wanted to believe that someone did survive the explosion. Moreover, she wanted to believe that someone could have been either Dakota or Grey. She lay there contemplating which woman could have survived, and she found herself in a quandary between the two women. There was a part of her that wished Grey lived because her innocence was taken by her willingness to love; while the other half of her heart poured out for Dakota, who immersed herself in loving and supporting her husband

to the point she put her own happiness aside. The fact that Dakota had a son who would grow up motherless caused more tears to drip from her eyes onto the pages of the book. She felt anger and sorrow toward Bland. The pain ran deep into her heart. Despite her angst, she couldn't stop herself from continuing to read.

—

After being on his knees for several intense minutes, Smith tried to lift Bland by the arm. Bland jerked away, then stood and took off into the darkness of the night. In a state of shock, for hours he aimlessly wandered the downtown streets of Washington, D.C.

23

MARGIE AND THOMAS FLEW TO WASHINGTON, D.C., a few days after they received the terrible news that their daughter was in a tragic accident. They tried to prepare themselves for the inevitable, but it was the uncertainty of not knowing if it was Dakota that devastated them the most. Although the anguish showed only in Thomas's eyes, deep fissure lines on Margie's face were testaments to her grief.

After a week of waiting to discuss Dakota in more detail, the three of them gathered in the kitchen. Margie had prepared a pot of coffee. Bland opened the discussion with apologies.

Margie interrupted, "It's not your fault, Bland. It's God's will." She offered him a soothing tap on the back before saying, "I can't believe she was having another baby."

Bland spoke quickly, "On Thanksgiving Day, we planned to surprise you guys with the news."

Margie's lips held tight as she began to sob. The reality of not seeing her daughter or unborn grandchild hit her hard.

There was a heavy desperation on Bland's conscience to tell the Gates why their daughter was at the office that night. However, he couldn't

bring himself to say it.

"What should we do about the burial?" Bland asked, as he took one of the cups of coffee from the counter.

"Well," Thomas's deep voice commanded the room. "We can't do anything until she is released for burial; that is, if it's her. First, I want to make sure it's my daughter."

Bland felt he had offended Thomas, but he didn't know how to approach a conversation about Dakota without talking about the possibilities of her really dying in that explosion, given the reality that only two people were on the floor during the explosion and only two bodies were found. Bland believed the faster a confirmation was that the body was hers, the faster they all would start their healing process.

Margie came to Bland's rescue even though she struggled to embrace the finality of her daughter being gone.

"Thomas, maybe we need to prepare ourselves for if Dakota is gone."

"I don't want to act too prematurely," Thomas sighed.

Bland was about to speak when the doorbell rang. He excused himself to get the door. From the peep hole, Bland didn't recognize the visitor. He watched as the man wiped donut crumbs from his mouth and jacket. With caution, Bland opened the door. A fairly stout man with a widow's peak and a unibrow stood in front of the screen door. The man had a full face that matched his size. Bland scrutinized the long, black rain jacket the man wore and tried to figure out who he was.

The man detected Bland's apprehension to open the screen door, so immediately he called Bland by his last name.

"Mr. Benthall?"

"Yes," Bland said, as he cracked the screen door.

"I'm Detective Rhodavack." The detective pulled his badge from his inside jacket pocket. "I would like to ask you some questions."

Bland took a quick glance at the badge, then glanced over his shoulder into the house. "What's this all about?" he asked.

"I just have a few questions I need to ask concerning where you were the night of the explosion. It's normal procedure for something of this nature."

"Normal procedure? What's normal about it? My wife was in an

explosion. She could be dead."

"Yes, I know about the explosion, and I apologize, Mr. Benthall, if my presence makes me seem insensitive." The detective paused, "It's kind of cold out here. Do you think we can talk inside?"

Bland glared from behind the screen door. He thought, how rude it was of the detective to show up at his house so soon after the explosion.

"Do you really think this is the appropriate time?"

"Like I said, Mr. Benthall, it's procedure to come by and ask a few questions. I must admit, Mr. Benthall, I am like an insect. I come out at the worse possible times, and I tend to get all up in your business. What can I say? I do what I do, and I do it well."

"Are you threatening me?" Bland asked.

"Not at all," replied Detective Rhodavack.

Bland looked at the detective, "I would prefer we spoke outside. My in-laws are here, and they are having a hard time dealing with the likely death of their daughter and grandchild."

The detective stepped back so Bland could step outside.

"How can I help you, Detective?" Bland asked, as he closed the front door behind him. He didn't want to bother the Gates with the sudden appearance of a detective, even though the detective's presence bothered him.

"Again, Mr. Benthall, I sure do apologize for coming to your home unannounced. I would have given you a call, but I was already in the area. So, I figured, why not drop by."

Bland offered Detective Rhodavack no response as he listened.

"The night of the explosion, where were you?"

"I already told this to the officers at the scene that night."

"R..i..g..h..t," he dragged the word out in an annoying fashion. "I'm sure you did, but I need for you to tell me. Sometimes uniformed officers are not as detailed as we would like them to be. I'm sure you understand, especially being a writer and all."

Bland gave the detective an intent stare before answering his question. "The night of the accident, I was at home."

"R..i..g..h..t, funny you should say accident," the detective corrected Bland, "because it hasn't been ruled as an accident. Well, at least not yet."

Bland was taken aback by his comment. "What do you mean? The fire chief said the explosion resulted from a faulty propane heater."

"It could have been part of the explosion but not necessarily the cause of the explosion. So, if anything, it was a premature response by the fire chief since the investigation is still underway. Any time a fatality results from a fire, it's important to make sure you dot your i's and cross your t's. Don't be too quick to say it is one thing when it could be something else."

Bland shifted his weight, "What type of detective are you?"

"I'm sorry, I thought I told you. I'm a homicide detective, Mr. Benthall."

"Are you saying there was some foul play involved?"

The detective pulled out a pen and a notepad. "I'm not insinuating or assuming anything. Just trying to determine what actually happened that night."

"I'm not sure what happened that night," Bland said.

"Then maybe we can help each other. So, you were at home around…?"

"About seven o'clock."

"Well, according to my notes," Detective Rhodavack flipped through papers that seemed to be in no particular order. "You have to forgive me; I was never a good organizer. Ah ha!" he bellowed. "Here it is. I'm told writers like you keep good notes. Well, I'll be the first to admit I never was good at writing, but I like to keep good notes. It has a way of keeping one on point. Don't you agree?"

When there was no answer from Bland, the detective continued.

"R..i..g..h..t. Anyway, I managed to get my hands on your company's phone records, in particular from your office. The records show that a call was placed from your office around 7:00 p.m. If you were at home, do you know who could have been in your office?"

"I was in my office," Bland replied.

"But you just said—"

Frustrated with the questions, Bland uttered, "I was confused with the time."

"Wooo!" exaggerated the detective. "For a minute there I thought my

notes were wrong. I tell you, I live and die by these notes."

Bland stood silent.

"So, who did you call, Mr. Benthall?"

"I called home to speak to my wife. Those records should also show that I received two calls from my house."

"R...i...g...h...t," he dragged the word out longer than usual. "I saw that. The call from your wife was regarding?"

"My wife was concerned about our son. I drove home to see about him. To my surprise, she wasn't there."

"She wasn't there, r..i..g..h..t. The detective scribbled in his book, then continued with his questions. "So, where was she?"

Bland looked at the man awkwardly as if the question was a joke.

Bland sighed, "It takes approximately twenty to twenty-five minutes to drive to the publishing house from our home. Given the time she logged in on the security register that puts her at my office. And me at my house."

"Mr. Benthall, you sure are good with details, maybe you should have gone into law enforcement, maybe become a detective. Then again, I was surprised to find out you are the author of so many suspense novels. I'm impressed. I heard you have a creative mind, especially the ability to think like a criminal. I guess you would have to, since you do write those types of books."

Bland remained silent.

"I also heard you have a way of making the detectives in some of your novels appear…" he paused and said, "what's the word I'm looking for, ah, incompetent. Yet, we always do catch our villain, even in your books, so I hear," said the detective, as he held up his index finger and continued, "but I'm confused. Why would your wife go to your office when she knew you were on your way home?"

Without expression, Bland replied, "I don't know."

"R..i..g..h..t," said the detective as he looked intently into Bland's eyes.

Bland had become annoyed with the manner in which the detective drew out the word "R..i..g..h..t."

Abruptly, the detective switched the conversation from Dakota to Grey. Somehow Bland knew the conversation would eventually turn to Grey.

"On the publishing house register, it showed you had another visitor that night. She arrived shortly after your wife, a Mrs. Greysen Brindle."

"Ms. Brindle," Bland corrected.

"A widow?" the detective asked.

"No, divorced," Bland replied.

"If you don't mind me asking, what was the nature of your relationship with Ms. Brindle?" The detective offered a list of choices for Bland to choose from. "Was she a business partner, a colleague, or a friend?"

Quickly, Bland retorted, "She is a friend," then remembered Grey was likely no longer with him. "Was a friend."

"A friend," the detective echoed. "R..i..g..h..t," he uttered softly. "Do you have any idea why your wife and," he glanced over his notes, "Greysen Brindle were meeting at your office?"

"That's an assumption, detective. I am not sure that they were meeting each other. There is a possibility that they just happened to be there at the same time."

Bland knew the odds of that were slim, and he was sure the detective wasn't buying it. Still, it was a good question, thought Bland. Since the night of the explosion, Bland had been pondering how Dakota and Grey ended up at the publishing house together.

"At the same time," he repeated with a laugh. "R..i..g..h..t, that's interesting, Mr. Benthall. I'm not one who believes in coincidences. For the sake of argument, let's say it was by chance they met at your office. You said you and Greysen Brindle were friends? Was she also a friend of your wife?"

"No!" Bland snapped.

"How would you categorize your friendship with this woman? Was it platonic, or maybe something a little closer?"

Bland knew what the detective was trying to insinuate. "We were just friends, Detective." Bland put extra emphasis on the word "detective" to let Detective Rhodavack know he was tired of his questions.

"How did you come to know Ms. Brindle?"

Bland's face turned sour with irritation, and he used extra bass in his voice with his answer.

"I met her twenty years ago, and I have known her ever since."

A partial truth, Bland thought, but hopefully enough to stop the detective's line of inquiry.

"That's a long time, and you've been married for how long?"

"Fifteen years."

"You went to college with your wife and married shortly after the two of you graduated?"

"Yes." From the questions, Bland realized the detective had been conducting some background checks on him that extended well beyond the fact he was a writer.

"You say your wife didn't know this Greysen Brindle?"

"No," Bland said, unflinchingly.

"I don't know if I asked this. Did you attend college with Ms. Greysen Brindle?"

Bland responded emotionlessly, "No, you never asked me that question and no, I never did."

The detective began chewing on leftover crumbs that had settled in his mouth. Bland paused to consider that Dakota and Grey had never met except for the one encounter in the boutique. As the detective sucked his teeth, Bland regained his composure and waited for another question.

Bland found the detective's questions to be unusual. It was like the detective knew something but wasn't revealing it.

There was a slow shifting of the detective's eyes as he looked at his notes again.

"Mr. Benthall, according to my notes, you stopped writing for a number of years. Then suddenly you were given a proposition to write again, I understand. The terms of that contract included a partnership in exchange for another novel. What an incentive!" Automatically, Bland knew the detective had spoken with the twins.

The detective looked up from the paper, "Now, at any time that you find my notes to be incorrect, please don't hesitate to correct me."

"Junior partnership," Bland corrected.

"Excuse me?"

"The contract was for a junior partnership."

"R..i..g..h..t." Then the detective continued, "Mr. Benthall, you stand

to make a lot of money from this junior partnership; that is, if you finish the book by the deadline. Given the situation, do you think finishing the book is even a possibility?"

Bland didn't bite on his question; he had an idea where the detective was going with the questions, but Bland wanted to be certain, so he asked.

"Where are you heading with this, Detective?"

"You'll know when I get there. Now, are you planning on leaving town any time soon?"

"That depends on the medical examiner's findings."

"R..i..g..h..t. I know what you mean. A lot of things hinge on those findings."

Bland didn't understand what the detective meant by the comment, but his constant use of the word "right" had more than irritated him.

"I know it appears I'm a callous man, but I am sympathetic to your loss. I mean losses. And, please give my condolences to your wife's family."

"That's if it's her," Bland was quick to correct the detective. "Remember a lot hinges on those findings, so I won't be passing on any condolences until I know it's my wife."

"R..i..g..h..t, and I apologize for my assumptions. As I stated before, I am not here to insinuate or assume." He stopped momentarily to check his notes. "Oh, did you know any of Ms. Brindle's family? The department is unable to locate any next of kin." He noticed Bland's annoyed facial expression and continued, "The department is trying to be proactive in case the medical examiner matches her to one of the bodies. So, as I was saying, you being such a longtime friend, surely you know someone?"

"No, I don't."

The detective looked at Bland suspiciously before saying, "R..i..g..h..t, I will be contacting you soon, Mr. Benthall."

Bland did not respond.

Detective Rhodavack turned and walked to his car. Bland waited for the detective's cruiser to disappear around the curve before heading back into the house. He wondered what would make a homicide detective interested in a case that was supposedly ruled as an accident.

Bland heard the front door open behind him. Thomas stood in the doorway.

"News about Dakota?" Thomas asked.

Bland tried to keep himself from crumbling to the ground as he talked to Thomas.

"Nothing, just the mail carrier."

"It's cold, Bland. Why don't you come inside?"

"I will after I get some more of this fresh air."

"Go right ahead, son," Thomas said, as he closed the door and headed down the hall.

Bland needed to be alone so he could muse over the reason for the sudden visit from the detective. He sat on the steps to question what connections the detective was trying to make. Abruptly, his thoughts dead-ended.

"Bland?" called John Scott, who was accompanied by his wife, Keri. Bland stood to his feet. There was a cake dish in Mrs. Scott's hand.

"We came to pay our respects, Bland," Keri whimpered. "I fixed this carrot cake."

"Can you take it inside for me? Dakota's mother and father are in the house."

"Sure I can." Keri made her way into the house.

"I'm coming, dear, I want to speak to Bland alone." John turned his head to face Bland. "How are you holding up, son?"

"The best I can."

"Any news?"

"Nothing," Bland shook his head.

"I want you to know that we are here for you. Whatever you need, don't hesitate to ask."

"Thanks, John, I really appreciate that."

John began moving toward the door, then stopped to say something. "Oh, my garage received the call to pick up your wife's car and take it to the impound."

"You did?"

"I didn't take it to the impound. It's in my garage," John paused on his words. "It would mean a lot to me if you let me fix that starter. I know

she's not around to drive it, but it would do my soul a world of good to fix it anyway."

"That's fine, John. I'd appreciate it if you did fix it." Bland noticed John beginning to chuckle to himself. "What is it, John?"

"That car managed to wake me up one last time, actually the night before she died. It was snowing so hard, but she was out there trying to start it." Suddenly, John caught his words, "I'm sorry, Bland, to keep implying that she's gone."

"It's okay, John. I don't want to believe she's gone either." Bland paused. "John, I want to go back to what you said about the starter. The car woke you up the night of the explosion?"

"No, it was the night before the explosion. As soon as she got it started, she skid-wheeled out the drive. The night of the explosion, I was at the shop all night."

"Around what time would that have been? I mean, when her car woke you?"

"I would say around 10 o'clock. Is something wrong, Bland?"

Slowly, Bland shook his head, "No, John."

"Well, son, let me go pay my respects. I'll talk to you later. Remember what I said, anything you need."

The door to the house closed, but Bland's mind was preoccupied with new thoughts. The situation was starting to develop some perspective for him. After John disclosed that Dakota left the house the night he rendezvoused with Grey, Bland was certain Dakota followed him to the train station.

Dakota knew I blew off our evening to be with Grey, Bland admonished himself. If she followed me, then certainly she recognized Grey from the boutique. That would explain her innuendos of an affair.

As he stared off into the dense greyish sky, a deep fog settled over his thoughts and clouded his thinking. Bland tried to correct his thinking with an assumption. Perhaps Dakota didn't see Grey; that's why she didn't reveal his mistress's identity to him. Still, the reality is that both were on the floor at the time of the explosion. How is that possible? he asked himself and continued his thought. Dakota didn't have a way of contacting Grey, even if Dakota knew who Grey was, Bland assumed.

His thoughts ended before he snapped his fingers and then he turned to dash into the house. He skipped stairs to head to his bedroom. Once in the bedroom, he ran to the house phone. Quickly he scrolled down the caller ID list of outbound calls. He frowned when he recognized Grey's number.

"What the hell?" He was unnerved with the idea of what may have been said. "She wanted to confront Grey, and she needed a place to do it. That would be the reason she called me home," he muttered. "Would that be enough to bring a homicide detective by my house?"

There was something missing, something that Bland believed the detective wasn't disclosing. In hopes of identifying the detective's intentions, he revisited their conversation. Slowly he began pulling out important words that the detective used like "lovers," "money," "anger," and "time." He wondered more about the timing because everything seemed to revolve around the time things took place. Things like him bolting home to find the house empty; Dakota and Grey at the publishing house around the same time; the deadline of the partnership and how he would gain a lot of money from it, and when he met Grey. Did the detective believe he had something to do with their deaths? Bland's mind seemed to stall. Maybe that's why the detective mentioned the money? Or maybe the detective was trying to attach the money as a motive for him to get rid of his wife, so he could be with Grey? He continued to mull over other possibilities.

Thomas stood at the bottom of the staircase calling Bland's name. Finally, the voice broke through Bland's frantic thoughts. "I'll be down in a minute."

Minutes later, Bland walked into the kitchen and saw the Scotts and Margie and Thomas sitting around the kitchen table having a cup of coffee.

"Bland, the missus and I have talked, and if Dakota is gone, we want to bring her body back home. We want to lay her to rest with her grandparents. Now, we value your opinion and—"

Thomas's words were cut short by Bland. "I figured you would want to do that, and I agree, Thomas. If Dakota is no longer with us, then her body needs to go back home. Honestly, this was never her home; being

in the countryside made her feel happier than any place in the world. She would have wanted that."

Margie was quick to walk over and place both her arms around Bland. "Bland, thank you."

Bland dropped his head.

The next couple of days were quiet around the house. Bland tried to stay busy to prevent his mind from creating an iota of hope that possibly Dakota wasn't in the explosion. He wanted to do the right thing and hang around the house in case Thomas or Margie needed him. More importantly, he refused to go anywhere for fear that he would miss the medical examiner's call.

As more days passed, the likelihood of his wife and Grey being dead was becoming more and more of a reality that he had no choice but to accept. Selfishly, he felt lonely.

Margie caught Bland drifting through the house.

"Bland, get out of this house and get some fresh air."

"I went out earlier." He tried to maneuver around her.

"No, get in your car and take a long ride and really get some fresh air."

Bland unwillingly grabbed his coat and keys. He drove aimlessly. Before he knew it, he found himself in the vicinity of the hospital. He considered stopping to see the medical examiner. He had been waiting over two weeks for someone to contact him. As he approached the hospital, he took a sudden turn into the entrance. The medical examiner could put to rest some of his fears. He needed to know for certain that it was Dakota and Grey in the explosion. That would be the only way he could let them go.

As he approached the hospital's morgue, he stopped when he noticed a security guard walking by the entrance to the morgue. He waited for the guard to disappear down an adjacent hallway before heading to the doors of the morgue. There was a pungent odor coming from the room. Bland bit down on his lip as he entered the cold room. A man in a white surgical uniform stood over a lifeless body. Bland watched from

a distance before gaining enough nerve to approach. With a surgical knife, the man cut down the center of the cadaver. Just to watch was making Bland sick to his stomach.

"Excuse me," Bland called from afar.

The man in the white uniform lifted his head up from the body. He pulled the protective goggles from his face.

"Can I help you, sir?"

Bland tried not to look at the dead body stretched out on the table but couldn't stop himself from taking a glance. A chill crept along his spine. Right away he said to the man, "I'm looking for the medical examiner."

The man pointed to an office near the back of the room with the shades pulled down. A dim light seeped through the cracks between the shades. Bland knocked on the door. Soon the medical examiner invited him into the office.

After entering the office, Bland immediately looked at the name tag on the doctor's coat.

"Benson Hatti, M.D." Dr. Hatti instructed Bland to close the door behind him.

"Hello," Bland's words stalled. He didn't know what he should say or ask. "Sir, I'm here about my wife."

"Your wife?" Dr. Hatti asked with little recollection. "Her name is?"

"I apologize. Let me start over. My name is Bland Benthall, and supposedly my wife was in a recent downtown fire. I mean an explosion."

"Yes, I recall that. Please give me a second." The doctor pulled a chart from the file cabinet. "Those bodies were found in the S&W building?"

"Yes, that would be correct."

"I was meaning to call you," the doctor said, as he opened the file. "You saved me a call."

"You were meaning to call me?" Bland was taken by the doctor's comment. Even though he was wishful that the medical examiner would have information on his wife, he really didn't expect that information so soon. The magnitude of the tragedy had given Bland the impression that the autopsy and its findings would take weeks to complete. At least in his novels it did.

"Doesn't an autopsy take weeks to complete?"

"An autopsy can take anywhere from three hours to twenty-four hours to complete. Sometimes writing out our findings can take longer. As for the bodies found in the explosion, identifying the bodies and determining the mechanism of death was vital."

"Mechanism of death," Bland repeated, then thought about what the detective said about the gun, "like a gun?"

"Like smoke inhalation from the fire. According to Detective Rhodavack, the gun to which I assume you're referring caused the explosion, but it did not directly cause their demise."

Bland's attention was piqued, "You spoke with the detective?"

"I tried to speed up the process after a Detective Rhodavack came by to inspect the bodies, and go over some forensic evidence, another reason for not getting back right away. I apologize, but the police have priority. As for the other female found in the explosion, do you know her as well?"

"Yes, I do." Then Bland asked bluntly, "So what were your findings, doctor?"

"My preliminary findings suggest that one of the bodies was closer to the initial blast or heat of the explosion than the other bodies, which means the body closer to the initial blast had a lower rate of identification.

"I compared your wife's dental records with what I found from the teeth of the body. Much of the frontal plate was damaged, but I was able to identify her by her dental records, as you can see here."

He handed Bland the dental x-ray for Dakota, then Dr. Hatti pulled out several grotesque pictures that had been taken of the body after the explosion. Bland forced himself to look at the charcoaled face with severe damage to the mouth.

Dr. Hatti began to explain the records. "The teeth act just like a fingerprint; it helps with identifying severely burned or decomposed bodies. The teeth are numbered." He pointed with his finger to a tooth on the dental x-ray. "This is the number three tooth. This tooth has a filling, which matches the number three tooth on this body."

Bland appeared surprised because he'd never known she had a filling. He continued to look at the x-ray.

"As a result of the force from the blast, your wife's fetus was detached

from her womb. Do you want to see those pictures?"

Immediately, Bland felt sick to his stomach. He quickly refused. "No." Slowly, he dropped his head. He struggled with the confirmation that Dakota was dead, and his baby was dead too.

"What about the other body?" asked Bland. Abruptly the door to the office opened and a beard-faced man entered. Quickly, Dr. Hatti stopped the man at the door.

"I'll be with you in a minute." The man looked at Bland and then closed the door as he left.

A strange feeling came over Bland. He wondered if he knew the man from somewhere, but the thought soon disappeared when Dr. Hatti went on with his findings.

"The other body," he repeated. "That would be," he went flipping through another chart, "Greysen Brindle. The physical description of the police report matches that of my observations of the body. The police couldn't locate any dental records. From my medical opinion, this body is the same person that signed the log-in sheet, which places her at the scene of the explosion."

"These are just your preliminary results, correct? Not your final determination of who might have died?" Bland tried to give himself some hope that the doctor might change his conclusion.

"Mr. Benthall, we do have a full house of bodies, so the full report of my findings will not be ready until several weeks from now. Frankly, my final report won't deviate from my preliminary report. I wish I had better news to give you."

Bland took a deep breath. "I just needed to hold on to something."

"I understand, Mr. Benthall."

Bland collected himself. "What are your plans for Ms. Brindle's body?"

"Normally, if the body isn't claimed, the coroner's office would donate it to a university with medical programs for students to study and learn from. This body, however, is too damaged to be kept for medical purposes. It will probably get shipped out to a funeral parlor to be buried or cremated. We used to do it here, but hospital cutbacks eliminated that. I'm sorry, young man, but no one has come forward to

claim her."

Bland nodded, "Thank you, doctor."

Bland began to feel queasy. Immediately, he felt his breath shortening. Quickly, he left the office and headed for the two steel exit doors of the morgue. At the other end of the room, the beard-faced man that barged into the office and the man in the white coat from earlier were huddled. The men made brief eye contact with Bland before walking into another room. The mere presence of them made Bland feel uncomfortable.

Outside the building, Bland took cover under a nearby tree to regurgitate. The cold air braced him against the reality of their deaths. There was no need to speculate anymore; his uncertainties concerning their deaths were now a reality. All he could think about now was how to break the news to Dakota's parents.

24

Dakota was buried two weeks before Thanksgiving. The day of the funeral was extremely hard for Bland. After they buried Dakota and their premature child, he wanted to isolate himself in the Gates's guest bedroom. Devin sat beside him, asking questions that Bland found difficult to answer. He tried telling Devin his mother was gone to a better place, a place that God had prepared. Tears slowly ran down Devin's cheeks.

"I will never get to see her again?" he asked in his soft voice. Bland hugged him tightly and did not respond.

Jane reached over for a few tissues to wipe her eyes before continuing to read.

Bland broke down when he saw Devin's tears. Thomas quickly came to his aid to take his grandson to another room.

Bland sat alone in the bedroom, weeping. Margie, who also was trying to maintain her strength, happened to see Bland from the doorway. She saw his tears drip over the photo of Dakota that he held

in a tight clutch. She watched in silence as he moved the photo to his chest. After standing in the doorway for a while, she went to his side to comfort him.

"Bland?"

Bland placed the photo back on the dresser and turned slowly toward the comforting sound of her voice.

"I know you're hurting, Bland. We all are hurting, but this is when family pulls together. Whatever you need, Bland, we are here for you."

He looked into Margie's saddened, damp eyes and wanted desperately to tell her the truth about Dakota's death. Yet, he couldn't bring himself to do it. Since reeling from the news of their daughter's death, neither Thomas nor Margie asked what actually happened that night. All they knew was what the police report said: Dakota went to the office to meet Bland, and suddenly there was an explosion, and she happened to be at the wrong place at the wrong time.

Like a coward, but worse than a coward, Bland was also a hypocrite. He accepted the police report when he knew the truth, and that caused him, in shame, to turn his eyes away from Margie.

Margie put her arms around Bland's shoulder. He mustered enough effort to say, "Margie, this is going to be hard on Devin, and I don't—"

Margie interrupted, "Don't worry. Devin can stay with us while you get yourself together."

"You don't mind?"

"Bland, the moment you married my daughter, you became family. This is hard for everyone, and we will stick together."

There came a soft knock on the door, and they both turned to look. It was Lou. Margie gave Bland a soft hug.

"I'll check on Devin so you two can talk."

Bland sat silently as she excused herself, but not before Lou kissed her on the cheek. Lou closed the door behind her.

"How are you holding up, old friend?" Lou asked as he moved toward the bed.

Bland shook his head as a gesture of not so good. "Lou, thanks for flying down."

"Hey, it's nothing; she was my friend, too. You want to talk?"

Since their deaths, Bland hadn't discussed the matter with anyone, including Lou. However, Lou pressed the issue until Bland's walls caved.

"Bland, you have to talk to someone about this."

"Dragging someone else into this was the last thing I wanted to do."

"You can't carry their deaths around as if it's your fault," Lou said.

"Isn't it my fault? They were at the office because of me. None of this would have ever happened if it weren't for me. Of course it's my fault."

"You can't say their deaths were your fault. Sure, you played your part in this, but who knows what happened that night."

Bland paused like he wanted to say something, then he stalled. Suddenly, he just came out with it.

"A homicide detective visited me. He pretty much interrogated me on my doorstep about Dakota and how I knew Grey."

"Homicide detective?" Lou repeated. "Why would a homicide detective be visiting you? I thought the explosion was due to a faulty heater."

"So did I, but I have a feeling this detective is trying to hold someone criminally responsible for their deaths."

"You're kidding me," Lou replied.

"He wouldn't let on as to what he knew. He kept asking about Grey, and if she had ever met Dakota before that night. Lou, all I keep thinking about is how they died."

As Bland's upper body slumped forward, his face plowed deep into his hands. He began to contemplate the explosion and their deaths.

"Their bodies were completely charred." He took a second to think about what he said, "My God, Lou. They were burned to death."

Bland thought of the fetus that was so graphically described to him the night of their deaths.

"I can't imagine anyone dying such a terrible death, and my unborn child died in that explosion," Bland cried.

"Bland, stop!" Lou interrupted. "Don't keep tormenting yourself."

Tears streamed down Bland's cheeks and into the palms of his hands. Lou clutched Bland by the shoulders, and Bland felt his body being pulled to his feet.

"Hold yourself together, Bland."

"I am trying, Lou," he sniffed. "What kind of man am I? What have I done? Look at what I have become. I can't even bring myself to tell her parents how their daughter really came to her death, and how it is all because of me and my selfishness and infidelity."

Lou whispered, "I can't see the good in telling them now. I know that sounds insensitive."

"Telling them could do my conscience some good."

"Bland, I am not telling you to conceal the truth forever, but allowing things to settle down would do everybody a world of good. The Gates just lost their daughter and their unborn grandchild, so you telling them would only compound the situation and make the matter worse."

"Waiting only brings pain later," he blurted, remembering Dakota's motto.

"Bland, you can't change it now. What's done is done."

"I can tell Margie and Thomas why she was even at my office that night."

"What good is that going to do now?" Lou reasoned. "Devin is their grandson and having them hate you isn't going to make things better for you. You'll find yourself in an awful custody battle, a civil suit, and who knows what else."

"I don't have any money," Bland cried.

"That isn't the point, Bland. If you confess your part in their daughter's death, they will look at you as the villain. You will become the scapegoat for their grief. Giving them time to heal may help with the process of forgiving you later. Your heart will tell you when to tell them and how to tell them. Don't do it on impulse or because of a guilty conscience."

Bland sighed, "That isn't what Dakota would say. She didn't like things to drag on." Bland stared out the window. "She would always say tell it now and get it out of the way so she could deal with it."

Somehow his thoughts transitioned from telling the Gates the truth about Dakota's death to him telling Dakota the truth about his affair when he had the chance. He let her pain linger, even when he knew she suspected him of seeing another woman.

Bland sighed, "I should have told her about Grey."

Unexpectedly, Lou asked, "What about Grey? Has anyone claimed

the body?"

"Grey," Bland whispered while still in his daze. He seemed to be outside himself. Amid such disorder, he thought about the medical examiner saying what might happen to Grey's remains. He felt sad that she wouldn't have a proper burial.

"No, her parents died years back, and even if I could find her ex-husband, he wouldn't give a damn. According to the morgue, the normal procedure is to donate the body to a university for medical purposes or send it to a funeral parlor. If it's sent to the parlor, I'm told if no one claims the body by a specific time, the funeral parlor would cremate it. I really need to go to her apartment and box up her belongings, but I can't seem to bring myself to do it."

Lou stated the obvious, "It needs to be done."

"I know, but the idea of it all gives me such an uneasy feeling."

"Do you need me to do it?" Lou offered.

"No, I have to do it. I have to face this."

"What are you planning to do with her stuff?"

"I haven't decided. Maybe donate it to some shelter. I'll go to her apartment when I return to the city."

"I am here to help, Bland, so call me if you need me."

A day after the funeral, the Gates and Devin drove Bland to the local airport. The ride to the airport was extremely quiet. All Bland could think about was what Lou said, so he decided to postpone his confession.

Once at the airport, he gave Devin a long hug. Devin was his only connection to Dakota and leaving him behind felt as if he were losing someone else. Margie and Thomas thought it would be best so Bland could get his house in order. If they only knew how out of order his house really was, they would take Devin from him, he thought. Somehow, he knew they needed Devin to help them heal as much as he did.

"Margie and Thomas, thanks again, and thanks for taking Devin."

"No problem, Bland," replied Thomas. "You just take your time to heal. Devin being down here will help us do the same. Are you coming back for Thanksgiving? We sure would love to have you."

"I don't know. I just need to get my mind together. I'm still supposed

to finish that book."

"Bland, don't worry yourself about that book."

"No, I have to because I promised Dakota I would finish it. I have to finish it for her."

"We understand, Bland. Do what you have to do, son," said Thomas, as he handed Bland his luggage.

When Bland returned home, the house was quiet, so quiet and so empty. He thought how desolate a house felt when there was no one there to give it life. The small things stood out the most, like not expecting a left hook to the body the instant he stepped through the front door. He dropped his bags and walked through the dark hallway to the flashing red light on the answering machine. There were a few messages on the machine. Lou had called several times, and the twins called telling him not to rush on the manuscript. The last call on the machine was from a stranger's voice that identified himself as the director of the Northeast Funeral Home. The man didn't say how he had gotten Bland's number, but somehow Bland had become the contact person concerning Grey's affairs. Bland thought maybe the medical examiner felt sympathy for him. Exactly what Bland planned to do with her remains was still undecided.

"Grey's remains," Bland repeated.

The message burned the reality that it all was real. Too real, both were gone. He tried hiding from the truth with the vodka underneath the kitchen sink. After returning from burying his wife, the vodka had become the best sedative to remove the guilt and nightmares. Days passed while he barricaded himself in the house and in the vodka.

After a week of wallowing, it was the knocking on the patio window that woke him. Scattered across the floor were empty vodka bottles. Slowly, he pulled himself off the kitchen floor. Standing and waiting for Bland to open the patio door was John Scott. Bland stumbled to his feet and fumbled with the door latch until it released.

"Son, what are you doing to yourself?" John asked as he passed Bland to enter the house. "You haven't shaved, and you smell like urine and stale liquor."

The cold morning wind blew the blinds back. Bland rubbed his eyes and blinked a few times to gather his bearings.

"What time is it?" he growled pathetically.

"It's seven o'clock in the morning."

"I must have passed out," he mumbled, but still loud enough for John to hear.

John picked up an empty vodka bottle and replied, "Yeah, and I wonder if this had anything to do with it."

Bland stared with no response.

"Son, let me give you some advice. This," he referenced the empty vodka bottle, "doesn't remove the pain. It just temporarily delays the pain until you're sober. When you're sober, you have to get drunk all over again to forget what's on your mind. Before you know it, you've slipped into a deeper hole. Bland, you're going to have to deal with your wife's death sooner or later."

John, of course, wasn't aware that he was also dealing with Grey's death and his guilt, as well.

Bland grabbed the bottle out of John's hand to toss it into the kitchen waste container.

"You're right, John."

"Get cleaned up, young man, and get out of this house. You need some fresh air, some sunshine. Plus, it stinks like stale liquor and urine in here."

John Scott exited the same way he entered. He closed the sliding door behind himself. Bland proceeded to the kitchen counter. John's words buzzed in his ear, and Bland knew he was speaking the truth. He would have to deal with both of their deaths if he were to start healing. He opened the cabinet and pulled out the coffee. The red light on the answering machine flashed. His fingers slapped at the machine until it came on. The funeral director had left another message. It seemed Grey's urn was ready four days ago, and Bland was just getting the message. If it wasn't picked up today, the funeral parlor was going to dispose of the ashes. As he dropped his head, the answering machine beeped again. It was Lou.

"Bland, I'm having a gig at the Marquette Club tonight with the high

society folks. I think it would be good for you to get out and mingle with some people. You may think it is too soon to be mingling with people but think of it as therapy. Now, if I don't see you by the earlier part of tonight, I will come and break your door down and carry you back to the club. Just so you know, I don't have any money to replace your door, so please don't force my hand."

Bland figured taking John and Lou's advice wouldn't hurt. First, he had to deal with Grey's remains.

After showering, he dressed and drove to the funeral parlor to pick up the urn.

A sense of fear and more guilt overcame him when he arrived in front of the funeral parlor. There was discomfort knowing why he was at the parlor, and that the business had nothing to do with his wife. Bland entered just as two men rolled a casket by him. He fought hard to shut out thoughts of Dakota when another man approached him.

"Sir, how can we help you?"

"I am here to pick up the remains of Greysen Brindle."

The man, giving nothing less than a serious facial expression, led him down a short hall. Once they reached the end of the hall, he pointed Bland to a cluttered room filled with old obituaries.

The sounds of a crackled cough came from behind a small disorderly desk. Bland's eyes rolled in the direction of the weaseled voice.

"We've been waiting on you for a couple of days to pick up the urn," the man said, as he revealed himself from behind the mass of paper and old boxes. He had a pointed face and nose. The rim of his glasses slid to the very tip of his nose. His small beady eyes peered over the top of the frame to have a better look at Bland.

"Sit down," the man ordered.

Bland sat in a cluttered chair across from the man's desk. This must be the director of the funeral parlor, Bland assumed.

He handed Bland a paper, "I need your signature before I can release the remains."

The moment he handed Bland the urn, guilt found a new way of attaching itself to his conscience. In his heart, Bland felt he should have

given Grey a more conventional burial. Again, he glanced around the room and noticed the clock on the wall. The clock read 6:00 p.m. If he were going to make it to Lou's performance, he had to be going. Frankly, any reason to leave the parlor was good for him. As the director escorted him to the front entrance, Bland remembered there were a few questions he needed answered.

"I am curious. How did you know to contact me?"

"Curiosity killed the cat," the old man laughed.

Bland didn't take the comment as being humorous, so he asked the old man if the medical examiner left his name.

"In this business, I've learned never to ask questions concerning anything other than payment, and what would you like for us to do with the body," explained the man.

"In this business," Bland repeated.

"What I can tell you is that when the body arrived there was a note attached with your name. The burial was already paid, even though we still cremated it. In these types of cases, it's a relief to get paid."

"What do you mean?" Bland asked.

"Normally, when no one claims the body, it's the city's responsibility to pay all expenses. Of course, the city only pays a small percentage of the cost. It's cheaper to cremate them than bury them. It's cheaper for everyone."

Bland thanked the man and left.

While Bland drove, he deliberated what he should do with the urn. Sporadically, he glanced over to the urn while in his mind he thought about who could have paid for Grey's cremation. He contemplated it being the firm that contracted her. Then again, maybe someone from the publishing house, but why would they do such a thing? No one really knew her from the publishing house except him. Or maybe it was a polite gesture from the twins. He continued to dwell on the matter until he heard the loud whistle of a train passing. It then dawned on him what he had to do with her ashes.

Union Station was busy as usual with cars and people fighting to

enter and exit the cold weather. Bland bought a ticket for the first train leaving the station. Once on the train, he bribed a porter with a few large bills to take him to the cargo cars. Nostalgia overwhelmed him as he passed through the lounge car and the sleeper cars. Once in the cargo car, the porter opened one of the doors.

"Make it quick or else it's my job. I'll be outside the door."

Bland walked to the edge of the open car door. Slowly he removed the cap from the urn and dumped the ashes into the air. He watched as the ashes floated with the wind. After the urn was empty, he took a seat on the edge of the boxcar to allow his thoughts to process.

It felt appropriate to release her ashes on the train, since that's where they first met. She would have liked that, he believed. His emotions began to take over. Without him realizing, the urn slipped out of his hand and fragmented against the gravel along the tracks.

"We have to go," said the porter, who had stepped back into the boxcar to make sure everything was okay.

Bland was already an hour late for Lou's gig. Luckily, the club was located somewhere downtown. Bland stopped a taxi driver to get directions.

"I never heard of a Marquette Club, but there is a Marquette Hotel downtown," said the taxi driver.

"I know the hotel. Do you think the club is inside the hotel?"

"Beats me, buddy," replied the man before driving off.

Bland jumped into his car and hurried to the Marquette Hotel. He had passed the hotel on many occasions, but he had never visited the inside. The hotel was one of the elites in the city. The price tag for a night's stay solidified its prestige.

The doormen stood at the entrance in nothing less than royal attire. A few well-dressed men greeted Bland when he entered the cathedral doors of the hotel. In awe, Bland passed through the large halls with their tall columns painted on both sides and ceilings in European designs. It was truly something to admire. Bland understood why a one-night stay in a regular room cost hundreds of dollars. As he wandered about the wide, long halls, he noticed an influx of very well-dressed individuals

entering a set of doors. That's when he realized he was underdressed for the occasion. When Lou mentioned gig, he automatically assumed it would be like the usual—a small to moderate size club with low lighting. In gold letters above the entrance were the words, The Social Room, not as large as a ballroom but, nonetheless, having the same appeal. Fortunately for Bland, he was wearing a black coat and black slacks. On the stage were Lou and a few unfamiliar faces. Disappointingly, Bland couldn't appreciate the music because of the loud chatter.

Bland moseyed to the back of the room to place distance between himself and the horde of people standing around. From behind him, a soft voice called his name. Immediately, he turned. It was Brandi McIntire, a high-profile executive director at Literature House Publishing, a competing publishing house.

"Hello, Bland, my condolences on your recent loss."

"Thank you, Brandi."

"I know this must be hard on you." She paused, "I am sorry, Bland. I'm sure this is the last thing you want to talk about."

"It's okay. I am told talking about it helps with the bereavement."

She shrugged her shoulders because she didn't know how to reply. "Well, I didn't expect to see you here, Bland."

"I didn't plan on being here, but my friend is playing in the band," Bland admitted.

"Frankly, if I didn't have to be here, I most definitely would be at home in bed. This is one of those things you do to please corporate, media, and the public. All the major corporations, non-profit organizations, publishing houses, and literary agents are in attendance. They are all willing to pledge their support to their communities. It's important that we care about our community. I'll be the first to admit off camera that it's all for show, but in the long run it equates to opportunity, sales, and good publicity. I guess in the long run everyone benefits."

"That's not so bad, is it?" Bland asked.

"The politics of it or everyone benefiting from it?" she countered.

Bland tried to answer her question with a question.

"Should everything we do be calculated on how we benefit from it?"

"When you ask me like that, then no," replied Brandi. "I truly hate

the politics of it all, but it comes with the business. As long as I benefit from the business, then it isn't all that bad."

"You're made for it," Bland commented.

"It's a handful, but the years have developed me into what I am, a mover and a shaker. On another note, what is this news I hear about S&W?"

Bland knew firsthand that Brandi was a pro at politicking. It was an instrument she utilized to move and shake and make deals under and above the table. She was ruthless in the publishing industry. Already, she had stolen three of S&W's editors and several prominent writers by offering them lucrative deals. Bland wasn't upset with Brandi because it was the nature of the business for publishers and directors at major publishing houses to offer good editors and writers large financial packages to relocate to other publishing houses. If S&W or any other publishing house wasn't willing to pay more to keep their writers and editors, then they normally jumped ship.

The moment she found out that Bland was the ghost writer known as Canis Lupis, Brandi expressed serious interest in his talent. Rumor had it that Bland was the big fish that she or any other editor or literary agent could not catch. And, yes, she tried and tried diligently to commit Bland to sign with Literature House Publishing. S&W offered Bland his first job, so loyalty went a long way in his eyes. The twins knew about her failed attempts and gloated on the fact that she was unsuccessful.

"What news did you hear concerning S&W?" he asked.

"My source tells me S&W Publishing is heading for the abyss."

"Going under?" he replied, but not stunned by the comment. Just one of Brandi's many tactics to create panic in a company, so editors and writers would leave for any deal. "You know the business, Brandi. Don't believe everything you hear or read."

"Bland, this is a small industry among giants, so information spreads quickly. The news of S&W contemplating bankruptcy has been floating around for the last ten to eleven months."

"Has keeping above competition boiled down to rumors and propaganda? What happened to good old-fashioned working hard?"

"The same thing that happened to those small publishing houses;

they either go out of business or get gobbled up by larger publishing houses." She smiled, "You'd better learn to listen to those rumors. They may help save your career one day."

"Well, as you and I know, S&W has a number of imprints under its belt, so I am sure they will keep S&W afloat."

She stared at Bland as if he were truly naïve. "You think?" Suddenly, her facial expression changed. "Well, to be fair and give the conversation some balance, I am beginning to think there could be no truth to the matter since they still have you."

"What do you mean?"

"What do I mean?" she stared at him confusingly, "I mean you are a bestselling author, whose books single-handedly propelled S&W among the giants in this industry."

"I am not the publishing house's only best-selling author."

Immediately, she retorted, "Your books alone have grossed millions on top of millions for S&W. Your international sales are astronomical. Your novels have been reprinted in at least 100 different languages. I know firsthand that S&W printed a combined five hundred thousand copies of your last two novels, and according to S&W, those numbers were considered a failure—given your prior books average first-day sales of $200 million. Maybe, the partners should have announced you were the author of those two disappointments; then the novels might have generated more sales."

"How do you know that?"

"I know what needs to be known if I plan on getting what I want. Like S&W selling six hundred million copies of your works worldwide. Trust me when I say this, many of S&W's imprints will make only slim profits on their authors. So that's why such news just can't be taken lightly, regardless of how many imprints S&W has under its belt. If my ship were going down, I would just get the most powerful writer of suspense fiction to write another bestseller. Even if the book flops, the announcement that you're writing another book would gross millions, enough to keep the company solvent. You know, Bland, if they are not treating you right over there, then I know of a publishing house that would love to have someone of your stature."

At first, Brandi had Bland considering her comments; that is, until Brandi's backdoor proposition. Nothing has changed, thought Bland. He listened with unwavering dedication to his publishing house.

"You do know those last two books you wrote—"

Bland interrupted, "You mean those disappointments. That is what you called them."

"I call it as I see it, Bland. Anyway, by writing those books you fulfilled your contractual obligations to S&W. S&W doesn't have an exclusive contract on any new works you decide to publish."

"I see you're still keeping up on me and my contracts." Her statement had Bland considering if she knew about his latest proposal from the partners.

"Indeed, it's my job."

"Don't you think that my writing a book for a competitor would be a conflict of interest?"

"You wouldn't be a competitor if you signed with me. S&W would be." She paused. "If for some reason you start to seek a business environment that offers lucrative perks, please don't hesitate to give me a call. I will make it worth your while." She handed him a card. "In case you lost the last one."

"Thanks, Brandi, but we've been down this road before. I am happy where I am. I've just been promoted to partner." Bland bent the truth and elected not to add the junior or the contingency.

"Partner?" she smiled. "Well, I think congratulations are in order. So the two old men aren't stupid after all. I guess some things do get past my ears."

Bland smiled. Very doubtful, he thought.

"Well, you can't knock a girl for trying. At least you can make me feel good by taking the card."

Bland slipped the card in his front pants pocket. As always, Brandi had given him something interesting to think about.

"I can do better than taking your card." Bland smiled.

"And how is that, Bland? You already rejected my offer."

"By giving you a counter-offer."

"Oh yeah, and what would that be?"

"Why don't you return to the publishing house?" Bland suggested.

"Bland that ship sailed many years ago."

"But the port is still here and waiting for the ship to come in."

"Like I said, the ship has long gone. I can go so far to say, it is lost at sea."

Bland detected the resentment in her reply. Years after Bland arrived at the publishing house, he had heard the stories of how Brandi helped build the publishing house's brand only to be rewarded by the twins with her walking papers. Bland believed that to be her impetus to steal all of the publishing house's writers and editors.

"I know you left on bad terms, but your coming back would mean—"

"Get your facts straight," she interrupted. "I didn't leave, I was fired and escorted off the premises. Bland, do yourself a favor; stop thinking those old men have your best interest at hand. They don't have your best interest in mind because they're too concerned about themselves. They will use you until you're used up. Get out while you can. Come to Literature House Publishing and your interest will always be put first."

Same Brandi, she could never turn off the pitch and sell, Bland thought. Lou appeared just as Brandi was about to continue speaking. Instead, she stood silent as Bland gave the introduction, "Brandi, this is Louis Nelson."

"Hello, Mr. Nelson."

"Call me Lou," he said, as he entered Brandi's personal space.

"Okay, Lou." Brandi smiled then turned her attention back to Bland. "Bland, I must socialize, but keep in mind what I said."

She gestured with a slight head nod and turned and walked away.

"What? I am not worth socializing with?" Lou asked, when Brandi created more distance between Lou and herself.

"You have that effect on women, Lou," Bland answered. "You didn't tell me it was a formal dinner, or it was sponsored by the industry I happen to work in."

"What difference does it make? No one comes to these things for the food. Plus, you missed the dinner. What are you complaining about when you didn't have to pay the $5,000 toward a plate dinner?"

"Five thousand dollars!" Bland uttered. "What are they serving,

endangered species?"

"As a matter of fact, yes, and the food wasn't all that bad," Lou joked.

"So how long is the gig tonight?"

"I don't get these types of gigs often, so I'm willing to stay as long as they need me. Anyway, how are you holding up?"

"It's hard, but I'm managing. One day at a time."

"Good and don't get caught in the bottle, Bland. Trust me, it doesn't help. It only makes things worse. Well, I'd better head back to the front. I see the pipsqueak waving for me," Lou grimaced.

Bland peered around Lou's body, "Who's that calling you?"

"He plays piano, but he also hired me for this gig."

"Looks as if things are getting better for you," Bland remarked.

"I hope so, but as you said, one day at a time. Anyway, I'm glad to see you made it out. For a minute there I thought you were going to shrug me off." Lou noticed the man waving again. "I've got to go."

A server happened to pass by carrying glasses of champagne, and Bland took the liberty of grabbing two. He swallowed the champagne quickly. He gazed around the room, spotting Smith and Wilkins huddled near the bar. The brothers had spotted Bland well before he noticed them. They waved for him to come over.

"Good evening, Bland," greeted Smith. He then handed Bland a much stiffer drink than the champagne he had consumed moments earlier. "It's good to see you out."

"It's good to be out," Bland responded.

Bland expected, but hoped the twins wouldn't ask anything about the explosion or the novel. The idea, however, crept in his mind to ask if they knew who paid for Grey's cremation, but asking that would open the issue he didn't want to talk about, so he elected not to inquire, at least for the time being.

"It seems as if you and Ms. McIntire were awfully chatty," Wilkins said.

"She was just offering her condolences."

Wilkins sneered. "You're telling me that ungrateful, cold-blooded varmint of a woman has a sense of compassion?"

Wilkins and Smith weren't fond of Brandi; more like they detested everything about her, including her less scrupulous ways of doing business. They knew her sentiments were the same about them.

Smith moved closer to Bland, "Did you get our call?"

Bland nodded. "I do wish to talk to you about that. The story was on my computer. As you know, my computer and laptop were in my office at the time of the explosion. I'm not sure if both were destroyed. Maybe the fire department was able to salvage something. There was a copy of the old draft on the laptop. However, if the computer was saved, then maybe the hard drive didn't suffer massive damage, and the file wouldn't be damaged. I'm hoping I saved it on the flash drive, but that too was left in the computer."

"Bland, do not worry about it right now. Just get through this time in your life, and we'll talk about everything later." Smith spoke with endearing sympathy.

"But what about getting the book on the shelves before Christmas?"

"If the book is meant to, then there's always Valentine's Day," Smith smiled.

Bland juggled the idea only to catch it partially, "I still have until the deadline, right?"

"Just come and see us when you're ready, and we will look at our options. As I said, the most important thing now is you getting through this difficult time in your life."

Bland had a feeling the partnership was the option that would no longer be on the table.

"Is the partnership still an option?" Bland asked.

"Bland, be serious, the deadline is days away. And you said your computer and laptop were in the blast," spoke Wilkins; then he paused to point his drink at Bland. "According to you, you can't write bestsellers at the last minute."

Bland could tell by his facial expressions that Wilkins was making fun of him and to some degree, daring him to try.

Silently, Bland hoped the flash drive, or the computer hard drive wasn't destroyed. The twins were very adamant that they wanted nothing to do with the old draft but, asked hopefully, the first chapter and only

chapter of his new draft was still on the flash drive, or hard drive of the computer so he could expand on it.

"By the way, a Detective Rhodavack visited our office for the second time inquiring about your whereabouts," Wilkins said, with a curious stare. "What's that about, Bland?" he added.

"He didn't say?" Bland asked.

"Unfortunately, no," Wilkins responded. "If he shows up again, I'll be sure to ask him."

There was an unsettling feeling in the pit of Bland's stomach. He had had enough of the entire scene and decided he didn't want to stick around talking to the twins or to wait for Lou. Waiting only meant having more conversations that he didn't particularly care to have. He excused himself from the men and left the club.

On the ride home, his mind zigzagged from Detective Rhodavack to Dakota's and Grey's deaths, then to his son. He decided the only way to keep his mind off of them all was to take Margie's advice and stay busy. Though he left the impression with the twins that he wanted to finish the book for the partnership, he really wanted to finish it for his wife. That would mean devoting most of the remaining time to writing, if he wanted to complete the book on time.

25

THE NEXT DAY, BLAND MUSTERED ENOUGH COURAGE TO return to the publishing house. He hadn't been there since the night of the explosion. When he arrived, he was confronted with the massive construction taking place on three floors. Rudy, the security guard, prevented him from going to the damaged floors.

"I just need to see if my computer and laptop are in my office. All of my work is on them," Bland said, hoping Rudy would let a friend have a break.

"I can't, Mr. Benthall. Ever since the accident, they have cracked down on everything. No more moonlighting, no more substitutions. Even with the extra manpower, I haven't been able to catch a game. By the way, the offices for the editors are now on the fourth floor."

Bland asked, "Can you tell me if anything was salvageable from the fire?"

"I don't know," answered Rudy. Suddenly, Rudy snapped his fingers, "Maybe Jesse knows. All week he's been moving boxes and furniture from all three damaged floors to the basement."

Bland heard his name called. He turned and saw that it was Penelope.

"Hey," she acknowledged him, as she walked past the security desk.

"Are you going my way?"

"I was heading downstairs to see what was salvaged from the fire."

"I was hoping to talk to you," she said.

"Okay. Rudy, thanks," Bland waved at Rudy.

Bland and Penelope moved away from the security desk. Penelope wore a deeply apologetic look on her face. Bland could tell something was bothering her.

"Bland," she spoke hesitantly. "I want you to know I am truly sorry. I had a tendency to flirt with you, and now looking back, I know it wasn't appropriate, nor was it respectful to your wife."

Bland gripped her by the hand and said, "It's okay, Penelope." He looked deep into her sincere eyes, "Thanks."

Penelope stepped into the elevator. "Bland, I need to talk to you about something that's important. I think—"

Before she could finish her sentence, Smith and Wilkins strolled onto the elevator. Their sudden appearance drew silence in the elevator. Penelope looked straight ahead as Smith said, "Good morning."

Bland looked at the men to reply, "Good morning, sirs."

Nonchalantly, Penelope made her way to the middle of the elevator. The door opened, and she politely said goodbye to them all. When the door closed again, the men began talking. Bland immediately wished he had followed Penelope off the elevator.

"Good morning, Bland. I'm surprised to see you today. After last night, I thought you were going to take our advice and get yourself some rest."

"I thought I told you that I have a novel to finish."

"That's a good spirit to have. Why don't you ride with us to our suite?" Smith said.

Bland reluctantly ignored his stop on the fourth floor. When the elevator doors opened on the penthouse floor, Bland smelled burnt debris. Once in the suite the men stood in the foyer to talk.

"Bland, the novel isn't what's important. Please, go home and get some rest," said Smith.

"You don't understand. I want to finish this novel. I need to finish this novel."

Wilkins frowned. "Let us be frank with one another. If you had wanted to finish this book, you would have completed it by now. So, please don't insult us by standing here telling us that you really want to complete this project. If the offer of junior partnership couldn't motivate you to write the book, and you had months to do it, what makes you think we believe you can do it in such a small window of time?"

"Because I have a new motivation," Bland retorted.

"You told us that before, Bland, about this new motivation that had sparked you to finish the book, and we were totally on board. Yet, we still have no book in our possession." Smith threw his hands open. "I think I understand the impetus that's now driving you to finish the book. We are not insensitive to what you are going through, but we are businessmen. We think it's best for both parties that we remove the offer of the junior partnership."

"I don't understand."

"It isn't good business to give away a junior partnership," remarked Wilkins.

Bland looked at Wilkins with an even more surprised expression. "You don't want me to finish it?"

"Hell, it's obvious from your last draft, and from you jerking us around about this new draft, which you refused to let us read, that you didn't have anything to give us before the fire. You won't have anything to give us by the deadline. And I shall remind you again, that deadline is quickly approaching. So why waste our time and yours?" growled Wilkins.

Bland had to know, so he asked, "Did you give the offer to someone else, another writer? Is that what this is all about?"

"Bland, we can get plenty of authors to write a book, but not just anyone would make a good junior partner. It wasn't the book that we wanted. It was the passion and the dedication that a person brought to their job that we desire. We wanted a partner who would believe in this house and would fight for its survival long after we're gone. It is our legacy, our father's legacy. We wanted a stakeholder who would make sure that the name S&W lives forever. We thought you were that person, but maybe we were wrong. We have been wrong before."

Bland looked straight-faced to the men and said, “I signed a contract, and that contract isn’t void until the deadline, correct?”

“Yes, we do have a contractual agreement, but we would have expected you not to fight us on our decision, given all that has happened in the recent weeks,” Smith replied.

“The contract stipulates an exchange between two parties before a deadline, so I have until the deadline.”

The two old men said nothing as they stared at each other. Finally, Wilkins nodded.

“Okay, but remember, Bland, no one is pressuring you to write this book. It’s your decision,” Smith restated.

“Can you finish it?” Wilkins asked. “And with a new plot?”

“I can finish it,” said Bland espousing a level of confidence that he knew he needed to possess.

Smith hit the button for the elevator and said, “Bland, I’ve been doing this work long enough to know the difference between a good writer and a great writer. You were once a great writer, but you’ve forgotten that what separates a great writer from a good writer is how they approach a story. You are now among the good writers who feel they have to wait for a story to come to them. When all the crucial elements of a great story are present such as love, passion, lust, infidelity, deceit, betrayal, tragedy, pain and misery, then a great writer takes the initiative to identify those things and writes the damn story. Just open your eyes and write. A story is right in front of us all. You are the master of your fate, so you hold the key to your destiny.”

“Time is almost up,” Wilkins said.

The elevator door opened not a second too soon. The twins said nothing as Bland stepped onto the elevator. Until the elevator door closed, they watched Bland as he watched them.

As Bland stepped off the elevator on his new floor, he gave a lot of thought to the twins’ remarks, especially Smith’s list of crucial elements of a great story.

When he heard Paige gasp and run from around her desk, he came out of his thoughts. The excitement of seeing him provoked her to throw her arms around his waist. When she pulled back from his embrace

tears filled her eyes.

“Mr. Benthall, when I heard, I tried…”

“It’s okay, Paige.”

Bland offered her his handkerchief while escorting her back to her seat. She sniffed and dried her eyes.

“Can you tell me where my office is?”

She sniffed again, “It’s the last on the right, across from Larry’s office.”

Bland frowned at the thought of his office being across from Larry’s. He knew Larry would have his nose in everything he was doing. As he walked to his new office, he noticed the blinds to Larry’s office were open and he momentarily stopped to take a peek. Nothing spectacular about his office, he thought.

Bland entered his new office and closed the door behind him. When he turned on the light he saw on his desk a new computer. Otherwise the surface of the desk was bare. Bland looked at the places where Devin and Dakota’s pictures would have been.

There was a knock on his door.

“What is it, Paige?”

“I forgot to give you this. Penelope dropped it off earlier.”

She handed Bland the sympathy card.

“Oh, thanks. She was kind of upset earlier,” Bland said.

Larry peeped into Bland’s office, “Who was upset?”

Bland looked up in a questioning manner, “How can I help you, Larry?”

Immediately, Paige excused herself.

“Bland, I know we haven’t always seen eye to eye, but I wanted to extend my condolences. If there’s anything I can do for you, please don’t hesitate to ask.”

To get the man out of his office, Bland smiled cordially. “Thank you, Larry.”

Bland suspected that Larry was the twins’ new eye in the sky. It wasn’t a coincidence to Bland that Larry’s office was directly across from his. Bland didn’t trust him, so he purposely kept his distance.

The intercom on Bland’s phone buzzed, interrupting his thoughts.

"Bland," Paige called through the intercom. "Detective Rhodavack is on line one. You want me to tell him you haven't returned?"

As much as Bland wanted Paige to say exactly that, he knew he had to deal with the 'elephant in the room'.

"No, I'll take it, Paige."

Bland glanced at Larry, "I have to take this call. Can you excuse me?"

As Larry backed out of the office, Bland gave a motion with his finger for Larry to close the door behind him.

Once again Bland thought about not taking the detective's call. If he didn't, Detective Rhodavack might make another impromptu visit, this time to the publishing house to question him. Yet, Bland was curious to know what other information the detective may have discovered about the explosion.

The detective's voice sounded through the telephone. "Mr. Benthall, you sure are a hard person to catch."

"You are saying that literally or figuratively, Detective?"

"Funny, Mr. Benthall, very funny. I've been reading your books, and like I said, you do possess a love for detail."

"Thanks, I will consider that a compliment coming from a detective."

"R..i..g..h..t, but sometimes too much attention to detail can cause a person to miss the big picture. I know that sounds like a paradox." There was a pompous laugh from Detective Rhodavack. "And speaking of the big picture, Mr. Benthall, according to my notes, your wife was admitted in the hospital a few days before the accident. A Dr. Robertson, the attending physician, says your wife had a nervous breakdown. And it wasn't until later that you were informed."

Detective Rhodavack just left the sentence hanging, so Bland attempted to explain.

"Yes, that would be correct. I found out about her nervous breakdown when I arrived at the hospital."

"No, Mr. Benthall, I was referring to her pregnancy. You didn't find out about that until Dr. Robertson told you." The detective's voice paused, but the popping of his gum continued. "You see, Mr. Benthall, I find it very strange that for six months a man doesn't know his wife is pregnant, especially when she knows, and when he is living in the same

house. Were you and your wife having some marital problems?"

"No more than any other husband and wife."

"I wouldn't know; I've never been married," the detective said. Bland elected to say nothing, so the detective continued. "According to the doctor, he felt your wife suffered from suicidal depression. Did you ever set an appointment to see the shrink the doctor recommended?"

This time, the detective waited for Bland to respond before continuing.

"No, we didn't think it was necessary because she wasn't suicidal."

"R..i..g..h..t, but life is complicated, isn't it, Mr. Benthall? I mean you thinking you know someone, then finding out you know very little about them." This time, he didn't bother to wait for Bland to respond before continuing, "So I guess I can no longer consider this as an accident. Maybe along the lines of a suicide, slash murder."

Bland rebutted the suicide insinuations because he knew how much Dakota loved life.

"As I mentioned before, the fire chief ruled the fire as an accident resulting from an exploding propane tank. What evidence do you have to support your conclusions?" Bland exclaimed.

Detective Rhodavack cleared his throat, "Again, I shall remind you that was before a thorough analysis of the blast was conducted. Given the projection and force of the blast, it has been determined that something struck the propane tank at great force to cause that type of explosion."

"Something of great force," Bland echoed.

"Given this new information provided by the arsonist investigator, we returned to the scene of the incident for a thorough inspection, and we happened to find a bullet casing. Now I find that very interesting, since we couldn't find a bullet. According to forensics, a bullet could ignite a propane tank and cause such a blast."

Bland stopped the detective immediately. "Was the explosion caused by a bullet?"

"According to the fire chief and now the crime scene investigator, yes."

"What happened to the bullet?" Bland asked, as he shifted uncomfortably in his seat. "Wouldn't it be lodged in the tank?"

"My guess is that it melted as a result of the extreme heat. But that's okay, because every gun has its own identifiable marks. Just as every barrel marks its bullet, so does the breech face leave stamped imprints on the base of the cartridge case. This impression acts as a ballistic fingerprint that can be used to match a casing to its original gun."

Bland knew the detective was purposely trying to irritate him to lose his temper and say something incriminating.

"Are you telling me this to scare or intimidate me?" Bland sounded perturbed.

"Not at all, I'm telling you because it's important that we stick to details without missing the big picture," said Detective Rhodavack.

"A bullet that was intended to provoke deadly harm on one person ends up killing two people. I'm sorry, three people. That's if you're one of these pro-life activists who considers a fetus to be alive. That brings me to my next question, Mr. Benthall. Do you possess a firearm?"

Suddenly a cold and delusional feeling overtook Bland as he wondered if Dakota had taken the gun to confront Grey. Bland wished now he had listened to Dakota's plea to remove the gun from the house. The fact she didn't like the gun in the house made Bland believe she wouldn't bother it. He was hesitant to tell the detective about the gun. In his gut, he had a feeling that the gun might not be in its place. If by some chance it wasn't, he was sure the detective would try to link the gun to him and fabricate some motive that implicated him in their deaths. Because he was fearful of knowing that, he lied.

"No, I don't."

The detective's voice rose in surprise, "You don't? Well, that's odd because according to my notes, you're licensed to carry a firearm. Why would a person be licensed to carry a weapon but not have a weapon?"

"I had a 9-millimeter, but I lost it."

"How interesting because the casing is from a 9-millimeter. Another coincidence, but again, I don't believe in coincidences. You think your wife found your gun?"

"Like I said, detective, I lost it. Plus, you know how many people have 9- millimeters these days?"

"Yes, the world is more dangerous, and one more gun lost doesn't

make it any safer. Let's say for hypothetical purposes that your wife found the gun. Would she use it?" His tone was serious.

"Even if she did find the gun, she wouldn't use it. She was afraid of guns, and I only had it for protection. Honestly, she hated the fact it was in the house."

"R..i..g..h..t," he sighed again. "It would help if you took another look to find it."

"I'm confused because if you found the casing, shouldn't you have also found the gun?"

"Unfortunately, a very large detail is missing, and that is why a ballistic test on your gun is so crucial to ruling you and your wife out."

"You said ruling me and my wife out? I didn't know we were suspects."

"Mr. Benthall, until we find that gun, everyone is a person of interest, including the dead. I leave no stone unturned, especially if there is foul play involved."

With the phone to his ear, Bland began to shake his head to the entire ordeal. He couldn't believe this was happening to him.

"By the way, I heard S&W had a break-in, and you were injured."

"I was attacked, but I only suffered a few minor injuries."

"But you didn't file a police report?"

"No. But I did notify the head security guard on duty."

"Mr. Benthall, do you often work late?"

"Depends, some days are later than others."

"You've been with the publishing house for a long time. You pretty much know the ins and outs of their building, wouldn't you say?"

"No, I wouldn't say that." There was brief silence. "Detective, I hope I've answered all your questions because I have a meeting to attend."

The detective seemed to ignore the comment. "How is the book coming?"

"The book?"

"The book for the junior partnership. Are you finished?"

After an uncomfortably long silence, Bland said, "No."

"I have no idea how you do it. I mean, writing under all that pressure. Wow, I was sure you wouldn't pursue it."

Bland waited a moment to respond. "Detective, as I mentioned, I am

late for a meeting. Is there anything else you want to say before I hang up the phone?"

Bluntly, Detective Rhodavack spoke, "Mr. Benthall, let me again express the importance of finding that gun and getting it to me. Purposely withholding information in an investigation is a felony that attaches serious prison time. If you know where the gun is, I will allow you the courtesy of bringing it to me."

Bland inhaled deeply and released the air through his nostrils just as hard. It was his way of telling the detective he had heard enough.

"Mr. Benthall, you have a nice day. And, please don't make me come to you." Then Bland heard the dial tone.

Bland sat there shaking his head. The detective was somehow trying to shift the cause of their deaths on him. But why? Bland didn't want to take the thought any further because he knew the truth. He desperately wanted to believe Dakota left the gun in its place. After saying that the gun might be lost and learning he was a suspect, he now hoped that the gun was in the shoe box.

"Paige," he said, as he walked past her to the elevator. "I'm going to get a cup of coffee. Would you like a cup?"

"No, thank you, Mr. Benthall. I've had my two cups for the day."

"Okay."

Bland made his way to the lobby. His main objective was finding Jesse to learn where the salvage ruins were stored.

Bland found Jesse in the food court dragging a mop back and forth across the floor. He headed in his direction. When Jesse saw Bland, he dropped his head to avoid eye contact.

"Hello, Jesse."

Jesse was slow to nod his head. It didn't take Bland long to notice Jesse's deliberate distance.

"You okay?"

With his eyes still centered downward, Jesse nodded and continued to mop. Bland believed that Jesse felt uncomfortable knowing Dakota died, and he elected not to discuss the matter. Instead, he asked Jesse where he had stored the salvaged ruins from the explosion. Jesse pulled the pad and pencil from his top left shirt pocket. Bland noticed the

unusual, uncontrolled shaking of Jesse's hand as he scribbled on the pad.

Bland peered at the note that read, Boxes in basement next to file room. He patted Jesse on the back, and Jesse went back to pushing the mop across the floor. The first thought that entered Bland's mind was the night of the attack in the basement, a place where he thought he would never again be alone. However, this would be his second time going to the basement since that attack. He was curious to see what was salvaged from the ruins. Nearby was the exit staircase. Quickly Bland darted through the door.

Inside the basement corridor was a strong odor of burned materials. Bland slowly walked the dimly lit, narrow hall. His heart began to race when he saw the sign for the file room ahead. A few feet beyond that was the storage room. Bland was apprehensive when he turned the knob to the storage room. He proceeded into the overcrowded room. Hurriedly, he rummaged through various boxes. He came across his laptop. It was totally scorched. He looked in another box. That is when he saw his computer. The monitor was cracked, and the outside case had melted from the heat. The board of the central processing unit was burned all the way through. Bland checked for his flash drive. It was also totally scorched. He tossed it back into the box. Any idea of salvaging the novel now seemed to be out of the picture.

Bland stood there for a moment thinking of his next move when the thought of the 9-millimeter flooded his mind. What if Dakota did take his gun? What if the police overlooked it, and Jesse, who isn't the sharpest nail in the box, tossed it amongst this rubble? His thoughts coerced him into a diligent search for the 9- millimeter.

Bland went scavenging through the other boxes hoping to find the gun. He didn't have any idea what he would do with the gun if he found it. He'd deal with that once he found it, he told himself, while pulling stuff from various boxes.

After searching for an additional thirty minutes or so in the hot room for the gun, he came up empty handed. Beads of sweat bubbled along his forehead. His facial expression changed from being indifferent to one of slight relief. The fact the detective made it clear that the weapon was not found at the scene of the accident offered Bland a sense of relief that

maybe Dakota didn't take it from the house. In his mind he removed the word "accident" and replaced it with "crime." In order to vindicate Dakota and himself of any wrong-doing, he needed his gun to be in her shoe box. The anticipation would drive him crazy until he returned home to look.

He spotted the security camera from the office. It was damaged, but seeing it sparked a thought. Maybe the tapes could tell him what actually happened on the floor that night. It would answer a lot of questions.

He rushed out of the storage room to the elevator. Once on the lobby floor, he walked over to the security desk and waved for Rudy.

Casually, Rudy made his way to Bland.

"Did you find the computer or laptop?" Rudy asked.

"What was left of them, which wasn't much, but I was wondering about the security tape recorded by the camera on my floor. Where do you store the tapes?"

"In the security office."

Bland breathed a sigh of relief. "The night of the explosion, do you have the footage from my floor?"

"It was confiscated by the police for evidence."

Bland's sudden relief dwindled. "What did the twins have to say about it?"

"They gave the police the tape, but there wasn't much on it."

"You saw it?"

"Yeah, but the tape was very grainy. Sometimes, you could see an image of a shadow or something floating and then there was a sharp light before the tape ended. Other than that, there was nothing."

"What about the surveillance footage from the main lobby floors?"

"Unfortunately, all the surveillance cameras on the main corridors and elevators were out."

Bland was outraged. "Out! Are you serious? Seeing the new camera in my office, I assumed they took care of all the camera issues as well. At least, I thought they replaced the outdated cameras."

"As I explained to the officers, this has been an on-going problem. I knew that one day it would cost those old men if they were not replaced."

Bland's body language showed that the cost of the twins' frugalness

extended way beyond the twins. Bland's hope of knowing what happened disappeared. He rubbed his forehead and briefly looked away from Rudy. Rudy soon came back into focus as Bland remembered something.

"Rudy, who worked the night of the explosion?"

The question caught Rudy by surprise, so he hesitated before asking, "What do mean?"

"The explosion happened on a Friday night, and I know the Wizards played that night. Did you catch the game?"

"I did."

"Since the cameras didn't capture anything, maybe the security guard who worked saw something. Do you know who worked that night?"

"I don't know. I had the entire day off." Once again, Bland's hopes of knowing what happened that night disappeared.

"Rudy, is the elevator the only way to gain access to the restricted floors?"

"You can take the stairs, but after business hours you need an access card to get on the floors."

"Access card?" Bland questioned.

"We gave access cards to your department. You didn't get one, Mr. Benthall?"

"No, I haven't been here to get it."

Rudy leaned down under the desk to swipe a card, which he gave to Bland.

"Is it that easy?"

"Yes, it is, Mr. Benthall, and that's between me and you, okay? If you lose it, we're supposed to charge you."

"Sure, and thanks," Bland said.

Bland jumped into his car and raced home. He began to feel a panic attack as he pulled into the driveway. He pushed open the front door and made a mad dash up the stairs into his bedroom. He ran straight for the bedroom closet. He looked on the top shelf for the box where the gun was stored. He spotted the shoebox and grabbed it from the shelf. Before opening the box, Bland paused to settle his nerves. Please be there, he thought. He opened the box. It was empty. His heart felt like

it stopped. He returned to the top shelf. He began to frantically pull at the inventory of shoeboxes in hopes the gun was in one of them. After opening all of the boxes, going through all of the bags, and searching the dark corners of the closet, Bland conceded that the gun was no longer in the closet. Yet, he wasn't ready to embrace the worst—Dakota taking the gun to hurt Grey. He looked around the bedroom, the bathroom, the downstairs closet, the sitting room, the kitchen, and in the kitchen drawers. In the process, he found the old draft of his novel and slung it across the kitchen counter. He then thought to search the basement. She may have moved it there to put it at a safe distance from Devin. He didn't find it there. Thinking he might have overlooked it, he returned to the bedroom closet.

Soon his demeanor went from calm to uncontrolled. Suddenly, shoeboxes and clothes began flying around the closet. After nothing was left on the shelves, Bland fell to his knees. It was finally his moment to grieve. He tried to hold back his tears as he remembered Dakota's beautiful smile. Vividly, he could see her laugh. How she slightly allowed her eyes and neck to shy away when she blushed. A thought of Grey unexpectedly crept into his mind. Her beautiful eyes would light up a room and her captivating charm matched her sweet fragrance. There was a throbbing pain that moved within his abdomen to his chest. His head and neck dangled with grief of never seeing either one again. Guilt consumed every part of him for destroying both of their lives. The more he remembered the two of them, the more anger and agony squeezed him from the inside out. He sobbed uncontrollably.

Hours later, the house phone began to ring. Bland pried himself from the floor to answer it. Instantly, he recognized Margie's voice.

"Hello, Margie. Is everything okay? How's Devin?" he asked. He cleared his throat and took a seat on the bed.

"I'm well, but Devin has been asking for you. He misses you, Bland. When can you come down?"

"I can leave immediately."

That was Bland's perfect excuse to get away and later deal with the publishing house, the novel, and the detective.

"No, Bland. I didn't mean to rush you."

"No rush, I've been missing him, too. Honestly, I was considering coming down for Thanksgiving."

"What about the book?"

"It will still be here when I return."

"That will be great, Bland. I'll let Thomas and Devin know."

"Don't tell Devin. I want to surprise him. I'll leave tonight so I can be there in the morning."

"That's such a long drive, Bland. I don't want you driving late at night. Why don't you fly? It will be quicker and less taxing on you."

"The drive will be therapeutic for me."

"Well, at least leave in the morning. It will still take the same amount of time and I will worry less if you did."

Bland glanced in the mirror across the room at his haggard face and decided he needed to rest for the night.

"Okay, Margie, I'll leave in the morning."

Early the next morning Bland spotted the manuscript on the counter. Sort of relieved, he grabbed it but knew very well he couldn't use it. Maybe he would have time to look at it and find a new idea to add to the first chapter of the new draft that was pretty fresh in his memory. His thoughts shifted to Devin and seeing him. A genuine sense of excitement filled Bland. The excitement, however, disappeared when he realized Devin would be without his mother for Thanksgiving and for the rest of his life. The feeling crushed his spirits. Never did he imagine his selfish choices could affect, and ultimately would affect, so many people.

While he packed his vehicle, Bland attempted to shift his attention from Devin and Dakota to a storyline that he pledged to have new energy to finish. Taking the long drive is just what he needed to devote time to developing the plot. As he put the last of his luggage in the SUV, John Scott happened to observe him.

"Happy Thanksgiving, Bland. So where are you heading?"

"To spend Thanksgiving with Devin."

"Now that's what I like to hear. How long will you be gone?"

"Just for the holiday. I have a big project to finish by Monday, so I will

return by Sunday."

"You might want to come back before Sunday. The weatherman is calling for a major snow and ice storm sometime Saturday or Sunday. Supposed to hit the entire East Coast."

"Oh, I didn't know that."

"Now you know, so be careful driving. Don't worry about the house. I'll keep an eye on it while you're away."

Bland climbed into the vehicle.

"Enjoy the time with your son. He's going to need you, and you're going to need him."

"Happy Thanksgiving, John, and thanks for everything."

"Don't mention it, Bland."

As Bland drove through the countryside, he thought his mind would concentrate on the story, but instead he reminisced about Dakota and the various places they visited when she was alive. With a smile, he recalled her spontaneity to stop the car whenever she felt the urge to do something outlandish. Her nature was to live life to its fullest. He felt he had cheated her by not taking her to spend more time with her parents. He looked out the window and over the corn and tobacco fields. He then realized he lost more than a wife. He had lost his best friend.

Before the day turned to dusk, Bland pulled into the Gates's long graveled driveway. Far in the distant field, Thomas was guiding in the cows. Margie and Devin were in front of the house. When Bland climbed from the car, Devin ran to him with shouts of joy.

"Daddy! Daddy! Daddy!" he shouted, as he ran to Bland. He jumped into his father's arms, and Bland held tightly to him. Margie could tell from Bland's reactions that he truly missed his son.

"Happy Thanksgiving! Long drive?" Margie asked.

"Daddy, I missed you."

"I missed you too, son." Bland's attention turned back to Margie's question. "The drive wasn't that bad."

Devin squirmed from his father's arms.

"Daddy, I want to finish playing. Come and play with me."

"First, let me speak with your grandmother, then we can play all

you like." He took a moment to watch Devin before asking, "How is he doing?"

"He asks about her every day. Some days you can see it in his face how much he misses her. Sometimes he speaks of her as if she were still here with us."

Bland's guilt drew him back from the conversation about Dakota. "I didn't know, he…."

"It's okay, Bland, kids sometimes do this to help keep the memory of a loved one alive." She stared out into the open field. "So do parents to remember a child." She swiped a tear from the corner of her eye. "Give him some time and he, too, will get through it. We will get through it together."

Bland dropped his head. "Margie, I miss her so much. I am so sorry."

"Bland, don't be sorry. It's all in God's divine plan."

She took Bland by the arm and walked with him to the front steps. They sat down and fixed their stares on the distant woods, watching the wind brush the treetops.

"This was Dakota's favorite time of the year." Bland smiled. "She would say it made her feel more alive than any other time."

Margie smiled, "You knew your wife."

Bland stared back into the open field. He didn't respond because he knew what truths he still hid in his heart. She tapped him on the knee.

"It's getting colder out here, so come on," she demanded. "I'm going to whip up some fresh homemade chili."

"That sounds good. I'm going to hang out with Devin. Then we'll be in." Bland gave a concerned glance to Thomas working hard in the field.

Margie noticed. "He's okay. Lately, he's been working a lot. I'm assuming that is his way of dealing with Dakota's death. The evening chill will bring him in soon enough."

That evening, Bland sat on Devin's bed, reading him a bedtime story. After the story, Devin crawled out of bed to say his prayers.

"Dear God, bless Mommy, Daddy, Granny, Grandpa and everyone else in the world. Amen."

He then crawled back into bed and underneath the covers. The

prayer was nothing new to Bland. He taught it to Devin; however, this time the prayer squeezed Bland's heart until the pain made him weep.

"Daddy, why are you crying?"

"Because I love you."

"You love me and Mommy?"

"Yes, I do, very much." Bland began to wipe the tears.

"Daddy, I miss Mommy."

"I miss her too, son."

"Grandma says Mommy is in Heaven."

"Yes. Your mother has gone to be with God." Bland stooped eye level to Devin. "You will always have her here. You will always feel her here." He placed his finger over Devin's heart. Devin smiled and wiggled under the covers.

It wasn't long before Devin drifted off to sleep. Bland gathered himself and walked to the doorway. He watched Devin before turning off the light in the room. Bland sadly thought about how much he had missed of Devin's growth in the months before Dakota's death.

Up ahead was Dakota's bedroom. The door to the bedroom was shut. When Bland approached it, his first inclination was to pass it. Yet, somewhere in that brief thought, a compelling feeling made him turn the knob. He entered the room.

He flicked the light switch and allowed his eyes to scan the room. Nothing had been changed. Bland stepped over to the dresser to look at one of her many photos. The longer he stayed in the room, the more his conscience attacked him. His thoughts ranged from why he ever put Dakota in such a position, to how he was responsible for her death. He wiped the tears that had bubbled in the corners of his eyes.

His body jerked when he heard Thomas's baritone voice behind him.

"Can't seem to bring myself to come up here and put her stuff away. I keep telling myself tomorrow. Maybe tomorrow, I'll get enough strength to put the stuff in storage, but when tomorrow comes, I just can't bring myself to do it."

Bland looked with shameful eyes as the pain consumed Thomas. He didn't know how to respond since he already felt like a hypocrite. Yet, he compelled himself to try to say something.

"It's…."

"You don't have to say anything, son. We all miss her. She was my all, and I am sure she was your all, too. You can spend as much time in here as you want." Bland noticed Thomas's aging posture as he turned and walked out of the room.

The next day Bland spent some precious time with his son. He even had an opportunity to sneak away to Dakota's gravesite. There Bland felt an overwhelming sense of guilt that caused him to repeatedly confess his sins.

After Thanksgiving dinner, the news of the coming storm was being promulgated on all the local channels as being the worst in eighty years. Bland began contemplating leaving before the weekend; however, the thought of leaving Devin made him ache all over. Bland felt he had no choice but to leave or get stranded in South Carolina for a week or longer. There were some things he needed to deal with back in the city, and Devin staying with the Gates would allow him to handle his business. That business was doing what seemed impossible—finishing the book once he returned.

That night after Bland packed his SUV, he swooped Devin into his arms. Margie and Thomas watched closely as Bland held Devin tightly. Margie begged him to stay.

"Bland, tomorrow is Black Friday. The traffic will be terrible, so please stay until Sunday."

"I can't, Margie. I need to return now before the bad weather strands me here. Plus, if I leave by daybreak, I will get back early enough to get into the office, so I can try to finish this book by the deadline."

"You have your laptop, so you can work from here."

Bland gave a desperate look that Thomas quickly noticed.

"Margie, Bland has to get back, so let him get on the road before the bad weather comes."

Bland looked deep into Devin's eyes. "We will be together soon, son," he said, while giving him a tight hug and kiss before putting him to bed.

26

BEFORE DAYBREAK BLAND STARTED DRIVING BACK TO the publishing house so he could work on the book. On his drive from South Carolina, he mentally rewrote what he remembered of the new chapter, and from there he would develop an outline for a new novel. Bland then mapped out a strenuous schedule for writing the rest of the novel. If followed, he convinced himself, there was a great possibility that he could finish the book before the deadline.

As he drove, his mind stayed occupied on the story and its plot, until he saw Interstate 64 and a sign toward Charlottesville, Virginia. Bland had a sudden whim to stop at his alma mater. It would only be a short detour, he told himself. Though he had many occasions to visit the university after he graduated, he managed to keep himself and Dakota far away.

After so many years of being absent, the campus was foreign to him. He was amazed at all the changes—even the place where he and Dakota found love was now a campus facility. He sauntered over the frozen lawn of the Thomas Jefferson Campus. Somehow, he found himself in front of Little John's Sub Shop, where he met Dakota.

Bland proceeded inside the building which housed a new and

improved twenty-four-hour deli. He sat in a wall booth and watched the activity of a few rambunctious students as they took him back to when he met Dakota. Bland was totally lost in the moment as his mind reflected on how they met.

Years ago, it was inside of Little John's when an intoxicated Bland Benthall had cut in front of the ordering line. Of all the people there, Dakota was the one that challenged him by tossing a saltshaker to the back of his head. It wasn't until his dorm mates used all the toilet paper that he saw her again. There she was, on page C8 of the campus newspaper; underneath her picture was an article she had written, entitled, "JERKS AND THEIR RUDENESS."

Even though she didn't blatantly use his name, he knew the entire article was about him. More importantly, he knew he had to find her. Though he had no intent of joining the campus newspaper, however, she was the significant motivation for him to consider it since that was the only way to get close to her. He knew he had to have her, so he landed a job with the university newspaper. As he reflected, Bland realized Dakota was not only the reason he joined the newspaper, but frankly, she was the reason he fell in love with writing. However, it wasn't until the end of his second year before she agreed to go out with him.

"Bland," a voice called out. "Is that you? Yeah, that is you!" shouted Alvin Snead.

Bland came out of the daydream and his eyes began to bring Alvin into focus.

Alvin raved on, "It's me, Alvin. I can't believe it. It's been what, at least sixteen, seventeen years since I last saw you?"

"How's it going?" Bland asked.

"It's going well."

"Are you still with channel 5?" Bland asked, as he slid out of the booth to greet Alvin with a handshake.

"Oh no, channel 5 became channel 3, and from there I was fortunate to land a gig with CNN. I've been with them for eleven years now."

"Alvin, that's great! Are you an anchor?"

"No, no, I'm producing, but enough about me. What brings you back to these parts?"

"I'm actually passing through, coming from South Carolina. And you? Why are you here?"

"They're honoring me with a broadcast award. Seventeen years in the business. A local that made it big, you know?"

"Congratulations, Alvin."

"Thank you," Alvin said, then pausing. "Hey, how is Dakota? I heard the two of you got married."

Bland choked on his question.

"I didn't receive my invitation," Alvin joked.

"Alvin, I'm sorry to tell you, but Dakota passed not too long ago."

He stood shocked. "Oh, no," his voice collapsed. "Bland, I didn't know. I…"

"I know, and it's okay."

The expression on Alvin's face was begging to ask, but he didn't. "You seem to be holding up well."

"Fairly well, but coming here is helping me to heal."

Alvin changed the subject. "By the way, congratulations to you on your surprise celebration, now I feel bad not making it."

"My what?" Bland eyeballed Alvin as he explained something that Bland should have known.

"February, I was approached by two men seeking to locate those who had an impact on your life. Something they wanted to incorporate into a surprise party honoring you."

Bland interrupted, "Two men? Are you sure it was February?"

"Yes, because my mother's birthday is in February, and I was about to leave work to go and purchase a gift when the men approached me. They said the party would be awesome. I couldn't wait to see you and Dakota, but they never got back in touch with me with the date. You look so surprised. Was it cancelled?"

"I never knew anything about it. So I guess it was cancelled," said Bland. He continued, "Alvin, I'm curious. Did those guys ever say who they were or who they represented?"

"I don't understand," Alvin looked baffled.

"Did they say they were from the publishing house?" Bland thought maybe it was the twins asking around.

"I am sure they did. I just assumed they worked for your publishing house. I mean who else would throw you a party of such magnitude? Too bad it was cancelled."

Alvin stopped immediately, then snapped his fingers. "Hey, they even asked about that girl named Greysen."

There was an uncomfortable look on Bland's face. He swallowed instantly when Alvin said her name.

"Hey, wasn't that the girl you met the summer before coming to college? You said you met her on the train. You used to talk about her all the time. Whatever happened to her?"

Bland didn't assume Alvin's question was rhetorical. He just ignored answering it by asking a more important question.

"So, what did you tell them?"

"I told them the story of how you met her on the train. They asked if I knew how to reach her. I explained to them I didn't know her personally. They asked if Dakota knew her, and I wasn't sure if she did. I mean, the moment you and Dakota became an item I never again heard you mention the name Greysen."

"Dakota had no knowledge of Greysen," Bland said sharply.

Alvin detected his tone. "Did I say something wrong?"

"Why would they want to find her?" Bland thought aloud. As Bland went into deeper thought, he began to block out Alvin's voice. Given Alvin's recollection that the men visited him in February, Bland was sure it wasn't the detective or his men. His thought persisted. Then who were they? Alvin's voice soon regained Bland's attention.

"I assumed they were trying to get in touch with her for the same reason they were contacting me, your celebration."

When Bland went silent, Alvin tried to move the conversation along. "So how long are you in town?"

"I was actually about to leave." Bland held out his hand to shake Alvin's. "I hope to see you in Atlanta sometime in the future."

"Please come by the news station anytime," Alvin smiled. He watched Bland exit the deli.

After leaving the campus, Bland drove the next two and a half hours

trying to make the connection between who and why someone would fabricate a story about giving him a party. More importantly, why did they want to find Grey? Before he knew it, he was pulling into the parking garage of the publishing house.

27

WHEN BLAND WALKED THROUGH THE MAIN LOBBY of the publishing house, Smith and Wilkins were returning from a late lunch meeting.

"Bland," Smith shouted from a distance. Bland turned his head in acknowledgment and waited by the elevator for the men to join him.

Bland tried gathering his composure. "Good morning, gentlemen."

"It's the afternoon, Bland," Wilkins corrected.

Bland didn't attempt to give a new greeting. His mind was tired of thinking about things that made no sense.

"How was your Thanksgiving?" Smith inquired.

"Fine."

"Did you spend it with your son?"

"As a matter of fact, I did."

Bland waited for the men to say something about the novel, but, to his surprise, they didn't bring up the topic. Still Bland mentally acknowledged the deadline. He then contemplated the amount of mental energy it would take just to finish the book. Was it more his ego and less a commitment to Dakota that he just had to finish the book? he questioned himself.

When the elevator arrived, Bland offered a flimsy excuse not to ride up with the men.

"Coming?" Smith asked.

"No, I think I want a cup of coffee."

"Hit the button," Wilkins growled.

As Bland walked to the coffee shop, he admitted to himself it would take something short of a miracle for him to finish the book they wanted. There was a brief thought to turn in the old draft anyway and let public opinion determine if it would be a bestseller or not, even though Bland knew the old novel in its present condition was subpar at best. He again reverted to the promise made to Dakota and hoped that would be the impetus he needed to finish writing the book.

While he stood in line, he heard a voice from behind him. Larry was walking up to him.

"Can you get me a double espresso while you're in line?"

Without replying, Bland added Larry's espresso to his order. The two men walked with their coffees back to the elevator.

"How are you this afternoon, Bland?"

"Fine." he wanted to give the man as little attention as possible.

"I guess the cat is out of the bag," said Larry.

"What are you talking about?" Bland frowned.

"When you were in my office that day, supposedly looking for a staple remover, I know you read those pages on my desk." Bland gave him a weird look as he waited for Larry to say something sarcastic. Larry continued, "What do you suggest, Bland?"

Surprised by his question, hesitantly, Bland ventured into a conversation with suspicion that Larry was only trying to get information for the twins. The first hint was the recently mounted camera in the office. What the camera didn't capture on tape, Bland was sure it was Larry's job to get.

"I suggest you follow your heart," Bland said, without smiling. He didn't have time to occupy his mind on small talk, not now, not when he needed to finish his own novel.

The moment the elevator door opened, Larry's voice clearly broke

through his thoughts and hearing Larry's small talk was starting to irritate him.

When the men exited the elevator, Larry looked at Bland, "I hope this stays between you and me."

Bland didn't know if the remark was meant to be facetious. "I wish you the best, Larry."

As Larry proceeded down the hall, Bland walked over to Paige, but before he could ask for his messages, she handed him a piece of paper.

"Bland, this Detective Rhodavack called five times and that's just this morning."

"This morning," Bland echoed. Bland knew the calls were about the gun.

"Thanks, Paige."

Bland walked down the hall. He noticed the blinds in Larry's office were open. Once in his office, Bland immediately closed his blinds.

He contemplated calling the detective. Later, he thought. He noticed as he moved around his desk, beside his personal computer, was a brand-new laptop with a white bow on top of it.

He picked up the phone. "Paige, who put this new laptop on my desk?"

"What new laptop?"

"Never mind," he hung up the phone. He plopped in the leather chair to consider who it was from. The PC flashed, interrupting his thoughts.

"You've got mail," the words flashed across the screen.

Bland clicked on his mail wizard. The message was from Penelope. She wanted to meet Bland in the atrium of the building around three o'clock.

The time on the computer read 2:55. Bland jumped from his seat, stuffed the new laptop into his satchel and rushed to the atrium. He saw Penelope waiting on a bench. When he approached, she moved over and made room for him to sit.

Bland frowned. "What's up?"

"I guess you didn't get the urgent message to give me a call?" She held a folder in her hand. "I had this for you at the beginning of the week."

"What is it?"

"I think you should take a look, but I have to get it back fast."

"Why so fast?"

"The auditors are here, and I need to get this back before they discover it missing. That's what the urgent message was about."

"I left the office early so I could visit my son for Thanksgiving." Bland opened the folder and browsed over the papers. "What is this?" He attempted to answer his own question. "Looks like a list of invoices. Some pretty expensive invoices, which appear to be paid to the same company."

Penelope interjected, "We like to call it a shell company."

"What's a shell company?"

"You can look at it in several ways. In this case our company paid this company, CS Printing, $700,000 within a seven-month period."

"What is strange about that? I mean this is a publishing company, and we do publish books to be printed."

"True, but we have an in-house printing company, which handles all of our printing jobs, except for international jobs."

Bland scanned over the name of the company again. "I've never heard of this company, CS Printing."

Penelope's face turned more serious. "Bland, I like to think our accounting system is akin to our federal government. It is a three-tier system of checks and balances. One branch checks the other to keep everyone honest, and it works the same here. When I first went through the file drawer, I found three out of place invoices. If an invoice needs to be paid by accounts payable, we check to see where the invoice originated. In this case, this particular invoice was from an outside printing company. Normally, we only pay a percentage of the invoice up front and full payment upon the receipt of the merchandise, but the Ordering Department hasn't received anything. That set off my internal alarm. So, I called the number on the invoice, but I was forwarded to an answering machine."

"CS Printing?"

"Right, and that immediately would have been the first tier in our system of checks and balances; however, the jobs were approved for payment."

"Who approved it?"

"The second tier of checks and balances, a partner. Only a partner can approve invoices over a certain dollar amount. Anything under $100,000 is approved by the department head, but when a partner's initials are shown on the invoice, it is automatically paid. No questions asked. That is not until auditing. And, that's the third tier of checks and balances. As I said, to keep all parties honest when doing business. Anyway, I went and pulled the old paid checks because I didn't recognize the initials on the invoice."

She took the folder from Bland and flipped to the last page.

"Look here," she pointed to a check. "You recognize the signature?"

Bland looked closely at the signature that was written in script. "That's my name," Bland acknowledged. "But I never signed this."

"According to this invoice document, you signed and approved the payment and six others like it."

"Could my signature have been digitally altered?"

"Bland, the signature page of this one invoice is in ink. I wasn't able to get the other six invoices, but I am quite sure those are also signed in ink."

Bland thought about all the papers that were placed on his desk that he never read, but signed.

"I thought only a partner could release funds of this magnitude."

"Bland, you are a partner."

"No, I'm not a partner until I give the twins my novel."

"According to this signature page and this invoice document of all the invoices, you are already a partner. It looks like someone has been benefiting since you've become a partner. Listen Bland, I did some research concerning your contract, and it appears a contract like yours gives you immediate power to make decisions in the best interest of the publishing house; however, it doesn't allow you the immediate financial benefits such as getting your contractual salary and shares of stock. Those things commence once you have fulfilled your contractual obligations. According to the first signature on this check, you've officially utilized your power. Is there a specific date when the novel needs to be turned over to the twins?"

"A few days from now, and no later than 12 o'clock," he divulged.

"Noon?"

"No, the deadline is midnight."

"Wow," she whispered in disbelief. "Well, if the novel isn't completed by that time, then both parties have the option of returning to their original positions. I call it the 'no harm no foul' rule. That's if no financial harm has been done, meaning no illegal activity has taken place. Your direct denial of the signature has me guessing illegal activity has or still is taking place."

"How do you know all this?"

"First year of law school and second semester of contract law."

"I didn't know," Bland said.

"That's the way I'd like to keep it, Bland. Anyway, it's only a matter of time before the auditors find the invoices. Once they find them, Bland, if the company is not legit, then you are likely to face embezzlement charges. I just wanted to inform you."

A baffled expression spread across Bland's face. "What! What's going on?" he exclaimed.

"I don't know, but Bland, you don't have much time to figure it out."

"When do you think the auditors will find these invoices?"

She shook her head, "It's hard to say, today, tomorrow, maybe not until next week."

"Tomorrow? When did the publishing house start opening on weekends?"

"The partners want us here all weekend to give the auditors whatever they need. I guarantee you they will find the invoices and the money trail." She paused, "Once it is determined where the money is going, subpoenas for bank records are issued, and lastly, indictments are handed down. Bland, I'm sorry," she said, shaking her head at the thought of the humiliation Bland would go through, especially after losing his wife just weeks prior. "But you do have a head start. Here," she handed him a slip of paper. "I wrote down the name of the shell company and its address. That's all I can tell you, Bland." Penelope stood up and glanced over her shoulder.

"Isn't there something like a check stub with an account number on it?"

"Bland, we're living in the new millennium; everything is digital. The publishing house uses electronic check payments to replace what used to be the paper check. It's the ultimate paper trail."

"That's perfect because there has to be a routing number and account number attached to those deposits. That will allow us to identify the owner or owners of CS Printing."

"Bland, I am not in charge of EFTs."

"EFT?"

"Electronic Funds Transfer, money transferred from our account to another account. Those accounts are handled by another area of the department. There might be a question of ethics just showing you these invoices, especially if you are charged with embezzlement. I don't want to draw any attention to myself. I don't want to lose my job, Bland."

"I understand, Penelope."

"Like I said, I plan on being here all weekend, so if you need anything, call me."

There was a sense of panic on Bland's face. "Penelope, I don't know what to do."

"Do what the auditors will do, follow the tracks."

"Follow the tracks?" Bland echoed.

"Yes, the tracks that lead to the money, and hopefully you will uncover who's setting you up."

Penelope then left Bland sitting in the atrium alone.

Penelope's words "follow the tracks" resonated in Bland's head as he took the back steps to his office. Concerning him was the company's name on the invoice, CS Printing. He had never heard of CS Printing. Equally concerning was why and how his name was attached to the invoices. Briefly he thought about the novel and how it would be literally impossible to finish, given the possible criminal findings concerning him.

Bland reached the exit door to his floor and yanked it open, only to stop and retreat into the stairwell. Standing at the receptionist's desk was Detective Rhodavack and other uniformed officers. Bland quietly closed the exit door, leaving a small crack. From the small opening, he could

see the detective and the police officers and hear their conversation with Paige.

"I have an arrest warrant for Mr. Benthall." In the detective's hand was a folded paper.

"He's not here," Paige said, as she sat up in the seat.

"*R*..i..g..h..t. Well, you tell Mr. Benthall that when he's least expecting, I'll find him."

Detective Rhodavack glanced down toward the end of the hall in the direction of the exit door that hid Bland. Rapidly, Larry came out from his office. When he reached the lobby, Detective Rhodavack was walking to the elevator.

Once at the receptionist's desk Larry asked, "Did I hear the word detective? Something about a warrant for Bland's arrest?"

Paige didn't answer. Bland closed the door and scampered down the steps. He knew he had to exit the building quickly. He jumped into his SUV and drove. Penelope's words "follow the tracks" again resonated in his head, but all he had was an address of the company. Bland studied the address, but he wasn't sure in what part of town the company was located. His wife's voice came to mind, and her nagging how one day he would need a smart phone. Bland shook his head. He needed a phone with a GPS that would take him to the address of CS Printing and save him the hassle of driving around Washington, D.C., to find it. Out of frustration, Bland broke down to call his service provider to get an exact location of CS Printing.

"An extra five dollars will be added to your account," remarked the phone representative.

"Five dollars," Bland cried. "Okay, fine," he said in order to get the information.

While waiting for the address, the operator replied that the address had a non-working number attached to it.

"I didn't ask for a number just the location of the address," replied Bland in frustration.

"It appears this address is located in the old warehouse district of the city."

He hung up the phone without saying goodbye. He put the car in

gear and drove to the warehouse district.

A lot of the buildings in the district were rundown and deserted. Soon he came upon the address that the phone operator gave him. Bland parked and walked to the front entrance of the building. Vigorously, he yanked the handle of the door, but it wouldn't budge. There were windows on both sides of the front door. Years of dirt and grime coated the windows, so they offered no immediate visibility inside the building. Bland used his sleeve to clear a portion of the window. He pressed his face against the spot to see inside the building. It was partially dark and mostly empty, but he could make out a desk with a phone and an answering machine on top of it.

Bland stepped away from the window, turned, and walked toward the back of the building. The charcoal sky was starting to turn darker. Bland approached the back door. It, too, was locked. He looked for another entry point. Off to the side was a set of steps that led to the basement of the building. As he proceeded down the steps, the light disappeared. At the bottom of the steps, Bland tried to nudge the door open. After several hard nudges the door gave way. He entered the half lit, cobweb-filled basement. Meticulously, he made his way across the floor. He stopped when he thought he heard something. The sound came from up ahead. It sounded like a door being opened. His eyes flashed around the basement, then into the dark space where the sound reverberated. In order to reach the upper level of the building, he would have to travel in the direction of the noise. Apprehensively, Bland walked along the dark area until he reached another set of steps. Slowly, he stepped on the bottom step of a long flight of stairs. He used the glowing light from his cell phone for partial visibility. Out from the dark, running at full speed in Bland's direction was a long-tail rodent. Bland jumped quickly, then dashed up the steps. His hard shoes echoed across the wood floor of the warehouse. When he reached the desk, immediately he hit the answering machine, but it didn't come on. He checked the phone, and it had no dial tone.

"That's odd." Then he looked around the empty room. "Everything about this is wrong," he muttered.

He searched through the drawers of the desk for anything that could tell him something about CS Printing. When nothing materialized, he

began to look around the desk. He noticed an aluminum trashcan filled with burned bank statements. He grabbed one that appeared to have some salvageable information on it.

On the top of the partially burned paper was the name "Washington Savings Bank."

"Washington Savings," Bland repeated. He knew the bank and its location.

Underneath the name of the bank were some burned out words that Bland assumed was the name of the account holder. He was fortunate to cull out what he hoped were the numbers of the account and the words "Closing Statement."

He checked his watch; banking hours were drawing near. If he rushed, he could make it before closing.

A thin woman was about to lock the door of Washington Savings, when Bland slammed his hand against the window.

"We are closed, sir. You will have to come back tomorrow."

Bland's eyes glanced at the hands on his watch. "It is five before six, and I am a customer."

The thin woman then turned to look behind her at another woman. She waved for her to let him in. He walked to her desk and noticed her name tag, "Cookie Zeller."

"Hello, and how may I help you, mister?" She waited for Bland to give his name. Before Bland knew it, he had given the woman his real name. "It's Mr. Benthall, Mrs. Zeller."

"It's Miss."

He hadn't devised a plan on how to acquire the information he needed from the account.

"Oh, my apologies, Miss Zeller, I know it's near closing, but I stopped by to retrieve some information on my account. Frankly, I'm surprised you're open being that it's Black Friday."

"That doesn't matter these days. Now everything is open, including the banks."

Bland noticed her stare at the clock.

"Is something wrong?" she studied the clock on the wall with impatient eyes.

"Well, I had a fire and most of my bank statements were destroyed in the fire. My quarterly taxes are due, and I need my statements to complete my taxes. This is the last day to mail off my tax papers. I don't play with Uncle Sam," he laughed.

"You do know your statements are online? All you need is your account number and the password used to set up the account. That will give you access to the account."

"That's the thing. I don't remember the password or where I hid it from myself," he laughed again, hoping to gain some sympathy.

He noticed the dry laugh Miss Zeller returned and knew he needed to do something if he were to get those statements.

"Miss Zeller, I can tell you are ready to get out of here. Trust me, I don't want to keep you. It has probably been a long day for both of us." She smiled in agreement. "All I need is a physical printout of all my statements."

"Of course, but that will take some time," she looked at the clock on the wall. "The bank is now closed."

Bland put on his charm.

"I can tell from your frequent glancing at the clock that you have a date."

"Is it that obvious?" she blushed.

"As beautiful as you are, yes. It is that obvious. I don't want to be the guy who keeps you from some lucky person."

There was a level of pleasure in her stare. "Okay, but for security purposes I will need the account number and some identification. I am sure you understand."

Bland didn't panic; he pulled from his inside jacket the partially burned statement and handed it to Miss Zeller. The lady typed in the numbers of the account.

"Can you verify the address on the account?"

"Sure," Bland smiled. A relief came over Bland the moment the woman asked for the address of the company.

He gave the address of the old warehouse. Miss Zeller performed several keystrokes and waited. The woman confirmed the address that Bland gave her as the address on the bank statement.

"Thank you so much." When the account came up, she looked up at Bland.

"CS Printing," Bland blurted the name of the account before Miss Zeller had a chance.

Miss Zeller stole another glance at the clock on the wall. From her facial expression, Bland knew she was worried about being late for her date.

"I'm sorry," Bland apologized. "I hope you don't have to go far to meet your date."

Miss Zeller offered him an impatient smile. "Mr. Benthall, do you have any identification? I have to verify you as the account holder."

"I thought that was done when I gave you the account number and address."

"No sir, business accounts are not that simple. Only the name on the business is on this account, not the name of the account holder. There is a separate business profile attached to the account that has the agent of the business. That information, along with the account number and address, is matched to the business account. I need your identification to verify your name on the business profile page. Otherwise, I am not permitted to give you any information on the account, such as monthly statements."

"That's all I need are the statements from the time the account opened."

"Once again, Mr. Benthall, I need to pull up your business profile and match that with your identification to verify you as the account holder of," she peered into the screen, "CS Printing." Once again, Miss Zeller glanced at the clock. To save time, she decided to abandon banking procedures and print the monthly statements while she waited for the computer to bring up the business profile. "Mary Ann," Miss Zeller called to one of the tellers. "I sent some statements to the printer. Can you grab them for me?" The two sat in silence for a few minutes until Miss Zeller looked up from the computer. "The profile isn't coming up under your name." She looked at Bland, "Did you find your ID?"

Once again, Bland began to pat his pockets for his driver's license.

"You do spell your name with one 'L'? "

At that moment, the teller placed the bank statements on Miss Zeller's desk.

"No, it is spelled Benthall, with another 'L'."

"Oh, two 'L's. Maybe that is the problem."

Bland watched as she made a few keystrokes. He contemplated a plan to get the bank statements once she found out the inevitable that he was not on the account.

"Did my name come up?" asked Bland, not wanting to show a look of desperation.

"No, the computer is running very slow."

"Maybe it, too, wants to go home."

She smirked at his attempt to humor her.

"I believe I left my ID in the car. I parked four blocks away but give me fifteen minutes to run and get it."

As Bland suspected, Miss Zeller glanced at the time again. "That won't be necessary."

"I was hoping you would not have me run and get that ID. I am not in the shape I used to be."

She laughed, then moved her eyes back to the screen. "No, that won't be necessary, it appears my computer has locked up."

Bland wasn't sure what to say. "Does it need to be rebooted?" He could not believe he just said that. He stared at the bank statements on her desk. A part of him wanted to grab the statements and run out of the bank. And he was about to do so. However, her patience had run its course as she glanced at the clock in pure frustration.

She grabbed an empty folder from her desk to put the bank statements in. "You have a pleasant evening, Mr. Benthall." Bland followed her lead and stood to his feet. He looked surprised when the banker handed him the folder. He shook the woman's hand. "I hope you have a wonderful date, Cookie."

"Well, thank you, and it was a pleasure serving you. If I can assist you in the future, please give me a call." She handed him her business card.

Bland carried the folder of statements with him to a restaurant across the street from the bank and took a seat in the back for privacy. He started separating the statements according to their months.

Quickly, he noticed from the most recent statement that the account was closed and had a zero balance. That made him scrutinize each month's bank statement, from the month he supposedly opened the account to the month it was closed, October. From the time the CS Printing business account was opened at Washington Savings in April, it received seven monthly automatic deposits from S&W Publishing House in increments of $100,000.

Bland looked closer at the business activity of CS Printing and saw upon its opening it had Washington Savings set up automatic withdrawals to three companies: Global Consultant Services, BLC Telephone Company, and Red Eye Investigation.

He then broke down the withdrawals that were taken out of the CS Printing account over the previous seven months by each company. CS Printing had a total of $132,000 taken by direct withdrawal by Global Consultant Services. A monthly withdrawal of $63.00 was paid to BLC Telephone Company. And within the second month of setting up the CS Printing account, a one-time withdrawal of $80,000 was paid to Red Eye Investigation.

He examined the closing statement to find that the remaining $487,559 in the CS Printing business account at Washington and Savings was wired to Global Consultant Services business account at National Financial & Holdings. Bland was fortunate that a copy of the wire containing Global Consultant Services' routing number and checking account number were included with the statement. However, banking hours had passed, so Bland was forced to wait until the next day before he could visit National Financial & Holdings.

He walked to the bar and asked for a phone book. He took it back to his table and began flipping through the pages. He wrote down two names: National Financial & Holdings and Red Eye Investigation. Strangely, Global Consultant Services didn't have a listed number or street address. After gathering all the scattered papers into one stack, he stuffed them back into the folder, then wrote the name Washington and Savings on the front of the folder and left the restaurant. Though he was too late to visit National Financial & Holdings, he figured he might catch someone at Red Eye Investigation before it closed.

As Bland drove, he was extremely vexed. He assumed Red Eye Investigation was a company hired to find people. But who paid a company $80,000 to find someone? More importantly, who could that someone be? Why was it being connected to him?

He pulled his vehicle into a parking lot adjacent to a dark brick building. There was a small sign on the door that read "Red Eye Investigation." With some caution, Bland entered the building. Automatically, a bell rang, and a woman came out of a back room.

"Hello, may I help you?" she asked.

"I think I may have utilized your services," Bland said.

"What service did we provide, sir?"

Bland looked puzzled, "I beg your pardon. Don't you find people?"

"The service provided, was it business related or personal?" Bland's eyes flickered with uncertainty. The woman tried to help. "What's your name, sir?"

"Bland Benthall."

"Mr. Benthall, yes, I remember your file."

"You know me?"

She assumed he was making a joke, so she laughed. "Only by email, but I hope you've been pleased with our services."

Bland looked at the woman suspiciously. He thought he would say something and see where the conversation led. "So, where are the two men that ran into my college crony?"

"You must be referring to Tim and Tom. They're brothers. Currently, they're out on an assignment."

"What type of assignment?"

"We can't divulge that information, you understand, given the nature of our business. So how is it that I can help you?"

"I want to retrieve my file." He recalled her mentioning his file.

"I am sorry, Mr. Benthall, but we don't give out files. All of our files are stored in our online sky database."

"An online sky database?" he questioned.

"Yes, it's a database that helps store and protect documents, photos, and other important things in case they are deleted from our main server."

"Well, can I have a copy from your online sky database?" he asked, before glancing at the file cabinets behind her desk. Bland was certain that companies like Red Eye Investigation kept hard copies of all their clients and would never totally rely on an online storage database.

"That's why we are highly recruited, because we don't give copies out. Mr. Benthall, you knew our policy. You signed a contract to these terms."

"I signed a contract?"

"Yes, you agreed to our terms when you filled out our online application."

"You have a website?"

"Yes, we're mostly contacted through the Internet. Our clients like to stay as discrete as possible."

Bland was expecting something more corrupt and underground about Red Eye Investigation; however, they appeared to be legit.

Bland sniffed the aroma of burnt popcorn that drifted through the air. "Is that popcorn I smell?"

The woman jumped, "Oh heavens, I left it in the microwave too long. Can you excuse me?"

The woman took off to the back, and Bland saw his chance to walk around the desk to the file cabinets. If he wanted any real answers, he would have to retrieve them himself. He had a narrow visual of the woman as she ran to the microwave. Cautiously, she pulled at the hot bag of popcorn. When she darted away from the microwave, she would disappear from his sight. Bland went down to the B section of the file order. The woman came back into his peripheral. He stole a quick glance. She was pulling the hot bag of popcorn out with a napkin. Again she darted from the microwave and from his sight. Quickly, Bland needed to find what he was looking for in the cabinet before the woman returned. As he turned toward the file cabinets, he hoped he was right about them harboring clients' files. His fingers dragged across the folders of B's until he saw his name. The sound of hard soled shoes approached him. He moved even quicker to get the folder out of the cabinet.

Seconds later, she walked in the waiting area. Her eyes raked over the lobby then on Bland, who stood in his original spot.

"Is it burnt?" he asked.

"Just on the bottom, I've never been good at popping popcorn, even in a microwave." She chuckled before moving behind the desk. "Anyway, I apologize that I can't be of more help."

Bland looked up and noticed he had left the file drawer slightly ajar.

"That's okay, at least I know the file is in good hands," he smiled.

Bland turned on his heels and left the building. He jumped into his automobile and hastily drove out of the parking lot. After driving fifteen minutes, he pulled over to the curb. He pulled out the folder that he concealed on the inside of his jacket.

He flipped through the pages in the folder. According to the notes there was an agreed amount of $80,000 cash to be paid in February. A second payment of $80,000 would be paid at a later date. Bland assumed that was the $80,000 that was withdrawn from the CS Printing's account at Washington Savings bank. "But what was CS Printing or the culprit who set up the account with Red Eye Investigation interested in finding?" Bland wondered aloud.

According to the notes on the paper, Bland, or someone purporting to be Bland, hired the investigation service a few months prior to the second payment of $80,000. Bland inferred that the first payment had to be an installment to start the investigation, and the later payment was for once the job was complete.

Bland flipped through the pages and stopped when he saw a picture of Dakota. The notes on the page revealed information on her background—hometown growing up, schooling, college degrees, marriage, and previous and current address. The next page was devoted to an article on his adoptive parents' deaths. On another page were pictures of his high school friends with scribbled notes beside each. He scrolled through a few more pages until he came to Alvin Snead's name. Paper clipped was a picture of Alvin by a full page of notes and in all caps the word "LOCATED."

Bland scanned the notes to read the personal comments made by Alvin. As Bland read the notes, they were consistent with his story. It wasn't until he started reading Alvin's direct comments that he became startled. He proceeded to read Alvin's quotes aloud.

"Yes, I remember her, or at least her name. He referred to her as Grey. I remember he couldn't stop talking about this girl he had met the summer before attending college. He joked he had lost his soul mate. If you ask me, he lost more than his soul mate. I mean the guy was in love. He was definitely consumed by her. He doesn't know I know this, but Bland even used the university newspaper's resources to search for her. Then he and Dakota started to hang out. I am not sure if Dakota knew about Grey. However, I am sure she suspected there was someone important he was looking for because she asked me. But men aren't supposed to disclose that information. Nonetheless, after Dakota stole his heart, I never heard him mention the name Greysen or Grey."

Bland's heart began to pound. At the bottom of the page was a star beside the name Greysen Brindle and in all caps the word "LOCATED" with the date beside it. There was a list of her demographics, marital status, occupation, and whether she had any living relatives or children.

Bland laid the folder down to think. Why would Grey be the intended target of a search for a surprise party that never took place? He looked at the date beside her name and calculated the date to be six weeks prior to their reunion on the train. Grey's name was now directly connected to Red Eye Investigation, and it connected to CS Printing, and CS Printing was acting as a shell company with money funneled through it from S&W Publishing house. Bland began to consider who these executives were that "so-called" hired Grey.

Although the connections indicted the twins, Bland wanted to weigh all the evidence before convicting them. His writing instinct began to take over. If he was setting up someone, the connections shouldn't be so easily detected, he believed. Therefore, suspicion drew him to believe there was more to this story. He opened his satchel and put the Red Eye folder with the Washington and Savings folder. Abruptly, he pulled from the curb and made a U-turn in the middle of the street. It was time for him to pay a visit to Grey's apartment.

28

WHEN BLAND ARRIVED AT GREY'S APARTMENT, HE retrieved the extra key to the apartment that was kept underneath the flower pot by the door. He opened the door and cautiously entered the foyer. Someone had taken the time to cover the furniture and gather most of her loose belongings into a few boxes. He focused on rummaging through the contents of the boxes in hopes of finding something that could identify the men that "so-called" hired Grey. He flipped through old utility bills and restaurant receipts. He thought about the contract that she referenced on several occasions. Then he came across a few of her notepads. One by one, he looked through the pages of each notepad, hoping something would catch his eye. Bland placed the notepad on the side to continue searching through the box when he found a book of matches on which were the initials "HH." He thought he knew the initials but when he couldn't pinpoint where, he placed the book of matches to the side and continued to search through the box. Eventually, he came across a note specifying a meeting with the executives that included an address of the Highty-Hole restaurant, a restaurant located in southeast D.C. Having found something of interest, he drew the paper closer to his eyes. The date for the meeting was for today and in

less than an hour. Immediately, he stopped giving the date and time of the meeting much thought, since Grey was deceased. He pulled out his wallet to save Grey's note and the book of matches. Also in his wallet was the book of matches from the floor of the file room. Coincidentally, both books of matches had "HH" and "Bar" on them. Bland focused on the address on Grey's note. He believed the initials "HH" on both books of matches could be the acronym for the restaurant, Highty-Hole.

"Who is really behind finding you and why?" he asked aloud.

He tried to put his mind around it all, the attack in the file room, both books of matches, and Grey's meeting that would have occurred in less than an hour. If he hurried, he could see who was meeting with her and maybe learn if there was a connection between Grey and his attacker.

A sound came from outside the front door. Bland tore the paper from the pad then tossed the notepad back into the box and bolted into the kitchen. He urgently searched through the drawers for a weapon. He discovered a hammer in the back of the drawer. He hid behind the wall next to the refrigerator and waited. The front door of the apartment closed, and someone was walking across the carpet. Bland squeezed the handle of the hammer. The closer the steps came, the tighter he gripped the hammer. When the shuffled feet turned into the kitchen, Bland's reflexes came down with the hammer. The woman screamed while moving out of the path of the blow. The flat face of the hammer smacked against the countertop, cracking the granite to resemble a spider web.

When Bland realized it was a woman, he attempted to aid her. That is, until she screamed again. Her frightened eyes settled on the hammer. Bland recognized it and laid the hammer on the counter.

He spoke calmly, "I didn't mean to frighten you, but you scared me."

"I scared you? You are the one with the hammer. Who are you, and how did you get in here?"

"The lady who resided here was a good friend. I stopped to see about her property. I have a key," Bland said in defense.

"I'm the manager of these properties. If you are here to get her stuff, then you should have stopped by the management office. Anyway, I

can't release it to you because you're not family."

"I understand, so what do you plan on doing with her things?"

"It will stay here until the end of the month. If no family member claims it by then, we will donate it to a local shelter."

"On her rental application, did she list a next of kin?" Bland asked. If there was a next of kin, it may lead him to more answers, he thought.

"No, she didn't. I already told this to the police."

"The police have been here?" he asked.

"A few times to look around," she moved into the great room of the apartment. Then she became very short with Bland. "I'm going to have to ask you to leave now. Please leave the key."

Inside the SUV, Bland took another look at the address on the paper. As he drove to the location of the restaurant and bar, it started to rain, adding a drab appearance to the cold and gray backdrop of the sky.

It was an old five-story building that lacked the five-star qualities that Bland believed would have attracted someone of Grey's stature. It happened to be in one of the rough areas of the city. Bland thought maybe he had the wrong address, so he looked out the windshield at the half-lit sign on the front of the building.

With disbelief, Bland mumbled, "This is it?"

He began to wonder why any executive would want to meet at this type of establishment. He wanted to leave, but then he thought of the old adage that Detective Rhodavack quoted, "Let no stone go unturned." Just being in the neighborhood gave Bland a sense of trepidation, yet he persevered. As he ran toward the building, he used his hands to shield himself from the cold rain.

With caution, Bland opened the door to the restaurant that had the ambiance of a dingy bar. The inside of the facility was dark and smoke infested with its normal barflies and very few customers dining. Sprinkled around the restaurant were a few small tables. When Bland glanced around the room, he saw a closed red door at the back of the restaurant. Near the door was an old man busing tables. Bland had no idea what or who he was looking for, so he grabbed a seat at the bar and was about to order a beer when two men with loud voices entered

the restaurant. Bland frowned when he recognized the beard-faced man from the morgue. What would be the odds of that, he thought? The men disappeared behind the red door.

Bland waited to make sure the men weren't coming back before walking over to the old man busing tables.

"What's through that door?"

"There are some offices upstairs." The man coughed. "You got a cigarette?"

Bland patted his pockets, knowing he didn't smoke. "No."

Again, Bland looked around before heading to the door. Having no idea what was on the other side, he approached the red door with caution. When he opened the door, he saw a flight of steps. The sounds of heavy footsteps traveling up them echoed along the staircase. Bland looked upward through the staircase and spotted two pairs of shoes. The shoes and the sounds emitting from the steps stopped at what seemed to be the third floor. Bland swallowed hard before thinking about climbing the stairs. What am I doing? he pondered. The thought almost coerced him to turn around, but he couldn't bring himself to do it. Instead, he started climbing the steps, which made whining and cracking sounds as he ascended. When he reached the third floor, Bland took a moment to catch his breath. He spotted a closed door with a sign on it that read, "Suite A." Slowly, he opened the door to the suite. Inside, at the beginning of a narrow hallway, was a restroom. Bland checked it to be certain no one would sneak up on him. Coming from the end of the hall were voices. Bland proceeded down the hall of the suite until he came to a perpendicular hallway. Along this hall were a few doors with numbers on them.

One of the doors was slightly ajar. Bland moved to the door. The small opening allowed him to see into the room. He caught a glimpse of a scar-faced man. The man's heavy voice alone caused Bland to panic.

These certainly didn't seem like the kind of people Grey would be doing business with, he thought. Instantly, Bland stepped back from the door when he saw a man with a corduroy jacket approaching from inside. If seen, Bland was sure the beard-faced man from the morgue would recognize him. He turned to leave the suite when the door he was

peeping through started to open. At once, Bland slid his body behind the opening door. Once Beard went to close the door behind him, Bland was sure he would be seen.

"You want me to shut this?" Beard already had his hand on the door and was starting to shut it.

"Naw, we'll lock the suite door, so you can leave that open. Let the room air out," Scar's menacing voice bellowed.

"But I left the key to the suite on the desk."

"Don't worry about it; we won't be gone long."

"But if Rich finds out that we left both the suite and the office door open again, he's gonna have a hissy fit."

"He ain't here, so come on," growled Scar.

When the man turned to show his entire scarred face, Bland didn't recognize him. Bland stayed hidden behind the door until he heard the suite door close. Once he felt safe, he came out from his hiding place. Temporarily, he stood in the adjoining halls before going through the open door of the office.

Inside the room was an old leather sofa and one chair in the center of the floor. The room reeked of a musty odor. When Bland walked, his feet squished over wet carpet. He leaned down to touch the moisture on the carpet. He looked down at his hand. On his fingers was a mixture of blood and water. The sight of the blood made Bland panic, and he considered what might have taken place in that room.

"What have I gotten myself into?" Bland whispered aloud.

There was a closed door inside the room with a dingy sign on it that read "STAY OUT." Despite this warning, Bland laid his ear on the door. Not a sound could be heard. The entire atmosphere reminded him of a movie. Never open a door with a sign on it that reads "STAY OUT" because that's where the trouble is. In every book he'd ever read, the trouble was normally behind the door that shouldn't be accessed. So, Bland decided to take a chance; he turned the doorknob and partially opened the door. He pushed his head through. Nothing happened. He figured it was safe to enter the room.

No one was in the room. He wasn't sure what he was doing and definitely had no idea what he was supposed to be looking for in the

office. However, Bland hoped that there might be a connection or clue that could lead him to some answers. With any luck, something might tell him what type of relationship Grey had with these men. Quickly, he erased the serious consequences attached to such illegal and risky activity.

In the room was a small refrigerator catty-cornered with a microwave on top and surrounded by empty frozen dinner boxes. On the opposite side of the room was a lounge sofa with shredded cushions. As he proceeded, Bland inadvertently kicked one of the many beer cans scattered about the floor. He stopped and waited to see if someone heard him. Hearing nothing, he looked around the room with no real thought of finding anything. His attention was diverted from the empty boxes and beer cans when the phone rang. The answering machine clicked, and immediately Bland felt nervous.

"Somebody call me back now, and I mean ASAP. I'll be at the farmhouse and bring that package," a scratchy voice said. "And hurry up!"

Bland believed these guys didn't sound like the kind of people that would call the cops if they found an uninvited guest in their office, more like the type that would bury him in the office's walls. Inside the room was a door that led to the hallway. To be careful, Bland chose to backtrack into the adjacent room he had previously traveled. He was sure to leave the office door open as he found it, then he made his way into the hall of the suite, and up the connecting hall. His nervous energy increased his speed. He stopped abruptly. A concealed bathroom door swung open as Bland approached it. He froze, and his heart raced while his tongue stalled. Out came a large man, who moved to stand directly in front of Bland. Bland recalled one of the roughneck men implying it was only the two of them, so who was this guy? How stupid it was to even enter the suite not knowing how many men were there. Bland didn't know what to think or do, so he stood there in silence. The two men faced off with no words exchanging. Finally, the large man spoke.

"I hope you don't mind; I had to take a dump, and our bathroom upstairs is broke." He turned and headed out the door of the suite.

Bland exhaled deeply with a sense of relief, then slightly relaxed.

He knew he had to get out of the suite and fast. When he made it out of the suite and started down the stairs, he saw one of the rough men heading back up the steps. Something told him not to return to the suite. However, before he knew it, he had backtracked into the hallway of the suite to avoid the man. He knew he couldn't go back into the office, so he had no choice but to enter the bathroom in the hall. A strong stench choked him as he entered. There was no lock on the bathroom door, so Bland placed his weight up against the door. He prayed the man wouldn't attempt to enter the bathroom.

The man opened the suite door and marched down the narrow hall. Bland squinted his eyes to see through a small opening he made with the bathroom door. The man passed and entered the open door of the office. Now out of his sight, Bland's olfactory took in the foul odor within the bathroom, which pressed him to get out. However, his trying to leave without knowing whether the thug would reenter the hall could be suicide.

Bland waited a few minutes before opening the bathroom door. Fortunately, he hadn't exited the bathroom because the outside door of the adjacent room suddenly opened. Scar walked across the open doorway of the room, which happened to be in a direct line and view to the bathroom. Scar noticed the answering machine blinking. He moved from Bland's line of sight to hit the button, and for a few seconds, stood over the machine with his back to the open door. Bland completely opened the bathroom door. He had decided to creep out while Scar's back was turned, but Scar suddenly moved from the machine back to the open doorway, and Bland quickly allowed the bathroom door to return to a cracked position. While the machine cued, Scar walked in the hall and headed directly for the bathroom.

Bland closed the bathroom door; he was sure it was only a moment before he and Scar came eye to eye. Bland feared this meeting would be fatal for him. Scar grabbed the knob to the bathroom door and tried pushing it open. Bland wedged his body up hard against the door.

The answering machine beeped before the message from the scratchy-voiced man repeated. Scar cursed and turned loose the knob of the bathroom door and quickly headed back to the office. He closed the

office door behind him. With both doors now closed, Bland slipped out of the bathroom and out of the suite. He made his way down the steps.

When he yanked open the red door to the restaurant, Bland and the old man busing tables crashed into each other. Bland was about to keep going when he saw the beard-faced thug coming through the front entrance of the restaurant. Not to be discovered, Bland bent down to help the old man pick up the cups and plates. When Beard disappeared through the red door, Bland stood up and sprinted out of the restaurant.

It was pouring rain as Bland exited the restaurant, but instead of jumping into his SUV and leaving, he slid down in his seat and waited for the men to come out of the building. He needed to know what business Grey had with these men, and whether that business had anything to do with the explosion at the publishing house and she and Dakota's deaths. Not to mention, he was curious to know what package the scratchy-voiced man referenced.

When Scar and Beard got into a tan 4x4 Jeep, Bland gave chase. The Jeep curved toward Interstate 495 North to 95 North. When the Jeep reached the exit for the Annapolis Naval Pier, it turned onto the ramp. Bland continued with his pursuit, even knowing the dangers of following such men.

It was dark and still raining hard when the Jeep pulled off onto a dirt road. Bland slowed his speed and was careful to turn off his headlights. He left his parking lights on to guide him along the muddy dirt road. The taillights of the Jeep indicated its position, and that it had stopped ahead on a hill. At a snail's pace, Bland crept up the hill to a safe point of stopping. From there, he decided to hike the muddy road that disappeared behind tall bushes. His feet sank the moment they touched the mud. He pushed branches and foliage from his face as he attempted to climb the muddy trail.

Soon he came upon the 4x4. Inside the Jeep was a collection of beer cans, cigarette butts, and the putrid stench of death. Up ahead, the muddy road opened into a wide field. Thankfully, the rain had lightened up to a mist, so Bland could see a dilapidated, rugged farmhouse in the middle of the field. The light in the house allowed Bland to see a

few shadows darting across the wall. Instead of returning to his SUV, he chose to eavesdrop on the men. Quietly he approached one of the downstairs windows. He could hear the voices of the men echo off the wall. Bland drew closer to the window to hear and see. He rose on the tips of his shoes to have a look in the room, but his height barely allowed him to see over the lower sill of the window. No one was in the room, but in an adjacent room there was a light hanging from a cord that swayed back and forth. A silhouette on the wall showed a person hanging by a rope from the rafters. He watched as another shadow began hitting the body of the hanging silhouette. The clap of a fist smacking against flesh echoed in Bland's ears. He watched quietly as another larger shadow pushed the smaller shadow out of the way; then he also began slinging punches to the head and body of the person hanging. Bland waited for the hanging body to rip out a scream or anything to express the pain it was receiving from the men, but the person hanging from the rafters didn't utter a sound. A steady flow of liquid dripped. The dark liquid flowed from the lit room, along the cracks of the floor panel into the next room where Bland watched from the outside window. He didn't need to see the color of the liquid to know it was blood.

Bland ducked as Scar walked into the next room, over to the window where he was peeping. Scar lifted the window and spit out a glob of tobacco. There was no time to move without being seen, so Bland pushed his body flat against the house, underneath the window. Residue of brown tobacco juice dripped on Bland's head and ran down his neck. Scar walked away from the window to the dark corner of the room. Again, Bland returned to the tips of his shoes to witness what he assumed was a murder taking place.

Breathing heavily, Scar wrapped his hand around something long. From the glow of light, Bland saw it was a wooden bat. The softer-voiced Beard yelled, "I'm getting tired of hitting him. He's starting to hurt my knuckles."

Bland didn't believe that the man hanging from the cord could still be alive, not until the body suddenly jerked.

Beard jumped back, "Did you see that shit? It jumped! It ain't dead."

"He's dead. Bodies sometimes do that when they die. It supposedly

has something to do with the nerves being the last thing to go," said Scar. However, he used the bat to strike the midsection and ribs of the hanging body.

Bland's toes were weakening. He lowered himself to glance around for something to stand on. He spotted an old crate among the thrown-out debris and snatched it. It wobbled a bit before he could balance his entire weight on it, but he managed to keep it steady.

"Give me that bat, so I can make sure he's dead," Beard requested.

Coming from somewhere else in the house was the loud, scratchy voice, but no silhouette to identify his size.

"You two morons stand over there until I tell you to move."

Bland recognized that the heavy scratchy voice belonged to the man on the answering machine, Rich. When a portion of Rich's body appeared in the doorway, Bland immediately noticed the broad frame of the man was much larger than the other two men. His frame and buzz-cut matched something out of a comic magazine thought Bland. As Bland leaned forward to get a better look at Rich, the old crate gave way under his weight.

"There's someone out there," Beard said.

"Come with me," ordered Rich to Scar. Instantly, the two men ran into the dark room and over to the window. They saw Bland running from the house. "Follow me," demanded Rich. He and Scar bolted through the back door of the farmhouse.

Bland had slipped and was pulling himself up from the muddy ground when he slipped again. As he picked himself up from the soggy dirt and mud, he heard a door to the house bang against the wall. The conditions were dire as he slipped, fell, and slipped again down the muddy drive. If caught, he knew that he, too, would hang from the rafters. Bland looked back at the two men giving chase. He tried to catch his balance as he slid down the narrow, slick path. Scar closed in and grabbed Bland's jacket, while Rich tried to stop himself from falling. As Scar yanked on his jacket, Bland jerked his body left, causing Scar to slide into a tree where he lay unconscious.

Bland fought to stay on his feet. When he felt his shoulder jerk backwards, both he and Rich fell and rolled down the muddy

embankment. Their bodies slammed into the front driver's side tire of the thug's 4x4. Rich slipped but held to Bland's collar while trying to climb to his feet. In order to break Rich's grip, Bland rammed his cell phone into the side of Rich's face.

Bland tried to run but instead found his body sliding along the side of the Jeep. After gaining control, he ran for his SUV. He looked back to see where the man was. Rich managed to use the bumper and hood of the Jeep to pull his broad body upright. The look Bland saw in Rich's glaring eyes showed he wanted to do him bodily harm. Rich dug inside his jacket and pulled his gun from his holster. He started running toward Bland firing the pistol at the same time. Bullets ricocheted off the hood of the SUV. Bland ducked. He slapped at his pockets for his keys. He looked into the car window and saw the keys hanging from the ignition. The bullets and Rich were getting closer. Bland began punching numbers in the security keypad on the driver's side door to release the lock. After two tries the lock clicked, and Bland dove into the vehicle. He turned the ignition, shifted the vehicle in reverse, and hit the pedal. A few more bullets struck the front bumper of the vehicle. Bland rolled the steering wheel and the SUV did about a 90 degree turn on the muddy road. Again, he slammed his foot against the pedal. More bullets could be heard hitting the trunk of the vehicle as it fishtailed along the mud-covered road. Rich stood and watched as Bland drove off. When Bland hit the brakes to avoid an all-out tailspin, the small lights over his rear plates illuminated his tags.

The cruel man pulled out a cigarette and stood there watching the speeding vehicle's brake lights gleam and dim. He smoked the cigarette down to the stub, then pressed it into the mud. Suddenly, Bland's cell phone began to ring, and Rich bent down to grab it out of the mud.

"Yeah?" he snarled. "You want to speak to who, Greysen Brindle? Who is this? Dr. Ford? She missed her appointment with Dr. Dows? Her blood work," he repeated. "Well, what type of medical emergency is it?" the scratchy voice asked. Rich's threatening eyes squinted. "Is that right? Yeah, I'll pass the message along." With a sinister smirk, Rich hung up the phone. He lit another cigarette. Then he dialed a number on Bland's cell phone.

The voice on the other end answered, "Bland?"

"No. It's me. You have a problem."

With an evil look, Rich turned and started up the muddy road. On his way back to the house, he assisted the other thug to his feet. They entered the house and walked into the light of the room where Beard waited by the hanging body. With the pistol still in hand, Rich walked over to the body to place the muzzle to its head. He pulled the trigger. Brains and skull fragments splattered across the wall and the silhouette of the body. Then the evil-faced man looked at Scar and Beard.

"Get the car. That's enough practice on a corpse. We got work to do."

29

FRANTICALLY BLAND DROVE AT HIGH SPEEDS TO PUT distance between himself and the sadistic men at the farmhouse. To be extra careful that he wasn't followed, he drove an hour out of his way before reaching the city limits. By the time he reached Interstate 495, traffic was bumper to bumper. Finally, he arrived at his house. Bland sat in his car staring at his dark house and thinking about what had just taken place.

Nothing made sense, such as the men trying to kill him at the farmhouse, not to mention, having seen the man from the coroner's office also at the farmhouse. Bland wondered if one of these men could have been the man that attacked him in the file room at the publishing house. Again, what did all this have to do with Grey? Why would she be meeting with such ruthless men? Exhausted, he got out of the vehicle but did not really want to enter an empty house.

He flipped the light switch in the foyer, but the room stayed dark. After almost being killed at the farmhouse, the stillness in the house made him feel extremely uneasy. Those men are miles away, and there's no way they know where I live, he reasoned.

Bland tried to focus on various objects in the darkness of the room.

A blown fuse, he assumed. Not wanting to venture to the basement to the fuse box, he decided to check a light switch in the kitchen to be certain it was a fuse. When he walked into the kitchen, he heard glass and other debris cracking under his feet. That feeling of security slowly turned into fear that began to creep along his spine. When the kitchen light didn't work, he felt his way through the dark to the counter drawers in search of a flashlight.

"Damn," he cursed, when the flashlight wouldn't come on. He remembered all the times Dakota told him to purchase batteries for the flashlight. "You will never know when it's needed," she would say.

He took a moment to consider all the times Dakota told him he would be sorry for not listening to her. At that moment, he wished his wife were there to berate him for not listening to her.

It scared him when he inadvertently kicked a chair and what he thought was the trash can as he made his way to the basement door. Instantly, he thought of the men at the farmhouse and the body hanging from the rafters. The long stairs that led to the basement squeaked as he made his way down. By sheer memory, he made his way to the fuse box. Suddenly, a hard blow struck him in his ribs. Bland fell to the floor. He looked up just in time to see the silhouette of a large foot coming toward his head and rolled over in time before the man's heavy foot could connect to his skull. The man kicked again as Bland backed into the staircase. He tried to focus his eyes in the dark, before stooping to hit the man in the kneecap. The man fell to the floor, and Bland came back with a hook to his attacker's jaw. Another pair of footsteps rumbled down the basement stairs. Bland grabbed the shoulders of the first man. Then he released the man when a forearm struck the small of his back. Bland fell back to the floor after an assault of kicks to his body and head. The sound of gunfire suddenly rang out in the basement followed by a flare of sparks.

Both assailants scurried up the steps to escape the buck shots. Bland crawled to his knees, then to his feet. He grabbed the back of his neck as he opened the fuse box. His hand felt across the inside panel to the switch on the main breaker. When the house lights flashed on, John Scott yelled and charged with a double barrel shotgun in his hand.

Bland couldn't make out his face, so he tackled John. His shotgun went sailing across the concrete floor. Bland pulled his fist back to punch, but stopped when John screamed, "Bland! It's me."

Bland held his fist in the air. He slowly pulled himself off John to help the old man back to his feet.

"What are you doing with that shotgun? You could have killed me, John."

"I saw someone was in the house, so I came over to investigate. When I heard scuffling…" John's voice raced as he tried to catch his breath.

"I know," Bland said as he dusted himself off.

"I saw two shadows darting from room to room. I got my binoculars, and I saw two burglars. They were going through everything. Then, the lights went out. That's when I got my shotgun and crept through the back yard. I decided to come in through the basement and surprise them. That's when I heard the commotion. I thought it was them."

"It was me."

"Well, I didn't hear you drive up, so I didn't know that at the time. Bland, I think I hit one. Look. I see blood."

Drips of blood led a path up the stairs.

"Thanks for coming when you did."

"Are you okay? I didn't hurt you, did I?" John asked.

"No. Five more seconds and who knows?" Bland said, as he began to climb the stairs. "Come on, let's go upstairs and see what damage was done."

"Wait," stopped John. "Let me get my shotgun. They might still be around."

"I doubt it. You're pretty good with that thing."

Upstairs, the main floor looked as if a hurricane had hit it. Sofa cushions were cut, and plates, pictures, and drawers were thrown about. Bland made his way around the room, not thinking who did the destruction, but contemplating that the men from the farmhouse knew where he lived.

He bolted up the stairs to the bedrooms, leaving John downstairs. In each bedroom, the beds were turned over, the drawers were emptied,

and items were tossed everywhere.

Bland turned quickly when John walked into the bedroom.

"They did a number up here. Look at this room. This doesn't look like a burglary, Bland. It doesn't look like they stole anything. All the appliances and electronics seem to be here. They must have been looking for money. Do you keep large sums of money in the house?"

"No. Never have."

"Well, they were looking for something."

As Bland looked around, he gave considerable thought to John's comment. And yes, nothing appeared stolen. What did the men from the farmhouse want? He was mulling it over when John shouted.

"I'm calling the police."

"No, John," said Bland, after thinking about Detective Rhodavack. He definitely didn't need any police involvement.

Bland had decided that staying at his house wasn't an option. It wouldn't be safe. He believed the men might return. "I'll deal with it tomorrow, John, but tonight, I'll stay at a hotel."

"You don't have to do that; we have a guest room, and you know you're welcome."

"Thank you, John, but I need the space for my thoughts. I need to figure some things out."

"Bland, are you in some sort of trouble?"

"I don't know," Bland said, honestly.

As Bland drove, he pondered the idea of the men coming to kill him. As he pulled up to the motel, he began to question how they were able to find him. Another thought flashed through his mind. During the scuffle at the farmhouse, did he lose his ID? He began to search for his wallet. Once found, he flipped it open to his driver's license. When he spotted his credit card, he had another thought. Those men tracked me to my house; surely they could track the credit card if I used it as a method of payment. He patted his pockets in search of cash. Abruptly, he stopped to stare at the motel. A feeling of trepidation came over him. Even if he used cash, he wouldn't feel safe at the motel. He contemplated his next move. Once he cleared that thought from his head, he drove to where he

knew he would be safe.

When no answer came after several knocks on the door, Bland thought maybe it was a bad idea to just show up unexpectedly at Lou's house. He started to leave when the lock to the door clicked and the door opened.

"Bland!" Lou said with surprise. "What brings you by so late?"

"I think someone is trying to kill me."

"What!" Lou sounded alarmed and then was stunned by Bland's disheveled appearance. "Come in."

Bland looked down at his dirty clothes. "Do you think I can take a hot shower and maybe borrow some clothes from you?"

"What have you gotten yourself into, Bland?"

"More than I can handle," he replied, as he stepped past the door. "I was attacked twice tonight by some really bad men."

After taking a quick shower and changing, Bland flopped his body in the large recliner and stretched back far enough to engage the bottom harness to support his feet. There was a long sigh of relief.

Bland updated Lou on all the latest events that had transpired since he saw him last.

"So, who do you think the men were that attacked you?" Lou asked.

"I don't know. All I know is that Red Eye Investigation was hired to find Grey. Those men could be working for Red Eye." Bland sighed, "According to the woman at Red Eye, I hired their services to find Grey."

"So why did you hire Red Eye to find Grey?"

"That's the thing, Lou. I didn't," Bland said with a serious stare. "Someone authorized a deposit of $80,000 in cash to have Red Eye look for her. CS Printing's bank statements show another $80,000 being withdrawn by Red Eye. I don't have that kind of money."

"I know that, but the police don't know that," Lou responded. "Now it appears you have plenty of money. Not to mention, two women and a baby are dead. Do you see the inferences this detective is going to draw, Bland?" Lou shook his head and continued. "What are you planning to do?"

"I don't know. I was told to 'follow the tracks', and it should take me to who is behind this."

"Follow the tracks? Did the tracks stop at the bank?"

"Actually no, since all the money was transferred to another bank, and it was past banking hours. Tomorrow is Saturday, so I will have to wait until Monday for the bank to open to get more answers."

"Bland, you don't have until Monday. Most banks are open until noon on Saturday. You need to check it out first thing tomorrow."

Bland nodded his head to the idea.

"Do you have any idea why those men broke into your house?"

"At first, I thought to harm me, but they ransacked the place as if they were looking for something."

"What could it have been?" Lou asked.

Bland looked blankly at Lou and said, "I don't know because nothing was missing." Bland's voice lowered as if remembering something important. "Could they have been looking for the gun?"

Quickly, Lou asked, "What gun?"

"The homicide detective said a 9-millimeter casing was found. According to him that casing can still identify the gun."

"You have a 9-millimeter?"

"Yeah, but it's not where it's supposed to be. Frankly, I can't find it. Now I'm wondering if they destroyed my house to find the gun."

"You said they were still there when you arrived, so maybe they didn't find it either."

Bland sat up in the recliner. "So what does that mean?"

"It means they know something that you don't know." There was a long silence between the two men. Finally, Lou asked, "So what's next, Bland?"

"Until I can figure out the connection between Grey and these men, I plan to visit National Financial & Holdings and find out what the connection is with me."

Lou walked into another room and returned with a glass of water. It surprised Bland.

"You're still hanging in there?"

"I've been faithfully going to those meetings," said Lou, as he walked over and took a seat across from the recliner. "Bland, the more I think about it, you have to find out the relationship between Grey and these

men before that detective does because I am sure he's going to paint an unfavorable picture of you."

Briefly, Bland shut his eyes. "I know. Because once he gets word of those invoices, it will be inevitable. He's going to say I'm either directly or indirectly the cause of their deaths."

"What about the book?" Lou asked.

"The book," Bland repeated, now forcing his eyes to stay open.

When Bland didn't elaborate further on the book, Lou assumed he had completed it. "So you have finished it?"

"I haven't typed a word since the night Dakota and Grey died. I had good intentions to finish it, but now all of this has occurred. I know a lot is riding on it, but I have to figure out this mess so I won't end up in jail."

Lou watched as Bland's eyelids dropped again.

"Bland, the book isn't important right now, but getting to the bottom of this is crucial. Why don't you get some sleep, you look exhausted. Take my bed, and I will take the sofa."

"I couldn't move from this chair if I wanted to." Bland's eyelids started to drop once more.

"I'll probably be gone by the time you get up. Dad has surgery tomorrow and I need to be there early so I can fill out some paperwork. Veteran stuff." Lou watched as Bland's eyes dipped. "Are you sure you want to sleep on that recliner? The bed is in the next room, and you'll get a better sleep."

"This is perfect," his eyes barely open.

"Do as you like, but your back will feel it in the morning."

Bland's tired eyes finally collapsed, and it wasn't long before he fell asleep. It was the first night since he buried his wife that he managed to get a good night's sleep.

The teakettle whistled long and loud enough to wake Bland. Lou removed the pot from the burner and grabbed two cups from the cabinet.

"Good morning. You were snoring, so I assume you slept well?"

"I needed to, but my neck and lower back are aching," Bland moaned. He made his way into the kitchen and sat at the small kitchen table.

"I tried to warn you," Lou smiled. "Coffee or tea?"

"I'll be sure to listen next time. Tea, please." He sipped at the hot tea, not wanting to get burned. "I thought you would have gone to the hospital by now. What time is your dad's surgery?"

"Eight o'clock." Lou poured himself a cup of coffee.

"Then you need to get moving," said Bland, after looking at his watch.

"You sure you don't want to come? It's a minor surgery; afterwards, we could head over to the bank and then to your house."

"I want to be at the bank when it opens. I need to follow this to wherever it ends. Who knows where that is, so I may need all the time I can get. I really need to get on my old floor at work to look around. Maybe something was overlooked. In case Dakota did take that gun, I need to find it before they do. Jesse stored a lot of damaged merchandise in the storage room, but the gun wasn't there. If it isn't at my house or in the storage room, it has to be on the floor. I can't shake the feeling that it's somewhere on the floor."

"How do you plan on getting on the floor?" Lou took another sip from his cup.

"Maybe I can get Jesse's keys to the service elevator, ride it to the fourth floor, and then take the steps."

Bland checked the time, then hurried to drink the last drop of tea. He followed Lou to the coat closet.

"Don't forget your computer bag by the recliner."

"My satchel," corrected Bland.

"Is that what they're called now?" Lou grinned. "Anyway, speaking of Jesse, I saw him a few months ago."

Bland looked confused. "You did? When were you at the publishing house?"

"I wasn't. I had to take Dad to the hospital for some tests when I saw him on one of the patient floors. Strange thing," Lou paused, "when I said his name, he looked startled. Then he took off in the opposite direction. I took it as his way of saying he didn't have time to bullshit. That's how I feel when I don't want to be bothered."

"Jesse has a mental issue, something to do with the war. He can go in and out at any time. I'm hoping he doesn't wake up one day and decide

to kill everybody at the publishing house."

"Post-traumatic stress disorder."

"Yeah, I think that's what he suffers from. Anyway, regardless of his issues, I need him to get me on that floor. By the way, these men know my car, can I—"

"You don't have to ask. Here are my keys," Lou said.

"Here are mine. Disregard the bullet holes."

30

BLAND IMPATIENTLY WAITED FOR SOMEONE TO OPEN the door of the bank. Following the tracks to the money had taken him to some strange places. Nonetheless, he was determined to find who was at the end of the money line, hoping it would tell him who was setting him up. He sat in the reception area waiting to be called. It wasn't long before a young man came to escort Bland to a cubicle.

"Welcome to National Financial & Holdings, Mister…" his voice trailed off as he waited for Bland to disclose his name.

As he did at Washington Savings Bank, he offered his name and hoped some promising information might be gained.

"Bland Benthall."

"Mr. Benthall, do you have an account with us?"

Bland wasn't sure how to answer the question, so he didn't. The man directed Bland to take a seat.

Bland started to fidget, moving from side to side, as he retrieved the Washington Savings folder with the monthly bank statements. He showed the account manager where money was automatically withdrawn from Washington Savings into an account at National Financial & Holdings. For a brief second, the man looked at Bland suspiciously then sat back

behind his desk.

"I need the information on this account," Bland said.

"May I see that account number again?"

Bland slid the paper over to him. The banker began striking the keypad of the computer. Within seconds, the name of the company was pulled up.

"Are you affiliated with the company in some way, sir?"

"Umm."

He noticed Bland's hesitation then asked directly, "Are you the account holder?"

"No."

"Since you're not, I'm not at liberty to divulge any information on this account. All I can give you on the account is the name of the business."

Maybe Bland saying he was not affiliated with the business was the wrong answer. Quickly he rushed to speak.

"I know the name of the company. It is Global Consultant Services. It is withdrawing funds from my account into your bank."

"Sir, nothing can be withdrawn from your account at Washington Savings without first getting your consent. So, regardless of how it appears, you must have agreed to the withdrawals."

"I understand that, but I don't recollect giving that consent."

"If there is some fraudulent behavior occurring, you need to discuss this with your bank or with the police. Since you are questioning the withdrawals, I am assuming you had your bank stop the automatic withdrawals."

Bland stalled, "Yes, but I still need that account holder's information."

"Sir, as I mentioned, I can't divulge that information."

"Is there anything you can tell me about this company?" Bland asked.

The bank manager looked across the desk at Bland. Suddenly, his eyes redirected from Bland back to the computer screen.

"Global Consultant Services is a DBA attached to a secondary account."

"What's a DBA?"

"It's when an account holder does business under a trade name rather than under their legal name," disclosed the bank manager. The

bank manager frowned as he studied the account more intensely. "That's odd."

"What's odd?" Bland replied anxiously, hoping whatever was found would be a lead.

"The DBA that is attached to this secondary account doesn't have an account holder listed," he looked closely at the monitor. He then scrolled through history of the account. He acknowledged what Bland had said about the monthly deposits, but then noticed a large wire transfer into the DBA. "Umm, large sums of money have been transferred from this DBA account into the attached primary account," he said. "Let me pull up the primary account holder."

When the account came up on the screen, the bank manager's interest grew, as did Bland's, to know more about the account.

"Umm," he sighed. "This account was closed a month ago. And, the money," blurted the bank manager without realizing his mistake of divulging personal information on the account.

While the banker's curiosity kept him interested in the account, Bland asked, "The primary account was in whose name?"

"She," the manager's voice stalled.

"Did you say the account holder was a woman?" Bland asked. Only when a confused Bland asked what happened to the money did the banker realize his error in revealing information concerning the account. Bland attempted to ask another question. "If the account is closed, where did the money go?"

The bank manager asked, "Do you have any identification, sir?" Suddenly, his head popped up from the screen to look past Bland. Bland turned to look.

"Excuse me for a moment," he said, then moved from around his desk. Bland watched as the bank manager and the police officer gazed back in his direction before entering a nearby room.

Nervously, Bland stood and quickly walked away from the bank manager's desk and out the door of the bank.

Bland stood on the side of the bank with the palm of his hand over his forehead. The moment he heard the bank manager say the word

"she," implying that the account holder was a female, Bland believed his situation was more serious than he had imagined. He had already contemplated who the "she" could have been.

As he walked to the car, he mulled over the idea that someone was going to great effort to implicate him of stealing money from the publishing house. Once in his vehicle, his thoughts went deeper. He laid his head back to focus his eyes on the ceiling of the SUV. He felt increasing pressure that time was running out to find more answers if he wanted to stay out of jail. He began to agree with the detective. It seemed that nothing was by chance. He opened the glove compartment to find some scrap paper. On the paper, he made two separate timelines and ran them parallel according to the months of the year.

The first timeline focused on all the events that befell him since he was offered the partnership. He labeled the timeline "Post Partnership." The second timeline focused on everything and everyone connected to CS Printing. He labeled that timeline "Paper Trail." He felt he could get no peace until he figured out all the pieces of the puzzle.

He started the Post Partnership timeline with the date he was offered the partnership.

That was in March, thought Bland. Then he looked at the Paper Trail timeline. The first invoice was paid to CS Printing in April. He scribbled in the date of the first invoice. "April 1," he whispered. "April Fool's Day, and I was the fool after all."

He reached into his satchel and pulled out the folder from Washington Savings. He emptied the contents of the folder onto the passenger seat. He looked over each statement where National Financial & Holdings had withdrawn money. On the Paper Trail timeline, he added important dates from both financial institutions to cross-match with events on the Post Partnership timeline.

He put the bank statements back in the folder and pulled out the folder he had stolen from Red Eye Investigation. According to Alvin, Red Eye contacted him in February, so on the Post Partnership timeline, he penciled in Alvin's name and the date when he ran into him at the university. On the Paper Trail timeline, he penciled in the date Red Eye located Alvin. From there, he began to add the dates he and Dakota took

their trip to South Carolina and when he met Grey on the train. Then he made a side note about Grey mentioning her being contacted about the job offer in Washington, D.C., which was prior to reuniting with him. According to the notes beside Red Eye, that job offer would have come after Red Eye found her, which he wrote on the Paper Trail timeline.

Again, Bland began studying the Paper Trail timeline. By April, the publishing house was making a large deposit into CS Printing's bank account at Washington Savings, and a few weeks later, National Financial & Holdings was making automated withdrawals from the CS Printing account into Global Consultants' bank account, which happened to be a DBA attached to a secondary account that transferred all its money to a primary account that is now closed. He concluded that the only true lead he had was that the account holder was a female.

On the Post Partnership timeline, he penciled in the date of the explosion and their deaths. Trying to figure some order of details, he once again cross-matched both timelines in hopes of identifying any connections. After important dates, people, and events were placed on both timelines, he held up both papers to study them. He hoped something would grab his attention. While looking at his notes, Bland noticed that the inception of the Red Eye investigation on the Paper Trail timeline correlated with his reconnection with Grey on the Post Partnership timeline.

Bland considered this correlation and thought aloud, "The fact that my name was on the invoices that paid this shell company, CS Printing, and CS Printing was attached to all those different business accounts, including its payoff to the investigative service that found Grey, could offer Detective Rhodavack the motive that I might have been involved in the deaths of Dakota and Grey." He thought deeper about who had the power and money to orchestrate such a thing, especially since a month after the installment payment to the investigative service, he miraculously ran into Grey.

Penelope's comment of how only a partner could sign off on invoices with high amounts flashed in Bland's mind. According to Penelope, contractually, he was a partner with the same power as the twins. By the

process of elimination, he knew he didn't set himself up, so immediately, his thoughts filtered to the twins, and whether they had knowledge of this loophole in the contract. Would the twins have set him up? Bland rubbed his forehead and wondered, why? Did it have something to do with him writing the book? He weighed that question and answer against Brandi's comments about the publishing house filing for bankruptcy. Bankruptcy happened to be a good motive to make two men do something so scandalous to save their company.

Bland pondered what he found out at National Financial & Holdings. He wondered what woman's name was on the account and he began to suspect Grey. Given the correlations between the two timelines, Grey seemed to be the common denominator of both timelines. He began to consider the embezzlement allegations and Grey's name possibly on the fraudulent account as the crux of the twins' scheme to frame him. "But that would mean Grey," he mused. Not wanting to even consider this line of thinking, he moved on to another thought. He tried to surround his thoughts on why someone would send two goons to vandalize his home. What was the connection? Bland muttered aloud, "What is it that these men know that I don't know?"

He put the key in the ignition, started the vehicle, and drove off.

Outside the publishing house were several police cruisers. An awful feeling settled in Bland's sore abdomen. Instead of pulling into the parking garage, he pulled to the side of a curb. He patted his jacket, then searched the entire car for his cell phone. He assumed he left it at Lou's place. He shook his head then looked across the street. To his surprise there was a pay phone on the corner. He climbed from the car and skipped through traffic to get to the pay phone. When he reached the phone booth, he noticed the phone was missing. He cursed before noticing he had parked in front of a café. He made a dash for the café.

Once inside, Bland caught a waitress's attention, "Do you have a phone?"

"We have a bubble phone in the back of the café."

"A what?"

"It's like a pay phone but takes half the number of quarters."

He dialed Penelope's office number, which was automatically forwarded to her business cell. Penelope was in a meeting when her phone rang.

The men stopped talking so she could answer it.

"Hello."

"Penelope, it's me, Bland; what's going on in there? I see several police cars in front of the building."

"Yes, I know. If you give me five minutes, I will come and show you where the file is, okay?" she said, to throw off the police officers, Detective Rhodavack, and the twins.

"I'm parked across the street from the building. I will be standing in front of a café," Bland said.

She quickly hung up the phone. "The auditors need a file," she said to the twins.

"They always call on your cell?" questioned Detective Rhodavack.

"According to my bosses, I need to be accessible at all times," replied Penelope, while glancing at the twins.

Detective Rhodavack then looked at the twins. "So how long had Mr. Benthall been embezzling funds?"

Wilkins snatched the folder that Penelope held in her hand.

"According to this first invoice paid, for at least seven months, and frankly, I can't believe it."

"How is something like this possible?" the detective asked.

"Anything is possible," Wilkins grunted. "He is a partner, so he has just as much access to everything as we do."

"This contract stipulates," Detective Rhodavack held it out in his hand, "Mr. Benthall's partnership isn't effective until he submits the novel. So how is it that he authorized such large dollar value invoices?"

Smith corrected, "We wondered the same thing, and after consulting with our attorney there was a loophole discovered in the contract, which stipulates that a person has all partnership rights once the contract is signed. The only thing Bland doesn't have is the salary that goes along with the junior partnership. Other than that, he has access to everything."

"R..i..g..h..t," Detective Rhodavack said, as he wrote in his note pad.

"But shouldn't you have known that bit of information, given that you created the contract?"

"Our lawyers drew up the language in the contract," snorted Wilkins. "This is our first time offering any kind of partnership in our publishing house, so mishaps like this can occur."

"A mishap that has cost you a lot of money."

"What do we do now?" Smith asked.

"Be patient and see where the money takes you," Detective Rhodavack responded. "Have you or anyone heard from Mr. Benthall lately?" The detective's eyes scanned the room. No one responded. "Well, if you do, please give me a call. By the way, gentlemen, when is the deadline for the novel?"

"Less than seventy-two hours."

The detective looked at his note pad. "What do you stand to gain if the novel is not finished on time?"

Smith answered quickly, "Nothing."

"And if he does finish it?" the detective asked.

"We get a novel," Wilkins replied.

"Wouldn't you also get a lot of money?" countered the detective.

"Only the public can determine that," Smith replied.

"R..i..g..h..t," the detective said.

Penelope turned to walk out the door when Smith stopped her.

"Penelope, send the auditors up, and tell them to bring the wire deposits S&W made into CS Printing's bank account. I want the detective to see them."

"Yes sir, right away."

Penelope left the office and skipped down the back stairs. She exited the west side of the building and came around to 3rd Street.

Bland stood in front of the café deep in thought when he heard someone calling his name. Penelope walked extremely fast toward him. She looked nervous and agitated as she approached.

"Bland," she said, while breathing heavily. "It's cold out here. Let's go into this café and talk." He escorted Penelope into the café. "Bland, I don't have much time. I have to get back." She scanned the cafe. "I've been calling your cell, but it goes straight to voice mail. I am assuming

it is full."

"I lost my cell phone, and I can't retrieve any messages without the phone."

"You can access your messages from another phone. All you have to do is dial your phone number and put in your password." Frustrated, she shook her head in disbelief. "Do you ever answer your texts or check your email? Your office voice mail is also full, so I couldn't leave any more messages on that. It was urgent that I speak with you."

"I haven't thought to check my office phone or email," he paused to look across the street at the publishing house. "What's going on in there?"

"Chaos!" she replied frantically. "Policemen are everywhere. A detective and the partners are looking for you. Bland, they found the invoices. As we speak, the detective is asking the auditors for the records on the wire deposits."

"Penelope, I did what you told me. I followed the tracks to the money, and the tracks led me to," he paused, not wanting to introduce Grey as a person of interest to the twins. "I have been thinking hard about some things, and I figured it out: The twins are setting me up."

"Why would they want to set you up?"

Bland thought before answering her. "They don't want me to have it."

"Bland, I am not following you."

"As you mentioned in the atrium, Penelope, if the twins honor their part of the contract, they are not in breach of it. As long as I turn in the novel on the specified date of the contract, I, too, am not in breach of the contract. Now, if both parties adhere to the specifics of the contract, I can only breach the contract by doing something illegal."

She finished Bland's sentence, "Like misappropriating funds from the company that pays you. That would allow them to keep the partnership, the book, and you'll go to jail," Penelope said.

"That's the problem. I didn't embezzle anything, but I will go to jail unless I prove they set me up."

"What's your proof to this theory, Bland?"

"It's simple. Their motive is my proof."

"And what's that?"

"The publishing house is going bankrupt, and that's the last thing they wanted to have happen. They needed money, and how else to get enough money to keep the publishing house from going bankrupt but to get their number one writer to write a bestseller. That's the reason they offered the partnership."

Bland revealed to Penelope everything that Brandi had told him.

"There is one problem with your theory, Bland. The publishing house isn't going bankrupt. Earnings have risen 8, 12, and 14 percent, respectively over the last three quarters, with all its imprints, and that's without your bestseller. Bland, the publishing house is financially sound."

Bland just saw his theory destroyed. He felt misled. The one time he believed Brandi, it turned out to be a lie.

"Fourteen percent," he repeated.

"Yes, that's why it makes no sense. They don't need you to write a book. They have plenty of money."

Bland ran his hand through his hair. "If the twins weren't filing bankruptcy, then why would they set me up?"

"That's if they set you up," replied Penelope.

Her comments brought about new thoughts accompanied by new theories that began to surface in Bland's mind. He began to second-guess his own theory.

"Bland, are you okay?" Penelope asked. Again, she looked around. "Listen, I don't know what's going on, but I have to get back before they become suspicious of me."

Bland nodded, "Yeah, I understand. Penelope, thanks for all your help."

"Bland, be careful." She rose from her seat, and Bland watched her leave the café.

Bland pushed back from the table, dug into his front pants pocket and pulled out two quarters. He thought as he walked toward the bubble phone, if the twins aren't behind this set-up, then who?

Bland slipped the money into the phone's slot. Quickly, his finger punched the keypad. He keyed in his access code when his office voice mail prompted the command.

"Your mailbox is full. To hear your messages, press 'one' on your touch-tone phone," the automated voice commanded. Bland did as instructed. The first message was from John Scott.

"Bland, I'm calling you at work because I have called your home phone and cell phone and left messages, but you won't call me back. I wanted to let you know I towed your wife's car to my garage." Bland skipped to the next message. "Bland, it's Penelope, I've been trying to reach you all morning. It's important that you call me right away." Bland deleted the message, "Mr. Benthall, this is Detective Rhodavack. I need you to give me a call ASAP." Before hearing the complete message, Bland skipped again to the next message. The next message was also "Mr. Benthall, this is Paige. I just wanted you to know; don't come to the office today. It's full of cops. And Rudy, the security guard, has been trying to reach you." From Paige, "Mr. Benthall, it's me again. The partners are pissed and looking for you. Also, that detective came looking for you. Oh! Can you please call Rudy, he says it's really important." The message suddenly stopped. There were several more messages from Paige, and Bland skipped them all. "Bland, this is John again. I really need you to call me concerning last night. I want to know if you're okay. You should call the police, Bland. Also, before I forget, Sharon from across the road has been looking for you. Please contact this woman because if she knocks on my door again at six in the morning, I think I won't be polite. She and a few of Dakota's friends wanted to have a memorial celebration in honor of Dakota. I think it's a great gesture. I hope you didn't mind, but I gave her both your cell number and work number. Call me." Bland's tolerance to listen to all the messages was drawing near. "Hello, Bland, this is Sharon, your neighbor. I saw Mr. Scott, and he gave me this number to reach you. Please give me a call. Thank you."

Message fifteen, the automated voice revealed.

"This is Detective Rhodavack. Mr. Benthall, I have given you ample opportunities to contact me. I don't have to paint you as being involved in stealing from your company; it appears you're doing a good job by yourself. Listen, I need to talk to you. If you don't contact me in the next day or two, there be a warrant for your arrest. You have my number." The detective's message ended abruptly. Then, there was another from John,

"Bland, call me ASAP!" Bland skipped to the last message and was about to hang up when he heard Greysen's name. "This is concerning Greysen Brindle. I am her gynecologist, Dr. Ford. Greysen listed you as a contact on her forms. Following HIPPA guidelines, I am able to contact you concerning Greysen's health. However, this information cannot be left on the phone. I will attempt to reach you on the other number listed. In case I can't reach you, it is vital that Greysen gives me a call or comes by the clinic. This is my cell number. Please give me a call. I relay this message with a great sense of urgency."

Bland memorized the doctor's number and quickly redialed it.

The phone rang several times before the doctor answered. "This is Dr. Ford."

"Dr. Ford, my name is Bland Benthall. You left a message on my phone about Greysen Brindle."

"Mr. Benthall, I'm confused. We spoke last night about Greysen."

"We spoke?"

"Yes. You don't remember? I called your cell phone after leaving a brief message on your work number."

My cell phone, thought Bland. It then dawned on him that he used it as a weapon to get away from the thug and never realized he had dropped it. Dr. Ford must have spoken to the thug, concluded Bland.

Bland grew nervous.

"Doctor, I'm sorry, but I was really intoxicated last night. Honestly, I don't remember the call or the conversation. Can you please update me on what the call was about?"

"We conducted a number of tests on Greysen, and some results were abnormal. I scheduled her to see a high-risk doctor, but she never showed."

"Dr. Ford, it saddens me to tell you, but Greysen died in a tragic accident."

"Oh, no!" It was obvious in her tone of voice that Greysen's death came as a shock to her. "Did this happen recently?"

"No, a few weeks back."

"Please tell me the baby survived?" her voice sounded desperate.

Bland turned his ear more into the phone, "What did you say?"

"She was six months pregnant. Did the baby survive?"

Bland simultaneously tried to gather his thoughts and words. "She was six months pregnant?" Bland shook his head. "Slow down for a minute, doctor. Did you say baby, like having a baby?"

"Yes, I did. As I mentioned to you last night."

Suddenly, recalling the medical examiner's report of the bodies found in the explosion, "Are you sure?"

"Yes, positive, Mr. Benthall. She was so excited; I assumed Greysen told you."

Bland dropped his head at the thought of the thugs receiving that information.

"What time did you call my phone last night?"

"It was sometime before my shift ended. My shift ended at 10:00 p.m."

Bland pulled the phone from his ear and stood there dazed while Dr. Ford's voice reverberated through the receiver. Bland felt a sharp pain in his gut as he slowly hung up the phone.

"She was pregnant," he muttered in disbelief. "That would mean…" Bland took a moment to entertain the possibility that the deceased body identified as Grey's wasn't her.

If what the doctor was saying bore some truth, then the body couldn't have been Grey's, he thought. If she was pregnant, surely the fetus would have been discovered like the other one by the fire department or by the medical examiner. Neither the fire department's report nor the medical examiner's report disclosed anything about finding a second fetus. That would mean, he paused his thought, not wanting to give himself hope of anything.

With his mind in a tailspin, he decided to call the medical examiner to settle any suspicions concerning Grey. Bland reached for the phone directory and started flipping through the pages until he found the hospital's coroner's number. Quarters fumbled in his hands as he put them in the dispenser. As he listened to the rings, he felt an increase in anxiety.

"Medical examiner's office."

"I'm trying to reach Dr. Hatti."

"Speaking."

"Hello, Dr. Hatti, I am the husband of Dakota Benthall. She was one of the two female bodies brought in after the explosion at the publishing house a couple of weeks back."

"Yes, you came by the morgue?"

"Yes, yes I did."

"How can I help you?"

"By some chance, could the other adult female found after the explosion have been pregnant? I mean, could you have known that?"

"The autopsy of…" the doctor paused, "what was her name?"

"Greysen Brindle."

"Yes, that's it. The autopsy of her death showed no signs of pregnancy."

"Nothing?"

"She wasn't pregnant, Mr. Benthall, only your wife."

Bland swallowed and decided to ask, "How certain are you that the other body found was my wife?"

"According to the medical report, very certain."

Bland was insistent. "But, is there any chance of error?"

Dr. Hatti replied, "There is a small chance of error, but it is not likely. Mr. Benthall, we know that a pregnant woman and her fetus died that night, and your wife was pregnant. And the dental records identified your wife."

Bland slowly closed his eyes, and said, "Thank you, sir."

"I'm sorry Mr. Benthall, I know it's a hard thing to accept."

"Thank you again, sir."

Bland sat silently. There were so many questions bombarding him that he didn't know where to start. His compulsion for detail began to structure his thoughts like it did when he wrote his bestsellers. He took a moment to reflect on how the OB-GYN's report contradicted the medical examiner's findings regarding Grey. Bland tried to find a plausible way for both reports to be accurate. According to the publishing house's log sheet, on the night of the explosion Dakota and Grey were the only two on the floor before the explosion.

His mind began to drift. Stay focused and think through it, he told

himself.

Bland then considered the bodies that were found. The new revelations from Dr. Ford raised doubts in his mind as to whether Grey's body was, in fact, one of the bodies found after the explosion. Given Dr. Hatti's confirmation of Dakota's death, and Dr. Ford's revelation of Grey's pregnancy, Bland couldn't bring himself to conclude that Grey didn't die from the explosion, just that her body wasn't found on the floor after the explosion.

His thoughts stalled again. He felt that increased anxiety of writer's block starting to engage.

Okay, take your time and tell me what you know, he told himself. He spoke aloud, "I know there were two female bodies and a fetus that died that night. I know the fire chief identified the bodies solely by the log-sheet. Yet, their identities were later confirmed by the findings of the medical examiner, who was emphatic that the body identified as Grey's wasn't pregnant. That counters Dr. Ford's findings that Grey was pregnant, unless someone other than Grey died in that explosion, an explosion that the detective is trying to link Dakota through my gun. If my gun is the cause of the explosion, why wasn't it found at the scene of the accident?"

Bland's thoughts shifted to the thugs that tried to kill him, and whether they had something to do with the explosion and his gun possibly missing from the scene of the accident. Why break into my house if they had the gun? he questioned. He drew the only possible conclusion, "They don't have the gun."

The fact the men were trying to kill him led Bland to believe they were willing to go to any extreme to find the gun. He was at a loss as to why they wanted the gun so badly.

He suddenly recalled what Lou said, "They know something that you don't know." Bland continued to think aloud. "Dr. Ford stated she called my phone during her shift last night; therefore, the information she gave to the thugs about Grey's pregnancy came before they ransacked my house. So, they assumed, like I did, that Grey died in the explosion. If they believe or know that Grey is alive, that explains what they knew that I didn't know. But what is the connection between Grey and the

men breaking into my house?"

He spoke aloud again. "If the thugs broke into my house to find the gun, wouldn't that infer that my gun wasn't the cause of the explosion? No, not necessarily," he answered himself. "Just because my gun wasn't found at the scene doesn't mean it wasn't used or didn't cause the explosion," he told himself. He closed his eyes to settle his thoughts. After a few seconds he opened his eyes. "Given the thugs urgency to find the gun, the gun could very well be the key to unlocking what actually happened that night," Bland assumed.

Bland thought about going to the detective with what he knew; however, all he knew was derived from two timelines that drew questions and assumptions but did not draw him closer to the truth. These thoughts brought Bland to the decision that going to the police was not an option, especially knowing there was a warrant for his arrest.

He feared it was a matter of time before the detective tried to connect the embezzlement charges to him, and him to the explosion. He assumed the detective would draw a conclusion that a jealous wife went to kill her husband's mistress. If Bland attempted to redirect the detective's investigation by introducing the new information about Grey being pregnant and conceivably alive, then it could further implicate him as a conspirator in killing his wife to be with Grey. Since Grey's body and Bland's gun were missing, Bland was sure the detective would draw such a conclusion.

One thing for certain for him to figure out this entire mystery, he believed important questions had to be answered: If Grey is alive, where is she? Who is the dead woman that everyone believes is Grey? If Grey is dead where is her body? Where is his gun? Is there any possibility at all that Grey died in the fire and Dakota lived?

Bland rushed over to one of the available computers in the café. He began to conduct a search for articles that focused on recent fires and explosions. There he found writings about the explosion at the publishing house and the ghastly bodies found at the scene. Bland retched when he read that a piece of scrap metal ripped open the pregnant woman's uterus, causing her to go into premature labor. Although the articles

were painful, he continued to read them in order to put his unanswered questions to rest.

No article provided Bland with information on any unidentified body resulting from a possible explosion. As a result, Bland searched for all public and private hospitals within a forty-five-mile radius of D.C. The search yielded a list of hospitals. Bland jotted down all the hospitals and their phone numbers.

He patted his pockets; he was out of change. He went over to the cashier to inquire if the man had change for a hundred-dollar bill.

"We can't break a bill that large, sir."

Sitting in the opposite corner of the café was a college student on his cell phone.

Bland walked over to the kid. "Hey, I need to buy your phone," Bland said.

The student looked up in bewilderment.

"Who buys someone's phone?" The student pointed to the bubble phone in the corner of the café. "There is a café phone. Use it."

"I am out of quarters."

"That phone takes quarters?" he remarked with amazement. "Dude, isn't there a pay phone on the corner?"

"As I said, I am out of quarters, and I really need your phone."

"Dude, we are living in the new millennium, these days you can buy a cell for a few bucks. Plus, I just got this phone. I haven't had time to explore it or switch over my contacts."

Bland was tired of going back and forth with the student, so he handed him the hundred-dollar bill.

"Man, this isn't a minute phone."

Bland reached into his front pocket and handed the student all the money he had.

With wide eyes, the student quickly counted the money and said, "Dude, you are crazy." Then he promptly handed Bland the cell phone.

Bland was about to turn and leave when the student called out, "Hey, don't you want to know the number? You paid for it." The student wrote down the number and handed it to Bland. "Hey, that number will only be good until the end of the month, unless, you want to pay me more."

Bland muttered, "Thanks for the courtesy warning," and turned and walked away.

Bland called the emergency room of each hospital. He asked each check-in personnel if a burn specialist or trauma team responded to an incident around the specific dates and times that corresponded to the explosion at the publishing house. The more hospitals he called, the more efficient he became with his inquiry. Any potential leads were eliminated due to the type of injuries the person may have sustained, or the date in which the person was admitted. After an exhaustive search, Bland finally dropped his head in defeat. Though the search didn't produce the answers he sought, it did confirm that no bodies were sent to any hospital. Bland worried that maybe he was going down the wrong track. Too much time had elapsed, and he desperately needed to find a new lead that could answer the questions that were haunting him. He held the cell phone in his hand and stared out from the large windows of the café.

As Bland was about to exit the café, he noticed a patrol officer about to ticket Lou's illegally parked car. Bland bolted out the door of the café to stop her.

"Oh, I'm driving that," Bland said. "Can you give me a break? It's not even my car."

The officer looked at Bland, "Do you work downtown?"

"Yes, I do," Bland replied.

"Then you know better than to park on the street in front of a fire hydrant," she said and continued to write the ticket.

"But it's a Saturday."

"It's still a fire hydrant, so it doesn't matter."

Bland knew it was hopeless to get her to stop filling out the ticket once she started. He erratically threw his hands in the air to demonstrate his frustration on getting a ticket. The officer rested the palm of her hand on her weapon. Bland diverted his attention to her gun, and immediately he restrained himself. As he calmed down, his attention was directed back to her firearm.

"Excuse me, is that a 9-millimeter?"

She looked at him strangely. "I suggest you move the car before it gets towed." He stared more closely at the officer's weapon. He was sure it was a 9-millimeter.

She tore the ticket from the ticket book and handed it to him before proceeding to the next car. Bland put the ticket in his pocket, then jumped into the car. He put his head down to think. Seeing the officer's gun immediately triggered a theory that maybe a security guard was on the floor at the time of the explosion. Bland tried to think like a writer, working all possible scenarios in his head to arrive at a plausible conclusion for a security person to be on the floor at the time of the explosion.

He revisited some previous information, such as Dakota being six months pregnant, and Dr. Ford stating that Grey was six months pregnant. But the medical examiner's report showed that someone other than a pregnant woman died in the explosion that night.

"It had to be a security guard," Bland mumbled to himself. "More likely a female guard making her rounds on the floor. That could prove the mix-up of the bodies." The facts that he had recently discovered seemed to support this theory.

He thought more about the reports from Doctors Ford and Hatti, which appear now to support each other, given his suspicions of the female security guard. Clearly Dr. Ford acknowledging Grey's pregnancy could very well put the guard on the floor, which would make Dr. Hatti's findings valid: The body thought to be Grey wasn't pregnant.

However, according to Rudy, the twins were adamant that security personnel could not carry firearms, thought Bland. "But could outside security personnel taking over in-house shifts possibly have a firearm?" Bland wondered aloud.

"Now, that could support my theory that a female security guard was at the publishing house that evening, possibly with a gun. If she had a gun did it cause the explosion? If so, what happened to the gun?"

Suddenly, he became excited when believing he was on to something. That excitement faded when he realized that neither the twins nor the police seemed to question whether any security personnel were missing the night of the explosion. Bland was now uncertain if his new theory

could shed light on who really died in the explosion.

Bland held to this thought for a few seconds. He looked over to the publishing house. Suddenly he visited a more pressing question. What if.... A tap on his windshield pulled him from his thoughts. The officer was motioning with the billy club for Bland to get moving. He quickly pulled his car from the curb and almost hit a police cruiser coming out of the parking garage of the publishing house. Immediately, the police cruiser's sirens flared. When Bland slammed on his brakes, he instantly had a flashback of the night of the explosion. When he was hurrying out the parking garage to get home to Devin, he nearly collided with Jesse who was turning into the garage.

"Jesse was there that night," he muttered. "When I was leaving the parking garage to check on Devin, Jesse and I damn near had a head-on collision. As nosy as Jesse is, I'm sure he saw something. I have to get in the publishing house to find Jesse," he whispered. It would be risky trying to get into the publishing house now, but what choice did he have? He realized that a lot depended on him finding those answers, such as his freedom and maybe even his life.

31

UNEXPECTEDLY, JANE'S EYES SLID OFF THE PAGE WHEN Constance pulled the book from her hands.

"That's enough reading for today. For the last few days, you have been totally consumed in this book. Is it that good?"

"Yes, so let me finish," she tried grabbing the book from Constance's hand.

"I have to change your bandages." Constance wheeled over a tray on which to place the old bandages.

"I want to see my face. Are you going to let me?" She answered for Constance, "No?"

The door to the room opened and Jane's voice dropped. She stood from the chair and walked over to the bed.

"Hello, Jane," Dr. Stewart said, as soon as he entered the room.

"Hello, Dr. Stewart. How are you this evening?"

"I'm hanging on by a thread. It's been a long day, Jane. I hear your physical therapy is going well."

"I can run now," she smiled.

"No running, Jane."

"It was a joke, Dr. Stewart."

Dr. Stewart smiled and pulled scissors from his pocket. He began cutting through the bandages. As always, Jane sat quietly as the doctor meticulously scanned her face.

"Everything looks good, Jane, and your voice sounds great."

"So I'm still scheduled for the cosmetic surgery with Dr. Moss?"

"I don't see why not. That is, unless something comes up."

"Then let me take a peek now, in case something does come up."

"Soon, real soon," Dr. Stewart smiled. "I really like your persistence."

"Men, they will tell you anything to shut you up," Jane scowled.

"I agree," said Constance.

"Okay, no male bashing," the doctor chimed in while checking Jane's hands and legs. He then moved so Constance could dress the wounds and start rewrapping her face.

Dr. Stewart began to make keystrokes on his medical tablet. Once finished, he scribbled additional notes on Jane's chart.

"Try not to stay up too late this week. I need for you to be rested," he said in a stern tone of voice.

After Constance finished wrapping the new bandages, she looked at Jane's disappointed eyes. "Do you need anything?"

"Where is my book?"

"It's in my pocket."

"I guess I have everything a woman needs to be fulfilled," Jane quipped.

"I am assuming you are referring to the book?" Dr. Stewart commented. "Given my hectic schedule, I prefer audio books."

Dr. Stewart caused Jane to remember the tapes under the mattress. She had gotten so deep into the novel that she forgot about them. She decided that once Constance and Dr. Stewart left, she would retrieve the tapes.

Constance threw out the bandages, then pulled the novel from her pocket. Jane's eyes lit up.

As he approached the door to the room, Dr. Stewart said, "I'll see you tomorrow, Jane."

"Okay, Dr. Stewart."

Constance tossed the book to Jane. "I want to read this after you finish."

"I will make sure you get it. Are you done for the day?"

"Unfortunately, I have two more hours before I can feel the comfort of my own bed. This split shift is killing me. I hate working late hours. Anyway, I'll see you later, okay?"

When Constance disappeared from the room, not a second passed before Jane dug under the mattress for the tapes and the tape recorder. She placed the player on the table and slipped in a tape. As before, she held the book in her hand to pretend to read in case someone rushed into the room.

Like the previous tape, Dr. Westfall's voice softly transmitted from the small speaker of the tape recorder. Jane expected to hear her own voice transmit through the speakers but was surprised when the voice belonged to Constance.

Gradually, Jane sat upright to listen, and the book slowly slid from her hand to the bed.

"Nurse Constance, our last session was very helpful. This time I want to return to the scene when and where you found Jane. I want to see if there was anything at the scene that can help identify her."

"Sure, doctor."

"Nurse Constance, I want you to lie back on the sofa and relax. Allow your eyes to focus on the ceiling fan. As you watch the blades of the fan, your body will relax, and the blades will gradually slow down. As the blades get slower and slower you will drift off."

For a few seconds, the magnetic strip of tape went silent. Then Dr. Westfall chimed back in, "Nurse Constance, I want you to return to the night when you discovered Jane in the bushes."

"I had just finished work and was very tired. I left through the emergency entrance. As I started walking, I heard sounds of moaning coming from the bushes. Whatever it was sounded to be in tremendous pain. I began to walk toward the bushes where the moaning and wailing were coming from."

"As you moved closer to the bushes, did you see anything that stands out?"

"I just saw this body with something covering it. The body was curled in a fetal position. I could smell the singe from the clothes."

"What are you doing now, nurse?"

"I'm moving the hand from the person's face." From the recorder, Jane heard the sharp breath taken by Constance, as if something had shocked her. Constance's voice screamed, "It's a woman! It's awful! Her flesh, the skin is coming off in my hand."

"Calm down, Nurse Constance, and tell me what you did next."

"I ran back into the hospital to alert the emergency room of a trauma situation."

Jane listened with pain in her chest and rage in her heart. Constance had lied to her about her involvement that night.

"She is burned so badly all over her body. She's moving her mouth. She is trying to tell me something."

"What is she trying to tell you?"

"I don't know. She keeps pointing at her midsection. It is so chaotic. Everyone is moving and talking so I can't hear her."

"Nurse Constance, shut out the disorder around you and focus only on her. Tell me what she is saying."

Jane gasped. "She is," there was a pause, "having a baby."

Tears ran down her cheeks when Constance started talking about the baby, suddenly an assault of questions attacked Jane. She forced back the lump in her throat and continued to listen.

Constance breathed heavily as the doctor pushed harder with questions about the baby.

"The baby is in distress," her voice rose. There was a slight silence before her voice came back through the speaker. "It's not breathing." Suddenly, Constance screamed, "Flat line."

Jane gasped as she listened, while tears poured from her eyes.

After twenty-five more minutes of tape, it finally clicked off. Jane was quiet, and her eyes fixated on the wall in front of her. Slowly, in sort of a daze, she grabbed the recorder and flung it into the wall. She began screaming and tossing random items across the room. After she exhausted herself, she sat down at the foot of the bed with her face in her hands and sobbed.

Abruptly, the door to the room opened and in rushed Constance.

"Jane, are you all right? I heard you screaming all the way down the

hall." Jane's eyes squinted with fury toward Constance.

Hysterically, Jane screamed at Constance, "Why didn't you tell me about my baby? Why Connie? Why didn't you?"

Constance stood back in shock. Her hands covered her mouth as the tears formed in her eyes, "I'm sorry. I'm sorry, Jane. We wanted to tell you." Tears streamed down Constance's face.

Two nurse techs and a station nurse bolted through the door when they heard the commotion. They went straight for Jane.

"No, no!" Jane yelled. "Please, no."

Jane became combative as they attempted to restrain her. A third nurse rushed in and pulled a needle from her medical jacket and stuck it in Jane's arm. Jane's fight disappeared, and her struggle slowed to the point that the techs could put her in the bed.

Constance watched the tension lines in Jane's face subside as her body grew more relaxed. How did Jane know about the baby? Had her memory returned? Constance's thoughts were interrupted by one of the techs.

"Nurse, do you want us to get restraints?"

"No."

"What about cleaning this room?" the tech asked.

"Call the custodian," Constance ordered, while she gazed around the room. She stopped when she saw the tape recorder that had settled in a corner of the room.

Constance picked up the tape recorder and opened it. She was astonished when she saw her name on the tape. It was the tape of her second session with Dr. Westfall. This is how Jane knew about the baby, she thought. Constance knew she had betrayed Jane's trust by saying she knew nothing about that night. She contemplated how to tell Jane the truth and explain why she lied.

It wasn't until the next day that Dr. Stewart heard about Jane's incident. He had Dr. Westfall meet him in Jane's room while she was still sedated. The two of them stood at the end of her bed discussing the various possibilities of what to do with her. What they didn't know was that the medication given to Jane had worn off, and she listened quietly

while they discussed her fate.

Dr. Stewart shook his head. “What do you think, doctor?”

“It’s my professional opinion that you send her to Memorial General. We can no longer provide the health care she needs, doctor. Plus, she will get twenty-four- hour supervision to prevent her from hurting herself or anyone else. Not to mention, Dr. Stewart, this will also help you. I know this has been a financial strain on you personally.”

“I believe you’re right. I will contact Memorial General today and work on getting her transferred by the end of the week. I need to contact Dr. Moss. I think the cosmetic surgery will have to be delayed. Now that the swelling has gone down in her face, I’ll take some photos and digitally remove the scars so I can circulate them in the community.”

“Yes, a picture of her may help. Make sure she gets plenty of rest. I also suggest frequent checks on her,” Dr. Westfall said.

Seconds after Dr. Westfall and Dr. Stewart left the room, Constance quietly entered. She approached Jane’s bed with a look of remorse across her face and gently called her name.

Jane’s eyes stayed shut.

“Jane, if you can hear me, I want to say I’m sorry for lying to you. Dr. Westfall believed telling you about the baby would send you into a state of depression. I only participated in the sessions because I wanted to help you. That night everything was moving so fast that some details might have been overlooked. Dr. Westfall and Dr. Stewart suggested that I return to the event through hypnosis. Hopefully, I would find something that I overlooked, something that could help us in determining your identity. I didn’t mean to lie to you, Jane, really, I didn’t. I wanted to help you recover.”

After minutes of silently watching Jane, Constance turned and left the room. After a while, Jane rolled out of the bed and went into the bathroom. She looked in the mirror at herself and wondered about who she was.

With the tips of her fingers, she felt the bandages over her forehead before she let her face sink into the palms of her hands. She began to cry. As she moved back from the mirror to grab some tissues, she spotted her water cup. She grabbed the tissues and began wiping the tears from

the corner of her eyes. When she bent down to pick up the water cup, something of interest caught her attention. Seeing the name of Walter Reed around the hospital never registered, that is, not until she read it on the hospital's water cup.

Quickly, she moved from the bathroom to the table near the bed. She was in search of the book. She remembered seeing the name Walter Reed in the book. She scanned the tabletop, then the floor. She dropped to both knees to tilt her head under the bed. There it was caught between the wall and the leg of the bed. She slid her body well underneath the bed to grab it. Without getting up, she flipped through the pages to where she recalled seeing the name. Once found, she read where Lou claimed to have seen Jesse, but Bland was unaware it was Walter Reed Army Medical Center.

Jane remembered Constance's words of smelling the singe from her clothes. According to Constance's session with Dr. Westfall, she was found severely burned and pregnant. According to the book, two women, one pregnant with a fetus, died in an explosion. From there she began to work backward in conjunction with the book. Quickly, she flipped the pages back to the confrontation between the two women the night of the explosion. Numbness inched along her limbs until her body felt paralyzed. Maybe it was a coincidence that her life was a reflection of this book, but the comparison between the book and herself was so overwhelming that she truly couldn't ignore the correlation. Rather, she wanted to believe there was a connection, and that the book was really about her life. Now thinking this story had something to do with her life, she asked a very profound question. Rather than who died, she wanted to know who lived. She believed, however, the only certainty to answering that question was to finish reading the book.

32

BLAND DIDN'T NEED THE CAR TO BE TOWED, SO HE decided to draw less attention to it and himself by parking it in the publishing house's lower level parking garage. For a moment, he sat in the car, contemplating how he was going to get inside the building to see Jesse without being detected. First, he had to find out where the cops were. He tried to call Penelope but there was no answer. Then he called Paige. When she answered the reception phone, his voice was racy and panicky.

"Paige, are the cops still there?"

"Mr. Benthall?" she questioned.

"It's me, Paige."

"What phone are you calling me from?"

"Did the number show up?"

"Yes, it did."

"Well, I can be reached on this line, okay. Listen, are the cops around?"

"They are with the partners in the accounting department," she whispered.

"Okay."

"Where are you, Mr. Benthall? Everyone is looking for you."

"I am sure they are. Remember, if you need me, call the number that showed up on the caller ID." Then Bland hung up.

Normally, Jesse spent most of his day in the main lobby and food court. Bland hoped that was still the case. That way, he could blend in amongst the crowd. His entry point would be the back door of the food court next to the trash disposal, which was also located in the lower level of the parking garage. Before heading to the back dock of the food court, he looked for something to disguise himself. He grabbed a cap from the glove compartment, slipped it on his head, and then pulled down on the bill to hide his eyes. He waited behind one of the dumpsters near the dock for someone to exit the back door of the food court. Finally, someone came to make a drop in the Dumpster. Bland charged the door to catch it before it closed and locked. He managed to catch the door with his fingertips.

"Hey you!" a voice shouted to Bland as he let the door close behind him. Immediately, Bland dropped his head. "That's not an entrance." As the security approached, Bland dropped his head in hopes of not being recognized by the security guard. "Mr. Benthall?"

Bland lifted his head and recognized the voice belonged to Rudy. Bland blew a big sigh of relief. "Rudy."

"What are you doing?"

"Honestly, hiding from the twins, security and all the police."

"We did get a notice to alert management if you are spotted." Rudy noticed Bland's eyes widen. "Don't worry, Mr. Benthall, I am not saying anything."

"Thank you, Rudy."

"Plus, I have been looking for you myself. The last time we spoke, you asked if I knew who worked the night of the explosion. I found out that it was our supervisor. When I questioned about the night of the explosion, he was shifty, like he didn't want me to know something. I think he wasn't even here."

Bland's attention rose, "So who do you think worked the shift if he didn't?"

"I think it was an outside security guard who worked that shift, but no one is going to say anything in fear of losing their job. Remember, what we were doing hadn't been approved by the twins."

Bland weighed what Rudy had just said. "Was the outside security personnel a female?"

"I don't know."

Rudy's answer did not confirm his suspicion of a female security guard present the night of the explosion. Bland was overcome with anxiety. "Well, can you tell me if outside security carry a gun?"

"Outside security guards aren't supposed to have a gun when covering any of our shifts. That's the deal when we get a substitute." After a long pause, Rudy hesitated, then admitted, "But some substitute guards do carry their weapon."

While Bland held to his thoughts for a few seconds, Rudy looked on with deep sympathy reflected in his eyes.

"Mr. Benthall, I am sorry about your wife. I wish I had worked that night."

Bland understood what Rudy was trying to convey to him. "Rudy, it's okay." Bland looked up the hall to the food court. "Have you seen Jesse?"

"He's probably in the food court."

"Yes, I was thinking the same thing."

"If you want, I will keep an eye out for him as I finish my rounds."

"I appreciate that, Rudy," said Bland.

Just then an announcement was broadcast through Rudy's radio. "To all security personnel, we are on high alert for Mr. Bland Benthall. If he is spotted, apprehend immediately."

"It's best you keep an eye out for security and the cops," said Rudy, before trotting up the narrow hallway.

Once in the food court, Bland sat at a table near the back to wait for Jesse to appear. The lobby seemed to be filled with extra security guards. Bland scanned the area for Jesse. When a security guard passed, Bland would casually drop his head. A few of the guards gathered and looked in Bland's direction. Bland glanced upward thinking he saw Jesse. When he realized it wasn't him, he again lowered his head.

"Where are you, Jesse?" he muttered.

If he didn't come soon, Bland risked being identified. Too late, Bland thought. The guards were walking toward him. Bland made subtle eye contact with the men as they approached. He lowered his chin to hide his face. He could see the feet of the men steadily approaching. Bland turned his body slightly as the men came extremely close. He was about to run when Rudy's voice broadcast through several of the security guards' radio.

"Mr. Benthall has just been spotted getting on the back-freight elevator. All available security guards head that way and fast."

At once, the guards turned on their heels and raced for the freight elevator. As Bland watched the security guards run off, he spotted Rudy who quickly motioned to Bland with his radio, then moved from behind a column.

Bland knew he needed to leave the area fast, so he got up from the table and casually slipped over to the trash cans. He decided to move in the direction from which he had entered the building, but that was before the custodian's door opened, and Jesse set out a dust mop. Bland rapidly walked to the area.

When Bland reached the open door to the custodian's closet, he heard water gushing into a bucket. Jesse was hunched over the sink. The moment Jesse heard footsteps coming from behind, he straightened his upper torso and turned quickly. Fear overcame his usually relaxed disposition.

Bland wanted Jesse to believe he knew about the intricacies of the accident. That meant opened-ended questions when needed but closed-ended questions were preferred.

"Jesse," Bland said in a non-confrontational manner, "can we talk?"

Bland noticed how Jesse's hand gripped around the mop handle. Jesse was about to strike him. Bland raised his hands.

"Wait, Jesse, I'm not here to hurt you. We are friends." Immediately, Bland questioned the reason for his defense.

Slowly, Jesse lowered the mop.

"Jesse, I need you to answer a few questions to help me figure out what happened the night of the explosion. Did you see anything out of the ordinary?"

Jesse pulled the notepad and pencil from his shirt pocket and began to write. When finished he handed the pad to Bland. Bland read the words aloud. "I don't want no trouble. I do my job and go home." Bland paused, "Jesse, you're not in trouble."

Jesse, with slight apprehension, grabbed the pad from Bland. After he finished writing, he held up the pad for Bland to read. You want to hurt me too. Bland looked up from the pad to reply. "No, Jesse, I would never do that. Who hurt you?"

Jesse scribbled on the pad: some men came.

"What did they want?"

Jesse had a frightened look on his face.

"Jesse, you and Dakota were friends. I just need to know what happened that night. If you know anything, please tell me." Bland looked desperate.

Jesse moved forward and maneuvered around Bland to grab the handle to the closet door. Bland stepped further into the closet so that Jesse could close the door. Jesse securely engaged the lock. Then he maneuvered, once again, around Bland to where they faced each other.

Bland watched as Jesse turned his back to him and started removing a number of boxes of disinfectant that happened to be hiding a small space in the floor. Jesse removed a loose piece of concrete. He retrieved a dirty cloth, then stood with it. His hands began to tremble as he unwrapped the material. All Bland could do was watch and wait. Well hidden in the inside of the old, dirty cloth, Bland spotted the charcoal handle of the gun that had been scorched in the explosion.

Bland's eyes lit up. "The gun!" he said suddenly.

Jesse handed him the cloth with the gun in it.

Bland looked up at Jesse to ask, "Where did you find this?"

When Jesse pointed to the floor, Bland tried to interpret.

"You found it in the closet?"

Jesse shook his head no.

"This is the gun that was in the explosion?" Bland questioned.

Jesse nodded yes.

Given the gun's condition, Bland couldn't distinguish if it was his or not.

"Jesse, whose gun is this?"

Jesse offered Bland a blank expression before scribbling on his pad. Once he was finished, Bland read the note aloud. It was war, I watched from the bush as the enemy engaged. My fighter was being overrun by the enemy, so I went and got backup.

"Backup?" asked Bland. "What are you talking about, Jesse?"

Visibly, the explosion that night caused Jesse's mind to flash back to the war. Bland's interrogating tactics were causing him to flash back again.

War teaches you to react to sparks, Jesse wrote.

Jesse dropped his eyes, he recalled as much as he could about that night. He wrote: I heard screams coming from the floor. My fighter was alive. I crawled through war zone, cuz' my fighter was on fire. I tossed a coat over the body to put out the fire, then I pulled it to safety. Snipers all around, so I had to stay low. Didn't want to die. I got to get the wounded out of here. It's important to drop off the wounded to the medical post and get back to the battle. My troops were out there without me. The battle was over when I got back. Medics brought out the dead. Nothing I could do but keep an eye open, cuz' the war ain't over.

"What do you mean, the war isn't over? Jesse, you keep referring to a fighter and an enemy, who are these people you are talking about?"

I'm talking about war, Jesse wrote.

Bland peered down at the gun in his hand. "Does this gun have to do with the war?"

When Jesse nodded yes, Bland remembered the chaos and the destruction from the blast, then realized Jesse had equated the explosion to an encounter of a battle that had taken place. The enemy, Bland assumed was Grey, since he had never seen her before, and Dakota was his fighter since he knew her. Bland's thoughts dashed back and forth.

"Jesse, did your other fighter have a gun?"

Jesse wrote, Don't know.

Immediately, Bland assumed Jesse's other fighter was the security guard.

"How many guns were found on the floor?"

Jesse put up his index finger.

"Only one?" Bland said. "Then it's either the security guard's gun or mine."

"Jesse, did one of your fighters die?"

Again, Jesse nodded yes.

Given all the information Bland had just learned about Grey's pregnancy, he automatically assumed it was the security guard that died in the explosion.

"Was it your fighter you saved?" Bland wanted to be certain.

Yes, Jesse nodded.

"Where did you take the woman?" Jesse looked at Bland strangely. "I mean, your wounded fighter. Was it a female?"

Jesse nodded.

"Was the enemy you were fighting as well as the reinforcement you went to get, female?"

Yes, he wrote on his pad.

"Where did you take the wounded fighter?"

To the medical post, Jesse scribbled.

"Is that like a hospital?"

Jesse nodded.

"But, Jesse, I checked the hospitals, I mean, all the medical posts in the area, but no wounded fighter was checked in." Bland considered Jesse's mental state could have caused him to fabricate some portion of his story. "Are you sure this even happened?" asked Bland.

Bland watched as Jesse scribbled on the pad. That fighter was brave and held her line until the backup came. The moon went black, when I heard the pop of the gun. I didn't see nothin' except a spark, then boom! He paused writing for a moment, then he continued, they were burnin'. His eyes were wide, as if in a trance.

"Then how do you know you grabbed the right fighter?"

Jesse shrugged his shoulders. Bland tried to interpret the meaning of Jesse's nonverbal communication.

There was a collective silence before Jesse began to write, Don't know, just gut feeling it was my fighter. She was fightin' to the death.

Bland became alarmed, "Did she die?"

I left the body, Jesse wrote, at the medical post.

"What medical post?" Bland cried in frustration.

He became frustrated because he didn't understand what was meant by the medical post or someone fighting to their death. Was she dead, or was she left to die but lived instead? he wondered.

Jesse confirmed Bland's suspicions that a body was taken from the floor, but where was it taken and who exactly did he take? Sure, Bland wanted to believe his assumptions of matching Grey's and Dakota's identities based on Jesse's allegiance to his own troops versus that of the enemy. Bland didn't want to rely on assumptions; however, his thoughts shifted to the idea of Dakota possibly surviving the explosion. His idea evaporated when he thought of Dr. Hatti's report confirming Dakota's death. What if he was wrong? thought Bland. What if there was foul play? There was that man—the man at the morgue who was also at the farmhouse. Who was associated with the men who tried to kill him? What if Dr. Hatti was in on it? What if? He stopped his thought. Bland knew without a body to support his theory he would look like an idiot if he brought this to the detective's attention. Plus, he wasn't sure of the detective's level of involvement. Who knows? The detective could be in on it, too, he thought. He returned his attention to the gun.

The gun could very well be the key to unlocking what happened that night, Bland assumed. He knew it had to be put in a safe place. He looked at Jesse. "Who else knows about the gun, Jesse?" He shook his head. Bland stated his intended word, "Nobody. Jesse, can I trust you to put this in a safe place?"

Jesse looked down at the floor.

"I mean a safer place?"

Yes, nodded Jesse. I know what to do with it, Jesse wrote.

He took the gun from Bland and began rewrapping it. Once finished, he put on his coat.

Bland watched as he stuffed the wrapped gun inside of the coat, then grabbed his fitted cap.

Bland paused, "What's that?" He looked at the fitted cap pulled down on Jesse's head. Highlighted were the words on the front of the cap, army, soldier, and vet. Bland's eyes grew wide.

"That's it. You took the body to the army medic post, Walter Reed Army Medical Center. I never thought to check there." Bland shook his index finger. "My friend, Lou Nelson, saw you at the hospital. You were looking in on someone's room. Was it your soldier?"

Jesse began to write. I left her there. Jesse looked at Bland, then commenced to writing again, Will I lose my job?

"No." Bland shook his head with a certain level of anxiety. "Jesse, have you told anyone else what you're telling me?"

No, nobody knows, he wrote. He moved his head rapidly from left to right.

That's when it hit Bland. It wasn't so much what the thugs that broke into his house to find the gun knew, but rather what they didn't know. They don't know who survived the explosion, since the only pregnant survivor was taken away by Jesse before she could be identified. Bland felt anxious because, once again, he believed he was on to something.

"Where at the hospital is she, Jesse?"

The sick building, not the crazy building, he wrote.

"Sick and not crazy," Bland repeated.

In the air, Jesse flipped up five fingers.

For a moment, Bland stood silent, wondering what he meant. Then it came to him.

"She's on the fifth floor of the sick building. What room?" Bland's voice raised.

This time Jesse tried speaking. His voice was muffled and hard to understand as he said, "Last room on right."

Suddenly, Jesse handed Bland the pad. I hope it's my soldier, Bland read.

An emotional Bland responded in kind, "I hope so too." Bland realized if these killers were also looking for who survived the explosion, then he needed to get to Walter Reed Army Medical Center quickly.

Bland unlocked the door to the closet. As soon as he stepped out the door, Larry was standing in front of him.

"Bland, why are you coming out of the closet?"

"Why do you care?" Bland said, hatefully.

"Just asking, no need to get an attitude." He moved aside so Bland

could pass.

"Well, since you must know, I lost something."

"Check the lost and found," he sarcastically replied.

Bland looked at the man menacingly, "It's strange how we keep running into each other."

"Yeah. I was on my way to the restroom. I drank way too much coffee, and I can't hold my water like I used to. I have to hurry, don't want to have an accident in the food court!"

Bland watched as Larry pulled his cell phone from his inside jacket. He believed it was only a matter of time before the twins and the police showed up. After Larry disappeared, Bland sauntered through the food court, being very discreet so as not to bring attention to himself. Up until that point, it appeared nothing was as it seemed, and no one or no information could be trusted.

Bland's shoes scuffed against the marble, then the concrete of the parking garage. He moved quickly across the open space to get to his car. He pulled the keys from his jacket and hit the automatic lock. After getting in the car, he felt a sense of relief. More relaxed, he slid the key into the ignition just as a crowbar smacked the driver's side window. Bland panicked and knocked the keys from the ignition. As he bent over to find the keys another blow shattered the glass. It was Scar from the farmhouse. Bland hurried to find the keys. Once he located the keys, he felt the man's large fist against his jaw. The force of the punch sent Bland sailing halfway into the passenger side of the car.

"Where is the gun?" Scar barked, then threw another punch toward Bland's ribs.

Bland quickly grabbed his satchel to protect his face. When Scar's fist hit the laptop inside the bag, he grimaced. Bland dropped the bag to reach for the glove compartment. Inside was the container of mace that Rudy had given him in case of an emergency. The man yanked at the car handle until the latch gave, and the door flew open. Just as he reached for Bland, Bland pointed the canister at him and the chemical mist from the container dispersed outward. Scar was temporarily blinded as he stumbled slightly away from the car. Instinctively, Bland slammed the

car door into Scar's knees. Scar hit the ground hard, then slowly pulled himself to his knees. This time Bland slammed the door into his head, knocking him out on the concrete floor. Finally, Bland was able to put the keys in the ignition. He hit the accelerator and raced out of the parking lot.

Scar gained consciousness, then stood. He pulled his cell phone from his pocket.

"He got away. I'm going back to see the mute."

Bland took as many back streets as possible to Walter Reed Army Medical Center. As he drove, he continued to contemplate why the men were so adamant about finding his gun. For several more blocks, he mulled over that question without getting an answer. His mind went into a deeper discussion with himself concerning the gun. Were there other reasons these evil men were so desperate to find it? Do they want it because it could declare my innocence? he thought. That's only if my gun wasn't the cause of the explosion, he believed, then suddenly challenged that thought with another. If my gun didn't cause the explosion, it would suggest what the thugs already knew, that someone other than Grey and Dakota was on the floor during the time of the explosion. Could the missing gun perhaps identify who survived? Bland pondered.

Bland hit the accelerator to make it through a stop light. The wheels of the car momentarily lifted off the pavement.

He thought about Rudy's comment that sometimes substitute guards have been known to carry a weapon. "What if the gun Jesse found wasn't his, but rather it was a 9-millimeter that belonged to the security guard? What if the casing found at the scene of the crime matched that barrel? Briefly, his mind flashed with a sense of clarity, understanding that if it was the security guard's gun, then it was the only connection that could link the security guard to the explosion. Given what he knew, he could only conclude that the thugs also knew about the security guard. And whether the guard had her service weapon with her the night of the accident. Because they still sought his gun, Bland assumed she didn't have one. Instead of the gun being the key to revealing what happened that night, he saw the gun shedding light on who survived the explosion.

His mind flashed to another thought that he had been avoiding: Who was behind it all? He thought of Grey. Was she a victim or was she the mastermind behind it all? He didn't want to believe it, but the evidence was stacked against her. He took a moment to consider both timelines: the hiring of Red Eye Investigation to find her, their reunion, her connection to the evil men that tried to kill him, and the latest, a female's name attached to the DBA account connected to the shell company, CS Printing.

He weighed a few more unanswered questions: Was Grey hired to set him up? If so, did the twins hire her? Did the twins find some clever way to frame him for stealing money from the publishing house? Was Grey the primary account holder of the DBA account at National Financial & Holdings? Bland realized many of his questions suggested Grey's involvement. He couldn't reject this as a possibility, not after discovering Grey may have been personally acquainted with the men that broke into his home.

Bland convinced himself that if these violent men were so desperate to locate the gun, they would be much more desperate to locate the survivor of the explosion. He had a strong feeling that the goons were on their way to the hospital, given they were always a step ahead of him. He believed the survivor's life was as much in jeopardy as his. He desperately needed to find the survivor before those men did.

He skidded across a few more intersections, barely avoiding head-on collisions. When Bland approached the gate of Walter Reed Army Medical Center, he pulled his ball cap over his eyes. As he approached the checkpoint, two heavily armed military officers approached the car on both sides. One of the men walked slowly around the car, being extra cautious to look in the back seat. The other noticed the broken window.

"What happened?" the guard asked.

Bland looked at the window, then at the guard. "What can I say, neighborhood kids."

"Why not get it fixed?"

"It just happened today," Bland said, while handing the guard his license.

Carefully, the guard looked at the license before handing it back to Bland. Bland stole a glance in the rearview mirror at the other guard checking underneath the car.

"So, what brings you to Walter Reed?"

"My father had surgery this morning. I am already running late." Bland impatiently twiddled his fingers for the guard to let him through.

"What is the name of the patient?"

"Is that necessary?" Bland asked.

"It is post 9/11; everything is necessary. So, the name of the person you're going to see, sir?"

"My father, Mr. Nelson, was admitted this morning."

The officer stood and looked at Bland with one long stare before looking at the clipboard of names. After finding Mr. Nelson's name, his stare was still as intense. He pointed toward the hill. "He's in that building, sir; get your window fixed." On those last words he waved for Bland to drive past.

As Bland drove to the front of the building, he went around obstacles of concrete barriers that made it look like someone was preparing for war. Bland parked, then jogged from his car to the side entrance of the hospital. He ran until he came to a four-hallway intersection. He stood in the middle of the intersection—going the wrong direction could be the difference between life and death for the woman. His mind wandered back to Jesse and their conversation. He recalled Jesse's words verbatim, "The woman was on the fifth floor of the sick building." It made no sense to Bland, but he was determined to find her.

In the meantime, the goons managed to gain access to the hospital. They made their way to the rear of the building and climbed the stairs. According to the information they beat out of Jesse, the woman was on the fifth floor.

Bland stood in the hallway intersection, contemplating Jesse's instructions.

"The sick building," Bland whispered. Bland stopped a passing nurse. "How do I get to the fifth floor?"

"Just take elevator B, over there," she pointed.

Bland started toward the elevators, then stopped, "This elevator is for the sick people and not the crazy people?"

"The sick, the crazy," the nurse appeared befuddled. She smiled after thinking, "You want to get to our regular patients located in the main hospital. No, don't take the elevator. Instead take this hall to the side doors. Then walk across the lawn to the adjacent building, the sick building as you called it. You happen to be in the "crazy" building, which is the psychiatric building for our mentally disturbed patients."

"I'm sorry," Bland apologized.

"It's okay. I never heard the buildings referenced like that."

Suddenly, the vibration from Bland's cell phone made him jump. He wrestled in his pocket until he found it.

He held the cell phone until the caller spoke.

"Bland! I can't believe you answered."

"Paige, is that you?"

"Yes, it is, Bland. The police are here looking for you."

"Yes, I already know that."

"You don't understand. Jesse was found dead at the publishing house."

"What!" he yelled, not believing what he heard.

"The police are looking for you, since you were the last one seen with him."

Bland responded in shock. "Do they think I killed him?" His heart felt like it was coming from his chest. "Larry," he whispered, then remembering running into him when he left Jesse in the custodial closet.

"Don't come to the office, Bland," Paige warned before the phone hung up.

Bland bolted down the hall and out the doors, just as the goons walked the corridor to the last room on the right in search of the woman. One goon clutched his gun, while the other pushed the door open. A curtain enclosed the bed. The men pulled their guns and connected silencers to the barrels before slowly approaching the curtain. The goons pulled back the curtains and were about to pull their triggers when all they saw was a pyramid of boxes on top of a bed frame. Angrily, the men ran out into the hall and grabbed the first person they saw in a medical uniform. Rich squeezed the woman's arm hard as he asked, "Is there another fifth

floor in this hospital?"

"There's the main hospital." She pointed to the building across the lawn.

He released the woman's arm, and the men took off in a trot to the other building. When the thugs were out of sight, the woman grabbed the station desk phone to call security.

Bland charged across the lawn to the next building. He burst through the entrance doors, then to the steps. He skipped every other step until he reached the fifth-floor exit door. The last door on the right, he told himself, as he opened the door to the fifth floor. He began to run down the hall, sliding slightly on the waxed floor before catching his balance.

Nervous and frightened, Bland stood before the last door on the fifth floor, unsure if it was Dakota or Grey in that room, and whether he had arrived in time to save whichever one it might be.

He pushed the door open. The room was slightly dark, and Bland expected to confront the ruthless men. What little excitement he had was quickly removed by his guilt of seeing a person lying in the hospital bed and knowing he put her there. From afar, the dim lighting in the room hid the face of the patient. Again, Bland inhaled deeply to prepare himself for what he thought would be the inevitable: the identity of the person. Quietly, he moved across the room to the bed to get a closer look. From a distance, given the contour of the body, the physique was a female. But the physique was not enough for him to determine who the person was that lay in the bed. His eyes moved slowly along her bandaged toes and arms and hands to her chest then to her masked face.

He peered down over the lifeless-like body, hoping to gain some advantage of knowing who she was from her scarred lips and dark eyelids.

—

"So, who is she?" Jane anxiously cried out as she read.

—

Someone pushed at the door. Startled, Bland turned quickly.

"Nurse Constance," someone called.

The forward movement of the door stopped, then moved in reverse. Bland moved from the bedside back to the door. He pulled the door open enough to see the nurse walking back to the nurses' station. He contemplated moving the bed but felt it was too conspicuous. Once more, he pulled the door back to see the location of the nurse. She moved out of his line of sight, but noticeable enough was a wheelchair against the wall. Swiftly, he pulled the door open to grab the wheelchair. He had to move fast. He knew it was only a matter of time before the men or the nurse showed up.

The angry men had made it to the first-floor elevator of the main hospital. The elevator doors opened, and they moved to the back and waited as others entered.

Meanwhile, Bland lifted the upper torso of the woman's body from the bed. Her body was heavy as he transported it from the bed to the wheelchair. He was surprised that the woman didn't wake up. To hide the bandages, he tossed a blanket around her shoulders and neck. The head of the body tilted forward as he pushed the wheelchair against the wall in the hallway. The nurse's back was turned. He tried to blend in with some of the patients who walked along the corridor. He couldn't help but hold his breath as he passed the few nurses who were busy with patients' charts.

The elevator door finally closed. The impatient men watched the numbers change as the elevator arrived at the next floor. They became more agitated with each stop the elevator made that wasn't the fifth floor.

Bland glanced up the hall at a few people waiting for the elevator. He began pushing the wheelchair in that direction. As he passed an adjacent hall, Bland spotted a patient transport elevator at the far end.

When the main elevator door opened to the fifth floor, the sadistic men exited in time to see Bland standing behind a wheelchair. Immediately, they reached into their jackets. Seeing the men, Bland forcefully turned the wheelchair then pushed vigorously against its handles. He and the chair began scurrying down the adjacent hall toward the patient transport elevator. The men gave chase and were closing in on him and

the wheelchair. Bland noticed that the elevator light turned orange as it was about to open. Still he was some distance from the elevator. Making that elevator was his only chance to escape the men. The elevator doors had opened. Bland could see someone exit and then turn down the adjacent hall. He knew it was only seconds before the elevator doors closed and unless he released the wheelchair with one last hard push, they weren't going to make it. He heaved the wheelchair forward and released his grip from the handles. It took off in a direct path for the elevator as the doors were starting to close. The width of the wheelchair fit perfectly between the steel elevator doors. The wheel of the chair hit against the side of the door, causing the steel doors to reopen.

The three men ran down the hallway at full speed and saw the wheelchair hit the back of the elevator. Again, the doors began to close. The men were on Bland's coattail. Beard reached out to grab him but stumbled and fell. As he slid across the slick floor his thick head rammed into the wall. Rich and Scar jumped over their unconscious partner.

There wasn't much time left before the elevator doors connected. Bland saw his opportunity slowly closing. He ran harder and managed to dive between the closing doors. At the last moment, Scar tried lodging his gun between the doors of the elevator, but it was too late.

"Tell me where it stops," yelled Scar to Rich.

The elevator didn't stop until it reached the first floor.

Rich bolted to the door to the stairwell and yelled to Scar who was scampering down the exit steps. "It stopped on the first floor!"

The palms of Bland's hands were sweaty. His entire left side had absorbed the impact and ached. He pushed the wheelchair from the elevator. He needed to find a place to hide. Up ahead, he saw two white coated physicians exiting a laboratory. He darted for the door. Bland caught the door and rolled the wheelchair into the room that was filled with prosthetics and a few plastic skeletons. In an adjacent room, he could see two doctors talking.

Bland knew he had to develop a plan and quickly.

When Scar reached the first floor, he spotted Bland at the opposite end of the hall pushing the wheelchair through a set of double doors.

Seconds later Rich stepped off the elevator. There was a loud commotion, so Bland turned to look. The men were knocking people out of their way to get to him. Bland saw them coming and pushed the wheelchair hard down a service walkway. The sudden turns Bland made with the wheelchair made the lifeless body move from one side of the chair to the other.

Bland hurried down a hallway that led to a dark boiler room. Once in the dungeon-like setting, he hid the wheelchair behind one of the large boilers. He then proceeded to cross under a few of the long pipes to separate himself from the wheelchair. Eventually, the sound of footsteps approached. Bland dropped to his knees and spotted the men's feet. They were a few yards away. Rich ordered that they split up.

Bland spotted a discarded steel monkey wrench underneath a boiler. He attempted to get it, but the handle was out of his reach. He lay flat on his stomach and extended his fingers to touch the handle. The tips of his fingers brushed just over its edge. He wedged himself further under the boiler and stretched as far as he could. He then used his fingernails to pull the handle of the wrench into his hand.

When Scar heard the sliding of steel against concrete, he stopped walking. Immediately, he pointed his gun in the direction of the sound and began to walk. Bland stood off in the shadow with his hand gripped tightly around the wrench. He waited. When Scar's shadow drew close to Bland, he brought the wrench down in a striking blow. He struck with full force across the man's shoulder. In slow motion, the thug fell. The gun could be heard sliding across the concrete floor. When Bland went to strike Scar again with the wrench, the thug was quick to sweep Bland's feet from underneath him. The wrench dropped from Bland's hand, and his head smacked against the hard-concrete floor. Scar reached over and punched Bland in the face. Bland spit blood as he grabbed the thug's wrist to avert being hit again. Scar managed to get his large arms around Bland's neck and position him in a neck choke hold. His forearm tightened around Bland's throat, constricting his air passage. As hard as he could, Bland rammed his elbow into Scar's side, hoping to get the thug to release his grip, but Scar squeezed tighter. Bland saw black spots as his air lessened. From the corner of his eye, he spotted the

wrench. With the little strength he had left, he reached for it. He curled his fingers around the tool and swung the wrench against Scar's head, knocking him out. Scar's grip released from his neck and Bland coughed and spit to catch his breath. As he stood to his feet, he heard the angry voice of Rich behind him and he turned to see the buzz-cut man from the farmhouse that tried to kill him. Rich looked at his comrade laid out on the concrete floor.

He pointed his gun at Bland and in his heavy voice demanded Bland to tell him where the woman was hidden. Bland looked past the man to the large boiler. Rich saw the direction of Bland's eyes and used his gun to force Bland in that direction. They walked to the wheelchair. The body was still tilted forward with the blanket cloaked over it. Bland turned toward Rich with part of his body shielding the wheelchair and the person underneath the blanket.

"You made this too hard," spoke Rich before pointing the gun at the wheelchair. Bland saw an opportunity to charge Rich. A single shot rang out and, instantly, Bland stopped to clutch his chest. Was I shot? he asked himself while dropping to both knees. The bullet had ripped through Bland, then into the blanket draped over the wheelchair.

With wide eyes, Rich watched the blanket over the body crumble. He looked at Bland with perplexed eyes. He pointed the gun at Bland's head and was about to shoot, when Rich dropped to his knees, then to the floor. The man gave Rich's head several more strikes before blood rushed from his scalp. Bland watched as Rich's body jerked. He was sure the man was dead.

A man Bland had never seen before stood over Rich with the wrench in his hand. When the man stepped over Rich's body and moved toward Bland, Bland was fearful he was next to get struck by the wrench. The posturing of the man's body over Bland instantly identified him as the assailant that attacked him in the file room.

The man's menacing eyes stared at Bland before they both heard Bland's name being called. The stranger turned, then disappeared behind one of the boilers. Seconds later, Lou ran up to Bland and helped him up from the floor. He glanced at Rich stretched out on the concrete with blood around his head, then back at Bland.

"Is he dead?" Lou asked.

Lou watched as Bland grabbed his side, "Yeah, I think."

"Are you okay?" Lou inquired.

"I've been shot." Blood dripped from Bland's side.

Lou was quick to lift Bland's shirt to inspect the injury. "The bullet grazed you. You should be okay."

"Yeah," Bland said, as he pulled the shirt down.

"Are these the men you were telling me about?" Lou asked, while bending down to see if the man was dead.

"Yes, but how did you know I was here?" Bland asked, rubbing his neck.

"The security desk called to see if Mr. Nelson had another son by the name of Bland Benthall. Then a raspy voice from the sergeant's radio said there were men with guns running down the halls of the hospital. Somehow, I knew you were involved. Then I heard what sounded like a muffled shot coming from this direction."

"You came just in time," Bland said, as he thought about the man that had just killed Rich.

"Looks like I was too late." Lou looked at the wheelchair and the blanket draped over the lifeless body. "Who's the dead person?" He was sure that the person under the blanket was dead.

Bland pulled back the blanket to reveal a plastic skeleton.

"I don't understand," Lou glared.

Bland held his side. "It's a long story, and I'm afraid I don't have enough time to explain it."

"I'm sure you are right. The military police are on their way, so you need to get out of here."

"What about you?"

"I'll be okay, but you need to get going. I'll tell them what happened."

"Before I forget, notify the staff that there is a woman in the prosthetic lab. She's wrapped like a mummy."

Lou looked puzzled.

"I will explain later," shouted Bland, as he took off in an all-out sprint.

Bland checked himself into a hotel because he was afraid to return

home. Despite the recent turn of events, he had decided to keep his promise to his wife. He believed a bestseller couldn't be written in less than two years; he would have the remaining days before the book deadline to do it. Before writing a word, he reflected on everything that had transpired in the last year of his life. What he would do about the partnership and proving his innocence, both to him were still equally difficult. Now, Jesse's death complicated things more. It was apparent that Detective Rhodavack would do all he could to link the fraudulent activities taking place in the publishing house to Bland. Whoever sought to set him up had done a pretty good job.

Bland gathered his thoughts, then adjusted his seat, and commenced to write. He finished the book a few hours before the midnight deadline. He pulled away from the laptop. Frustrated and filled with heavy emotions, he sent an email and waited for a response before deciding to visit the twins.

33

S&W APPEARED DESERTED AS BLAND APPROACHED THE revolving doors. He walked through the halls, uncontested by security guards. There wasn't a police officer in sight. He stepped on the elevator and rode it to the penthouse suite.

The elevator to the penthouse opened, and Smith and Wilkins were waiting.

"Bland, come on back," they directed.

Once in the study, Bland elected to stand rather than take his usual seat. He looked the men straight in their faces and placed the manuscript on their desk.

"This is what you wanted, and I lost everything so you could have it, but you already know that."

Neither of the old men grabbed the manuscript, but the pleasure of having it on their desk was in their eyes.

"Bland, we knew you could do it."

Before Smith could finish, Bland was asking, "At what cost did I do it?"

"Bland, everything has its cost. Unfortunately, you experienced the ultimate cost, and our condolences go out to you," said Smith.

Bland looked down at the hardwood floor. Then he looked back to Smith.

"Your condolences go out to me?" he said scornfully. "How can the two of you stand there in good conscience, knowing the part you played in this?"

"What do you mean, Bland? What part did we play?"

"You know damn well what I am talking about."

"Bland, stop fishing for answers; we have nothing to hide. So tell us what you're insinuating." Wilkins' heavy voice carried from across the room.

"I must admit it was a clever plan, and I was thrown off after discovering the company was financially sound. Nonetheless, I figured it was the two of you that set me up to make it look like I embezzled money from the publishing house."

"Why would we do that, Bland?" asked Wilkins.

"Because you wanted to protect your interest, and in order to do that, you needed a back-up plan. That back-up plan involved Greysen Brindle. I contemplated the level of her involvement, whether she was an innocent pawn or involved in the plot to set me up. The more I thought about her reuniting with me on the train, and right before her job proposal and right before Red Eye investigators located her, and the fact she was meeting with your goons were too many coincidences. I didn't want to believe it, but she played me well. The three of you played me well."

"You only came up with this theory after the bankruptcy conspiracy didn't fly," Wilkins retorted.

Bland looked surprised.

Wilkins noticed, "Don't look so surprised. When will you learn that nothing gets past our ears or our eyes?" Wilkins then snapped his fingers. "It was you who said we were clever like foxes. Just call us the *Urocyon cinereoargenteuss*," Wilkins gloated.

"The Gray Foxes," Bland whispered.

"Sly as a fox, and yes, I do like the irony in that saying." He glared at Bland, "You're not the only one who can come up with a Latin name to call yourself." Wilkins smiled, "Did you know the fox is a solitary hunter

and very, very intelligent?"

"You found that out all by yourself? And your point is?" Bland asked, sarcastically.

Smith recognized Bland's sarcasm and waved Wilkins off. "Bland, go ahead and finish what you were going to say."

"Yeah, finish," Wilkins snorted. "I'm curious to know where you're going with these accusations."

Bland gathered his wits. "When your goons destroyed my house in search of the gun, I assumed it was needed to identify who survived the explosion. After giving it much thought and considering all scenarios, I couldn't understand how my gun or the security guard's gun could provide such information. At the most, the guard's barrel matching the casing, or my gun's barrel not matching the casing, could only identify that someone other than Greysen and Dakota was on the floor that night. Unfortunately for you guys, that would have sparked an investigation as to whom these bodies belonged. That led me to question the connection to the gun."

"So, what was the connection?" Wilkins blurted.

"Greysen's death benefited you guys, since now the threat of blackmail by Greysen was no longer an issue. That is, until you found out that someone may have survived the explosion. Finding the survivor was just as important as finding the gun because the two of you needed both the gun and the survivor to disappear to cover your tracks."

Smith smiled. He nodded for Wilkins to search Bland for any police wires or other recording devices. Once it was noted Bland was clean, Smith commenced to speak.

"Bravo, Bland, so it appears you followed the evidence, and got your own set of answers; however, we did, too, and the wrong answers will cause you to draw the wrong conclusions. This in turn can have you writing the wrong version of a story," smiled Smith. "I always told Wilkins you aren't as good a writer as you are a storyteller. Truly, you are the best I've ever known; however, I am afraid you weren't writing the story that was put in front of you." Smith moved slowly around the room as he talked. "Bland, some writers can imagine such a story full of pain and misery, but when a writer personally suffers such pain and

misery, that's a gift you should be thanking us for."

"So, the two of you did put this entire chain of events into motion?"

"No, Bland, we didn't put it into motion, but we saw it through in hopes you would write our bestseller; if not, then we will make some adjustments before it hits the stores," Wilkins said.

"Some adjustments like whether or not Greysen Brindle died?"

"That's where your story would stray from the novel we hoped you wrote." Smith glanced at the manuscript on the desk.

"Contrary to your belief, we didn't give a damn about Ms. Brindle. Our interest wasn't with her. Um, I see that glare in your eyes. You know the glare when you think you know exactly what's going on, or when you have it all worked out in your head, but then something hits you unexpectedly," puffed Wilkins, suddenly tossing Bland a folder. "That is the direct money trail. Take a look at those bank statements."

"This has your fingerprints all over it," Bland implied, as he looked at the two of them.

"No, Bland, not our fingerprints," Wilkins barked.

Bland perused the papers to read what he already knew. He looked away from the papers, then back to Wilkins.

Wilkins instructed him to look at the last page in the folder. "Do you recognize the name of the bank?" When Bland didn't answer, Wilkins continued, "Republic Bank of Washington, D.C. is a small bank within walking distance of the publishing house."

Bland kept studying the bank statements, thinking this wasn't the bank to which the tracks had led him.

Smith chimed in. "All the money that was funneled through all those accounts ended up in an account at this bank. Do you recognize the account holder's name?"

Bland's eyes widened before uttering in disbelief, "Dakota Benthall." He peered up from the paper to look at the men.

"That's who held our interest," Wilkins snapped.

"What interest would you have had with my wife?"

"A business interest," Wilkins replied.

"Why?"

"You were broke and she was desperate," Wilkins bellowed.

"Who do you think put this idea into motion?" asked Smith.

"I don't understand."

"Let me help you understand, Bland," offered Smith, in a more civil tone of voice. "A few months before we offered you the partnership, Dakota came to us seeking help. Your bad investments and poor financial management had jeopardized everything the two of you had worked so hard to accomplish. The bank was threatening to take your home for a second time. I could see it on your wife's face; she was willing to do anything for a sense of financial security."

"Security?" Bland questioned, debating whether to trust what the twins were saying.

"Why yes, something that would offer her some peace of mind," Smith clarified.

Bland couldn't bring himself to believe it. "My wife came to you for a handout?"

"Don't be so offended by the truth, Bland," Wilkins snarled.

"Whose truth are we talking about?" Bland questioned. "My wife wouldn't come to you for a handout."

"Are you sure? It was inappropriate. Besides, we don't believe in charity unless it benefits us," gloated Wilkins.

"So, what was she willing to offer you for this so-called 'peace of mind'?"

"According to your wife, an opportunity of a lifetime," Wilkins pointed his cigar at Bland.

Bland was confused, "A what?"

"A deal," Wilkins smirked. "In exchange for a partnership, we would get a bestseller."

Smith turned toward the large window in the office. "Not just any bestseller, a bestseller that would sell more copies than any of your previous novels. That kind of language translated into a lot of money, so it captured our attention. Of course, we had our doubts, since we never possessed the power to get you to write again, and it appeared money didn't seem to be a great motivator, even in the face of tremendous debt."

Bland peered out the large window in disbelief. He thought about Dakota's request to handle the banking.

Smith noticed, then said, “Her offer was certainly inviting, but how would she possibly get you to write again?”

Wilkins offered the answer, “A secret.”

“A secret?”

“That was my reaction as well. It is something about the word itself that makes it mystifying.” Smith paused to take a sip of scotch, then repeated, “A secret.” He grinned as Bland looked from the window back to him. “She said she knew something you didn’t think she knew. What could she have possibly meant? If you could have seen her face, you would have been as baffled as I was. The statement was strange, yet very intriguing. I was in suspense to know what it was, but she refused to reveal her secret. Smart lady.”

Smith shrugged his shoulders, “Perhaps you had already written another novel, and you didn’t think she knew. Maybe desperation caused her to put aside her pride and come to us with this strange offer. Or, maybe it was something else entirely. As long as I have been in this business there is one thing I know, secrets make excellent stories. I must admit, she even had me believing in you again.”

Wilkins offered Bland a pathetic glance. “You know, Bland, I have never known a woman to fight so hard for a man. Your wife fought for you, even when she knew your best days of writing were behind you. That’s why this entire,” he waved his hands, “whatever you want to call it, didn’t fit with me. I believe the two of you contrived this bestseller crap only to squeeze more money from us. As far as I am concerned, you confirmed my suspicions with those awful drafts. When we discovered your wife’s name and yours attached to the account where all the money was funneled, I knew we were being taken.”

Smith interrupted, “I am not as cynical as my brother, but when you submitted those drafts, I was extremely disappointed. As for your wife, well, I do believe her actions were out of desperation.”

“It wouldn’t have mattered what I submitted. The two of you weren’t signing off on that partnership.”

“We are not like other publishing firms, we don’t give out partnerships like they are certificates of appreciation,” barked Wilkins. “But you are correct in your assumption; there was never any plan to honor our

agreement with you or your wife. On the contrary, we found a way to keep it all—the partnership, the novel, and the money. We owe it all to you."

"To me?" Bland echoed. Momentarily, Bland looked up from the papers in frustration, realizing what Wilkins meant by his comment. "If you suspected me of embezzling funds from the house, why did you allow it to continue?"

Wilkins smiled, then added, "To allow the plot to thicken."

Smith explained. "What my brother is trying to say is a secret did come across our desk that definitely grabbed our attention and allowed us to exploit your unscrupulous behavior. That secret was Greysen Brindle. The question is, was she the secret that your wife refused to share? If so, what were your wife's intentions with her? Someone had done their research on Greysen Brindle, and we were hoping there was a scandalous story waiting to be told. As you could imagine, we were so excited and expecting to read about her as a love interest in your first draft. Unfortunately for us, and Dakota, she wasn't even alluded to. Nonetheless, we decided to give you a chance and see where you were going with the novel, but the more we read, the more we frowned upon the direction the book was taking. What befuddles me is how you've become blind to the elements of a great story, while in the presence of those crucial elements."

"Are we on that again? 'Elements,' " Bland repeated sarcastically. "What were they? Love, passion, deceit, truth, pain and misery, revenge, envy, lust, lies, tragedy, and, oh yes, don't forget secrets? I can name some more if you like."

"Something like that, but you forgot them all," blurted Wilkins, before continuing. "We decided that if you no longer possessed the ability to imagine a great story and write it, then we would orchestrate the perfect true story that you would have no choice but to write. After learning of Ms. Brindle's connection with you, we thought it would be perfect to stage an event like the bomb threat to help put the two of you in the same place at the same time."

"The train," Bland murmured.

"Are you a betting man?" Wilkins asked.

"No, I don't gamble."

"You did gamble on your family by betraying them and committing adultery. It is suggested that three out of four marriages have a cheating spouse. Sure, we used Ms. Brindle to bring love and passion to the story, and yes, we were surprised when she gained your attention as quickly and as easily as she did. I mean, knowing the love you had for your wife, your swift betrayal was pretty impressive," Wilkins smirked. "Even seeing her here at the publishing house was a shock."

Smith leaned against a chair, "As for the deceit? There were multiple levels of deceit that just evolved as the plot evolved. From the outside looking in, we would never have expected such things. You always did say that a great story must have a strong element of truth to support it. Who knew you were going to deceive Dakota, and who knew that both women would deceive you? Wasn't that a delightful twist to know that both women were pregnant at the same time? I'm sure you enjoyed your lustful self, but if you ask me, that's a big secret to bear. And we know the tragedy that resulted from it has tormented you with pain and misery."

Bland blurted, "Did you orchestrate their deaths, too?"

"I will admit, the explosion was an unforeseen accident that might have brought about their early demise, so we thought. But no, we didn't personally kill them; however, a detective could imply that we had a motive, given our business arrangement with your wife. So, it would be in our best interest that she stays dead. You see, we needed the gun only to make sure it stayed missing, just like Dakota. Without the gun, who can prove who died or survived that explosion?" Smith acknowledged.

The way the men spoke of the gun caused Bland to wonder if they knew it was in Jesse's possession.

"We couldn't have written the story any better," smiled Wilkins. He then added, "Actually, Ms. Brindle's demise benefits us as well because then you are suspected of both their deaths. Frankly, it doesn't matter who survived; they just needed to die." Wilkins bluntly replied. "And now, that too has been taken care of."

The twins must not have known their plan failed, thought Bland. Immediately, Bland began to suspect the twins killed Jesse for the gun.

"Like you killed Jesse?" Bland blurted.

"Once again, you are crediting us for something we know nothing about," remarked Wilkins.

"You didn't have him beaten to death?"

"No," Wilkins replied, his face devoid of emotions.

Smith chimed in, "The police weren't looking at us as suspects; they were looking at you."

"I didn't kill him, but I'm sure you know who did kill him." Bland thought about the men that tried to kill him. He sounded off, "Forget the gun, surely there is someone out there searching for the female security guard," Bland finished. "The last place she was seen was here. Eventually that is going to raise some flags. Definitely when her gun is found."

"Where is your proof that she had a gun or that she was even here? There is no surveillance footage of her being here. Moreover, she was not an employee of the publishing house, so why would she be here?"

Bland suddenly remembered Rudy, and that he would back up Bland's allegation of an outside security guard working the night of the explosion. "I'm sure Rudy would contest that," Bland said, fishing again.

"You threaten a man's livelihood and freedom, and you'll be surprised what he remembers and what he doesn't," Wilkins said, with a menacing stare at Bland.

"Fortunately for us, the tracks trace back to you," Smith grinned.

Wilkins interjected, "With the embezzlement charges looming over you then..."

Bland finished his sentence, "You don't have to honor the partnership."

"Correct, my boy," Wilkins agreed, in an arrogant tone. He sipped his brandy. "As my brother said, we get to keep it all."

"Indeed," Smith exclaimed. "So instead of turning you over to the police, we gave you space and time to rekindle your relationship with Ms. Brindle and allowed your fraudulent activities to continue.

"You really don't get it, Bland; the name Canis Lupis is a multi-million-dollar business. Hell, the name is a corporation in itself, and you were so selfish and willing to throw it all away. I often berated myself for not securing the ownership of Canis Lupis long ago," Smith complained.

Wilkins took some papers from his desk drawer. He stood from his chair, pulled the cigar from his mouth, and presented Bland with

another opportunity.

"You see, Bland, we are all creators of opportunity. Given the situation you are facing, we are willing to offer you one last opportunity. Sign over the rights to Canis Lupis, and we can make all your problems disappear. We will make you richer than you could ever imagine."

"Is it that easy to destroy peoples' lives? Make promises you never intend to keep? Get your goons from Red Eye Investigation to kill at will to protect your interests and your secrets?" Bland hissed.

"You think you know everything. We never hired Red Eye Investigation. We have individuals that we pay very well to protect our secrets. You already met them, so take the deal, Bland," Wilkins suggested. "Your last book didn't get published, and the two before that were flops. Thank goodness, we never published them under your pseudonym; otherwise, Canis Lupis would have been finished."

Bland often wondered how Dakota knew about his unsuccessful novels, and now it made sense. His heart sank at what appeared to be his wife's betrayal.

Bland shouted at the men, "Your actions were reckless, irresponsible and cost people their lives, all for a story. You're just as guilty of their deaths as I am. Maybe even more so."

"Again, where is your proof, Bland? It all implicates you. Once the detective gets these final bank statements with your and your wife's names on them, he will have no choice but to connect you with the deaths," Smith declared. "Without either a gun, or a body, how can you disprove it? You see, Bland, I admired Dakota for her good intentions. What she did, she did out of love and desperation, but don't confuse our motives with hers. What we did, we did for greed. That is the final element of a great story. As we said, we weren't sharing it with anyone. This publishing house was built on the sweat of our family, so we will always protect it."

"You still needed me to write the story," declared Bland.

"No, we needed your name to be on the story we wanted told," Wilkins sneered.

"How did you know I would finish the book?"

Smith started to chuckle, "Because you are predictable. Whatever

elements are missing in the book, we made arrangements for someone to add those elements."

Bland believed that someone would be Larry Peterson, given his itch to write and his constant sucking up to the twins.

"With the addition of their deaths added to your story, that means more money. Think of the potential sales this book will generate," Wilkins chuckled.

Smith smiled in victory as he picked up the manuscript. Wilkins watched in silence as Smith scrutinized the title of the book, then turned to the first page. While Bland flipped through the bank documents, he could hear the pages of the manuscript being turned.

After reading several pages, Smith peered up from the book. "Bland, this is good, really good." Then he went back to reading.

Wilkins didn't crack a smile as he looked at his brother, then slowly toward Bland.

"Well, it appears another writer won't be necessary," Wilkins said, with a sarcastic expression.

Before Wilkins could say another word, Smith cried out, "What's this?" he asked, as he looked up from the pages.

"That's your novel," Bland responded, while still studying the bank documents. He noticed from the bank statement a large sum of money was taken to pay off his house.

Smith began flipping through more pages, "Bland, where is the rest of the novel?"

"That is your novel," Bland said again.

"After the first chapter there are only blank pages." Smith flipped to the last numbered page of the manuscript, "Three hundred and sixty blank pages."

"What's the problem?" Bland asked.

"They are blank pages!" Smith shouted.

"No, they are pages of the main characters' endless thoughts. More like abstract thoughts. What's good about this book, you can't change it because I sent out copies to individuals stating it was the final copy of Canis Lupis's new novel."

Wilkins hurried over to grab the stack of pages from Smith's hand. He flipped through the pages. "Bland, what the hell is this? Enough with the nonsense! Where is the novel?" barked Wilkins. When Bland didn't answer, Wilkins went on a rant. "None of this will hold up in court. The contract states a partnership for a novel."

"I'm not sure how many pages constitute a novel, but I'm sure it's less than the pages I gave you. Even though you guys never planned on honoring the contract, I never cared about the partnership. I never did. As you said, my wife wanted it more than I did. But I made a promise to my wife that if it is the last thing I do, I would write that story."

Wilkins's hand smacked the surface of the manuscript, "Whenever you write it, remember we will own it. We lived up to our contractual obligations, so that story belongs to us. Whatever revenue is derived from it will be ours. You belong to us," Wilkins screamed.

"You will never own Canis Lupis. You see," Bland pointed to the manuscript in Wilkins's hand, "you forgot another element of a great story, having nothing to lose."

"If you were going to betray us, why show up with a blank manuscript?"

"I, too, had to meet my contractual obligations. Plus, I wanted to see the look on your faces when the two of you realized all your efforts were in vain."

Wilkins hurled the manuscript across the room and wanted to do the same to Bland. Bland watched as it wedged itself between the wall and the bookcase. Wilkins moved toward Bland, when suddenly the men heard the elevator door open.

"You think this is over," Wilkins shouted.

"I am sure it isn't," Bland shouted back at Wilkins. "If what you're telling me is the truth about Dakota, Red Eye, and even Jesse, then I'm sure it isn't over, but I am running out of time to prove my innocence, and I need answers that will allow me to separate what is fact from what is fiction."

Smith quickly defused the situation. "Gentlemen, please. It has come to my attention that both the fox and the wolf have been outwitted. It appears we are not the only players in the game."

Bland questioned, "If not the two of you, who could it be?"

"A clever rabbit," Wilkins answered.

"Clever indeed," Smith echoed. "But don't be too quick to chase it down a rabbit hole. The character behind this plot moved at a different speed, a speed that allowed time to dictate the outcome."

"What do you mean?" Bland asked.

Smith was about to speak when the door to the study opened. Seconds later, Detective Rhodavack and two uniformed officers walked into the study.

Smith moved to Bland's side to whisper in his ear. Bland's eyes wandered off in a daze as he listened.

"Arrest this man," the detective pointed to Bland. The officers placed Bland's hands behind his back and commenced to escort him out of the study. Detective Rhodavack looked at Smith and Wilkins, "Thanks for letting me know he would be here."

The End.

34

THAT WAS THE END OF THE BOOK, AND JANE FELT cheated because a number of her questions weren't answered, such as Bland's outcome, the twins' fate and, most importantly, her identity. She needed to find these answers, and she knew her time was limited. At any minute, Dr. Stewart could walk through the door and have her transported to Memorial General. According to the doctor's conversation, she would be under twenty-four-hour supervision there, preventing her from finding out the truth. She needed to act fast.

Jane picked up the novel and flipped to the publisher's information. Her only chance of finding her identity lay with Bland Benthall, she thought, or rather his new pseudonym, the author of the book, *Sipul Sinac.*

She was able to find the phone number of the publishing house. From her room phone, she dialed the number and waited with a high level of anxiety. When the phone stopped ringing, Jane heard someone trying to dial out.

Quickly, Jane started saying hello.

"Oh, I'm sorry. I didn't know someone was on the line. Were you holding for someone?" the voice asked.

Jane thought to go with the flow, "Is this the publishing company?"

"Yes, it is."

"I wanted to speak with Sipul Sinac."

"I'm not the receptionist, so if I make a mistake in transferring you to his office, please call back. Just give me a second."

Jane heard a button being punched, then seconds later a man's voice answered. She didn't recognize the voice. After reading the book, she had her idea of what Bland would sound like, and this man's voice wasn't what she expected. However, not knowing his voice, she couldn't exclude the man as being Bland.

"Hello, is someone there?" the man asked.

"Is this Sipul Sinac, the author of *Path to the Past*?"

"Yes, this is he."

Jane's voice stalled because she didn't know how to ask if the man was truly Bland.

"Mr. Sinac, do you know Bland Benthall?"

There was a moment of silence before the man responded. "Who is this?"

"Bland, is it you?" Jane asked.

"Who is this?" the man asked again.

Something was wrong, Jane thought. "You're not Bland, are you?"

"No, I'm not. But—"

Before he could finish, Jane asked, "Is Bland even a real person?"

"Yes, but—" The next thing the man heard was a click, then silence.

With disappointment and confusion swirling about her head, Jane sat in the chair, stunned. Her eyes blinked as her attention moved from the phone back to the novel that was in her hand. That small possibility of reading a book with a parallel of her life made her question her own sanity. She, however, still hadn't totally accepted that the novel might not be about her. Quickly, she reread the page where Bland was handcuffed and taken away by Detective Rhodavack.

Detective Rhodavack, she repeated to herself. Since the book was based on a true story, she hoped that it was really his name. She called information for the police station and was given eight precinct numbers.

After calling each of the precincts, she finally was able to track down the detective.

"This is Detective Rhodavack."

"Detective, my name is...," she paused to think of a name, "Molly Tanberry. I am trying to locate Mr. Bland Benthall."

"Bland Benthall," Detective Rhodavack said, as he cracked his gum between his teeth. "You'll find Mr. Benthall at the State Penitentiary."

"He is?" she said with surprise. She didn't think they would have convicted Bland, believing he found the gun that could prove his innocence.

"Molly Tanberry, what's your interest in Bland Benthall?" the detective asked.

Before the detective could receive an answer, Jane hung up the phone. Later that evening when the floor was quiet, she waited for the nurses' station to clear before creeping up the hall. She slipped around the desk and grabbed a white jacket with a name tag that read "Michelle Learn, RN." As she was leaving, she spotted a purse. It took only a second to swipe two hundred dollars and slip the bills into her pocket. Quickly, she wrote an IOU on a blank paper and stuffed it back into the nurse's purse.

She put on the jacket and bolted down the exit stairs. Once on the first floor, she slipped into a custodian's closet where she found a box cutter. She began cutting through the bandages on her face. The custodian's closet was without a mirror, so Jane still had no idea what she looked like. She spotted a ball cap on a box of tissues and stuck it on her head. She pulled the bill down over her forehead to hide the scars and stitches that may have stood out. She tossed the bandages into a trash can, then exited the closet. As Jane approached the security checkpoint outside the hospital, she feared she would be caught.

Constance, meanwhile, returned to find Jane gone. She dashed into the hall, then to the nurses' station. The secretary hadn't returned from break, but the shift nurse had just returned from making her rounds.

"Did you see where Jane went?" she asked.

The shift nurse was reaching into her purse when she discovered the IOU note.

"Someone stole my money," she shouted and added, "and my medical jacket."

"Let me see that," Constance said. She shook her head. "How long were you gone?"

"The time it would take to do my rounds and a five-minute break."

Constance looked at the nurse, "Who was watching the station?"

Immediately, the nurse responded, "Becky. I'll bet she's sneaked off to the cafeteria again."

Constance had a strong notion that Jane was trying to leave the hospital grounds, so she tried calling the security checkpoint.

While the military guards inspected employees' badges, the checkpoint phone began to ring. After it rang several times, the officer turned his head to acknowledge the phone and finally went to answer it.

Constance let the phone ring one more time before slamming the receiver down. She looked at the exit doors and took off in a fast pace down the hall.

The guard was annoyed when he answered the phone to only hear the dial tone. Slowly, Jane approached the security checkpoint. The military guard immediately asked for her badge. She took a deep breath and began to pat over the medical jacket.

"I must have left it on my floor," she said, while trying to stay calm.

"Ma'am, I can't let you leave without seeing your badge."

She could tell from his demeanor he meant what he said, so she went back to searching her coat and hoped she hadn't dropped the badge when hurrying off the floor, or even left it in the closet where she tossed her bandages.

By this time, Constance exited the staircase. Up ahead, she could see Jane standing in front of the security checkpoint. Constance tried yelling to get the guard's attention, but she was too far away to be heard.

The worried lines in Jane's face lifted when she felt the badge in the inside pocket. She handed it to the military guard, who looked at it and Jane curiously.

"Looking at you in this picture, Mrs. Learn; it appears you lost a lot of weight."

Jane smiled, "Yes, a little."

"More than a little, if you ask me. Your face appears swollen and red. Are you okay?"

"Just a cold," she responded, with her head tilted downward.

He took a few additional seconds to inspect her. Meanwhile, Constance was running and calling with flailing arms to get the MP's attention.

"I'll let you pass this time, but you need to get an updated picture, or someone could mistake you for a psych patient." He handed the ID back to Jane.

Once Constance reached the security checkpoint, Jane was outside the gate. When Jane heard the MP scream for her to stop, her walk turned into a sprint. Constance watched as Jane hailed a passing taxi. Constance knew she was too late to stop her. She wondered where Jane was going.

35

THE TAXI PULLED UP IN FRONT OF THE STATE PENITENTIARY. Jane glanced at the fortress of barbwire and tall walls patrolled by officers with loaded weapons. Once inside the cold, colorless building, she announced her presence and signed in to see Bland Benthall. The guard asked Jane for some form of identification. In Jane's hand was the nurse's badge. She handed the guard the badge and waited to be escorted to a visiting area. As she waited for the prisoner, emotions of anger, sadness, and rage filled her. There were some questions she wanted to ask Bland. The question that lingered deeper than the others concerned her identity.

"Lady," the prison guard interrupted her thoughts. "It's time." The guard led her to another room with a row of partitions. There she sat in a small confined space with only a telephone and a plastic window that would separate her from the prisoner.

Through the thick plastic window, she saw a man in a brown jumpsuit approaching her cubicle. A middle-aged, handsome man sat down. Bland gasped when he saw who was sitting in front of him, and from his sudden reaction, she knew it was Bland. Her heart felt like it stopped when he took his seat.

Jane's anxiety increased as she waited for him to call her real name.

"Greysen." Bland sighed before he reached for the phone. Because of Bland's hesitation, she sensed he was expecting to see someone else.

"You were hoping to see Dakota?"

Bland was taken aback by the scars around her face and her raspy voice that made her sound totally different. Shamefully, Bland's head drooped. Slowly he lifted his head to look at Jane.

"Yes, I was hoping to see my wife. The reality of knowing Devin has to grow up without either parent is even more painful."

To some degree, Jane possessed the same anxious feeling that captured Bland. Until now, she had no idea of her identity. Some hope had lingered that she would be Dakota, and then she would have been wanted and needed by her son, her parents and, to some degree, by Bland, too.

As Jane, all she knew about herself was what Bland had written. There was a sliver of hope that there was some inaccuracy in his book, and as such to remove the despair that her life wasn't as he portrayed. According to Bland, she was alone in the world with nowhere to go, with no one seeking to discover her. Just the thought caused a tear to roll down her cheek.

"I know you have a lot of questions, Grey," he said, as he looked into her eyes.

Jane thought about his comment. Still not wanting to believe she was alone or a mistress in some real-life tale, she peered directly into Bland's eyes and asked, "Is the book a lie?"

"What do you mean?"

"How are you able to write in an all-knowing perspective of the characters without experiencing what we suffered, without living such devastating events, or without going through the mental or emotional trauma? There has to be some inaccuracy to your story, such as my life."

"I wish I was wrong about your life—where you come from or that you had family waiting for you. Much of what I wrote about your past life came directly from you. I was able to capture what we experienced together, such as your feelings, your emotions, and even your heartbreak. Does that mean, at times, I embellished to give the story some dramatic

effect? Sure, I did. However, as a writer, I have a responsibility to be as accurate as possible and portray the truth of the story, its characters and even the events that characters have succumbed to. Unfortunately, the story is as accurate as possible. I mean, it is based on a true story, and you did find me in this place."

Her head collapsed. He had culled out what iota of hope she possessed, and simultaneously replaced it with pain, and the inevitable truth that she had to surrender to the harsh reality that she was alone. She prepared herself to embrace the truth by asking another question.

"Why did you lie to me?"

She watched as Bland swallowed the words before trying to answer. Slowly his mouth began to move.

"I fell in love with you the first time we met," he replied, without a blink of the eye. "I never stopped loving you. After seeing you again, I wanted you. I had to have you. Grey I want you to know my love for you was genuine. I had no intent to hurt you. I know you're innocent in all of this, and I am sorry I had you caught up in a love triangle, but I love my wife, and I miss her so much," Bland said, his tears beginning to fall. "Sometimes people go out looking to replace something that's already at home."

"I'm sorry it took losing your wife for you to realize what she meant to you. But, as I am sure you know, I lost a lot too. I have you to thank for that, so forgive me if I don't appear sentimental." Jane could only assume what she thought Grey would have said.

"I don't expect you to be sympathetic. I just wanted you to know that I didn't mean for any of this to happen. My objective was to love you, not hurt you."

"What did you think would happen when you played with two women's hearts and emotions?" Her words charged at him. "How dare you sit behind that window and act innocent of this, claiming it was love!" She noticed the elevation in her tone, and then she lowered her voice. "It was anything but love. It was a game to you. So, don't sit there and toss love around like it is casual sex, although maybe, to you, it was."

"I wanted to tell you the truth, Grey."

"Bland, you were living in lies rather than in truth. This fear you

possessed about telling me the truth somehow didn't stop you from telling me a bunch of lies."

"I can't justify my actions, Grey. I did what I did. I am where I am. I lost what I lost. I never intended for this to happen. I don't expect you to forgive me, but I am sorry," he expressed with extreme contrition attached to his plea for forgiveness.

Jane surprised him with a rhetorical question.

"Would your wife have forgiven you?" Since Dakota could never ask him, Jane felt she had to be her voice as well. "You destroyed her, and she loved you, Bland. You abandoned your wife and your son. How do you justify your actions by saying it was for me?" She shook her head with disgust at the thought of a man doing such a thing. "Yes, you are where you are, and you have suffered, and your suffering is merited. But you will never suffer what we have suffered. I lost my baby, and she lost her life, and her unborn child. So, every day while you're in this place, you need to think about those losses."

"I can't stop thinking about them and the truth—"

"The truth." A sudden display of anger erupted from within her. "You and those awful men ruined my life! Don't you believe in fate, Bland? Wasn't it fate that brought us together? Maybe it was fate that caused me to read the book, so I could learn the truth."

"I wasn't sure you were going to get the book." He looked down, then back into her eyes. "Maybe it was fate that exposed the truth about the twins." His thoughts shifted to Dakota. "Fate," he said the word, as he looked deep into Jane's eyes, then he connected the word to Dakota. "The night of the explosion, I learned that Dakota had found a picture that outraged her. She used her cell phone to call our neighbor Sharon to watch Devin. However, Sharon's voicemail picked up. It seems as if Dakota was attempting to leave a message for Sharon, the twins called our house phone. Since our bedroom handset did not work, Dakota answered the twins' call on speakerphone.

"Right after I was arrested, Sharon visited me in jail and told me about a phone conversation between Dakota and the twins. The entire conversation was recorded on her cell phone's voicemail. The recording helped expose Smith and Wilkins' entire plan to deceive Dakota of the

partnership, the book, and the money at any cost, and how they planned to use you to do it. Of course, they were more specific on the recording."

"I don't follow. You had the recording, so why are you in jail? And what happened to the twins?"

"Though the recording helped convict the twins and their goons of conspiracy to commit murder, it didn't vindicate me of the embezzlement charges. My signature and my wife's signature were still on that last checking account, so the jury looked at our dealings with the twins as two parties criminally deceiving each other for economic gain. The court also believed our acts helped to cause the deaths of everyone in that explosion."

"I'm still confused. The gun should have helped prove your innocence of our deaths. You told Jesse to hide it. You suspected the twins of killing Jesse to get it." She paused. "Speaking of Jesse, were you convicted of his death? The cops did suspect you of killing him."

"The cops tried to pin Jesse's death on me, but the recently installed cafeteria cameras showed Jesse leaving his custodial closet thirty minutes after I left. The cameras showed him getting on the elevator. His body was later discovered in the basement of the building. That video footage from the cafeteria cameras and video of me running through the buildings of Walter Reed around the time of Jesse's death exonerated me of his death.

"As for the gun, the twins never produced it. They claimed they knew nothing about a gun. I believe they killed Jesse because he refused to give the gun to them. Fortunately for us, the gun would have opened an investigation as to who died that night. Truth is, if Dakota had survived the explosion, I'm sure the detective would have charged her, the twins, and me for your death and the death of the security guard. The sole purpose of hiding the gun was to protect you and your identity."

"At the time you didn't know I was the one who lived, so you were really protecting your wife."

"Based on the medical findings, it was more likely that you survived, rather than Dakota. So, I want to think I was protecting you both. As the twins said, without the gun, who can prove who died or who survived that explosion?"

"As you said in your book, there was the female security guard."

"She was never reported missing and another gun was never found."

"How certain are you that it was your gun that Jesse hid?"

"My gun is the only weapon connected to the explosion."

"Where is the gun now?"

"I have no idea where it is. If the twins don't have it, then Jesse took that information to his grave."

She said nothing for a few seconds, then she surprised Bland with another question. "In the novel, the twins suggested they didn't hire Red Eye Investigation to locate me, so who hired those men to find me?"

"I don't know, and that's where the tracks to the truth keep eluding me. I could tell from the twins' reaction that they weren't expecting to be the deceived."

"You mean, you fooling them about the book?"

"No, not that," his eyes widened. "Some things Smith whispered to me before I was arrested has been lingering with me."

"What did he say?"

"Deception that hides in the dark is far less dangerous than the truth that hides in plain sight."

"What does it mean?"

"A rabbit likes to hide in a dark hole, so I'm sure he was referring to the characteristics of a rabbit, not equating to whom he believed would have been the culprit that set us up. If you ask me, a rabbit is exactly what could out sly those foxes. Smith was correct, neither the foxes nor the wolf would have seen that coming."

"When you keep referencing people to animals, it sounds like a children's fairytale wherein you and those men keep considering yourselves…as characters in this fairytale," she said, when considering such a ridiculous comparison.

Bland tried to explain. "I'm trying to find the truth."

"Through fairytale characters?"

"If I can discover the truth through the eyes of fairytale characters, then yes."

"No, Bland, this isn't some fairytale. The truth about what happened to me or your wife or who set you up isn't found in some fairytale

characters. If anything, I am living a real-life nightmare and the only thing true about the foxes and the wolf is their own contribution to take innocent peoples' lives while destroying the lives of others, and what for—greed, love?" She wasn't sure if she wanted Bland to answer her questions.

He gave her an apologetic stare, "Grey, I am sorry. I never meant for this to happen to you."

"Shouldn't that be me and Dakota? She didn't deserve this either. It's strange, but after reading your book, part of her will live through me."

"I hope she does," Bland said, sympathetically.

"As for you, Bland, I guess you reap what you sow," Jane retorted.

She put down the phone, rose from the seat, and walked out of the room. Bland stood to watch her disappear behind the steel door.

Once Jane was back in the taxi she began to sob. Her anger for Bland was real and painful, now knowing who she was and what she had lost. More and more the reality of her situation came full circle. There was no one waiting for her or expecting her to show up.

The taxi driver looked through the rearview mirror and asked, "Are you okay?"

Jane reflected on her life and compared it to that of Dakota's life, and how Dakota's life seemed to be more worthwhile than her own.

The taxi driver's question ended her thoughts. "Where do you want me to take you?" She had arrived at the inevitable—she had only one place to go.

Jane looked up from her hands. "Take me home, please."

"Where is home?"

"Walter Reed Army Medical Center."

Jane arrived back at Walter Reed's security checkpoint where she gave the military guard Dr. Stewart's name. Within minutes Constance and Dr. Stewart were rushing out of the building.

"Jane, you're back," cried Constance, who was shocked by her appearance.

"My name is not Jane; it is Greysen."

The nurse stood confused. "What did you say?"

Dr. Stewart took Grey by the arm, "Come with me."

That evening Dr. Moss, along with Dr. Stewart, came by Grey's room.

"Dr. Moss is here to look at your skin and face."

"I just want to make sure you didn't do any damage to yourself," said Dr. Moss, as he inspected her face.

Grey's eyes fluttered as Dr. Moss began to touch her skin.

"You don't have any idea the damage you could have caused to your skin by taking off those bandages."

Grey watched as Dr. Moss shook his head. She could tell from his eyes how extremely upset he was.

"Greysen, allow me to share with you why I am so upset. You underwent several surgeries to repair some damaged facial features. This included scar revision and fracture repair; even a few bones in your face were damaged from third-degree burns, so I did work there as well. A few split skin grafts were performed. That's when shaved pieces of skin were taken from a healthy section of your body and applied to the bones on your face and secured in place by stitches." He took time to point out the stitches. "Since the grafts weren't large, you suffered only minimum scarring. But if you had gotten an infection, we could be facing some serious problems. Thank goodness the scars look clean, and the skin looks good." He continued to rotate her face from side to side. "The skin grafts have done a good job attaching themselves to the cells beneath the skin. Some of the more vivid scars, like here and here," he pointed out with his hand, "will improve with some cosmetic surgery. I want to get on that tomorrow before you decide to disappear again. So, you get some rest tonight."

Grey sat up in the bed, "Dr. Stewart, are you still sending me to Memorial General?"

The doctor was slow to respond; he wondered how she knew. "Jane," he stopped abruptly to correct himself. "I'm sorry, Grey, as of right now, I'm not sure what's going to happen with you. What I do know is that Dr. Moss needs you to be rested for tomorrow. After your surgery, I want to schedule an appointment with Dr. Westfall to determine what is going on with your memory. After we do that we can talk about Memorial General."

Later that night Constance checked in on Grey, who happened to be

lying restless.

"Can't sleep?" Constance asked.

"No."

"Greysen," Constance said carefully. "You're starting to remember?"

"Call me Grey. I wish I could say I am, but no."

"But you remember your name?" Grey looked at the novel on the table and was about to reveal to Constance her source but elected to keep it to herself. She was still upset with Constance for betraying her.

"It's a long story, Connie."

"I tell you what, why don't you tell me when you're ready?"

A few weeks after the cosmetic surgery, Grey was sitting in Dr. Moss's office for a follow-up. Dr. Stewart and Constance joined them. As Dr. Moss removed the last bandages from Grey's face, he noticed her slumped shoulders.

"Grey, take this mirror and look at yourself."

Constance released her grip from Grey's hand so she could take the mirror. She saw her face for the first time. Her cheeks lifted, and her eyes seemed to brighten before them.

"What do you see?" Dr. Moss asked.

She was expecting to see burned and flawed skin like on her hands and legs, but to her amazement the skin appeared smooth except for some swelling and stitches. She moved her fingertips across her forehead, down her cheekbone, and along her jaw line. She looked in amazement while considering the novel and her reflection as a path to her past. Grey laughed, "Without a memory, it's like discovering me for the first time."

Dr. Moss noticed Grey's long gaze. "Is something wrong, Grey? Are you disappointed?"

"No, doctor, it's not that. I was wondering why I still don't remember." She glanced toward Dr. Stewart. "I thought you said my memory would come back once I saw myself."

"Grey, seeing your reflection may or may not trigger your memory. Frankly, we were hoping the memories would resurface, but Dr. Westfall said that really depends on the individual. A number of things can trigger it. I'm still trying to figure out how you know your name is

Greysen. Nevertheless, we plan on taking some pictures and circulating them in the community. I'm sure someone will recognize you."

Again, Grey peered up from the mirror. "You think so, Dr. Stewart?" she asked, while knowing the truth.

"I'm positive, Grey."

She returned her eyes to the mirror.

"Grey, put the mirror down," Dr. Stewart insisted. "I wanted to wait until after your visit with Dr. Moss to tell you that you will be transferred to Memorial General."

Grey's voice trembled as she shouted, "No, Dr. Stewart! Why?"

"Grey, there is no more we can do for you here. If you want any chance of finding out your identity, that is, beyond your name, you need the services of those who specialize in memory loss. I already spoke to Dr. Westfall, and she agrees."

"But you all are my family. I'll never get to see you again." Grey thought of how lonely her world was about to become.

Constance smiled, "No, that's not what Dr. Stewart is saying, Grey. I will make it my duty to visit you, and I am sure Dr. Stewart will do the same. You are our family, too."

Grey positioned the hand mirror back to eye level. As she looked at herself, her thoughts roamed on telling them about the novel and how she came to know her name. She began to entertain the idea of going to Memorial General. Possibly it was a chance to learn more about her past, beyond Bland. Her thoughts were interrupted by Dr. Moss, who interpreted her facial expressions as continuous concerns about the stitches and other marks on her face.

"If you are worried about the incisions, don't be," Dr. Moss said, as he tried to quell her fears. "Once the scars heal, they won't be as noticeable."

"I think Dr. Moss and his team did a great job," spoke Dr. Stewart. He beamed as he looked at Grey's face.

"Yes, you did a great job, Dr. Moss," Grey agreed.

"Now, I would be remiss if I took all the credit," Dr. Moss smiled. "Because of the severity of your injuries, Dr. Stewart and his team of doctors and nurses reacted quickly, which played a crucial role in saving your life. As for the injuries sustained to your face, there was one

important thing that helped with the surgeries."

Slowly, Dr. Stewart moved slightly away from Grey and extended his hand to Dr. Moss.

Dr. Moss approached Grey. "Do you recognize this, Grey?" He opened his hand.

Grey took the grainy object that appeared to have taken on a lot of damage.

"What is it?" her eyes widened as she tried to make it out.

"It's part of a locket, Grey," Constance said.

"Grey, I figured the locket would be significant to you, maybe resurrect some memories once you saw it," Dr. Moss offered.

Grey moved the locket closer to her eyes. She noticed that the locket was heavily damaged. She opened the locket to find the picture slots were empty. Though she did not recognize the locket, she did remember it from the book. A cold chill came over her body. She peered up at Dr. Moss. "How was this so important in helping you help me?"

Grey studied the locket some more as Dr. Moss continued. "There was a picture of you found that was definitely beneficial to the reconstruction of your face. Fortunately for you, it was found."

Grey's eyes went from the locket back to Dr. Moss, as he retrieved a very smoke damaged photo that revealed a lighter silhouette of a face. Grey took the picture from the doctor to inspect it.

Grey squinted. "I can't see anything."

"Well, the computer saw a lot. I created a mold of your face from this picture. From that mold, a facial reconstruction program rendered a digital markup of your bone structure. The computer came back with a pretty good structural pattern for me to follow," he smiled, then continued. "This would have never been possible twenty years ago, but technology has its benefits."

"How did you know it was me in the picture?"

"Before the facial reconstruction surgery, the structural pattern of your face closely matched that of the mold created from the picture."

She turned the picture over, to see only a layer of soot. Grey handed the damaged photo back to Dr. Moss so she could continue to study the locket. She turned it over. She studied the engraving on the back. She

licked her thumb to remove some dirt.

She read the words aloud, "my soul mate." She looked at Dr. Moss to ask, "Where did you say you found it?"

"The night I found you in the bushes," Constance answered. "I found the locket and that photo in the front pocket of the somewhat burned blazer found beside your body."

"A blazer," she softly repeated. Grey's thoughts shifted to Bland's novel, then to Bland and Dakota's bedroom. She seemed alarmed and stared distantly. "A blue blazer and a torn picture?"

Constance looked stunned. "Yes."

Instantly, camera-like scenes of her traumatic past and her dreams flashed through her mind. After the mind's film had completely run its course, she sat there with a moment of clarity before passing out.

When she regained consciousness, she screamed. "This isn't me… this is not my face!"

"Grey, settle down," Dr. Stewart said, as he tried to control her flailing arms.

"My name isn't Grey," she screamed again. "You gave me her face. You gave me *her* face."

"Calm down, Greysen," Dr. Moss said, as he struggled to control her.

"My name is not Greysen! My name is Dakota Benthall!"

Suddenly, she felt her skin being pierced. Dr. Moss had stuck her with a needle. Her body went limp, and she fell over in Dr. Stewart's arms.

36

DOCTORS STEWART AND MOSS ESCORTED THOMAS AND Margie Gates to a waiting area before seeing their daughter. He asked them to sit before going any further.

"I hope you had a pleasant drive," Dr. Stewart said.

Margie began to ramble, "When I received your phone call, I thought someone was playing an awful joke."

"Margie, that's not what the man asked you," Thomas said.

"That's quite all right, Mr. Gates. She's just happy to know her daughter is alive."

There was a knock on the waiting room door, and Dr. Westfall entered. "I'm sorry to be late."

"Actually, you are just in time," Dr. Stewart replied. Dr. Stewart began introducing the credentials of Dr. Moss and Dr. Westfall and their roles in their daughter's care. "I know you've been updated on how your daughter arrived in my care, and what injuries she suffered. These doctors will further explain what they have done to help Dakota along on her journey to recovery. Dr. Moss," waved Dr. Stewart.

"Thank you, Doctor." Dr. Moss stepped forward to speak. "Mr. and Mrs. Gates, your daughter went through an extensive amount of

reconstruction to correct serious damage to her face. Unfortunately, the damage was compounded by a very flawed facial mold. However, after knowing your daughter's true identity, we gained access to a photo of your daughter, and I was able to restore her original facial features. For the last month, she has been recovering from that, as well as from some minor cosmetic surgery. She does have a few slow-healing scars, but that's nothing to worry about. It is important, however, that she stays indoors for at least another four to six weeks."

Dr. Moss gave the floor to Dr. Westfall, who began to explain the psychological trauma their daughter had undergone.

"While your daughter has been healing from her recent surgery with Dr. Moss, she has also been a resident of Memorial General where she has been undergoing therapy with a memory specialist. Unfortunately, only a small portion of her memory has returned. And much of that deals with her trauma. I have put together a packet for you to take. The packet explains what dissociative amnesia is and what memory exercises Dakota can perform daily to help with more memory recovery. It is important not to expect too much too soon. As time progresses, she may remember more, but only time will tell."

"Dr. Stewart, you mentioned something about her voice," Thomas said.

"According to Dr. Tucker, the ear, nose, and throat specialist who performed surgery on Dakota, your daughter's larynx was severely damaged in the fire. As a result, a large amount of scar tissue has built up on her vocal cords. That's the reason for her hoarse sounding voice. Unfortunately, the tone of her voice will not likely get any better."

"I don't care about any of that. I just want to know when I can see my baby?" Margie asked.

"Sure, they are in the patient's room." Dr. Stewart escorted them across the hall to another room. He turned the handle to the door, then slowly poked his head inside the room. He looked back at Margie and Thomas, "She and the nurse are watching their favorite television program—Jeopardy!"

Dakota lay in the bed laughing at Constance missing another Jeopardy! question. When the door to the room opened and Dr. Stewart

and the other doctors entered, Dakota immediately sat up in the bed. When Thomas and Margie walked in the room, Margie broke down the instant she saw her daughter, and Thomas's strong resolve folded as well. Dakota's excitement exploded.

Tears flowed from Constance's eyes. She watched as the family reconnected with tight hugs and kisses. Constance glanced at Dr. Stewart, who also had choked up while watching the reunion. After the excitement settled, Dakota looked around before asking, "Mother, where is Devin?"

"He's coming, baby. The doctors wanted us to see you first."

After twenty more minutes of reuniting, a nurse came in with discharge papers. "I need you to sign these so you can go home."

"Home," Dakota repeated in a skeptical whisper.

"Yes, home," responded Margie, then she gave her daughter a tight hug.

"We wanted to surprise you," Constance said, before a wide smile came across her face.

Dr. Stewart asked Mr. and Mrs. Gates to leave the room with him to go over some additional treatment follow-up information for Dakota.

The departure of Dr. Stewart and Dakota's parents was soon followed by Dr. Moss and Dr. Westfall, who politely excused themselves. As Constance moved toward the door, Dakota grabbed her by the hand to stop her from leaving.

"You want me to hang around?" asked Constance.

"If you don't mind."

"Sure, Jeopardy! is still on," Constance giggled. "How do you feel?"

"Excited but also very scared."

"It's okay to be scared, Dakota." Constance replied, hoping to lessen Dakota's concerns.

The door opened and in walked Dr. Moss with two strangers.

Dakota and Constance observed the man and woman as they walked into the room.

"Hello, Mrs. Benthall. My name is Brandi McIntire, I represent Literature House Publishing Company, and this is my associate. I know

this is a very exciting day for you, so I will take only a few minutes of your time. I was wondering if the three of us can talk alone."

Constance looked at the strangers. "Let me give you some privacy. I will be across the hall, in the nurses' station, if you need me." She winked.

The moment Constance left the room, Brandi signaled to her assistant to place two duffle bags on the floor.

"Allow me to explain, Mrs. Benthall, the reason for my visit. The night Bland was supposed to submit his novel, I received an anonymous email from a person inquiring if I was interested in purchasing a bestselling novel. If so, it would cost me," Brandi paused. "Well, let's say a lot of money."

"You agreed to pay someone money before knowing who wrote the manuscript and before reading it?" Dakota asked, displaying her skepticism.

"I had a hunch." Brandi's eyebrows rose.

"So, you normally do irresponsible things based on hunches?" Dakota noticed her own behavior. "I apologize for being rude."

"It's okay, and you're right, it was irresponsible. Sometimes you must go with your gut feeling," replied Brandi. "However, we faced a problem because Bland was under contract with S&W Publishing to write one last novel. Bland couldn't afford to put his name on the book or my contract because it would directly attach him to Literature House Publishing and possible legal obligations. So, to answer your earlier question, that is where my associate came into the picture in hopes of rationalizing my irresponsibility. It was he who signed the contract. Plus, both Bland and my associate had a common purpose. It served Bland's purpose to get the book published, and at the same time, the book would serve as a launching pad for my associate's career."

"I'm confused. How did it serve as a launching pad for his career? Since the book was about Bland's life, and Bland did write it, wouldn't the twins have rights to it?"

"Just because the book is about Bland's life doesn't mean it couldn't have been written by another writer. As I mentioned earlier, S&W had a contract to publish one last book written by Bland, but it didn't have the rights to stop someone else from writing Bland's personal story.

Frankly, one could argue that Bland fulfilled his legal obligations to S&W Publishing by handing in a manuscript before his deadline, but it was better to be safe," Brandi answered. "So Sipul Sinac was created as the author to tell that story."

Dakota turned to look at the man. "And this is Sipul Sinac?"

Brandi took the opportunity to introduce the man, "My associate, Mr. Larry Peterson."

"Thank you, Brandi," said Larry.

Dakota did not recognize Larry. "I don't understand. Larry Peterson," Dakota whispered under her breath. "You were in the book. Bland didn't like you."

"You don't have to like someone to need someone."

"You were a spy for the twins."

He smiled. "Yes, I read that, too. When I caught your husband in my office, he happened to see my manuscript for a new novel and my personal letter I was writing to Mrs. McIntire for her support. Shortly after starting with S&W, I was approached by Mrs. McIntire to sign with Literature House Publishing. I refused her offer, mainly because of Bland. Ironically, Bland's story didn't share that I have admired your husband's work for a long time. I wanted to write and edit like your husband, so I figured if the twins allowed Bland to ghost write, given his success, they would encourage me to do the same. However, I couldn't have been further from the truth."

Dakota exclaimed, "How am I supposed to believe what you are saying? You weren't very friendly toward Bland."

"Yes, to put it mildly. I was made to believe by the twins that Bland threatened to leave S&W Publishing if they gave me the opportunity to ghost write. Bland had made the Stumps a lot of money so, of course, they weren't going to ruffle any feathers with him. I couldn't believe that Bland would stifle another writer's creative freedom, so I became bitter toward him.

"Knowing Bland and I didn't always see eye to eye, I was surprised when I received the call from Mrs. McIntire asking me if I wanted to further my career. She told me about Bland's contract with the twins and the dilemma she and Bland faced."

Brandi chimed in, "Larry could very well put his name on Bland's book without injury to himself, to Bland, and, most importantly, to Literature House Publishing since he had no contractual obligations to the S&W Publishing House. So, I persuaded Bland to go along with my idea."

"Without Canis Lupis as the author of the book, it doesn't generate as much money," Dakota asserted.

"We thought about that before publishing the novel," Brandi admitted. "Fortunately for us, Larry found a way to connect the two authors and hopefully protect Bland from any legal issues."

Larry interjected, "Bland was a ghost writer, and only a few knew his true identity, so I figured changing his name to something his fans could still identify with was our best option. I considered several names, then it came to me." He paused to gather his thoughts. "It is funny how life's experiences can come full circle. Years ago, I served in the Peace Corps, and my stay was in a small village called Sipul, Honduras. It dawned on me that's how we can make the connection between Canis Lupis and our new author, Sipul Sinac. So, you see, Sipul Sinac is Canis Lupis. The name is in reverse order and spelled backwards.

It didn't hurt that someone leaked to the press that this new author, Sipul Sinac, just completed a new story based on the personal tragedy of Canis Lupis.

"Who is going to believe that?"

"I guess that would depend on the reader," Brandi replied.

"Again, we are back to square one. If the fans can make the connections that these two authors are the same person, surely—"

Brandi interrupted, "For the success of the book, we hope the fans do."

"Then, surely, the twins will make the same connections and have a legal argument." Dakota blurted, "You're going to get sued."

"They would first have to prove the two authors are the same person. Again, Larry Peters is the ghost writer known as Sipul Sinac. Nonetheless, Literature House Publishing is willing to take on S&W Publishing if and when that time comes. Until then a deal needed to be made and books needed to be sold."

Brandi waited for Dakota to absorb all that had been said. "After Literature House and Bland agreed on the terms of the deal, I received an email with some important details concerning the funds, and when to publish the manuscript."

"Given your scandalous character in the book, why did you pay Bland? I mean, you had the novel in your possession."

"Your husband is smarter than you know. He didn't email me the novel until the money was verified in Mr. Peterson's bank account. Still conscious of any legal ramifications by S&W Publishing, Literature House Publishing made the check payable to Mr. Peterson since Sipul Sinac is his pseudonym. He could have betrayed both Bland and me and disappeared with the money; instead, he cashed the check, and now we're here." Brandi looked down at the duffle bags on the floor.

Larry bent down to unzip the duffle bags. Inside the bags were stacks and stacks of money. When the money registered with Dakota, she looked up with stunned eyes.

Dakota looked at Larry. "What stopped you from keeping the money? I'm sure the twins would have made it worth your while to tell them what Bland was up to."

"My word," he firmly said. "Bland didn't have to like me, but he had to trust me. Plus, the twins had deceived me about Bland, so I had a score to settle."

Dakota directed her attention back to Brandi. "I'm curious, how did you find me?"

"I received another anonymous call telling me where you were. I spoke with Dr. Stewart and, again, that put us here."

Dakota paused, then looked down at the large duffle bags.

"I'm confused. How would Bland know to give me this money? He didn't know which one of us survived."

"We were instructed to give the money to you. It appears your survival worked in your favor."

Dakota thought about the remarks Brandi made. Again, she glanced at the duffle bags. "So, how much is there?"

"That's the first of five payments, so let's say, money should never be an issue for the rest of your life," Brandi grinned. "Bland wanted you to

be well off. We all have to trust someone sometime, Mrs. Benthall.

"It has been a lucrative venture for us all. So, you see, we honor Bland's wishes for you, and Literature House Publishing is satisfied to know that Canis Lupis will live on as Sipul Sinac—the pseudonym for our newest suspense writer and senior editor, Mr. Larry Peterson. Not to mention, Mr. Peterson writing as Sipul Sinac strengthens our legal position in case S&W attempts to sue us for contract infringement."

Dakota looked off in a daze. "I can't believe Bland was willing to give up Canis Lupis."

Brandi replied, "He would say you were worth it."

Dakota considered Brandi's comment. Then another question entered her mind. "What did the twins receive?"

"Well, in their attempt to withhold vital evidence in a crime, they received twenty-five years in a federal prison as co-conspirators to commit murder. Currently, the publishing house is being run by a third, younger brother, who was suddenly discovered. It appears that the twins' father, Old Man Stump, had a secret of his own. You see, Mrs. Benthall, we all gain something, and sometimes it may not be what we want, but we gain, nonetheless."

The door to the room slammed into the wall just as Dakota was about to speak.

"They couldn't contain him any longer," smiled Constance, as she followed Devin into the room.

"Mommy," Devin came running into the room and hugged his mother.

They all watched as tears streamed down Dakota's face. Moments later, she reluctantly let Devin pull back from her embrace.

Brandi was quick to grab the box of tissues from the table and hand it to Dakota.

"Mommy, don't cry. Heaven can wait, Mommy."

His remarks caused more tears to run down her cheeks. She dabbed them as Constance grabbed a tissue to wipe her own eyes.

"I agree, baby." She wiped away the last of the tears.

"Mommy, Granny said you're coming home today."

"Yes, I am," she nodded.

"Yeah! Can you read me my favorite story tonight? Please, Mommy?"

"Sure, I can, *The Big Bad Wolf*? Does Granny have that book?

"No, Mommy, that is not my favorite book. You remember it?" he asked with excitement in his voice.

Dakota looked to Constance, then back to Devin. She squinted as she tried to remember the story.

Brandi's inquisitive nature was piqued because of Dakota's inability to remember the name of the book. Her eyebrows drew inward as she intently watched Dakota struggle to remember. She moved in closer to the side of the bed to get a better look at Dakota.

Dakota stared blankly at Devin as an uncomfortable silence filled the room.

After noticing Brandi's offensive body language, Constance moved to the foot of the bed. She deliberately broke the silence by diverting attention away from Dakota to the perfume Brandi wore, which seemed to inflame her nostrils the instance she walked into the room.

"What is that fragrance you're wearing? Is it lilac?"

"Yes." She was amused the nurse could identify the fragrance.

"It is a familiar scent," Dakota interjected. Her nostrils spread to remember where she first smelled the fragrance.

"It comes in this body gel that my staff orders online. We give it out as a gift to new business prospects. I liked it so much that I decided to keep a couple of bottles for myself," she laughed softly. "If you like, I can have a few bottles sent over."

"No, thank you," Constance replied. She was lashing back in response to Brandi's demonstrable, mocking facial expressions toward her friend. "The fragrance of lilac doesn't sit well with our allergies." She looked toward Dakota, "Wouldn't you agree?"

Dakota's eyebrows lifted when she noticed Brandi's full smile reshaped into an ominous frown. Within seconds, another uncomfortable silence permeated the room.

The silence was broken when the television came back into focus. The host of Jeopardy! read his final question. "This folktale demonstrates how cleverness and deception are employed by an opponent to win a race against a stronger adversary."

Constance managed to grab everyone's attention in the room when she smacked her hands together. "I know the answer."

While Constance struggled to answer the Jeopardy! question, Dakota struggled to identify where she first smelled the fragrance that Brandi wore.

Dakota's fixed stare on Brandi was broken when Constance cried, "What is that rabbit's name? It's on the tip of my tongue." Constance shouted out an answer. "What are the Tales of Peter Rabbit?"

Before each contestant had the opportunity to reveal their answer, Brandi replied, "What is the Tortoise and the Hare?"

"What is the Tortoise and the Hare?" echoed the Jeopardy! host.

Devin looked at Brandi and screamed with jubilation. "That's my favorite story. How did you know the answer?" he asked, as he stared up at Brandi with big wide eyes and a big smile.

Brandi peered down at Devin. "An old colleague once told me that sometimes the answer is right in front of us, but we fail to see it because we fail to comprehend the question.

"What?" frowned Devin, who was lost at the beginning of Brandi's explanation.

Constance narrowed her eyes since she believed the comment was directed to her. "What you said makes no sense, well at least not to me."

From the perspective of the fairytale, however, the comment made perfect sense to Dakota, who now understood Smith's remark to Bland on the night he was arrested in Smith's study. That only the patience of a tortoise could have outmaneuvered the greedy foxes, the amoral wolf, and the arrogant hare. She also believed that she had just witnessed the tortoise poke its head from its shell.

"I will wait outside and let you all finish your conversation," Constance offered, as she moved to the door.

"Can you please take Devin to my parents?"

When Constance took Devin by his hand, Brandi suddenly turned and looked at Larry. "Can you get the car? I would like to speak to Mrs. Benthall alone."

"Sure," Larry said. Before leaving, he extended his hand to Dakota. "It was a pleasure meeting you."

Dakota gestured with a polite smile as she shook his hand.

Brandi waited until the room cleared before speaking. "The doctor said you suffered or you're suffering from some form of amnesia?" The two women locked eyes and held their gaze for a few seconds. "In case you need me to refresh your memory," Brandi replied, "is there a question that Mrs. Benthall would like answered?"

"Are you willing to answer it?" Dakota asked.

Brandi smiled, "I am listening."

"Why would the tortoise engage in such a deceptive scheme?" she asked, then wondering if Brandi would admit she was the culprit behind this intricate plot to set up both Bland and the twins.

"I'm sure this is not about fairytales, so your question has to be hypothetical?"

"You're right, it's not about a fairytale."

"Then do you mind if I use your fairytale analogy to answer your hypothetical question?"

Dakota smiled as she was willing to play Brandi's game if it meant the truth would be discovered. "Sure, it should be thought-provoking."

Brandi returned the smile. "I believe great fairytales have unequal characters that possess a certain level of tolerance and discipline that allow such characters as the foxes, the wolf," she slowed her voice, "and the hare to have center stage, creating an illusion of no-control, that allows the manipulation of the foxes' greed, and the use of temptation to snare the wolf and to exploit the presumptuous nature of the hare. So, while all eyes are focused on the stronger opponents, there is a tendency to forget that there is another and more cunning opponent in the race." Brandi stepped closer to the bed. "I read in the book that you are a good chess player."

"I don't know. I can't remember."

"Then I'll remind you that the game is about patience and position. It takes steady patience when setting up your opponent. Sometimes it requires you to think several layers deep to anticipate a move so you can position yourself to make the right move."

"The right move?" inquired Dakota.

"A move that creates the right opportunity." Brandi leaned in to

whisper to Dakota, "such as allowing your adversaries to exploit a perceived weakness that allows them to get comfortable and complacent, so they'll make a mistake. It took a long time, persistence and a lot of patience, but I got my revenge on those old bastards, and I finally got Bland, well, Canis Lupis, their most lucrative author. We now own the rights to his name and the rights to Sipul Sinac. Also, you're looking at Literature House Publishing Company's first female partner." A sinister yet satisfied expression blanketed Brandi's face as she stood straight and folded her arms in satisfaction.

"It sounds like the tortoise benefitted the most from this scheme?"

"That depends on whom you ask. Wouldn't you agree?" There was a brief silence. "I am sure the wolf would disagree."

"Why is that?"

"Isn't it obvious?" she paused to wait for a response, then remembered, "Oh, that's right, I forgot you're suffering from memory loss. Well, besides the more unobvious reason, there is the fact that my assistant saved his life at the hospital. And, if for no other reason, I would hope a sense of redemption in knowing he did the right thing by you," Brandi replied.

"You protected Bland, so he would do right by me?" she questioned.

"I protected my interest," Brandi countered. Now wanting to test Dakota's memory, Brandi asked, "How about you, Mrs. Benthall? As I recall, your interest was to gain peace of mind and a sense of security. Did you achieve that?"

"I don't follow," Dakota replied.

"In the book, you made a deal with the twins for peace of mind and security, right? So, are you at peace with all the outcomes, as well as your own? I hope, besides all that money, that you are able to obtain some semblance of peace," Brandi said, when an awkward expression appeared on Dakota's face.

"Peace?" she frowned. "I lost my unborn child and my life."

"Don't forget you lost your husband," Brandi remarked.

"Was he ever mine?"

"Mrs. Benthall, there is a saying that 'All is fair in love and war.' "

"Maybe, but it's a shame that innocent people had to die for the

interest of others."

Again, Brandi paused to look intently at Dakota. "Yours as well." She didn't give Dakota a chance to reply. "We all found ourselves characters in the same fairytale, Mrs. Benthall. And we all had a part to play."

"What part did Greysen Brindle and Jesse play? Except two innocent people dying?" Dakota retorted.

"That's the thing about fairytales, they offer this grand illusion of a magical and wonderful tale, but most fairytales mimic a grim reality, and casualties of war are necessary for the sake of a moral and happy ending. Sometimes you must sacrifice the queen for the sake of the win. As for Jesse, it appeared he had something that was desperately needed."

Immediately, Dakota muttered, "The gun."

"The gun is at the center of the problem; it is the key to all the answers so, of course, the gun. It can expose everyone, it is the one thing that keeps everyone in control," said Brandi with a very direct face. "No one needed any loose ends. Whoever possesses the gun wins the war." She smiled before tossing up her hands.

"So, whoever killed Jesse has the gun?" Dakota asked, with serious insinuations behind her tone.

"One can only assume in this enchanted fairytale." Brandi offered an equally firm tone, along with a cold stare.

"The novel implied a second gun. Are you sure there isn't another gun?" Dakota questioned.

"Let's hope it's the only gun for everyone's sake." With a devious and threatening smile, she said, "We don't need any more casualties of war, do we?"

"Why are you telling me this? Aren't you afraid I would go to the police?"

Brandi replied, "Mrs. Benthall, I didn't get this far not knowing what could happen, but you losing your memory was a surprise. A surprise that is keeping a loose end from getting snipped."

"Is that a threat?"

"Let's say it's an observation. I am sympathetic to those you lost, but before you go running to the police, let me remind you that the gun protects you, too."

"So I keep hearing."

"Then I suggest you start listening, since your memory and the book are no longer references to whom your allies or enemies are."

The two women stared at each other without speaking a word. No sooner did the silence consume the room, than Devin ran back in at full speed.

"Mommy, we are waiting for you."

Dakota's eyes stayed locked on Brandi's as she reached out to grab Devin and pull him close to her.

Brandi smiled seeing the two of them embrace. "I see you did get what you wanted. Some things are worth the sacrifice. What greater peace than having a family?" she asked, then suddenly paused as if her words had given her new insight to some information. "Mrs. Benthall, I realize now that a person could gain peace through death; just as well out of death could come an opportunity of life. Would you agree?" she asked.

"I guess that would depend on who died," retorted Dakota, then added, "Would you agree?"

There was an inquisitive silence on Brandi's behalf. "Mrs. Benthall, did you know that many people think the rabbit and the hare are one and the same? True, they are from the same family, and contrary to your nurse's belief, neither is a rodent. Both are charismatic, yet cunning. Both have docile appearances that beget your trust, but they are very different. While the rabbit is meticulous and tremulous, the hare is audacious and rather a risk-taker. When in the presence of danger, the hare must blend with the environment since it has no burrow to offer it refugee. As the danger approaches, it uses maneuvers and speed to outrun the predator. The rabbit, on the other hand, has a dark burrow as shelter. However, when the rabbit cannot reach its burrow to escape the threat, it does something very interesting. It does not panic like the hare and run. Instead, it becomes the hare by camouflaging itself to hide in plain sight. The use of ingenuity is where some say the rabbit is keener than the hare.

"I would surmise that if it is possible to distinguish the rabbit from the hare, then it is possible to discover who gains peace or the opportunity to

live another day. Until then, it appears we have a cliffhanger. Personally, I never liked cliffhangers. They're like loose ends that are sure to unravel at some point, causing all kinds of unwelcome problems. But that is why writers use them, to insinuate, to dramatize suspense to a book's ending, leaving the reader to ponder some unanswered question or ambiguous statement. Frankly, I have had a lingering curiosity to know what Smith whispered to Bland the night he was arrested. That information could affect people's lives. And not always for the best." She placed emphasis on her last words. Dakota showed no reaction as Brandi continued.

"Mrs. Benthall, maybe you can answer a hypothetical question that can possibly alleviate our cliffhanger? If you could be a hare or a rabbit, which would you be?" There was a stillness as Brandi waited for the answer.

Dakota, with an ingenuous face, answered, "I would be me, Dakota."

Brandi smiled, then uttered, "Touché." She chose not to challenge the answer. She put forth her hand to shake Dakota's. "Well played. It appears we have a draw, for now," she smiled. "So, you do know how to play. Now, I look forward to playing chess with you some day." Brandi saw her opportunity to escape presented itself. "Let me excuse myself, so you can enjoy your family." She proceeded to the exit. Once in the doorway, she stopped to turn toward Dakota. "Don't forget to read your son's favorite book tonight. He is really looking forward to it." She looked at Devin. "What was the name of it?"

Devin yelled out, "*The Turtle and the Rabbit*."

"Yes, that's it," Brandi smirked, then repeated, "*The Turtle and the Rabbit*." Her eyes settled on Dakota's eyes, "What a tale that could have been."

Brandi left the room as Constance entered. Dakota turned her affection to Devin. She squeezed him tightly.

"Mommy, I missed you so much. Promise you won't go to Heaven again until you are very, very old."

Dakota commenced sobbing, "I promise, baby. I promise."

Constance turned her head to avoid crying. Once she gathered control over her emotions, she said to Dakota, "Your mother and father are waiting in the hall with the doctors."

"Okay," she said, as she paused from kissing Devin to look up at Constance.

"Come on, Mommy, it's time to go home. I want you to meet my pet cricket, Riley." Devin jumped from the bed and ran out of the room.

Dakota lifted herself from the bed and walked into the bathroom. She wanted to let having her identity and family back sink in. Then she thought about Grey.

Dakota heard the door open again. "Tell them I'm coming, Connie. Can you please have someone help carry these bags?"

"Dakota, can you step out of the bathroom for a minute?" asked Constance. When Dakota came out of the bathroom, Margie stood in the middle of the room.

Dakota looked from Constance's face to the child that Margie held.

"What's going on?"

Quickly, Constance spoke up. "Dr. Westfall thought this would be a great time for you to meet your son. He should help you with your overall healing."

"My son?" She was flabbergasted. "I thought the baby died."

Constance interrupted, "He was in bad shape, just as you, but he's a fighter, just as you. He weighed less than five pounds and was in an incubator for four months. Since then his home has been with a foster family. He's small, but he's tough. He's been getting a lot of love while you got better." Constance gestured toward the lady that accompanied the baby. "This is Mrs. Zarr, the social worker assigned to the child."

Dakota registered the social worker with a quick look, then slowly, Margie walked over to give a stunned Dakota her son.

The touch of the child in her arms against her chest lifted her spirits with joy.

"What's his name?" Dakota asked.

"Well, everyone on the neonatal and intensive care unit and the foster family refer to him as Miracle; however, naming him is your duty." Constance stood back and smiled.

Dakota's total attention was on the child. She touched his fingers and then his toes. Then her eyes began to tear up.

"Please, can you give us a moment?" Margie said to Constance.

"Sure. I'll notify the doctors that you'll be out in a minute. I'll get someone to help you with your bags."

Constance turned and left the room, recognizing it was no longer necessary for her to be a surrogate family member, as Dakota now had her real family.

The room became quiet for a few seconds while Margie watched Dakota hold her son with such love and compassion.

"I want you to know you're not alone anymore. I am so sorry you had to go through all that pain and suffering by yourself, but your family is here now, so you don't have to face this alone. Ever since you were a little girl, I called you my optimistic opportunist because whatever you encountered, you knew how to roll with the punches and make the best of the situation. Baby, this will be no different. You keep your head up and stand proud," she said, as she lifted Dakota's chin with her finger. "Remember, they say everything happens for a reason."

"I love you, Mother," she cried.

Margie leaned over to hug them both, "I love you too, baby." She helped wipe the tears that streamed down Dakota's face. "Look at you. Well, I have another little man to spoil. Devin is going to love having a little brother." Margie's eyes moved from the child to Dakota, "He looks just like you, so what do you plan on naming him?"

Dakota peered at his bright eyes. He blinked several times as he looked into hers.

She paused for several long seconds before answering.

"His name is Grayden."

"Hmm, that's cute. Where did you come up with that name?"

After kissing Grayden on the forehead, Dakota broke her glance, then shifted only her eyes toward Margie with a slight, hollow grin. Dakota's eyes twinkled, "It's a long story, but it's the perfect name."

THE END

MW01504690